"That was a foolish thing you did."

Kieran's voice was rough with emotion. "I feared you were lost to us forever."

"Would that matter, my lord?" Tears sprang to Megan's eyes. "Your journey would be easier without another to worry about."

He drew her fractionally closer and brought his lips to her temple. "I am not a man given to worry or fear. But something about you terrifies me, Megan. You are too bold, too brave, too headstrong. And though I know you are capable of taking care of yourself, I have this perplexing desire to watch over you."

"You should not have come after me."

"And why is that?"

"Because you nearly gave up your life, as well."

His voice, low and tender, was warmed with a smile. "Would that matter to you, lass?"

"Aye."

"Oh, Megan." With a sigh, he drew her into the circle of his arms.

FIRESIDE BOOKS
4201 S. Noland Suite H
Indep., MO 64055
816/373-9169

Dear Reader,

Welcome to Harlequin Historicals. This month, Harlequin brings you some of your favorite authors.

Highland Fire, the next title in Ruth Langan's popular Highland series, tells the story of Megan MacAlpin. The winsome Scottish noblewoman is rescued by an Irish chieftain, and the two join in fighting their common British enemies.

With *Forever Defiant,* the team of Susan Yansick and Christine Healy, writing as Erin Yorke, have written about a young Englishwoman who follows her new husband to Egypt and finds herself caught in a world of danger and political intrigue.

In Elizabeth Lane's *Birds of Passage,* an indentured servant falls in love with a sea captain on a voyage to America, and they must overcome countless obstacles in order to find happiness. And in *Gold Fever,* Ann Pope has set a marriage of convenience story smack-dab in the middle of a rough-and-ready gold-mining town.

Keep an eye out for all four September Harlequin Historicals.

Tracy Farrell
Senior Editor

Highland Fire

Ruth Langan

Harlequin Books

TORONTO • NEW YORK • LONDON
AMSTERDAM • PARIS • SYDNEY • HAMBURG
STOCKHOLM • ATHENS • TOKYO • MILAN

Harlequin Historicals first edition September 1991

ISBN 0-373-28691-0

HIGHLAND FIRE

Books by Ruth Langan

Harlequin Historicals

Mistress of the Seas #10
Texas Heart #31
*Highland Barbarian #41
*Highland Heather #65
*Highland Fire #91

*Highland Series

Harlequin Books

Harlequin Historical Christmas Stories 1990
"Christmas at Bitter Creek"

RUTH LANGAN

traces her ancestry to Scotland and Ireland. It is no surprise, then, that she feels a kinship with the characters in her historical novels.

Married to her childhood sweetheart, she has reared five children and lives in Michigan, the state where she was born and raised.

To Tom, Maureen and little Tom III.
The circle is unbroken.
And to the Tom who owns my heart.

Prologue

England
Fleet Prison, 1566

At the sound of booted feet echoing hollowly along the vast chambers, every prisoner looked up in fear. Most of the beatings were meted out at night, when there would be few witnesses.

When the footsteps halted outside the door of their cell, the two brothers glanced at each other, then turned to face the wrath of the jailer. While two men stood guard outside the cell, the one with the whip turned the key in the lock, then stepped inside. Rats scurried away as the light spilled into the dank cell. With feet apart, hands on hips, the jailer stood regarding his latest victims. The flickering light of the torch cast his face into the twisted mask of the devil.

"Who'll be first?"

The taller of the two prisoners stepped in front of his younger brother.

"Nay, Kieran," the younger one protested. "He'll lay you open again."

"If he's man enough." Kieran O'Mara touched a hand to his torn flesh and prayed the jailer would expend most of his energy on him before turning to the lad he tried to shield.

"Move aside," the jailer shouted. "I know yer game. Ya've taken his beatings for the last four nights. This time I'll start wi' the weakling."

As the jailer raised his hand, it was caught in a grip of steel. His eyes widened at the raw strength of the prisoner.

"Ya dare to defy me? Seize him," the jailer shouted.

Instantly the two guards dropped their torches and wrestled the man to the floor of the cell. While they pinned him, the jailer sneered, "Now I'll tell ya the truth, since ya'll not live to repeat it. We've been ordered to see ya never leave this place alive, O'Mara, you and your brother." He gave a shrill laugh. "And the best of all is that ye were betrayed by one who calls himself friend to ye." The jailer's lips curled into a sneer. "And ya musn't concern yerself about yer lovely mum. She'll be well taken care of. So long as she pleases m'lord. If ya know what I mean." With a laugh he brought the whip down upon the younger prisoner again and again.

Kieran was suddenly filled with such rage that even the two guards could not contain him. With a burst of determination he broke free of the hands restraining him and battered the two men until they fell to the floor. Then, with a cry of fury, he brought his arm around the jailer's throat.

With his lips close to the jailer's ear he snarled, "Tell me who betrayed us."

The jailer gave another evil sneer and defiantly clamped his mouth shut.

"His name, damn you, or I swear you'll die."

Again the jailer grunted and refused to speak.

Kieran's fury boiled over. "Then take your bloody secret to the grave." He heard the bones of the neck snap. As the jailer crumpled to the floor, Kieran knelt beside the bloodied form of his younger brother.

"Hold on, Colin. We are leaving this prison. We are going home."

With a tenderness that belied his massive size he lifted the battered body of his brother in his arms and carried him along the maze of passageways until they were free of the prison they had shared for the past year.

Kieran trudged through narrow streets and filthy passages until the city was far behind. He walked all night without stopping. And when the dawn light touched the horizon, he climbed to a hayloft and cradled his brother's body to his chest to keep him warm.

"I give you my word, Colin. You'll not be buried in this godless land."

At Colin's slight nod, Kieran felt a wave of relief. At least he was still conscious.

By evening, his brother's lips were blue. Kieran knew there was little time left. But he had never been one to break a promise. Though the journey before them would shatter the spirit of most men, he never flinched. As soon as the sun dipped below the hills, he lifted his brother in his arms and began the trek that would not end until dawn. He passed through villages and tiny hamlets, waded through streams and crossed fields of grain, stealing food to sustain their strength. And through it all, his mind worked feverishly. He did not yet know who had arranged their imprisonment in Fleet, but if it took him a lifetime, he vowed, he would learn the name of his enemy. And seek vengeance.

On the sixth day they had left England behind. When they reached the banks of the River Tweed in Scotland, Kieran wrapped the feverish lad in a stolen cloak and turned to study the Highlands looming in the mist.

"It's not Ireland, but it's not England, either. Do not fear, Colin. I will only leave you long enough to find food and weapons." And a sturdy horse, he thought. For the journey home was far from over. It had, in fact, only begun.

Chapter One

᷈᷈᷈᷈᷈᷈

"You make me proud, lass," Duncan MacAlpin commented, standing as tall as his seventy-six years would allow.

Beside him on the balcony, the golden-haired leader of her clan, Megan MacAlpin, blinked away the sudden tear that threatened. Looking out at the sea of dear faces, she was overcome with emotion. The grounds of MacAlpin Castle were filled with the people who had come to pay their respects to this man.

Megan's eldest sister, Meredith, was here with her husband, Brice Campbell, and their two wee bairns, as well as an entourage of Highland warriors, and of course Brice's foster son, Jamie MacDonald, now grown to manhood.

Megan's middle sister, Brenna, had come from England with her husband, Morgan Grey, who hovered by her side, seeing to her every need. His tender ministrations toward his wife, who was swollen with their first child, brought a smile to Megan's lips. Who would have ever dreamed that two such ruthless creatures as Brice Campbell, the infamous Highland Barbarian, and Morgan Grey, the English Queen's Savage, could be tamed by the love of two very different women?

That quiet power wielded by her sisters was alien to Megan. If there was some secret potion that a woman used on a man, Megan had not yet learned of it. She wanted no part of the silliness that went on between lovers. Love, she thought with a sudden frown. Look at all the turmoil it created. She glanced at the man who stood proudly beside her.

Old Duncan had served faithfully as man-at-arms to Megan's father and grandfather, as well as to her sisters Meredith and Brenna. Yet it was not advanced age, nor failing health, that had finally robbed him of his position of importance. It was the care of the woman he loved.

"My Mary's steps are faltering. She needs me with her night and day. 'Tis the only reason compelling enough to take me from your side. I hope you understand why I must step aside, lass."

Megan did understand. She had seen that same kind of love shimmering between her father and mother until their deaths.

The old man's voice broke. "You are so young to be leader of our people. I had hoped to stand with you."

Choosing to disregard protocol, Megan wrapped her arms around the old man's neck and hugged him fiercely. "I know, Duncan." For a moment her voice caught in her throat and she stroked his head. "You have been brother, father, grandfather to me. I know what it has cost you to give up this place of honor. Especially," she murmured, "since your own son and grandson lie buried in the ground."

"Aye. There is no one left to carry on the tradition."

"You have given all that a man can give." In loud, clear tones she called out to those below, "I give you the most loyal soldier in all of Scotland. Duncan MacAlpin."

The crowd roared their approval. Megan stepped back, leaving the old man alone to face his cheering friends. When she made her way inside, one warrior disengaged himself from the others and followed her.

As the crowd surged forward Brice Campbell leaned down and whispered to his wife. Meredith nodded. A moment later Brice threaded his way through the throng and strode into the castle. He paused outside the door to the library.

From inside came the sound of a man's voice raised in anger.

"I am the strongest warrior in our clan. No man can best me in a fight."

Brice recognized the strident tones of Malcolm MacAlpin, a distant cousin to Megan.

"Aye." It was Megan's voice, unusually calm, quiet. "Especially if 'tis fought your way."

"My way?" The words were spoken in anger.

"In a fair fight, there are probably several who could best you, Malcolm."

"When my life hangs in the balance, I do not care about the fairness of the fight. I care only for survival."

"As well we all do. But my man-at-arms must be above reproach. There are those who say you would use any means to achieve victory." She leveled her gaze on him. "There are even those who say your true loyalty lies with England."

He flushed. "I am a Scot, born and bred. But I am no fool. Our future must be tied to England's. That is no reason to reject me as your second in command. We are not at war with England. Our Queens are cousins."

"As are we."

"Aye. I am Duncan's nephew. Since he has no more sons or grandsons, I am the logical choice to replace him."

"Your logic, mayhap. But the choice will be mine alone."

Malcolm's voice rose. "If you do not choose me, I will be disgraced among our people."

"Understand me, Malcolm. I do not call disgrace upon your name. But neither will I choose you to be my man-at-arms."

For a moment Malcolm was too stunned to speak. Then he found his voice, and his tone held an edge of fury. "Mark me well, Megan MacAlpin. If you do not grant me this honor, you are no longer my leader. Nor are we family. From this day forward, I shall serve only myself. And someday—" his voice lowered ominously "—you shall pay dearly for this slight upon my name."

The door was yanked open and a wild-eyed Malcolm pushed past Brice and strode away.

Stepping into the library, Brice found Megan standing before the fireplace, her head bowed in contemplation.

A cozy fire burned on the hearth, sending occasional sparks up the chimney. The scent of leather-bound books and ledgers hung in the air. Despite the tranquil setting, raw energy flowed from the young woman.

As he closed the door, she turned toward him. "So, Brice. Have you had enough of the celebration?"

"I might ask you the same."

Megan shrugged. "'Tis Duncan's day. And his Mary's. They have no need of me for a while."

"I could not help overhearing Malcolm's words. Be on your guard, Megan. He could prove to be a dangerous enemy."

"I will not be threatened by every vain peacock who desires a place at my side."

It was like her to dismiss the threat. Had Megan, he wondered, ever been truly afraid of anything? "Who have you chosen to replace Duncan?"

Before answering him she turned to glance at the rolling lawn, alive with the brilliant hues of the men's saffron shirts and Highland plaids and the colorful gowns of the women. "I have several young warriors in mind. 'Twill be difficult to fill Duncan's boots."

"Aye. Your man-at-arms must be willing to lay down his life for you."

"As I would for any member of my clan. He must be skilled with longbow and broadsword, as well as sword and dirk."

"Mayhap most important, he must be loyal to the death."

"Aye." Megan paused for a moment, then gave him a smile. "You are not a man to seek me out for small talk, Brice. Nor to eavesdrop on my... discussions with my unhappy clansman."

Brice found himself wondering how many hearts would be broken by that dazzling, beguiling smile. "Nay. I have come to offer a candidate for your consideration."

She arched an eyebrow. "A Highlander?"

"Not by birth. But in his heart he will always be one."

Her eyes widened as she realized where this was leading. "Surely not Jamie MacDonald?"

"And why not?"

"He is your son, Brice. As you yourself said, if not by birth, then at least in his heart. And in your heart, as well."

"Aye. I do love him like a son. And always will. But now that I have wee bairns of my own, I yearn for the quiet of home and hearth. Meanwhile, Jamie grows restless. He yearns to be in the thick of battle."

"Battle," she scoffed. "We are at peace with the English. Or so our Queens have decreed."

Brice's smile grew. "For the moment. But you and I know, lass, that such a fragile peace can be broken at any time. Living here on the border, there is a sense of anticipation, a sense of adventure that is missing these days in the Highlands. Here you must be ever ready to fight for what is yours."

She met his smile with one of her own. "I need no lectures on the dangers of living on the border, Brice. I am always prepared for a fight."

"Aye," he said dryly. "As is Jamie. You are two of a kind, Megan. Your blood heats at the very thought of war. That is why I offer him for your consideration. He would make a fine man-at-arms. I have taught Jamie all I know. He is a skilled warrior. If I were to find myself in battle, I would want him by my side. And I would trust the lad with my life and that of those I love."

"How would Jamie feel about leaving the Highlands? Would he not feel isolated from those he loves?"

"We have already talked of it. Perhaps one part of him will always stay with us in the Highlands. But another part of him needs to be here, where his father and his father's people lived."

Megan turned away to gaze into the flickering flames of the fire. For long moments she was silent, pondering the choice that lay before her.

In the past few years, since her sister's marriage to Brice Campbell, Jamie and Megan had grown close. Being just a few years apart, they had played like frisky colts, wrestling and racing, burning up energy in endless teasing. Megan was completely comfortable in Jamie's company. He was the closest thing to a brother she would ever have.

She turned and met Brice's gaze. "It is a generous thing you offer, Brice, to give up the lad who is like a son to you. If Jamie MacDonald is willing, I should welcome him by my side."

Brice nodded. "I will send him to you and the two of you can seal your pact."

He opened the door, then paused with his hand still on the door pull and turned to Megan. "A word of caution. Duncan's zeal was tempered with age and experience. Though Jamie is an able soldier, he is perhaps too much like you. You are both young, hot-blooded and headstrong. Beware that you do not lead each other into dangers that are best left unexplored."

"Aye."

Her quick, impish smile did nothing to dispel the thread of doubt that tugged at Brice.

When the door closed behind the Highlander, Megan glanced at her father's sword hanging over the fireplace. Her sword now, and she would handle it with all the skill of a seasoned warrior. With Jamie MacDonald at her side, she would welcome any army that dared to invade.

She lifted her skirts and resumed her pacing, eager to welcome her new man-at-arms. Suddenly she felt like joining the others in celebration. The threat from Malcolm MacAlpin was quickly forgotten.

* * *

Kieran O'Mara knelt in the shade of the forest and studied the herd of deer that grazed a short distance away. He had fashioned a stick into a crude knife. That and his hands were his only weapons; he needed nothing more. He forced himself to remain perfectly still as his gaze roamed the thick foliage. He would allow the doe and fawns to pass by unmolested and take the buck that brought up the rear. The meat from such a kill would sustain him and Colin on the long journey ahead. The thought of his weakened brother gave him renewed strength. Colin trusted him to bring them safely home. Kieran would not let him down.

The deer suddenly lifted their heads in alarm. Kieran's eyes narrowed as he peered through the forest to see what had startled them.

Two riders approached. Kieran felt a rush of anger and frustration. He had been so close. So close. Hunger gnawed at him. His hand tightened on the wooden weapon as he strained to watch and listen.

"Now then. Do you not agree that the game is more plentiful here?"

Kieran studied the lad whose voice carried on the wind. Though the youth was tall and heavily muscled, Kieran had no doubt he could best him in a fight. The lad had youth on his side, but Kieran had something far more compelling—desperation.

"Aye." Megan agreed, patting the bag that dangled from her saddle. "We have caught more quail and dove in the past hour than I often see in a day."

As they urged their mounts across a stretch of flat meadowland ringed by gently rising forests, Megan gave a quick glance over her shoulder. "Keep a close watch out for the MacDougals. Though this is open land, they have long considered it theirs. They will be spoiling for a fight if they find us stalking their deer."

So they were poachers, like him. Kieran kept the lass in his line of vision. From this distance he saw that she rode like a man, with her gown hiked up to reveal tanned, shapely limbs. Her gown was a shimmering shade of amber that caught the sun's rays. The shirred bodice hugged her high firm breasts and tiny waist. Her mane of wheat-colored hair danced against her shoulders.

Jamie touched the sword at his waist. "If it is a fight the MacDougals want, I will be more than happy to oblige."

Megan's laughter rippled on the breeze. "Brice was right. Your blood runs as hot as mine at the thought of battle."

As he watched from his place of concealment, Kieran's eyes narrowed at the woman's laughter. How long had it been since he had heard such a wondrous sound. For one brief moment it stirred something in his heart that he had thought long dead. He had feared that a year in Fleet Prison had destroyed everything human in him.

Jamie gave a sound of disgust. "Someone has to be prepared to fight. Your sister has poor Brice so besotted, he would rather lie by the fire and bounce his bairns on his knee than tend to the work of a warrior."

"Aye. But you should be grateful that the old ones are willing to step back and give us the chance to take our rightful places."

"Old? Brice?" Jamie threw back his head and roared. "If Brice ever heard you say that, he would wring your pretty little neck."

"You know what I mean." Megan shot Jamie a look. "Something terrible happens to people when they fall in love. Look at Brice and Meredith. They have turned into complacent married people. And look at what Brenna has done to Morgan Grey. He spent the entire fortnight at our castle hovering around her like a clucking hen."

"Aye." Jamie met her frown with one of his own. "It fair tears my heart out to see a warrior like Brice Campbell wiping spittle from a wee bairn's chin and talking about peace with the enemy."

Megan could not help laughing at Jamie's apt description. Dear Jamie. She understood his frustration. And he was the only one who understood hers. She glanced at the proud man beside her and tried to picture the lad she had met years before. Jamie had been but a slender lad, all elbows and knees, with a shock of red hair that had rivaled the sun. Now, scant years later, his shoulders were wider than a broadsword, his back and arms rippling with the muscles of a warrior. His pale skin had turned to bronze, and his red hair had darkened to a rich, warm auburn. Already the Highland lasses fluttered their lashes when he rode past their villages, and they vied for his attention. Thankfully, he had not yet noticed. Or at least had given no indication that he had. But one day soon he would fall into love's silken web like all the others. Then she would be the only sensible one...

"Look." Megan leaned from the saddle and touched Jamie's arm. "In those trees."

Both of them caught sight of the antlers disappearing among the foliage.

"I bet you a sovereign that I bring him down before you," Megan called, sliding from the saddle and dropping the reins.

Before Jamie could react she was across the meadow and following the buck into the forest. He leaped to the ground and ran after her.

As the two disappeared, Kieran turned to where their horses stood grazing. A slow smile touched his lips as he stepped from the forest and moved cautiously toward the animals. But before he could take up the reins, he heard the thunder of hoofbeats. At the far side of the meadow rode a line of armed men. Leaving the horses, Kieran slipped into the cover of the forest.

"The herd has slipped away," Megan concluded.

"We could follow them," Jamie eagerly suggested.

"Aye. And end up torn by brambles and halfway up the mountain when daylight fades."

"We have slept under the stars before."

"That we have. But I much prefer my own bed, Jamie. Besides, our bags are already swollen with game. I have had enough of hunting."

"Do not tell me you are turning into a weak-kneed female."

"You know me better," she said, laughing.

Megan pushed her way through the underbrush until she stepped into the brilliant sunshine of the meadow. Instantly her smile was wiped from her face.

"God in heaven. Jamie. Look."

He turned to where she pointed. The riders had already spotted their horses and were racing toward them.

Megan and Jamie drew their swords and waited for the first attack. Without their horses, they were at a distinct disadvantage. What was worse, they were vastly outnumbered.

"I count at least a dozen of them," Jamie said under his breath.

"Aye. That leaves eight for me," Megan said, planting her feet squarely. "And four for you, my lad."

From his position in the forest, Kieran heard the low rumble of laughter before the two bravely faced their attackers.

Fools, he thought. What chance did a lad and a lass have against a dozen men? They would surely be dead before half the men had even raised a sword. Yet, he reminded himself, the fight was not his. And even if he wanted to go to their aid, he had no weapon.

He intended to turn away and make his escape before anyone had time to discover him, but found he could not. As he watched from the cover of the forest, his curiosity slowly turned to surprise. The two were skilled warriors.

Though he watched both with admiration, it was the woman who held his attention. She danced, parried and thrust until the first attacker found himself unseated from the saddle and backed up to a tree. A second attacker soon joined the first, but the lass bested them both and sent them to their knees.

She fought with dirk and sword, and though her attackers towered over her, she refused to back away.

"Are these the MacDougals?" Jamie asked as several more of the horsemen closed in for an attack.

"Nay. These are not Scotsmen. They are bloody English."

At Megan's words, Kieran's eyes widened. He had thought the shabby men to be Highlanders, but as he studied them, realization dawned. The long hand of English justice reached even beyond its own borders. They were here to bring him and Colin to Fleet Prison.

He thought of Colin, alone and wounded. If he did not soon return to tend him, the lad would surely perish. For Colin's sake, he yearned to escape, but it was not in his nature to run from a fight. Especially knowing that these two innocents were being attacked because of him.

Though they fought with great skill, it was apparent that the two would soon be overwhelmed by the sheer number of their attackers.

Without a thought to his own safety, he stepped from the forest. Bending, he retrieved a sword from the hand of one of the Englishmen.

From the corner of her eye, Megan saw the stranger join in the fray. When she realized that he was standing with them against the attackers, she returned her attention to the task at hand.

The fight had now become a deadly game of skill.

"Behind you, lass."

At Kieran's words, Megan turned and found herself facing another swordsman. With quick movements she drove him back, then dodged his thrust. By the time she had disposed of him, two more faced her. Backing up, she found herself pressed against the stranger, who was fighting to hold off two other swordsmen.

"Good work, lass," Kieran called as she sent her opponent to the ground.

There was no time to reply. The swordsmen were everywhere, some still on horseback, others leaping to the ground to aid their fallen comrades.

Suddenly Jamie saw a man leap from the forest and race toward Megan. In the blink of an eye he knew that this man was not one of the English, but Megan's cousin Malcolm, and he was headed toward her with serious intent. Jamie shouted a warning, then turned to his own battle.

"Malcolm! You traitor!" Megan felt the pain, sharp and swift, as her opponent's sword pierced her shoulder. That only renewed her efforts. She felt her breath coming faster as she drove her attacker back with quick thrusts. Beside her Jamie fought gamely to hold off two swordsmen.

Megan watched in horror as Jamie lunged forward just as one of the attackers raised his weapon. The impact plunged the blade into Jamie's chest, stilling his words. With a gasp, Jamie dropped to his knees in the heather. Both of his hands closed around the hilt of the sword. But he had not the strength to pull it free. An ever-widening river of blood stained his tunic and formed a pool among the blossoms.

"You have killed him! God in heaven. You have killed him."

Had not Brice warned her about leaping into battle? Jamie's blood was upon her hands. With tears of rage blurring her vision, Megan sprang at Jamie's attacker, her sword raised.

Kieran was stunned by the lass's desperate struggle. Could he do less than this girl? If it cost them all their lives, they had to fight on until there was no breath left to draw.

He saw the Scotsman come up behind her. But before he could shout a warning, Kieran found himself cornered. With a skill born of desperation he fought off his attackers. Colin was depending upon him. He was fighting not only for his own life, but for that of his brother. He had come too far to be defeated by a handful of English.

Now only three attackers remained. Seeing the fate of the others, they fell back and disappeared into the forest. The sounds of battle stilled, and the land became strangely silent.

Kieran turned toward the girl, who lay beside her fallen comrade.

Kieran knelt beside her and probed her wounds. She was bleeding from several cuts. Worse, she had sustained a terrible blow to the head.

Gingerly touching the swollen mass at the base of her skull, Kieran whispered, "Can you hear me, lass?"

She lay as still as death. Kieran touched a hand to her throat and felt the pulse. It was faint, feeble, but a heartbeat nonetheless.

He turned to where the lad lay, moaning softly.

"Can you hear me?"

Jamie stared beyond the stranger at the still form of Megan. "Does she live?"

"Aye. Barely."

"Praise heaven. You must save her," Jamie whispered urgently. "I was sworn to see to her safety, and I have failed her."

"You cannot blame yourself. You fought bravely."

"It was not enough. You must save her life."

"First I must rid you of this knife." With quick movements Kieran pulled the dirk from Jamie's chest and felt a wave of relief that the wound was not mortal. From the back of Jamie's saddle he removed a flagon and poured a small amount of the liquid from the flagon over the raw flesh. Ignoring Jamie's hiss of pain, he tore strips from his own shirt and bound the wound. Then he removed a cloak from Jamie's saddle and wrapped the lad carefully.

"The wound is clean. With rest, you should be able to sit your horse by morning."

He saw that the lad was fading quickly. Within minutes he would surely be beyond thought.

"The lady. You must see to her."

Kieran lifted his hands in frustration. "I am a stranger passing through your land. I have nowhere to take the lass."

Jamie shook his head. "You do not understand. The lady is of noble birth. Her life must be saved at all cost. You cannot leave her here. There was one among the attackers who is her sworn enemy. He would end her life."

"What would you have me do?"

"Stay with her. See to her." Jamie's eyes were bleak. "I have failed my first task as the lady's man-at-arms. Without Megan's safety, my life is worth nothing." His hand clutched Kieran's sleeve. "I beg you. Do not leave the Lady Megan here to die."

Kieran saw the fierce light in the lad's eyes before his lids fluttered, then closed.

He pressed his lips close to the lad's ear. "Who are her people? Where is her home?"

Jamie had lapsed into unconsciousness.

With a muttered oath, Kieran gathered the weapons of the fallen soldiers. They were his now.

He studied the still figure of the girl. Except for the faint rise and fall of her chest, she made no movement.

Lifting the lass in his arms, he pulled himself into the saddle of one horse and caught up the reins of a second horse.

There was no time to tarry. Colin had been alone too long.

As the horses picked their way through the forest, his mind raced. What cruel game was fate playing? He had already given his word to Colin that he would take him safely home. And now he was saddled with this helpless female, as well. A female who was a complete mystery to him.

Chapter Two

Megan felt pain as sharp as the blade of a knife.

So this was what it felt like to die. Aye, she must be near death's door. It seemed only right that she sacrifice her life. Jamie was dead, and it was her fault. She must now die also.

Jamie. She saw his dear face, heard his joyous laughter ring through her mind. Jamie. Rogue. Tease. Brother. Friend. She felt a sudden shaft of pain around her heart. Jamie gone. It was too much to bear. But even as she mourned the loss of him, she felt his image fading from her mind. It was replaced by a physical pain. And then, as the pain grew, she knew another wave of fear. It was not death she feared, but the pain of dying. The pain was everywhere, exploding through her. She tried to absorb it, to ignore it, but it would not let her be. It was there, in her shoulder, her arm, her head. Especially her head. Surely her skull had been split.

She was hot, so hot. And her limbs were too heavy to move. Even her eyelids were heavy. It was too great an effort to open her eyes.

"Easy, lass."

A deep, masculine voice washed over her. Megan did not recognize it, and yet she knew she had heard those deep tones before.

Someone touched her. She stiffened, determined to resist. But she could not. And then the fear subsided. It was the angels. She felt the angels come for her. And though she had always thought she would fight against dying, she found herself welcoming their tender touch. Their firm hands reached out for her. She was floating, then drifting. They lifted her as lovingly as if she were a wee bairn. Their strong arms cradled her in a warm cocoon. She felt a heart beating. Hers? It must be. Angels had no hearts. It was strangely comforting to hear that steady, even heartbeat. Perhaps it was her last.

Suddenly she breathed in the familiar musky scent that she had always associated with her father. She felt his arms, strong, muscled, cradling her against his massive chest. She felt his cloak, rough and scratchy against her cheek. It smelled faintly of horses, and of the fields. Father. Somehow the angels had managed to bring him along to welcome her. A soft smile touched her lips, and she sighed as she wrapped her arms around his neck and clung to him. The pain was forgotten now. She was with the angels. And Father. She was at peace.

Kieran stared down at the lass in his arms. Blood matted her hair, and her skin was so pale he could see the blue veins just below the surface. She appeared tiny and fragile and as helpless as a wounded bird. Yet he knew her looks were deceiving. He had seen her face her enemy with fire in her eyes.

A woman of noble birth, the lad had said. Kieran had no reason to disbelieve him. Still, he had never known a high-born woman who could fight like a man.

He thought of his mother, a noble Englishwoman, accustomed to the luxuries of life at court. Though she had given up much out of love for her Irish husband, Kieran could not picture that gentle woman wielding a sword against invaders.

He heard the lass sigh and saw the slight smile that curved her lips. Where had her mind taken her? He hoped it was a kinder place than the bloody one she had just left. Even if the pain was forgotten for only a few minutes, it was a blessing. For when she returned to the land of the living, the pain of her head wound would not be easily ignored.

He was concerned about all her wounds, but especially the one to her head. It was bad. He had seen men die of lesser wounds. But the lass was a fighter. Somehow, he felt, she would not go willingly into that other world. He drew her close against his chest and wrapped his arms around her to ward off the chill air and nudged his mount into a trot.

As they made their way through the forested countryside, Kieran studied the occasional castle or manor house in the distance, wondering which one belonged to the woman in his arms. Because he had spent so much time in Fleet, forbidden to speak, he found himself needing to talk. The girl could not hear him, but it made no difference. The freedom to speak was too precious.

"Your people will soon miss you, lass. There will be concern about you in your household, and then worry. Mayhap they will send out soldiers in search of you and your man-at-arms."

Kieran glanced at the woman who rested so easily in his embrace. "I would be pleased to give up my burden to those who would care for you." It was a lie, he knew. At the moment she was not a burden. In fact, holding her in his arms was an altogether pleasant experience. More pleasant than he cared to admit to himself. How long had it been since he had held a woman close to his heart? "But I cannot afford to reveal myself. There are those who care about nothing except returning me to an English prison and an English justice. And if they harm you in the process, they will shed no tears. So, my lady, though I would wish your people good fortune in locating you, I fear that throughout the journey I must keep to the shelter of the forest. Any who challenge me will have to answer to my sword."

The figure in his arms sighed and burrowed closer to his chest. A thrill of pleasure shot along his spine and he fought to ignore it. She was, after all, unconscious and unaware of what she was doing to him. But there was no denying that she was a rare beauty, and just holding her in his arms made him feel truly free. He knew that she had not heard his words, but it gave him an odd sense of independence to talk to her.

The sun was setting as they approached the River Tweed. Kieran urged the mount carefully among the trees that grew close to the water's edge. Without warning he brought the steed to a halt and slid from the saddle. The movement jarred Megan awake. Her mind was befuddled. She could not seem to distinguish between the hot, searing pain in her body and the one in her mind.

This could not be heaven. She felt a moment of terror. Had she lived such an evil life that she was being condemned for all time to the fires of hell? Nay, there was someone, someone important to her, who was taking her to a safe haven. But who?

Though she struggled, she could not see the image of that important person in her mind's eye. She saw only a terrible blackness that threatened to envelope her in its web.

With a tremendous effort she forced her eyes open.

The glint of the setting sun reflecting off the water sent pain stabbing through her. She quickly closed her eyes, then set her teeth against the pain and forced them open again.

She was being carried in a stranger's arms. As he bent and deposited her in the grass, she caught a glimpse of dark hair and a face covered with a growth of dark beard. The eyes, too, were dark, piercing, as they glanced at her a moment before dismissing her. She had a sudden flash of memory, of seeing the man holding a sword and fighting beside her. As the stranger walked away, the image was erased.

Megan's eyes adjusted to the dim light of the forest. She saw what appeared to be a bundle of rags lying beneath a tree nearby. She watched as the stranger knelt beside the rags.

"Colin." Kieran touched a hand to the still form and felt a wave of relief when his brother moaned softly. "I've brought food. And horses and weapons," he added softly.

"I'll build a fire now, and we will eat. 'Tis what we need to regain our strength."

Gathering twigs and dried grass, Kieran soon had a fire burning. From the bags slung across the saddles he removed several plump doves and placed them over a spit. While they cooked, he fetched water from the river and knelt beside his brother, bathing his fevered body.

From her position nearby Megan watched and listened. She had no idea who these men were. From his condition it was plain to see that the one called Colin had been badly beaten.

Was that why she ached so? Had she been beaten, as well?

She thought about crawling to the safety of the underbrush, but found that her body would not respond to the simplest commands. When she attempted to sit up, a moan escaped her lips. Instantly Kieran hurried to her side.

"Are you in pain, lass?"

She tried to focus on the man who towered over her, but it was too much effort. Though her gaze met his, he could see the vacant look in her eyes.

"You'll be fine. You've taken a blow to your head. You need rest."

She nodded, too weary to speak. But the questions that plagued her would not permit her to sleep. Instead she lay, wide-eyed, watching as the stranger moved around, preparing food.

When the fowl was roasted, Kieran cradled Colin's head in his lap.

"I cannot eat," the man protested.

"You must."

"Who is the lass?"

While Kieran broke off pieces of fowl and fed his brother, he explained, "She and her companion wanted the same deer that I had spotted. Unfortunately, we were denied the pleasure by a band of English soldiers."

"English." Colin pushed his brother's hand away and shot him a questioning glance.

"Aye. Lucky for me, the lass and her friend were no strangers to sword and knife."

At Colin's look of surprise, Kieran gave a low chuckle. "I do not jest. The lass handled herself like one raised on the battlefield."

Megan's hand clenched, and she tried to imagine herself holding a sword. Could the man be speaking the truth? She could not seem to remember.

"What of the English?"

"We bested some. Those fortunate enough to evade the lass's sword sought refuge in the forest. But we are not rid of them yet. They are like dogs with a bone. They will continue to search until they find us."

"Sweet Mary. We must leave this place." As Colin made a move to stand, his brother restrained him.

"Nay. We have eluded them for the moment. You must regain your strength before we begin the journey home."

"And the girl's companion?" Colin caught his brother's hand in a surprisingly strong grip. "You did not—kill him?"

Megan went very still, dreading the stranger's reply.

"Her companion was only slightly wounded. I dressed his wounds and covered him with a warm cloak. By now he is able to sit a horse and return to his home. But he feared for the lass's safety. Her wounds are much more severe. Since she is of noble birth, I consented to return her to her people before we begin our journey home."

Colin gave a sigh, unaware that the object of their discussion was breathing a sigh of her own. "Praise God," Colin whispered. "Ours is a dangerous journey, Kieran. 'Twould not be fair to involve this innocent lass."

"Aye. I'll keep my promise to the lad."

Kieran. Megan turned her head, trying to focus on the stranger. At least now he had a name.

Kieran tore off another piece of fowl and watched in satisfaction as his brother continued to eat. His appetite was a clear sign that his wounds were healing and his strength was returning.

"No more, Kieran." Colin pushed his hand away when he attempted to give him more food.

"You must eat, Colin. We have miles to go."

"Aye. Tomorrow. But now I must sleep."

Kieran held the dipper to his brother's lips and watched as he drank deeply. Wearily Colin lowered himself in the rags that served as his covering. Within minutes his breathing was shallow.

From the saddle Kieran removed the cloaks he had taken from the dead in the meadow. He spread one over his brother, then wrapped another around the girl.

Megan shivered inside the warm cloak and tried to concentrate on the things she had heard, but the effort was too great. She seemed unable to hold a single thought. With a sigh, her eyes closed and she fell into a troubled sleep.

Satisfied that he had done all he could to make both of the wounded comfortable, Kieran sat down, resting his back against a fallen log. He ate quickly until his hunger abated.

In her dreamlike state, Megan struggled along a dark, narrow tunnel. The heat inside the tunnel was stifling. Each movement forward was slow and painful. But she could not go back. Up ahead there was a pale, flickering light. She had to reach the light. There she would find relief from the heat and darkness.

Her hands tore at the cloak that threatened to suffocate her. She felt the night cool her heated flesh. Her lids fluttered, then opened. A small flame danced in a bed of glowing coals. Overhead a million stars shone in a black velvet sky. The moon's glow trailed a patch of gold across the dark waters of the river. She drew in several long, shuddering breaths, relieved that her nightmare had ended. Or had it? A snap of a twig had her stiffening as she peered through the darkness. Though she did not recognize her surroundings, it was neither the darkened outlines of trees nor the creatures that prowled at night that caused her uneasiness. It was the presence of the stranger.

Megan watched as a tall, broad-shouldered man walked to the river's edge and removed his ragged shirt. A gasp escaped her lips. Even from this distance the moonlight clearly illuminated a patchwork of scars that crisscrossed his back.

When all his garments were removed Kieran dove into the river and disappeared beneath the waves, surfacing some distance away. The cool water was like a soothing balm to his wounds. As he swam effortlessly he felt the tension of the day slowly dissolve. With powerful strokes he swam across the river and back. When he reached the shallows he rose up from the water and shook his head, then waded the short distance to shore.

Megan could not tear her gaze from him. His body was splendid, with massive shoulders and a hair-roughened chest that tapered to a narrow waist and trim, flat stomach. He dressed quickly, tucking a dirk into his waistband, then bent to retrieve a sword that lay in the grass.

When he reached Megan's side he surprised her by bending close. Moonlight glinted on the drops of water that clung to his dark hair. His eyes were narrowed, questioning, as he studied her.

"So. You are awake. Is the pain tolerable?"

"Aye. Barely."

His eyes softened with a hint of a smile as he touched a finger to the swollen mass at the base of her skull. "You sustained quite a blow."

She pulled away from him, attempting to evade his touch. "From you?"

Her question startled him. "You do not remember?"

"Nay." She found his touch to be gentler than she had expected. "Why have you brought me here?"

"I could not leave you on the bloody battlefield. You were too badly wounded. And I could not stay to tend you. My brother needed me. I could not tarry."

She glanced at the young man asleep beneath the tree. "Your brother?"

"Aye. He has been badly wounded. I left him to search for food. That was how I encountered you and your companion in the forest."

"My companion." The pain in her head was beginning to throb. She smelled the fowl still roasting on the fire and felt her stomach lurch. She was going to be sick, and she was too weak to turn away.

Kieran saw her discomfort and realized what was happening. Pouring water onto a rag, he pressed it to her fevered brow. When the sickness had passed, he cradled her head in his arms and held a cup of water to her lips.

"You need to eat. Else you will become so weakened, you will not have the strength to recover from your wounds."

She knew the wisdom of his words, but the thought of food sickened her. "Please. No food. Not yet."

"Water then."

She nodded and drank, then slumped weakly against him. The warmth of him gave her comfort. Though she did not know this man, she instinctively trusted him. The fragrance of the forest surrounded him. He smelled of cool green grass and river water. Soothing perfumes that reminded her of something . . . something forgotten. With her eyes closed she touched a hand to his beard and gave a soft sigh of contentment.

Kieran was startled by the feelings her touch aroused. Throughout the long nights in prison he had dreamed of a tender woman. Even now, holding her, he was afraid he only imagined the soft sigh, the gentleness of her touch.

"Rest now, my lady. I will keep watch and see you safely through the night."

A smile touched her lips. She sighed and brought his hand to her lips.

He experienced a rush of heat that left him shaken. The simple brush of her lips on his flesh had him trembling with need. He glanced at the woman. Her eyes were closed. By the time he had her wrapped in the cloak, she had once more slipped into unconsciousness. She had no idea that her simple touch had unlocked a flood of feelings in the man who had saved her life.

Thin sunlight filtered through the branches, warming the figures who lay beneath the trees.

Kieran awoke instantly and lay very still, listening to the sounds of the forest. Birds chirped, insects hummed, water lapped rhythmically against the shore. The setting was so tranquil, he longed to stay here and put off what lay ahead. But he could not delude himself into thinking that there was safety in this peaceful setting.

Those who had trailed him here would not give up their search so easily. As soon as Colin was strong enough to travel, they must begin the perilous journey home. And as for the lass, he thought, turning to where she slept, she must be returned to her people this day. She would recover more quickly among her own.

Yesterday, in the confusion of battle and the rush to return to Colin's side, there had been no time to appreciate her beauty. Now he allowed himself the luxury of studying her. Up close, her complexion was flawless. In the early morning sunlight her hair gleamed like fine ale. In her fevered state she had thrown off the cloak, and his gaze moved slowly over her slender body, noting the tiny waist, the flare of hips. Her shimmering gold gown was open at the throat, revealing the dark cleft between her breasts.

In repose her relaxed features were perfectly etched. Her upturned nose and haughty chin gave her a regal appearance. But it was her lips that held his attention. Such inviting lips. They were full, pursed in a little pout and appeared to be as soft as the dew that beaded the heather.

He watched as her lids fluttered, then slowly opened. The first glimpse of her amber eyes startled him. Yesterday they had appeared more emerald. This morning they gleamed like a cat's eyes.

Kieran could read her confusion as she struggled to recall where she was. "Are you in pain, my lady?"

"Pain? Aye. Who are you?" she asked.

"My name is Kieran O'Mara."

He spoke the name with a sense of pride that was not lost on her. Though his name meant nothing to Megan, he was obviously a man of some importance. "Why am I here?"

Kieran thought they had settled all this last night. "You were wounded in a battle with some English soldiers, my lady. And your companion asked me to see to your safe return."

"My companion?"

"Aye. The lad who fought by your side. He said he was your man-at-arms. He was wounded but not seriously. He insisted that I take you with me and deliver you to your people." He read the bewilderment in her eyes and forced his tone to remain gentle. "If you will tell me who you are, my lady, and where you come from, I will see that you are returned to your home. Your companion told me only that your name was Megan."

"Megan. That is my name?"

What game was the lady playing? he wondered as he watched a range of emotions contort her features. Mystification, anger, then sudden, wrenching fear.

This was not a game, he realized with a sudden clenching of his jaw. Something was wrong. Very wrong. "What are you saying, my lady?"

"God in heaven." He saw the flash of fire in her eyes before the realization sank in and they clouded with tears. "I do not know my name. Nor where my home lies." She buried her face in her hands. Her words were muffled as she began to weep. "Sweet Mother of God. I can remember nothing." She fought back a sob. "Nothing."

Chapter Three

Kieran was rocked back on his heels by her words. For long moments, while the lass wept, he studied her in silence. He had heard of warriors who sustained blows in battle that left them momentarily confused. He had even heard horror stories about some who never seemed to recover.

Her tears left him feeling helpless. Could this be the same girl who had fearlessly faced her attackers with a laugh of disdain? If he had been surprised by her skill with a weapon, he was equally surprised that she could dissolve into tears at this unexpected upheaval in her life.

When her tears were stilled, he touched a hand to her shoulder. "It will come back to you, my lady."

"But I cannot remember even the simplest facts. My name. My family. This companion you speak of. Even my home."

"It will return in time."

"Do you truly believe that?" She looked at him, the tears still damp upon her lashes.

"Aye. I do. For now, you must rest and regain your strength. And as your body heals, so shall your mind."

Megan swallowed the fear that tugged at her heart. It would do no good to give in to the weakness. But this was the worst terror she had ever encountered. Did she have family, friends? How had she spent her days? Was anyone mourning her disappearance? Would she ever discover her past? Or was it forever erased from her memory?

"My name is Megan," she told herself firmly. This was what she would cling to. She had a name, even if she did not know anything about herself.

"There is cold meat and little else, my lady. But you must eat something."

"Aye. Thank you." Megan accepted a joint of fowl from him and forced herself to chew. But the fear that clawed at her insides left the food tasting like ashes.

Kieran handed her a dipper of water and watched as she emptied it. His mind was working feverishly. He and Colin were not safe here. They must leave soon, else they would be found and returned to the hell of Fleet Prison. It would not be fair to involve this innocent lass in their troubles. The journey they were about to undertake was a long and perilous one. And yet how could he leave her here, alone and defenseless, not knowing who she was or where her home lay? She might wander these forests, close to her people, and never find her way back.

Megan saw the hard set of his jaw and knew that he was troubled. But her fears were too great to let her care about this stranger's problems. She glanced at the turrets of a castle that rose out of the mists across the river. If only she could see something familiar. Something that would trigger her memory.

It would have broken her heart to know that she was staring at the turrets of MacAlpin Castle, the home of her ancestors for over a hundred years. Within its walls Jamie MacDonald was even now preparing an army of men who would sweep from the borders of England to the forests of the Scottish Highlands. He would not rest until Megan MacAlpin was returned to the safety of her home.

"We can tarry no longer." Kieran's voice was muted, to avoid waking the sleeping woman.

"One more night will make little difference to our journey, Kieran. But it may be what the lass needs to regain her memory of herself."

"And if she still remembers nothing?"

Colin rejected the unpleasant thought. "You said yourself she was badly wounded. Give her time."

Kieran's voice grew rough. "It would be lovely to give her time. But we have none to give. Unless we leave here soon, we will be facing something far worse than the company of a lass with no memory."

Colin shivered and turned away. With his back to his brother he whispered, "You are correct, as always. We leave on the morrow. But I do not think the lass should accompany us."

"Would you leave her here to fend for herself?"

Colin shrugged. "Could we not hand her over to some of her countrymen and ask them to look after her?"

"Aye." Kieran thought about the conversation he had overheard between Megan and the lad when they were poaching in the highlands. They had been prepared to fight the MacDougals if they were caught. "And if we happen to hand her over to her enemies, will we justify it by saying that we had no choice?"

Colin gave a long sigh. "If she suffers because of us, her blood will be on our hands."

Kieran stood. His eyes narrowed. "Hers will not be the only blood on my hands."

Colin watched as his brother picked up a stone and began to sharpen the blade of his knife. He marveled at the inner strength of his older brother. Kieran had always made the difficult decisions for all of them. He was rarely wrong. But if he was wrong, he bore the weight of his errors in private.

It must be lonely, Colin thought, to feel responsible for so many lives. Yet he had never known Kieran to complain. Or to let down his guard for even a moment.

* * *

Kieran cooked all of the game, divided some to be eaten for their morning meal and carefully packed the rest in a pouch, to be eaten on the long journey as they needed it.

While Megan ate she watched Kieran saddle their horses. The two men had spoken of a journey, but neither had told her where they were headed.

"Is your home far from here?" She found it easy to converse with Colin. Why then the difficulty in speaking with his brother?

"Aye. It will be a treacherous journey." Colin struggled to pull a tattered tunic over his head. Megan saw him wince as the rough fabric tore at his raw flesh. She let her food fall to the grass.

"Let me look at your back."

"Nay."

He pulled away but was not quick enough. Lifting the cloth, she let out a gasp.

"God in heaven. These wounds are festering. You cannot ignore them."

"We have no time. I cannot cause any further delay."

"If you do not take the time to let these wounds heal, you will soon be unable to even sit a horse. Now lie still."

Megan walked to the water's edge and began picking herbs, flowers and roots. Then she located a flat rock and a smaller stone. Kneeling, she began sorting through the herbs and pounding them into a paste.

When the horses were saddled and ready, Kieran returned to the clearing. For a moment he was taken aback by the sight that greeted him. Megan was tenderly applying a salve to his brother's wounds. What was more amazing, Colin was offering no objection.

Leaning against the trunk of a gnarled old tree, Kieran stayed out of sight, watching and listening.

"Where did you learn the craft of healing, Megan?" Colin asked.

"I cannot remember."

Hearing the thread of fear in her voice, the young man's tone soothed. "Do not fret. It will come back to you."

Kieran saw the set of her jaw as she muttered, "Aye. It must. I cannot bear not knowing who I am."

She completed her ministrations, then helped him with his tunic. "Can you stand?"

Leaning heavily on her arm, Colin managed to get to his feet. Megan saw the effort it cost him. Sweat beaded his forehead and upper lip. His jaw was clenched. His eyes mirrored his pain.

"You are not ready to ride," Megan said softly.

"I will ride," Colin said fiercely. "And if I cannot sit a horse, I will order Kieran to tie me to my mount. We can tarry here no longer."

Both of them looked up as Kieran approached.

"Are you ready, Colin?"

"Aye."

Megan glanced at the frail, sandy-haired youth, whose handsome face, though hidden beneath a growth of red-brown beard, had a look of innocence about it. Then she compared him with the man beside him, who towered head and shoulders above any man she had ever met. His face was covered by a growth of dark beard.

Upon close inspection, she realized that the brothers shared the same startling dark eyes ringed with deep slate, and the same full lips. But apart from those similarities, they were very different. Kieran carried himself like a warrior. His instincts were those of a soldier. His voice rang with authority. It was obvious that he was a man accustomed to giving orders and having them followed without question. Colin appeared to be a gentle youth, with quiet voice and almost shy demeanor. From his speech she knew him to be an educated man.

Kieran helped his brother into the saddle. With quick, impatient gestures he lifted Megan onto the back of the second horse. At that simple touch, both of them felt the

pull. And both fought to ignore it. Kieran pulled himself up
behind her and caught up the reins.

As the horses moved out, Megan held herself stiffly in
Kieran's arms. It had been his arms holding her on the long
trek here. She breathed in the musky scent of him and knew.
He had held her as tenderly as a mother holds a bairn, and
she had clung to him like some helpless maiden and had
even buried her lips against his throat. Her cheeks colored
at the memory.

Seated behind her, Kieran fought his own demons. Damn
her for being so soft and inviting. Now, throughout the long
journey, he would have to double his efforts to feel nothing. His home, his family, his very life were in peril. He
could not afford to be distracted by this stranger.

They rode for hours, keeping to the cover of the forests.
And though Megan had thought Colin too weak to sit a
horse, he surprised her. Kieran, too, was amazed that his
brother found the strength to cover such a distance. When
at last they halted, Kieran helped Megan down and hurried
to his brother's side.

Weariness was etched on Colin's features. When his feet
touched the earth, he slumped to his knees.

"We will stay the night here." Kieran caught up the reins
of the horses and led them toward a small river.

When he returned, Megan had already spread a cloak
beneath a tree and was helping Colin to lie down.

Kieran tore a strip of fowl from the bone and tried to
hand it to his brother, but Colin waved his hand feebly.

"Nay. I am too weary."

"You must keep up your strength."

When Colin shook his head, Megan took the food from
Kieran's hands and placed it in the lad's mouth. Without
protest, Colin chewed. The action was repeated several times
until he held up a hand in protest.

"No more."

"Roll to your stomach," Megan commanded. "And lift your tunic. Your wounds need tending."

Kieran smiled as the lad obeyed. Perhaps, he mused as he busied himself preparing a fire, the lass would prove useful on the journey. With that infuriatingly commanding tone, she would be difficult to refuse.

When Colin was asleep, Kieran handed Megan some food and leaned against the trunk of a fallen tree.

She watched him as she bit into the cold fowl. Throughout the day they had spoken only when necessary. "Where will this journey take us?"

"My land lies across the North Channel."

As yet, that meant nothing to her. "Is it a great distance?"

"Aye."

"And what about my land? My people?"

He had anticipated her questions and had put her off as long as he could.

"I regret that you must leave this place. I realize that at any moment your memory may return. But my brother and I cannot stay."

"You are being hunted." She watched his eyes carefully. "You are escaped criminals?"

So she had heard much more than he had thought. "Aye. We escaped from Fleet Prison in London."

"Have you committed terrible crimes?"

"I would suppose that depends upon whose version you hear, my lady. The English would say we are enemies of the Crown. I would tell you that we fight for the freedom of our people. And you..." He filled the dipper and drank. "I know not what you would call us."

"Have you taken the life of another?"

"Aye."

"That is a most serious business, the taking of a life." She felt a moment of panic, wondering if she might be guilty of the same crime.

"Aye." She saw the fire in his eyes. And the truth. He did not deny. Neither did he offer excuses.

He filled the dipper with fresh water and handed it to her. "I must see to the horses." He strode quickly away.

Megan lifted the dipper to her lips and drank. Then, with a glance at the sleeping Colin, she turned toward the river. While Kieran was busy with the horses, she intended to pick more herbs and roots for a salve.

For long minutes she searched the riverbank, singling out those herbs and plants that held healing power. When she had gathered enough for several days, she set them on a rock.

The water beckoned her. With a quick glance around to determine that she was truly alone, she stripped away her dirty gown and scrubbed it, then hung it on the branch of a tree to dry. She pulled off her kid slippers, untied the ribbons of her chemise and watched as it dropped to her feet in the grass. She took a tentative step into the water. It felt cool and wonderful against her fevered flesh.

Oh, it was good to wash away the dried blood that crusted her wounds. She lifted her hands to her hair and scrubbed the strands until all traces of blood were gone. Then, ducking beneath the water, she came up feeling gloriously clean.

She touched a hand to the lump at the back of her head. The swelling had subsided considerably, though the pain was still there. She cautioned herself to be patient. Soon enough the pain would be gone. And, she hoped, her memory would return.

She peered at her reflection in the water. Through the ripples she saw a small, oval face and wide eyes. She traced a finger across her small nose and high cheekbones, then pulled her long hair away from her face for further study. Regret poured through her. It was the face of a stranger.

She ducked beneath the waves and swam hard and fast to vent her frustration. When at last she surfaced, she swam in a leisurely fashion from one bank of the narrow river to the other. It pleased her that she could swim. She smiled, wondering what other talents she possessed. For now, until her memory returned, she was a blank parchment, with nothing written on it. There was so much to learn about herself. But she would learn. She was determined to learn all she could about this woman called Megan.

From his position down the river, Kieran watered the horses, then tied them. His gaze was drawn to the figure in the water. She tossed her head, sending a spray of water into the air. Her hair settled on the waves like a veil of spun gold. Kieran watched as she strode from the water and pulled on a drift of ivory chemise. In profile her youthful body was perfect. And enticing. His gaze slid from her high, firm breasts to a waist so narrow his hands could surely span it. He felt the familiar churning deep inside as she draped a warm cloak around herself.

Kneeling, Megan proceeded to grind the herbs and roots into fresh salve, which she placed in a small square of fabric.

When she walked away, Kieran removed his clothes and walked into the river. There was nothing better than a swim in the cold waters of the river to restore his common sense.

A short time later, when he returned to the clearing, he found Megan kneeling beside the sleeping figure of his brother, applying the salve to his wounded back.

She stood. "His wounds are beginning to heal. But it will take a long time. They are deep. And they have been allowed to fester."

"Aye." As he began to pull on his shirt, Megan touched a hand to his arm.

Instantly she regretted her impulsiveness. The heat was like a lightning bolt, jarring her.

Kieran, too, felt it. And struggled not to.

"I . . ." Megan touched a tongue to her lips. "I could not help seeing the marks upon your back. Let me apply my ointment."

She was already regretting this. But there was no turning back.

"There is no need."

He turned away and she saw the raw, torn flesh before he could pull on his garment.

"Kneel down, Kieran. Even in this dim evening light I can see the signs of infection."

Reluctantly he knelt in the grass, and Megan began to spread the ointment over his wounds.

She started at the base of his neck and spread her hands open, moving them in slow, circular motions until the ointment was on each shoulder. How wide his shoulders. How muscular his arms. It was odd that she had such thoughts with Kieran. There had been nothing like this while she applied the salve to Colin's back. She felt her mouth go dry and forced herself to swallow.

She moved her hands lower and spread the ointment on a patchwork of raised scars that marred his flesh.

"Were these all inflicted in prison?"

"Aye." He found it annoying to have to reply.

How long it had been since a woman had touched him? He had forgotten the wonder of it. Though her hands were small, they were surprisingly strong. As they pressed, kneaded, soothed, a sigh was dragged from deep inside him.

"Anyone who could inflict such horrible pain on another is not a man," she said, her voice low with anger. "He is an animal who deserves no mercy. Is this why you escaped from prison?"

Kieran was silent for so long that Megan began to think he had not heard her. But then his voice came, and she recognized the hard edge of fury. "Nay. I could take the beatings. But I knew that Colin could take no more. Especially when our jailer confessed that we were to be beaten until we died."

"God in heaven. What was your crime?" Megan was unaware that her hands had stilled.

"Having the name O'Mara."

"I do not understand."

"You will." He turned to face her. A mistake, he realized immediately. But it was too late. Now that he could see those eyes, reflecting the gold of the moonlight, he was held by a force much stronger than his own will. "When you see what is happening in my land, you will understand why being an O'Mara is a crime the English will not tolerate."

"There is so much anger in you."

"Aye." But the anger was already being replaced with something else. Something far more dangerous. From the moment he had looked into those amber eyes, he had known it. Needs, desires long buried, now burst free.

He was determined not to give in to the feelings that churned inside him.

His gaze was arrested by the wound at Megan's shoulder. "It is your turn, lass. Give me the salve and kneel."

With a questioning look, she held out the square of fabric and knelt in front of him. Dipping his hand into the ointment, Kieran began to smooth it over her shoulder. Megan jumped as though burned, then forced herself to kneel perfectly still. But the man who knelt facing her was causing terrible havoc to her nerves.

"Lower your cloak, so I may spread this on your other wounds," he ordered.

"Nay. They are healing nicely. I have no need of the balm."

"You will do as I say, my lady. Or," he added with a slow smile, "I will remove it for you."

Very carefully Megan lowered her cloak and bent forward just enough to allow him to reach the wounds on her back.

Kieran knew this was a dangerous position. He needed only to lower his head and he would find her lips. He felt his stomach muscles contract and forced aside such thoughts. When he had finished, she pulled the cloak up quickly.

"Now lift your hair, my lady."

Megan did as she was told, gathering her hair in both hands and lifting it away from her neck.

Kieran's arms came around her as he spread the ointment on the swollen mass, gently probing as he did so.

Her breath was soft against his cheek. He struggled to ignore the invitation of her lips. "The blow to your head is improving. Can you feel it?"

"Aye."

He breathed in the fresh, clean fragrance of her and struggled to keep his touch light. "Have you any other wounds, my lady?"

"Nay." She lowered her hands. Her hair spilled over her shoulders and tumbled to her waist in a riot of damp curls.

Kieran studied her in the moonlight and thought her the most magnificent woman he had ever seen. For a moment he thought about drawing her into the circle of his arms and tasting her lips. She would taste of cool river water. Her lips would be soft, her mouth inviting. He clenched his hands at his sides to keep from reaching a hand to her.

"I will say good-night now. I would advise you to lie as close to the fire as possible. The breeze carries a hint of a cold night."

"I will. Good night, Kieran."

"Good night, my lady. Sleep well."

Kieran rolled himself into a cloak on the opposite side of the fire and firmly closed his eyes. But an hour later, while Megan slept peacefully beside the fire, he was still awake, agonizing about the way she felt, the way she smelled. If he did not soon taste her lips, he would go mad thinking about her.

Chapter Four

The early morning sunlight could not pierce the dense forest. Beneath a canopy of vines and tangled underbrush Megan awoke very slowly and lay quietly, absorbing the warmth of the fire. She was grateful that someone had stirred the ashes and added fresh wood. Despite the heavy woolen cloak in which she was wrapped, she felt the damp chill of the forest.

"My name is Megan." Those words had become a litany in her mind. She hugged them to her heart. They affirmed that she had once had a home and family who loved her. Reaching up through the cobwebs of her mind, she struggled to remember something, anything that would stir memories. But to her dismay, no images formed. The words "father" and "mother" produced no pictures. Her home might have been a hovel or a castle. She had no recollection at all. She sat up, holding the cloak around her for warmth, and she bit her lip, deep in concentration as she tried to picture her childhood. A friend perhaps. A pet. But her mind remained blank. She had been born, it would seem, in Kieran O'Mara's arms, nursing wounds from a battle they had fought together.

From his position on the other side of the fire Kieran watched the play of emotions on Megan's face. He did not wish to intrude upon her private, troubled thoughts. Though she had made not a sound he knew everything she was feeling. Had he not experienced many of those same emotions in Fleet Prison? There his captors had stripped him of his identity, his dignity and his hope, along with his freedom.

"Good morrow, lass." Colin awoke and sat up stiffly. "Has anything come back to you?"

"Nay." Megan struggled to shake herself from her somber mood. She would do her grieving in solitude. "How are your wounds faring?"

"Much better. Thanks to your herbs and roots."

Her smile returned. She had no idea what effect that smile had on men. But Colin did. As did Kieran, who sat watching them.

"Then you no longer object to my attempts at healing?"

"I am most grateful, my lady." Colin threw off his cloak and reached for his tunic. Before he could pull it on, Megan crossed the space between them and knelt.

"You cannot dress until I apply my precious salve."

"I suppose I must now endure this ritual every day?"

"And every single night."

"Are you saying I must suffer this indignity until every wound has disappeared from my flesh?"

"Aye. Every single one, my lord. I have appointed myself your physician."

"Physician? Or guardian angel?"

"Use whatever term you prefer."

"It would do no good to argue, I suppose."

"No good at all. Now roll over."

As she began rubbing the ointment into his wounds, Colin gave a sigh of contentment. "If you did not have such wonderful hands, my dear physician, I would refuse to allow that bloody salve within smelling distance." He gave another sigh of pleasure. "But since I must countenance all this, at least you could rub the rest of my back, as well."

"Mayhap I will apply the rest of it to your tongue, if you do not hold it still, my lord."

Colin burst into gales of laughter.

Kieran watched the ease with which Megan and Colin sparred with each other. He had not seen his brother this relaxed in over a year. Many years, in fact. The lass did have a way about her. At least in the company of his brother. The more they bantered good-naturedly, the darker grew his own mood. Could he be jealous? The very thought of such a foolish emotion as jealousy had him jumping to his feet in need of something physical to do. Jealous. How could he be jealous of his own brother? Even if the lass was breathtakingly beautiful. He had no time for such nonsense.

Kieran prepared enough food for their morning meal, then went to saddle the horses. When he returned he saw Megan walking from the river. Her face was freshly scrubbed and her hair had been pulled to one side with a sprig of wildflowers. It was difficult for him to reconcile this innocent waif with the fiery creature who had faced her attackers with such courage.

As always, Megan felt tongue-tied in Kieran's presence. And his scowling demeanor did nothing to ease the situation.

"How..." She paused and tried again. "How are your wounds this morrow? Would you like me to apply a little more of my salve?"

"There is no time." Kieran hadn't meant to be so brusque, but something about her made him tense, impatient. The fact was, her ointment had taken much of the sting from his wounds. But some perverse sense kept him from admitting it to her.

Her temper surfaced, surprising both of them. "If you are too arrogant to admit you need help, I will have to force it upon you. Remove your tunic."

"I have no time for this."

"You will make time."

For a moment they stood facing each other like two angry rams. It was Colin who broke the tension.

"Unless you do as the lady says, Kieran, we will never complete our journey this day."

"Aye." As Colin walked toward the river, Kieran grudgingly removed his tunic.

Megan smeared her salve on his wounds. At first, her touch was deliberately rough, mirroring her feelings. But it gentled as she continued to apply the ointment.

Kieran steeled himself against feeling anything. Struggling to hold on to his anger, he reminded himself that their lives were in peril. But even that compelling reason could not keep him from feeling every movement of her fingers.

"Your wounds are already beginning to heal." Her voice was so close, he felt his nerves leap.

"Aye. I am grateful, my lady."

He turned. Instantly she dropped her hand and began to turn away from him. But his hand shot out, stilling her movements.

His voice was strangely rough. "You have a healing touch."

She was afraid to speak. Her heart seemed lodged in her throat.

"I wonder if you could heal hearts and souls as easily as you heal bodies."

He cupped her face in his hand and forced her to meet his look. What she saw frightened her. His eyes were dark, compelling. His lips parted as he lowered his face to hers.

God in heaven. Was he going to kiss her? She did not know what to do. Her heart thudded painfully in her chest. This man both frightened and intrigued her. And though she was loath to admit it, she wanted him to kiss her. She could feel the tension vibrate in the air between them.

Now that he was this close to her, Kieran had to taste her lips. One taste, he promised himself, then he would turn away.

His lips brushed over hers, the merest touch of mouth to mouth.

God in heaven, she was sweet. She smelled like the heather that bloomed on the distant meadows. Her lips were cool and fresh as a morning mist. They trembled against his, and he felt her awkwardness as she held herself stiffly in his arms.

She had never before been held in a man's arms. The thought raced through his mind, adding to his arousal. Lost in the taste of her, he took the kiss deeper.

For a moment Megan tried to pull away, but he held her firmly as his lips moved over hers. He heard her little gasp of surprise and pulled her close, wrapping his arms around her.

She was trembling, and he did not know if it was from fear or excitement. He knew only that he could not let her go. Not just yet. He needed one more taste of her, one lingering touch of her lips against his.

The sweetness in her was laced with a wildness that inflamed him. Though she was an innocent, he could sense a smoldering passion slumbering just below the surface. She would be no docile maiden, accepting a man's kisses and then turning away. Nay. He felt the passions that hummed through her, as alive and vital as the very air she breathed. With this lass, a simple kiss would never be enough.

With a little cry of alarm Megan suddenly pushed him away. One glance at her downcast eyes and flushed cheeks convinced Kieran that his instincts had been correct. She had never before been with a man. The thought left him stunned and reeling.

"I cannot even heal myself." Megan was surprised at how difficult it was to speak. "So how could I heal you, my lord?"

Breathless, she found the courage to lift her gaze to his. Had he just experienced the same things she had? Was his pulse racing like hers? Were his palms sweating; was his throat constricted? She could tell nothing from his dark, shuttered look.

Kieran took a step back, as if to prove to himself that he was still in control. The truth was, he needed to put some distance between himself and this woman.

His hands, he noted, were not quite steady. And his voice, when he finally spoke, was gruff.

"If Colin and I are to elude this hangman, we must make haste."

He brushed past her and called to his brother, who knelt by the river, "It is time to ride."

When he turned to her, Megan was still standing rigidly, watching him with a look that was unreadable. His nerves were as unsteady as his hands.

Colin scooped up his cloak and strode toward them. His gait was firmer this day. The lad was mending, Kieran noted with a detached sense of satisfaction. He watched as Colin pulled himself into the saddle.

Kieran lifted Megan up onto his horse, then pulled himself up behind her and caught the reins. Once again it was there, that quick, unsettling feeling at the mere touch of her. He resented it. He thrilled to it. With heroic effort, he pushed it aside.

Within the hour they had plunged deep into the forest, far from any sign of civilization.

They rode for hours in silence, picking their way over rocks and fallen logs, wading through icy streams. The silence was broken by the occasional cry of a bird or the swift stampede of deer when they came upon them feeding on the forest floor.

This was home, Megan thought, as her gaze swept, searching for a fleeting memory. Had she walked here, played here or perhaps fought here? Though nothing seemed familiar, she had no fear of these woods. If she had been here before, she had come as master of all she could see.

She tried, with great difficulty, to keep her mind on her surroundings. But with Kieran's arms around her, holding firmly to the reins, and his body warm against hers, he was never far from her thoughts. How would she endure being this close to a man who made her so uncomfortable? And why did he have this effect on her?

She turned to glance at Colin, riding slightly behind them, and Kieran's dark, probing eyes caught and held hers.

"Do you wish to rest, my lady?"

"Nay."

She regretted her terse reply, but she could think of nothing to say. Why was it that she could laugh with Colin and tease him with the ease of an old friend, while she could hardly speak when in the presence of his brother?

Had she ever met a man quite like Kieran O'Mara before? He was abrupt, tense, angry. He was a villain, it would seem, who had spent time in prison, and was even now being sought for the crimes he had committed. And yet his touch could be surprisingly gentle. With his brother, he showed great care and compassion. And with her...she thought of the fire, the passion that he had uncovered with that first kiss.

Megan shook her head, trying to sweep him from her thoughts. She was unaware that the gesture caused his eyes to narrow in appreciation. Her hair danced around her face and shoulders, then drifted down her back. He clenched a fist to keep from plunging a hand into the tangles.

Suddenly, Kieran caught a sound. Pulling back on the reins, he gave a curt order for his brother to halt.

"What is it?" Colin brought his mount up beside theirs.

"I heard something. A man's laughter, I think."

The three fell silent as they strained to hear anything out of the ordinary.

"There." Megan pointed toward a small clearing up ahead.

Kieran nodded.

"It could be crofters or hunters," Colin whispered.

"Aye. Or it could be the hangman's emissaries." Kieran slid from his mount and withdrew his sword from its scabbard. "If I do not return before the sun slips behind those trees, you must go on without me. Colin," he added fiercely, "you know the way. You will take the lass to Ireland."

"I will not go without you."

The anger Kieran kept coiled inside him was evident in the way he moved, catlike, to grasp the front of Colin's tunic. "You will do as I order. I have no fear of giving my life. But I will not give it in vain. One of us must make it home. They cannot take the land as long as there is an O'Mara alive to claim it." His words were an angry hiss. "Do you understand?"

"Aye." Colin studied the hard set of his brother's jaw and clamped his hand on his shoulder in a gesture of unexpected tenderness. "I understand." He stared deep into Kieran's eyes before murmuring, "Do what you must. God go with you."

"And you."

Kieran did not look at Megan before he strode away. He needed no distraction. But if he had, he would have seen a look of surprise mixed with understanding and admiration.

"He has been gone too long." Megan prowled from tree to tree in the forest, unable to contain the restless energy that drove her.

Colin lay with his back to a tree trunk, his eyes half closed. "I would give anything if I had but half your strength, lass."

She turned on him. "How can you lie there when your brother's life could be in peril?"

Colin shrugged. How could he explain the weakness that had plagued him these past months while he languished in that filthy prison? The lack of food, sunshine and freedom. And worst of all the endless beatings. All had taken their toll on his health, which had always been fragile. "He said we are to wait. And so we must."

The oath that issued from her lips would have shocked even his jailers. "You can wait." She strode to where the horses were tethered and removed a sword and knife from their place of concealment.

Colin sat up. "What are you doing?"

She shot him a look that reminded him of Kieran. "I intend to go to see why your brother has not returned."

"But he ordered us away."

"Perhaps you are obliged to follow his orders. No one orders me."

For a moment the young man was torn with indecision. In all his years, it had never occurred to him to defy Kieran. His older brother was a warrior, trained in the art of killing. Colin's own training had been far different.

He watched as the lass strapped on a scabbard and hid the knife beneath the folds of her waistband. As she disappeared into the woods, he paused for a moment longer. Then he followed her lead, retrieving weapons from behind the saddle of his horse and moving quickly to catch up with her.

When they neared the clearing, they heard voices raised in anger. Peering from behind the protection of a tree, Megan saw Kieran lying on the ground. His hands had been bound behind his back. His shirt was stained with blood. A man stood over him, his voice raised in anger.

"You will tell us where your brother is. Else you will die."

"Kill me then" came Kieran's reply.

The man kicked him, again and again, until one of the others put a hand on his sleeve to stop him. "Hold. He is no good to us dead. The brother cannot be far. We will search the woods until we find him."

Seeing the pain in Colin's eyes, Megan put a hand on his arm in a gesture of comfort and caution. "I know what you are suffering," she whispered. "Though your brother is being forced to sustain another beating, it would do no good for the two of us to charge into the clearing yet. There are too many of them. We must bide our time."

He nodded his agreement, but she saw the suffering it cost him.

Megan and Colin watched as several men mounted and urged their horses into the cover of the forest. When the hoofbeats faded there were only two men left guarding their prisoner.

"Now?" Colin asked.

Megan shook her head. "First we must wait and observe."

The soldier who had savagely kicked Kieran was as tall and solid as a tree trunk. His eyes, Megan noted, had lit with satisfaction at every act of cruelty. He held a bloody sword in his hand. She had no doubt whose blood it was. At his waist gleamed the dull gold of a knife. A bloody whip hung from his waistband.

The other guard was lustily eating a roasted partridge. He took no notice of the man who lay bound and bleeding nearby. A sword rested in the scabbard at his waist. He used his knife to cut his food, then jammed it into the bark of a tree.

After carefully assessing the situation, Megan leaned close to Colin and whispered, "You will wait here. See that you remain carefully concealed. When I reach the other side of the clearing, I will give you a signal. Do not move from this spot until you see the guards leave. Then you must reach Kieran's side and cut his bindings."

"Why would the guards be foolish enough to leave?"

She shot him a quick smile. "I have not as yet thought it through. But it will come to me."

Before he could issue a protest, she was gone.

Megan made her way from tree to tree, often crawling through the underbrush to avoid being seen. When at last she had made it to the opposite side of the clearing, she got to her knees and studied the scene. The one guard was still eating. But the other had sat down on a boulder and was taunting Kieran. She scooped up a handful of stones, then poised, awaited the right moment to create a disturbance.

"When we deliver you and your brother back to prison, we have a little celebration planned for you." The burly guard poked the tip of his sword against Kieran's chest and grinned when it pierced his flesh, drawing blood.

Kieran clamped his teeth against the pain. He would not give the guard the satisfaction of a reaction.

"Simmons told us that you thought you were some fine and noble warrior, taking beatings for your puny brother. We shall see how you endure the beatings meted out by the friends of Simmons." His eyes glittered. "The guards told us how you killed poor Simmons. Snapped his neck, did you?" He laughed, and the sound of it was high and shrill, like the cry of a seabird.

"Do you see this?" the guard asked, pointing to the whip tucked into his waistband. "It is how I got my name. Whip. I made it myself," he said proudly, running his hand over the thin strips of leather that would tear a man's flesh. "We plan to put a noose around your neck and hang you from the top of your cell. And then, while you are helpless and dying, we will each take our turn beating your puny brother with this until he has no flesh left on his bones." His laughter became a shrill cackle. "Is that not a fine celebration for a noble warrior?"

Kieran made no reply as he worked feverishly at the ropes that bound his hands. A glance at the tops of the trees told him that the sun had not yet set. Megan and Colin would be dutifully waiting for him not far from here. It would be no task at all for the soldiers who were searching to find them. He and Colin would be returned to Fleet, this time to face certain death. He shuddered to think of the fate awaiting the lass. When these animals were done with her, she would be better off dead.

"Simmons was friend to me. If it were not for the entertainment you will provide for us in London, I would most assuredly kill you here and now." Whip spat, standing and giving Kieran a mighty kick. "But I cannot deny the others their pleasure."

Whip was about to kick again when he heard a rustling in the forest just beyond the clearing. He and the other guard looked up in surprise.

"See to it," Whip said.

Pulling his sword from the scabbard, the other guard set down his food and moved off to investigate.

Just as he stepped into the woods, there was a rustling from the other side. Taking careful aim, Megan continued to toss the stones into the dried brush, knowing they would cause the necessary distraction.

"Who goes there?" Whip glanced across the clearing in time to see his friend disappear. He turned to where another sound disturbed him.

When the rustling continued, Whip stormed across the clearing and peered into the dense woods. "Speak up. Who dares to defy me?"

He heard the rustling, just out of reach. Vexed, he used the sharp blade of his sword to cut down the brambles that tore at his legs as he pushed his way through the underbrush.

Kieran looked up to see the flash of a sword as Megan stepped into the clearing. He felt a tug on the ropes that bound him, and was astounded to see Colin bending over him, cutting him free.

"I ordered you to hide yourselves. By whose authority...?"

"Make haste." As Megan beckoned to him, she saw the first guard returning from the woods. Moving swiftly, she stepped into his path and lifted her sword.

Kieran, still bound, was unable to go to Megan's aid. But he watched with grudging admiration as she faced an opponent who towered over her.

For a moment the man was so surprised he could only stare. Was he dreaming, or had this beautiful creature just dropped down from the heavens? Then he saw the blade flash in the sunlight. His lips curved into a smile. "Do you mock me, woman?"

"Nay, sir. I challenge you."

His smile disappeared when she lunged, catching him unawares. Her blade sliced into his shoulder, opening a gash that bled profusely.

With a look of fury he tried to drive her back, but she would not retreat. Instead, she lunged again, causing him to sidestep. Though he fought gamely, he was no match for her skill. His fury quickly turned into fear as he realized that his friends were too far away to come to his aid.

Hearing the sounds of blade hitting blade, Whip came rushing out of the forest. But when he entered the clearing he skidded to a halt. The prisoner was no longer lying on the ground, his hands and feet bound. With the last of the ropes cut, Kieran was struggling to get to his feet.

"Toss me your sword," Kieran shouted to his brother.

A moment later Kieran faced the man who, only minutes before, had taunted him mercilessly.

"I believe you planned a celebration," Kieran said softly. The blade of his sword glinted menacingly.

Whip rushed forward, intent upon ending this quickly. Kieran easily avoided his thrust and countered with one of his own. His blade slashed through the guard's sleeve but missed his flesh.

"I captured you once, O'Mara. I can do it again."

"Last time you had the help of four men. This time 'tis just you." Kieran neatly sidestepped the man's lunge and drove his blade into the soft, fleshy part of his upper arm. "I do not think your skill equal to the task."

The guard's mouth became a thin, tight line of concentration as he struggled to match his opponent's mastery. But though he was a powerful man, Whip soon found himself tiring.

On the other side of the clearing Megan fought with equal skill against a man who found himself amazed at the lass's agility. Each time he saw an opening for his blade, she managed to dance aside, and her blade seemed to find its mark each time she jabbed. Though his wounds were not fatal, he was bleeding from a dozen different places, and the effort to dodge her was draining him. He knew he could not hold on much longer.

It was Colin who heard the sounds of approaching horses. "Kieran. Megan. We must flee. The others are returning."

Though Kieran heard his brother's words, he refused to turn away from the man who had bloodied and taunted him. The need for revenge boiled through his veins, heating his blood.

"So. You would hang me from my cell." Kieran's sword sang until the guard found himself backed against the trunk of a tree. "And you would beat my brother until there was no flesh left on his bones." He felt a savage sense of release as his blade sliced through the man's shoulder until it encountered bone.

"Kieran." He felt Colin's hand upon his arm, tugging. His voice entreated, "Leave him. He is beyond fighting. Vengeance is Mine, sayeth the Lord."

"Aye." Though Kieran heard his brother's words, the need for revenge still bubbled dangerously near the surface.

"Please, Kieran." Colin's voice took on a note of desperation. "There is no time for this. We must flee."

Kieran felt the pain in his chest and stomach and knew that his ribs had been broken when he'd been overpowered by his attackers. He tightened his grip on his sword and faced the man who had caused his terrible pain. "If I were half the animal you are," Kieran said, his gaze dark with fury, "I would kill you where you stand."

He saw the man swallow and freeze, awaiting his fate.

"But so that you can tell the others that Kieran O'Mara is a man of honor, I will spare you your miserable life."

With a final thrust, he disarmed the man and tossed the sword to Colin. The guard fell to his knees and grasped his bloody hand.

Kieran glanced over to where Megan stood, pointing the tip of her sword at her opponent's heart. "We must go, my lady. His life or death is in your hands." He waited before adding, "The choice is yours alone."

Megan studied the man whose eyes were wide with pleading. "Do not accost us again," she said firmly. "Call off this need for retribution." She took a step back and saw the relief that transformed the man's features. "Or," she added, "we will not show you the same mercy when next we meet."

Relieved, Colin began to lead the way into the dim forest, followed by Kieran. With a last glance at the two subdued guards, Megan turned to follow them. But as Colin and Kieran disappeared into the shelter of the underbrush, she heard a man's voice call out, "Will you look at what we have here, lads. The gods have sent us a female, just for our entertainment."

As the cluster of ragged, dirty soldiers stepped into the clearing, she felt the press of strong hands around her throat. And as she caught at the offending hands and fought to pry them loose, a man's voice rasped, "Go ahead, woman. Fight me. 'Twill give me the excuse I need to slit your throat."

Chapter Five

Megan felt the hands at her throat gradually tighten until she could not breathe. Her struggles only made it worse.

As she fought her attacker, she saw a cluster of men dragging Kieran and Colin into the clearing. Both men had been disarmed and had no weapons except their fists. But they fought with every last ounce of energy until, bloodied and beaten, they fell to the ground. Their captors fell upon them and continued pummeling them while they bound them.

She did not know which sight tugged more at her heart, Colin, so weakened from loss of blood that he did not move, or Kieran, bloodied but unbowed, still raging against the men who bound his hands and feet.

"How kind the fates that sent us this reward for our day's labor." The man who held Megan tightened his grip around her throat until black specks danced in front of her eyes.

She knew that she must cease fighting him, else she would lose consciousness. That would lead to a loss of control, and above all, she must not lose control now. Her very life depended upon it. As well as those of Colin and Kieran.

When she stopped struggling, her captor loosened his grip. For a moment she stood very still, sucking deep drafts of air into her burning lungs.

She was aware that the men had formed a circle around her, looking at her with a kind of hunger that sent a chill racing along her spine.

"A comely lass," one of them said with a smile.

"Aye. She would bring a man much pleasure."

Megan's mind reeled with the enormity of the task before her. Somehow she must overpower a dozen men and free Kieran and Colin from their bonds.

She thought of the dirk hidden at her waist. One puny knife would not be enough. She needed to relieve the men of their weapons and find a way to get those weapons into the hands of the two men who lay just beyond the circle of firelight.

One of the soldiers reached out a hand to her, and she stepped just out of his reach.

"So. The lass dances." A second man reached out for her, and the entire company laughed as Megan pulled away.

"Dance for us, woman." As the men reached out their hands, grabbing at her hair, her skirt, her bodice, she dodged and whirled until, leaping onto a rock just out of their reach, she stared down in defiance. One by one the men grew silent.

"I will dance for you." She saw the look that came into their eyes. Lust. She recognized it and forced herself to continue. "But I would be much more fetching if I were given a chance to clean myself in the river." She glanced at the dirt and blood that stained her gown and clung to her hands and arms.

"Aye." One man separated himself from the others, and Megan knew that he must be their leader. His heavy beard did not hide the cruelty of his mouth or the puckered scar that had formed over his eye and cheek, where an enemy's sword had left its mark. The eye that could still see was narrowed upon her. "And I am just the man to see to the lady's toilette."

The men sent up a howl of laughter.

He bowed to Megan. "I am Wilkes, captain of the guard. It will be my pleasure to accompany you."

The men roared their approval. Their captain often saw to it that women were brought to their camp for their pleasure. His savage treatment of women was legend. Many a woman had begged to die rather than be returned to Wilkes a second time.

From his position on the ground, Kieran stared at the figure on the rock in disbelief. A sheltered woman of noble birth could scarcely be expected to understand her fate at the hands of men like these. Would the lass entertain them, in order to save her life? He quickly dismissed the thought. She was neither vain nor frivolous. Nor was she a fool. Was she, mayhap, stalling for time to make her escape? He had had little chance to really know her. Yet, from the time they had spent together, he had come to admire her courage. He had no doubt she would do all in her power to escape. He wished her well. She did not deserve this fate. In his heart, Kieran had little hope that she could succeed. The odds were sorely weighed against her.

Kieran watched and listened as the leader of the group caught her in his arms and lifted her to the ground. Yanking her roughly by the arm, he called, "This will take but a short time."

"Especially since you have been away from your woman for many days," one of the men shouted. "And many nights."

Everyone laughed.

"Do not tarry long," another added. "Else we will be awake all night awaiting our turns with the woman."

"Dudley," the leader ordered. "Prepare a meal for the men. With our task completed—" he gave a smug glance toward the two prisoners, securely bound "—we will feast and be entertained by the woman before we begin our journey home."

"Aye. 'Twill be a night to remember." The one called Dudley dropped the carcass of a deer, which he carried on his shoulder. With the blade of his knife he began preparing it for roasting.

Megan cast a quick glance at Colin and Kieran. Both men were watching her. Both wore identical frowns of concern. She could give them no reassuring look, no smile of confidence.

Though she was aware of the risk involved in her plan, she would not allow herself to dwell upon it. She could see no other way out.

As Megan was led away by Wilkes, several of the others went to the aid of the guards who had been overcome by Megan and Kieran.

Whip, who had been spared by Kieran, spat upon the two men who lay tied and helpless. With a sneer he told the others, "I should have killed this one when I had the chance. But now," he added with a laugh, "he can watch while I take my revenge upon his woman."

With the whip still dangling from his waistband, he was helped to a pallet spread beneath a tree. There, one of the men began to tend his wounds.

The other guard, remembering that the lass had spared his life, remained silent. He was almost sorry the captives had not made good their escape. The woman had fought bravely. And it was, after all, simply her bad fortune to be with these two rebels. Despite her skill with a sword, she appeared to be a young innocent. Her innocence would be gone after tonight, he knew. And though he missed the village wenches, he vowed to take no part in what would be done this night. When his wounds were bound, the guard rolled himself into his cloak and fell into an exhausted, troubled sleep.

Many of the men busied themselves cleaning their weapons. Others set aside their weapons while they rested. Soon, the aroma of roasting meat and the satisfying knowledge that their task was completed had them relaxed. Most of them dozed.

For the moment, Kieran and Colin were forgotten.

Kieran worked frantically on the vines that bound him. They tore into his flesh, cutting open old wounds, starting the bleeding afresh. He clenched his teeth and ignored the pain. Beside him, Colin drifted in and out of consciousness.

Brambles tore at Megan's flesh and snagged her skirts as her captor dragged her toward the river. Her hair caught on the branch of a tree, yanking her head back sharply until tears stung her eyes. She barely noticed. Her mind seemed frozen. She had no plan. She would simply deal with each hurdle as it arose. This man would be the first.

"Here is the river. Wash yourself."

They paused at the shore. Icy water spilled over rocks. Further downstream it formed a waterfall as it tumbled out of sight over a rock-strewn cliff.

Megan studied the treacherous riverbed. This was not what she had anticipated. She glanced at the man and said nervously, "I must have some privacy."

"Do you think me a fool?" Wilkes leaned against the trunk of a tree and crossed his arms over his chest. "Clean yourself. I will watch. It is why I came. That," he said, running his tongue over his lips, "and other reasons."

Ignoring his leer, Megan removed her kid boots and touched a toe to the icy water. Lifting her skirts, she took a tentative step, then another. Water swirled around her ankles.

From his position on shore, Wilkes enjoyed the view. The lass was stunning as she bent and scooped water over her arms and face.

As she adjusted to the cold, Megan forced herself to step farther into the river. When she realized that the man on shore was too caught up in watching her to notice that she had moved away from him, she became bolder. She began to leap from one rock to another. When she was in the middle of the river, Wilkes called, "That is far enough."

"And what will you do if I go farther?"

He was smiling. "I will order my men to kill your companions."

"Then do it," she said, forcing her tone to remain even.

"What are you saying, woman? Would you have me kill your friends?"

"Those men mean nothing to me." The lie nearly stuck in her throat, but she was determined to go on. "I am with them against my will."

For a moment Wilkes was struck dumb. This was not what he'd expected. He had thought that the threat of harming the men would keep her in line. He could not let the woman escape now. He would no doubt face a hostile group if he returned without her. Besides, he wanted her. Now. And he did not like the idea of chasing her through the icy water. Not that there was any doubt he could catch her. Stupid female. She could never outrun him, even with half a river between them.

He studied the swirling rapids and let out an oath.

"Would you like to join me in the water, Captain?"

"Nay. Return to shore."

Megan lifted her hand to the bodice of her gown and began to unbutton it. For a moment Wilkes was astonished. Then his eyes narrowed. Of course. She had done this sort of thing before. She was a camp follower. And she had singled him out because he was the leader. What good fortune. She was attracted to him. And why not? He had snagged his share of village wenches before. They were all hungry and knew that the Queen's soldiers always had coin in their pockets.

"I care not for the water. You come here."

As he watched, she undid a second button, then a third, until the bodice of her gown fell open to reveal a pale chemise.

"I was hoping I had chosen a man strong enough to carry me to shore."

The icy water, the slippery rocks were forgotten. He stepped into the river and struggled to make his way to her.

Megan felt her throat go dry. The man was twice her size.
The hilt of his sword gleamed in the scabbard at his side.
Did she really believe she could overpower him with noth-
ing more than the knife at her waist?

As he drew near, she felt a rush of energy. All fears were
pushed aside. She grew strangely confident, as though some
other hand guided her. She would not fail. She could not.

She waited until he reached her side. The rock upon which
they stood was smooth to the touch. She curled her toes,
determined to keep her balance.

"You are a strange lass." He stood facing her and reached
out a hand to her shoulder. "But I knew you could not resist me."

She moved a step closer, until their bodies were almost
touching.

"You realize, of course, that I must share you with the
others."

His smile grew, and Megan was repulsed by the stench of
filth and sweat and ale that clung to him. "But at least I will
be the first. Come."

As he took her arm he caught a flash of sunlight glinting
on the knife in her hand. He felt momentarily confused by
the warmth in his midsection, followed by a sudden sharp
pain. Bewildered, he looked down in mute fascination at the
blood that formed a warm, dark stain across his tunic.

Megan, too, seemed overcome by the enormity of her
deed. All she could do was stare at his ugly face and watch
while his look of puzzlement slowly turned to one of understanding, then rage.

For a moment his grip tightened on her arm, and they
both swayed precariously on the slippery rock. Then Megan remembered what it was she had to do to survive.

Pulling her arm free, she shoved against him with all her
might. He teetered, and his arms flailed in the air as he tried
desperately to catch hold of something, anything, that
would stop his fall. His fingers curled into the sleeve of her
gown and he held on tightly. Megan recoiled, and she heard

the sound of fabric ripping as the sleeve tore away. Megan neatly sidestepped and watched as he dropped into the swirling rapids, still clutching the torn piece of gown. For long minutes the river was stained crimson. Then even the stain disappeared as the body washed over the falls and the rushing water cleansed itself.

For what seemed an eternity Megan stood straight on the rock and stared into the river. Her feet, numb with cold, had lost all feeling. Her mind, too, seemed unable to function.

At last, wrapping her arms around herself, she began to shudder violently.

"We never should have forced the lass to accompany us." Colin could not seem to shake off the cloud of doom that surrounded him. "She would have been better off stumbling about in the forest, lost to herself and others, than staying with us. All we brought her was pain and humiliation at the hands of that animal."

In silence, Kieran continued to struggle against his bonds. There were no words he could speak in his defense. Everything Colin said was true. At this moment the lass was being brutalized by the captain of the guard. Soon she would be returned to the camp and passed around to every man who wanted her. And here he lay helpless. Helpless. The very thought sent him into a frenzy of activity. But their captors had chosen well. The vines, instead of fraying, only dug deeper into his flesh, until they found bone. He was beyond pain. But he was not beyond thinking. The thought of Megan with Wilkes tormented him until he thought he would go mad.

"Your captain has ordered the feasting to begin."

At the sound of Megan's voice, every head in camp turned to where she stood.

Kieran's eyes narrowed as he studied her carefully. Her gown had been torn viciously, leaving the front of her bodice gaping, revealing a pale chemise beneath. The hem of her gown was dark where the water had soaked it. It clung to her

ankles as she strode into the clearing. The front of her gown
was smeared with a dark stain. Kieran's stomach muscles
tightened. Blood. The bastard Wilkes must have hurt her
badly. Kieran's hands curled into fists.

Megan kept her head lowered, avoiding their eyes.

The men fell silent for long minutes as they stared at the
woman. They recognized Wilkes' handiwork.

"Where is our captain?" one of the men called.

"He is . . . resting." Megan lifted her head and stared defiantly at the circle of men.

"Exhausted from his latest conquest, is he?" Dudley removed the deer from the spit and began cutting off strips of
meat.

"Aye. He said to break out the ale for these men." Megan prayed there was ale among their supplies.

When Dudley hurried to the horses and returned with
several jugs, she breathed a sigh of relief.

The men gathered around eagerly, accepting their portion of food and drink.

Using that moment of distraction, Megan walked to
where Kieran and Colin lay. Pretending to be adjusting the
torn bodice of her gown, she removed the knife from her
waistband and dropped it into Kieran's hand.

He looked up in astonishment. "Were you badly hurt,
lass?"

"I was not hurt at all. But the captain will not be returning to his men."

For a moment Kieran could only stare at her. Then, as her
meaning became clear, he shot her a look of stunned
amazement tinged with admiration. For the first time since
this ordeal began, he felt his hopes begin to soar.

Megan moved away quickly and bent to adjust her boot.
As she did she picked up a sword that had been left resting
against the trunk of a tree. Hiding it beneath her skirts, she
sauntered past Kieran and let it drop soundlessly into the tall
grass.

"When will you dance for us?" one of the soldiers called.

She whirled and felt her heart pounding. "Now. Your captain ordered me to begin entertaining you as soon as your feasting began."

The tall, ugly Whip gave a knowing glance in Kieran's direction. "You can dance if you wish. But when I finish this feast, I intend to be the first to sample your charms. And I shall do it where your two brave warriors can see and enjoy."

Kieran worked the knife through the vines until at last they fell away. Then he brought the knife to the vines of his ankles. Within minutes he was free, and he hurried to free his brother.

"Lie perfectly still and pretend to be asleep."

Colin nodded.

"And watch for a chance to go to Megan's aid."

Colin shot him a look of agreement.

Both men lay just beyond the ring of firelight and watched as Megan began to move slowly among the men. Taking several of their swords, she placed them in an intricate crossed pattern on the ground. Then, asking for their knives, she added them to the pattern by sticking them, blade down, into the ground. Intrigued, the men watched as she lifted her skirts and began stepping, toe-heel, toe-heel, through the maze of weapons. Soon she was whirling, dancing, faster and faster, her skirts swirling around her ankles.

Each time the men caught a glimpse of her leg they would clap and shout words of encouragement to her, urging her to show them more. And each time she would lift her skirts higher, causing the men to roar their approval.

With a delicate movement she kicked her foot at a knife and watched as it flew through the air, landing in the grass where Kieran and Colin lay. With the men shouting encouragement, she followed it with a second kick, and a third, each time sending another knife flying through the air.

The soldiers were intrigued by her complicated footwork. Never had they seen anyone so dazzling.

Cheered by their reaction, Megan stepped into the maze of swords and danced around them until she managed to catch one on the toe of her boot. In one swift motion she kicked it high in the air. The men laughed and cheered as it landed by the tip of the blade in the tall grass just beyond the glow of the fire. She repeated the complex movement until all the swords were gone. Then, giving the men a smoldering look, she began a slow, seductive dance around the fire.

In the darkness, Kieran and Colin collected the weapons, then moved toward the horses, tethered beneath a tree. The soldier who was assigned to the care of the animals had long ago joined his friends at the feast.

"How do we get Megan away from those men?" Colin whispered as he trailed his brother toward the horses.

"I do not know. Yet." Kieran crawled through the tall grass, untying every tether. When the horses were free, he handed the reins to Colin. "If we are to make good our escape, we must see to it that every horse is gone save the ones we ride."

"Aye. Leave that to me."

Kieran touched a hand to his brother's shoulder. "Are you strong enough to ride?"

"This moment I even feel strong enough to wield a sword."

Kieran shot him a look of surprise. "Has the lass done this for you?"

"Aye. Never have I seen such courage."

Kieran nodded. "Nor I." His glance skimmed over the woman who continued dancing, though by now she must be beyond exhaustion. Courage? Aye. And much more. She was the most stunning, the most magnificent creature he had ever met.

At the sound of someone coming, Kieran motioned for Colin to duck down behind the horses. Turning, Kieran saw one of the soldiers step behind a tree to relieve himself. Kieran lifted the sword. The soldier gave a gasp of surprise, then dropped to his knees, his eyes wide with fear, his mouth agape. They left his body hidden in the tall grass.

"Take the horses now," Kieran whispered. "Meet us on the far side of the river. And Colin..."

His brother paused.

"Take whatever coin and other valuables you can find in the pouches behind their saddles. We may need them to assure our freedom."

Colin nodded. Without a word he led the horses deep into the forest.

Kieran pulled himself into the saddle of the remaining horse and tucked a knife into his waistband. In his hand was a gleaming sword. He gave one last glance over his shoulder, to be certain that his brother was safely away. Then, with a flick of the reins, he urged his mount into a run.

Megan had no idea what Kieran and Colin planned. But she had seen them crawl away in the direction of the horses. Though her body protested every move, she forced herself to continue dancing while the men shouted obscenities.

She saw the black steed looming up out of the mist of the forest. As it headed directly for the fire, she could make out the rider. Kieran. She braced herself as the horse leaped over the circle of men and landed directly beside her. She lifted her arms and Kieran scooped her up, holding her firmly with one hand.

For a moment the soldiers were too startled to react. When they realized what was happening, they leaped to their feet. But their weapons were gone. While they milled around in confusion, searching the tall grass for their swords and knives, Kieran and Megan disappeared into the safety of the forest.

Chapter Six

Colin stood on the far side of the river, anxiously awaiting the arrival of his brother and Megan. When he was far enough from the soldiers' camp, he had released the horses. Now they stood, singly or in pairs, calmly foraging. Several stood in the shallows, drinking. Others had disappeared into the forest. It would take the men hours to retrieve their mounts. By then, the three would be safely away.

Colin's pockets bulged with the gold sovereigns he had taken from the saddles. The hangman paid his men well. There was enough here to feed a family for a year.

His musings were interrupted by the sound of muted hoofbeats.

The black horse entered the river at a run. His pounding hooves sent a spray of water that caught the reflection of the full moon.

When the two approached, Colin's face lit with a smile. "You were splendid, lass."

Kieran took one look at Megan's ashen features and called, "There is no time for talk. We must ride."

"Aye." Colin pulled himself into the saddle and urged his mount into a run.

They raced across an open meadow, mindful of the fact that they were easy prey in the moonlight. On the far side of the meadow the forest rose up again, offering them sanctuary.

As they entered the woods they slowed their mounts, picking their way carefully in the darkness. Hearing the rush of a waterfall, Kieran led the way until he found a small clearing beside a river.

"We will rest here and tend our wounds. But we will leave again before dawn."

He dismounted and reached up for Megan. When he lifted her to the ground, he realized once again how small and fragile she seemed. She swayed and struggled to regain her balance. Instantly Kieran lifted her in his arms and carried her to the banks of the river.

"Bathe your wounds, lass. And then you must rest."

Kieran tethered the horses, then spread his cloak and helped his brother to lie down. "I will see to your wounds."

"They are nothing. See to the lass."

Kieran lifted his head in surprise. Megan was still sitting beside the river. She had not moved. He tended his brother's wounds quickly, then went to Megan. When he approached, she said nothing. Kieran studied her pale features. He recalled that she had been strangely silent during the long ride.

"What is it, Megan? Where are you hurt?"

She shook her head. "I am not wounded." Tears filled her eyes, and she tried to blink them away.

Instantly Kieran was on his knees beside her.

"Tell me where you are hurt."

She shook her head and refused to meet his eyes. "I do not understand this weakness that holds me in its grip."

Kieran touched a hand to her cheek and wiped away her tears. "It is exhaustion, lass. You have pushed yourself beyond the limits."

"Nay. It is more." She glanced at the torn bodice of her gown, stained with the blood of the captain of the guard. "I cannot wear this."

"What are you saying, lass?"

She began tearing at the buttons. "I cannot bear to look at this gown. I must be rid of it."

"I understand." He strode to where the horses were tethered and rummaged through their saddles. When he returned he carried a man's breeches and tunic. "These will be too large for you, Megan. But they are clean and serviceable."

He watched as she discarded the gown and pulled on the men's garb. When she was finished, she fell back exhausted. Kieran carried her to the place beside his brother and wrapped her in her cloak. As he started to stand, he whispered, "Rest now, and you will feel better on the morrow."

"Nay." She caught his hand and clung to it.

Startled, he dropped to his knees and studied her anguished look. "What is it, Megan?"

"I know not." Her lips quivered. "Nay. That is untrue. I know what troubles me. I have taken a life. That is a most serious thing, the taking of a life. Is it not?"

"Aye. A most serious thing. But you had no choice. It was the captain's life or yours."

She turned to Colin, who knelt beside them, his face etched with concern. "You said that vengeance belonged to the Lord."

Colin nodded. "Aye. But Kieran has just explained, lass. You had no choice."

"You still do not understand." The tears started again, and she was powerless to stop them. Her words were slow and halting as she struggled to swallow back the sobs. "I was not afraid. I knew I could kill him."

What a strange lass she was. Kieran found her words a puzzle. "Is that what troubles you, Megan?" He caught her by the shoulders and felt the tremors that rocked her.

"Aye. What sort of training did I have, that I could feel so confident in battle? What kind of person am I, that I can so easily take a life?"

"What kind of person? Oh, Megan." Kieran wrapped her in his arms and drew her firmly against his chest. As her tears soaked the front of his tunic, he touched a hand to her hair and rocked her as gently as if she were a child. "Though I do not know of your past, you have proven to me that you are a brave, courageous person." He felt her shudders slowly subside. Though he was not a man of words, he knew that he must find a way to console this woman. In low, soothing tones he murmured, "Without knowing anything about our past, you have tended our wounds. That takes a kind and generous spirit. And when we needed your help, you have saved our lives. That takes courage, lass. My brother and I are forever in your debt."

"Aye, Megan." Colin patted her shoulder. "We do not forget what you did for us."

Though he wished to offer her something more, Colin was too drained by what had transpired. With great effort he rolled himself into his cloak and struggled to fight the weakness that robbed him of his last ounce of strength. But the effort was too great. He was beyond exhaustion. His eyes closed and he slept.

Megan sniffled. Her words were slurred, as though talking had become a great effort. "You do not think me too young, and hot-blooded, and headstrong?" She wondered idly where those words had come from. But her mind was muddled by all that had happened.

Kieran chuckled, low and deep in his throat. "Aye, lass. All those words apply to you. And I am most grateful they do."

His laughter soothed her. She sighed softly and wrapped her arms around Kieran's waist.

The rush of heat was swift and unsettling. Kieran swore, low and fierce in his throat, and called himself every kind of fool. They had just escaped certain death because of this lass, and he suddenly found himself thinking of things that had nothing whatever to do with death. Things that would shock her.

In his mind's eye he could still see her, facing that horde of hungry men, lifting her skirts and dancing. He had wanted her. As had every man there. He could tell himself that his own lust was somehow nobler than theirs, but he would be lying. He struggled to push aside his base instincts and focus on her needs. "You are perhaps the first truly good thing I have found in this cruel world. You are everything fine and noble, my lady. And you are the most stunning, the most magnificent, the bravest woman I have ever met. And until you regain your memory of yourself, I pledge to protect you as I would my brother or myself."

He heard the soft, even breathing, and realized that she had not heard a word he had spoken. He felt her gradually relax in his arms. Her lips were pressed to his throat, sending a quivering need pulsing through his veins.

All her tension seemed to have dissolved, and he touched a hand to her cheek. Her tears had dried. He lifted his head and studied her. Her eyes were closed; her lips parted in a smile. Her breast rose and fell with each measured breath. She was sound asleep.

He could lie here all night, wrapped around her like this. But he would never survive the temptation. In his mind's eye he could still see that slender, feminine body she had revealed when she had torn away her gown. It was not an image he would soon forget.

With easy, gentle movements he drew away. Draping her cloak around her, he lowered her to the ground. Then he sat beside her, his back to the trunk of the tree, and kept watch while she slept. But though he listened for any sound that would alert him to the presence of danger, his gaze was often drawn to the beautiful creature who lay beside him, lost in her dreams.

He knew not who she was. Nor why the gods had thrown them together. But for now, he was most grateful.

Kieran stirred. He had allowed himself a few hours of sleep. But it was time to move on, before the soldiers could find their trail.

He touched a hand to Colin's shoulder and saw him stir. Then he turned to Megan. Though he disliked having to disturb her sleep, he had no choice. Gently he roused her.

Megan was instantly awake. Her eyes opened wide, studying the strange surroundings. Though she appeared not to move a muscle, he noted that her hand had gone to the place where a sword would rest in a scabbard at her hip.

His eyes narrowed. She woke like a soldier.

"We must make haste." Kieran bent and rolled his cloak, then tied it behind his saddle. "Even now the first light of dawn touches the sky."

Megan helped Colin to his feet and was pleased to see that his wounds caused him little discomfort. "Tonight I will grind more herbs and roots for a salve," she promised.

"I would much prefer deer roasted over a fire." He shot her a quick smile. "Last night I was too distraught over our circumstances to give much thought to the food those soldiers were enjoying. But this morrow, I would give much for just a taste."

"We shall eat." Kieran tucked a knife into his waistband and carefully wrapped the gold coins in a pouch. "Let us ride. Before the day is over, I promise you I will find food."

"Do you think the soldiers will follow?" Colin paused, while his frown suddenly turned to a hopeful smile. "Perhaps, with their leader dead, they will return to England."

"Mayhap." Kieran frowned. "But they claim to be friend to the jailer I killed." He saw Megan watching him and wondered how much to reveal. "I think their lust for our deaths is too keen to persuade them to give up the chase now."

He helped Megan into the saddle, then pulled himself up behind her. When Colin had mounted they urged their horses to follow the path of the river.

"Where do we go?" Megan was achingly aware of the arms that encircled her. Kieran's big hands, holding the reins, rested at her ribs. The same hands, she thought, that had held and soothed her last night.

"We must find a port. If we are to reach Ireland, we must cross the Irish Sea."

The breeze lifted her hair, and he breathed in the fragrance of lake water and wildflowers that clung to her.

Thoughts drifted through his mind. Thoughts that caused him much discomfort. With great effort he forced himself to study the terrain. They had to find the sea. And then they would go about finding a boat to take them home.

Home. That was one of the things that intrigued him about Megan. Her loss of memory about even the simplest things. Her name. Her home. What must it be like to lose one's memory of home?

He could see his own clearly. And with every image, there came the renewed determination to return as quickly as possible. But, he knew, with every mile they took, Megan drifted farther and farther from her own home.

"The river widens," Colin called.

"Aye. We will follow it to its mouth. There will lie the sea."

The terrain leveled. Gone were the rocky craigs and rugged forests. Here the land gentled to graceful hills and rolling green meadows. Soon even the hills disappeared, until a flat stretch of land could be seen in every direction.

Already the air had grown cooler. It carried with it the tang of the ocean, which could be seen on the horizon.

"Do the soldiers know where your home is?"

"Aye."

Megan shivered as they reached a rocky coast. It was the chill, she told herself. "Then they could have already determined that you will need a boat to reach your destination. They could be riding here ahead of us."

"Aye. It has crossed my mind. We will need to be cautious."

When they spotted a village in the distance, Kieran slid from the saddle. "They will be looking for two men and a woman. I will walk to the village ahead and inquire about a boat. If the soldiers were here, someone will have noticed them. If I think we are safe, I will return for you."

"And how will we know if you walk into their trap?" Megan's eyes flashed. "You left us once before and managed to get yourself trussed like a boar. I do not fancy staying here again while you get yourself captured."

Colin's voice was warm with laughter. "What do you say to that, my brother?"

"You are a most vexing woman." Kieran frowned at her as she steadied the restless horse.

"I may be vexing, but your plan is weak," she said calmly. "You should send me into the village. They will not be looking for a lone woman. No one will notice me."

He studied the soldier's garb, the wild mane of golden hair, and threw back his head with a roar of laughter. "No one will notice? Forgive me, my lady. You cannot help but turn heads."

Megan had never before heard him laugh. It was a rich, warm sound that oddly pleased her.

Colin joined in the laughter. "Aye, Megan. My brother is right. You could not possibly enter the village without notice."

She glanced at herself and was forced to make a grudging admission. "Aye. I suppose I would draw attention in men's clothing."

It was her rare beauty that would draw the stares of the villagers, Kieran knew. But he wisely kept his thoughts to himself.

"But know this." Megan kept her gaze fixed on Kieran's eyes. "If you do not return by the time the sun is directly overhead, Colin and I will ride to the village to see what detains you."

"Very well. Since you force me to change my plans," he said, bowing slightly toward Megan. "Find the village inn. I will be waiting there. With a tankard," he added with a smile. "There we will refresh ourselves and chart our course for Ireland." He turned, then flung an admiring glance over his shoulder. "Has any man ever told you that you have the instincts of a warrior, my lady?"

She felt her cheeks flushing as he began to make his way toward the distant village. He could not have given her a nicer compliment. But she had not the slightest notion of why his words had pleased her so.

As their horses plodded along the dusty lane, Megan pulled her cloak tightly around her to hide the strange clothing she wore. She had been agitated since Kieran had left them. They should have gone together. There was safety in numbers. Besides, she could not shake the feeling that something was very wrong. Their journey here had been too easy. And now, as they approached the row of aged cottages that looked out over the dark waters, the feeling grew.

"There, Megan." Colin pointed to the weathered sign that hung over the last building. "The Lion's Head."

She nodded and brought her horse to a halt. As she dismounted she whispered, "I do not like it, Colin. Something is amiss."

"There are only two other horses tethered here."

"Neither of which is Kieran's," she reminded him.

Colin glanced around. "Where could the soldiers hide that many animals?"

She had no answer to that.

"Come, lass. It has been a difficult journey. But food and ale will lift our spirits."

The Lion's Head was a small, cozy tavern. A fire burned in the fireplace, driving away the chill. The aroma of freshly baked bread perfumed the air.

A quick glance showed only two elderly gentlemen seated in one corner and a cluster of fishermen fresh from their boats seated around the fireplace, lifting tankards.

"I do not see Kieran." Megan frowned.

"Nay. Nor do I. But do not fret. He said he would meet us here. He will be along soon."

They followed the innkeeper through a small alcove. There a table was set in front of a cheery fire. When the innkeeper left, Megan studied the young man across the table. "Are you so trusting of everyone? Or just of your brother?"

He grinned. "Kieran is a man of his word. I have no doubt he will be here."

"And the boat?"

Colin shrugged. "Kieran will find a way. He will bribe or bully or buy what is needed."

They looked up as the innkeeper entered, carrying a tray containing a decanter and goblets. When he left Megan filled both their glasses. Before they could lift them to their lips, Kieran entered and took a goblet from the tray.

"We drink to a safe journey," he said.

"I told you he would come."

Kieran glanced from Colin to Megan. "Was there a doubt?"

"Aye. The lass is edgy."

"And well she should be. But I encountered no trouble."

The ale burned a path of warmth from Megan's throat all the way to her stomach as she felt her taut muscles begin to relax. She knew not why the feeling of danger did not go away, but soon enough, as Colin said, with food and ale, it would be gone. "Have you located a boat?" Megan asked softly.

"Aye. 'Tis small but seaworthy. The owner, a fisherman, knows these waters. He offered to take us across the Firth of Clyde to the Island of Arran."

"And then?" Colin asked.

"We will need something bigger than his small fishing boat to see us across the North Channel. But at least we will have a body of water between us and the hangman."

The innkeeper entered, bearing yet another tray. This one contained smoked haddock and steaming rolls fresh from the oven.

"Does this have a name?" Kieran asked as he helped himself to a large portion.

"Aye. Finnan haddie." Both the innkeeper and Megan spoke in unison.

"You are a Scotswoman. I can tell by your manner of speech. What is your clan, my lady?" the innkeeper asked.

Megan felt a moment of panic. But before she could respond, Kieran said, "MacDougal."

"Ahh. A Highlander. You are far from home, my lady." The innkeeper gave Megan a long, lingering look before bowing from the room.

When they were alone, Kieran answered her arched look. "When you and your companion were in the Highlands, I heard you warn him to beware the MacDougals. 'Twas their deer you were poaching." He took a bite of fish. "It is grand, my lady. You must have eaten this before."

Kieran watched as she tasted, then began enjoying, her meal.

"Aye. Though I do not remember. But I remembered what it was called."

He heard the disappointment in her tone. "Remembering a word is not the same as remembering a lifetime, is it?"

"Nay." She fell silent.

"It will come in time, Megan."

"Time." She glanced out the window to the dark water that reached to the far horizon. When they left here, there would be no more time. She would leave her home, her country, for a strange new place.

Kieran saw the look in her eyes and wished there was some way to ease her burden. But their celebration had suddenly taken on a somber note.

When they had finished every morsel on the tray, the innkeeper brought them scones with clotted cream and dishes of fruit conserves. They ate until at last their hunger was abated.

"We go now to the boat." Kieran lifted his tankard and emptied it, then dropped some coins on the table and led the way. Colin and Megan followed.

Along the shore they picked their way carefully amid the fishermen who sat on rocks, mending nets. Kieran stuck out his hand to a rangy man whose skin was the texture of aged leather. Fine lines creased his forehead. His cheeks bore deep hollows of sunken skin. His white hair was in sharp contrast to his sun-bronzed skin and pale blue eyes.

"Is the boat ready?"

"Aye."

They followed the old man to a small craft that bobbed at anchor in the foaming surf. If they had doubts as to its seaworthiness, they kept their fears to themselves.

Megan cast a quick glance at the dark clouds that billowed on the horizon. Not a good omen. She felt a sudden, quick flash of fear and wondered if she had ever before been in a boat on the ocean. The fear grew. Something about this day was not right.

Stepping into the water, they made their way to the boat. Kieran helped Colin into the stern, then turned toward Megan. Without warning an arrow sang through the air and landed in the boat's hull, missing Megan's head by mere inches.

Racing toward them along the rocky shore were a dozen men on horseback.

Most of the fishermen, having seen the approaching soldiers, ducked out of the way. Those few unfortunate enough to be too slow to escape gave out cries of pain and fear as they sustained wounds from flying hooves and singing arrows.

"Launch your boat," Kieran shouted to the fisherman.

"There are too many of them." The captain, too afraid to move, stood paralyzed on shore.

"You can go with us, or we will take your boat across the Firth of Clyde alone. Either way, we go now."

Hearing the challenge in Kieran's tone, the fisherman responded by leaning his shoulder into the boat. Kieran joined him. But with both men pushing the boat against the incoming tide, Megan was left alone to face the approaching attackers.

She pulled her sword and faced the first horseman. As he raced toward her she sidestepped and caught him on the tip of her sword, sending him sprawling into the surf. The next two horsemen came up on either side of her. But though she was outnumbered, she fought valiantly, toppling one and wounding the other.

"Megan. Come."

At Kieran's cry she turned. Already the boat rode the waves. As she watched, the fisherman hauled himself over the side and took up an oar.

Two more riders were thundering toward her. She dared not turn her back on them and try to make it to the boat.

"Megan. Hurry." Colin's voice was carried to her on the wind, like the call of a seabird.

She faced the next attackers and felt her hopes dim. Kieran and Colin would be forced to leave without her. But at least she would have the satisfaction of taking some of these bullies down before they managed to overpower her.

As she lifted her sword, another horseman came up behind her. Before she could turn, she heard the sound of blade meeting blade. She caught a glimpse of Kieran. He had returned to her side to join in the fray.

As she fought back another attacker, Kieran caught her by the arm, dragging her into deep water. "There is not time to waste. The boat leaves now."

"But what about the soldiers?"

"They will have to be powerful swimmers to catch us."

A huge wave rolled over them, taking them both down. Megan felt herself being pounded against the sand and rocks that lined the ocean bottom. Then, when she thought she could hold her breath no longer, she surfaced. A hand caught her, drawing her even farther into deep water.

She glanced toward shore and saw that the horsemen had halted. Even those brave enough to ride their horses into the water were driven back. The surf pounded the rocks, sending a foaming spray several hundred feet into the air.

"The boat..."

"Out there."

Megan felt a moment of panic. But as she cut cleanly through the water, Kieran stayed close beside her. Several times she felt herself being pummeled by the waves. But each time, when she surfaced, Kieran was there, shouting encouragement, staying close to her side.

By the time they reached the boat, Megan had no reserve of strength left. She felt strong hands closing around her wrists as the fisherman and Colin dragged her into the boat.

When Kieran pulled himself over the side, he touched a hand to her as she lay heaving and struggling for breath.

"Well done, Megan."

The tiny boat was lifted on a giant wave. For long minutes it hovered, riding the crest. Then, as the wave dipped, the boat seemed to shudder, then dropped hundreds of feet, where it bobbed gently, until the next giant wave caught it and tossed it around like a child's toy.

Megan felt her stomach heave as sickness enveloped her, leaving her weak and drained.

Kieran glanced at her pale face and, dipping a strip of cloth in the water that rolled about the bottom of the boat, pressed it to her fevered brow.

"It will pass."

From the depths of her misery she summoned as much anger as possible. "The next time you plan a journey," she said between bouts of retching, "I should like it to be in a pony cart."

Kieran's eyes danced with laughter. Even in a time of crisis, she could be counted on to have the last word.

Chapter Seven

By the time they reached the rugged shores of the Island of Arran, a cold, steady rain was falling. The sky grew black as the storm moved in. The waves, lashed to a frenzy by the storm, pounded against the shore.

While the captain steered the little craft between rocks and boulders, Kieran and Colin leaped over the side and set their shoulders to the task of bringing it in. Megan could only lie and watch. The seasickness had left her as weak as a newborn.

When the craft was anchored, the captain accepted his pay from Kieran. Eager to return to the mainland, he turned toward Megan, who clung weakly to the side of the boat. "Can you stand, lass?"

She gripped the edge of the rail and struggled to pull herself up, but her legs were unable to support her weight.

Seeing her distress Kieran lifted her easily in his arms. Now she truly was as frail and helpless as she had first appeared. It tugged at his heart to see her like this. He splashed through the shallows toward shore. There he deposited her in the grass and turned to Colin.

"Stay with her. I will return as soon as I find another craft to take us across the North Channel."

"What about food and shelter? Megan looks as though she has need of both."

"Aye." Kieran glanced at her, then met his brother's questioning look. To spare her further distress he kept his voice low. "It is what we all need, especially the lass. But the men who follow us will be but the stroke of an oar behind us. We dare not tarry here. We must set out immediately for Ireland."

"In this storm?"

Kieran hated what the crossing had done to Megan. She had not the strength to lift her arm, let alone wield a sword. But there was nothing to be done about it. They were no safer here than they had been in the highland forests.

"We leave as soon as I find a boat and a fisherman willing to sail it. Until I return, keep watch along the shore. At the first sign of a boat from the direction of the mainland, get her to safety and get word to me."

Colin nodded. As Kieran walked away, he knelt beside the girl, whose teeth were chattering uncontrollably.

"Here, lass." He lifted her into the small shelter formed by two giant boulders. When she was safe from the full fury of the storm, he wrapped her in his cloak and went in search of driftwood. Though the wood was wet, he found enough dry kindling to get a meager fire started. Soon Megan was no longer shivering, though her skin still had that sallow, sickly pallor.

A short distance away the waves slammed against the rocks piled up near the shore, creating a deafening roar. Overhead, angry black clouds rolled and billowed. An occasional flash of lightning split the heavens, bathing the shore in an eerie glow.

"I wish I could make you some tea," Colin said. "Or beg some spirits from a fisherman. 'Twould soothe you."

"There is no need." Megan gave him what she hoped was a reassuring smile, but he saw the way her lips trembled. "I could not keep it down. But do not fear, Colin..." As lightning streaked across the sky, her words died in her throat. Her fingers closed around his wrist. With her other hand she pointed toward the shore. "God in heaven."

Colin turned, but the world had already gone dark again. "What is it, Megan? What did you see?"

"Our pursuers. They have reached shore." Grabbing a handful of sand, she began to quench the fire.

"Are you certain? Did you see them clearly?"

"Aye. I have no doubt."

Colin was silent for a moment, then whispered, "The darkness can work to our advantage as well as theirs. If they did not spot our fire, they have no way of knowing we are here."

"Aye." She could see the wisdom of his words.

He reached a hand to her. "Can you stand?"

"With your help."

Accepting his outstretched hands, she got to her feet. With the rain pelting them, they picked their way among the rocks and boulders littering the shore and prayed that they could make their escape before another bolt of lightning rent the heavens and revealed them for all to see.

They walked in the direction Kieran had taken and soon found themselves in a small fishing village. Making their way along a narrow path, they wound their way among small cottages until they came to an inn.

Inside a cheery fire chased away the gloom of the storm. A candle burned on a table in the corner of the room where two men sat with heads bent close in quiet conversation. A young tavern wench stood behind one of the men, her hand draped across his shoulder in an intimate gesture.

As their eyes became accustomed to the light, Colin and Megan saw the three heads jerk upward and turn toward the door. It was then that they both realized one of the men was Kieran. The one upon whose shoulder the girl's arm rested.

Kieran shot his brother an angry scowl. "Why have you come here?"

"We..." Colin swallowed, wondering how much to reveal to these strangers. "We had agreed that if we—needed to escape the storm, we should come for you. Kieran, we must leave immediately."

Kieran's eyes narrowed. "You can speak freely. I have already told these good people the truth. They know that we are emissaries from the Queen, who has instructed us to pay a fortune to the one who assists us in her quest."

Colin felt his cheeks flame. It was obvious that Kieran had spun a story in order to procure a boat. But it was not in Colin's nature to lie. In fact, it went against everything he believed in. He felt himself stammering as his cheeks grew hotter. "The Queen . . . the fortune . . ."

Quickly assessing the situation, Megan cut in quickly. "We must leave now. Else all will be lost."

Kieran took in the drenched lass, whose soaked men's clothing and dripping hair made her look more like a homeless waif than a woman of noble birth. He saw the way she studied the tavern wench and wished there was something he could do to explain. But there was no time. She would have to go along with the charade.

"Captain MacLachlan," Kieran said smoothly. "My brother, Colin, and my sister, Megan."

Sister? Megan's mouth dropped open in surprise. Now what game was Kieran playing?

"This is Captain MacLachlan," Kieran continued. "He has agreed to take us across the North Channel to Ireland, on our secret mission for the Queen." He turned to the wench whose arm rested possessively on his shoulder. "And this is the captain's lovely daughter, Nola."

The wench dismissed Megan and Colin with barely a glance and turned to Kieran. Her voice dripped honey. "It was most kind of you to agree to share the Queen's treasure with us. But you cannot ask my father to risk his life on such a night. I urge you to heed his advice and stay the night. On the morrow the storm will have passed. You will be refreshed and ready for the perils of a channel crossing. Besides—" she moved her hand through the hair at Kieran's nape, her fingers soft and seductive "—it would be our honor to have you stay in our humble inn."

Megan studied the woman in the scarlet gown, whose small waist and ample bosom were perfectly displayed. Then she glanced at her own coarse tunic and breeches, which dripped water on the polished wood floor. She felt a rush of anger, and some other, deeper feeling she could not identify. "Mayhap you should do as the lady suggests and...refresh yourself in this cozy inn, brother, while Colin and I seek shelter from the storm under the rock where you left us."

Colin nearly burst into laughter at the dark scowl that crossed Kieran's face. Leave it to the lass to show her claws.

Quickly recovering his composure, Kieran turned to the captain and his daughter. "The lass has a tongue like a viper, but I promised our mother I would never forsake her. Of course," he added without looking at Megan, "I fear that one day she will push me too far and I will do something I will later regret. For her own good, of course."

"The child is fortunate to have a brother as brave and noble as you," Nola said with a dismissive wave of her hand. "I am certain we can make room for them on the floor near the fireplace. You will be snug and warm there, child."

"Child! How dare—"

Before Megan could say more, Colin cut her off. "There is no time left, Kieran. We must go at once."

"Aye." Kieran turned to the captain. "I fear we cannot wait until the storm passes. If you cannot take us across the channel now, we will be forced to seek another boat."

Captain MacLachlan glanced at his daughter, then drank down a tumbler of whiskey. He knew that Nola was taken with the charm and rugged good looks of this stranger. Her husband had died in a shipwreck over two years ago, and there were few men on this island who were interested in a widow with two small bairns. He studied the man who sat across from him. A night with a lusty lass like Nola could convince the stranger to stay. On the other hand there was the gold. Captain MacLachlan did not want to lose his chance at the Queen's fortune. If, as the stranger had implied, there were many coins, his daughter would be well taken care of. And she could buy the attentions of a few dozen island lads who could assuage her loneliness.

The captain filled his glass and emptied the contents in two swallows.

His daughter chewed her lip and prayed he would refuse to set sail tonight. It had been a long time since a stranger as handsome as this one had arrived upon their shores. She had no doubt that she could please him, if only her father would insist upon waiting out the storm. But though she was headstrong, she would never defy her father. Whatever decision he made, she would have to abide by it.

Colin and Megan fought to keep their nerves at bay. At any moment their pursuers could burst through the doors and all would be lost.

Megan glanced at Kieran and cursed the fact that he seemed not at all concerned. Not once did he glance her way.

"I do not relish facing the angry seas this night," the captain said slowly. "But the Queen's fortune is a worthy goal. One I cannot resist."

"How soon can we leave?" Kieran asked.

"As soon as you and the lad and lass have refreshed yourselves."

Kieran turned a charming smile upon the captain's daughter. Lifting her hand to his lips he murmured, "I regret that there is not even time for refreshments. But perhaps, if you would prepare some food for our journey, I can tell the Queen about your kindness. Perhaps I can even return one day and thank you properly myself."

Nola's face was aglow as she said with a seductive smile, "I shall hold you to that, my lord."

As she walked away, her father called, "Prepare food and ale. And some sheepskins, girl. 'Tis a foul night to be on the water."

"Aye, Father."

A short time later the captain led the way toward a dark, hulking shadow on the beach. The boat was twice the size of the small vessel that had carried them to the Island of Arran. Megan glanced at the black, boiling waves and shuddered. A craft twice this size would still not be big enough to suit her. The thought of what they were about to undertake sent terror rushing through her veins.

As she was helped into the boat, she turned and saw the way Nola clung to Kieran before bidding him a safe journey. The man was a scoundrel. He was flirting shamelessly with the captain's daughter. And enjoying every moment in her company.

She sank down against the sturdy planks that lined the vessel and closed her eyes against the lurching of her stomach. She had never felt so miserable in her life. It was merely the seasickness, she told herself firmly. It was not because of this hateful man and the strange feelings he aroused in her.

A flash of lightning revealed a score of men running along the rocky shore toward their boat. Megan glanced toward Kieran and knew, by the hard set of his jaw, that he had seen them, as well. He shouted to Colin and the captain, and the three men braced their weight against the hull of the boat. It scraped along the sandy bottom, then caught a wave and began to float. As the three managed to scramble aboard a series of waves carried the boat far out into the channel.

Megan peered through the darkness but could not make out the figures on shore.

What would Nola say when she discovered that the Queen's emissaries were escaped criminals, wanted by the executioner? A shudder passed through her. Worse, what would the English soldiers do? Would they finally give up their quest? Or would they follow across the water to Kieran's land?

Megan felt the boat catch a giant wave and skim along the crest. Suddenly the boat dropped, falling, falling, until it was caught by another wave and lifted high. She fell to her knees in a fit of weakness, then crawled to the forward section of the boat where a small, makeshift shelter offered some protection from the storm. Under it Megan huddled, wrapped in a warm sheepskin. Each time the boat rode another wave, Megan faced another bout of sickness. Each time she managed to swallow it down, determined to fight this terrible feeling. She would not give in. She would be as strong in this fearsome battle as she was in those battles fought upon the field of honor.

When they had been at sea no more than an hour, the storm broke upon them with all its fury. Thunder crashed with deafening force. Lightning danced across the waves, blinding them with its intensity. The wind and waves tossed the boat around as though it were a leaf. Megan huddled in a corner. Terror gripped her. The sickness rolled over her, wave after wave, until she threw off the sheepskin, got to her feet and rushed to the side of the boat to retch.

"Nay, Megan." Alarmed, Kieran dropped his oar and started toward her. But his words were whipped away by the force of the wind.

As he raced the length of the boat, he saw her lean over the side. At that moment a wave crashed across the prow of the boat and swept her overboard.

The captain and Colin, having seen what happened, raced toward the railing.

"A rope," Kieran shouted above the wind. "I must have a rope."

The captain struggled with a coil of rope until one end was free.

Quickly tying it around his waist, Kieran braced himself for a moment against the wind, then plunged into the frigid waters.

Megan felt herself being dragged down beneath the icy water. For long moments, as she struggled against the angry waves, she felt as though she was suffocating. Her burning lungs ached for a breath of air. Struggling against the force of the water, she moved her arms and legs in a frantic scramble. When at last she broke the surface, she took in a long, deep breath. But before she could take another, a wave rolled over her. It was impossible to catch her breath. The more she struggled against the walls of water, the more her lungs demanded air. A sense of panic seized her. Soon she would be too exhausted to struggle.

A crash of thunder was followed by a flash of lightning that danced across the water. Megan saw the huge black waves rolling toward her and braced herself. Tons of water poured over her, slamming her down so hard she felt the rough scratch of sand at the bottom of the channel. With all her might she struggled upward, toward the air that her lungs craved.

As she surfaced she heard a man's cry and felt strong hands reach for her.

"God in heaven. Megan, I thought I had lost you."

"Kieran." She coughed and choked as she struggled to suck air into her starving lungs. "Is that you, Kieran?"

"Aye. Do not speak." He dragged her close and wrapped her in his arms.

Safe. The first thought that flew into her mind was that she was safe now as long as Kieran held her. But as the storm-tossed waves continued to swamp them, her relief turned to despair.

"You should not have come after me. Now we will both be lost."

"I have no intention of giving up when the goal is this near. Can you hold tightly to me, Megan?"

"Aye."

"Then hold on, and no matter what, do not let go."

At his command, she wrapped her arms around his waist and clung to him. Kieran strained against the rope, slowly, painfully pulling until they were drawn close to the boat.

Megan saw the effort it cost Kieran to struggle against the forces of nature. But though his muscles strained until his face was contorted in pain, he continued to pull against the rope.

"We have you, Kieran. We can pull you in."

From across the waves came Colin's voice. Megan felt a tremor of fear as another flash of lightning illuminated the two men in the boat. They were still so far away. But both men were bent to the task of reeling in the rope that was their only line to the two in the water.

Kieran felt Megan's hands begin to slip as a giant wave washed over them. His voice was a rough command.

"Hold on to me, Megan. A little while longer, lass, and we will be safe."

"Aye." Rain pelted her face, blinding her. And as they inched their way toward the boat, she clung to him, grateful for his quiet strength.

When they reached the side of the boat, Kieran handed her up to the men who reached for her. When Kieran was safely aboard as well, the captain shouted to Colin, "Man the oars, lad, while I handle the tiller. Else we will find ourselves swamped."

Colin and the captain struggled to keep the boat on course.

Beneath the shelter in the prow of the boat, Megan and Kieran lay, taking in deep drafts of air. When their breathing had returned to normal, they huddled together beneath the sheepskin until the trembling subsided.

The storm continued to thunder and rage, but for a few brief moments they forgot about everything except each other.

"That was a foolish thing you did." Kieran's voice was rough with emotion. "I feared you were lost to us forever."

"Would that matter, my lord?" Megan's throat was raw as she tried to speak. Tears sprang unbidden to her eyes. "Your journey would be easier without another to worry about."

"Aye." Beside her, Kieran lay very still, his arms wrapped possessively around her. "It seems I spend far too much time worrying about you, lass. And thinking about you."

He drew her fractionally closer and brought his lips to a tangle of hair at her temple. "I am not a man given to worry or fear. But something about you terrifies me, Megan. You are too bold, too brave, too headstrong. And though I know you are capable of taking care of yourself, I have this perplexing desire to watch over you."

As he spoke, his fingers moved along her spine. She trembled, aware of him as she had never before been aware of a man.

"You should not have come after me." She had no idea why she was suddenly crying.

He put his arms around her and drew her close. "And why is that?"

"Because you nearly gave up your life, as well."

His voice, low and tender, was warmed with a smile. "Would that matter to you, lass?"

"Aye." The tears were stronger now, bringing with them a rush of shame that he should see this weakness in her.

"Oh, Megan. What am I to do with you?" With a sigh he drew her firmly into the circle of his arms. While she wept he ran soft kisses across her temple to her eyelids. He tasted the salt of her tears and moved his lips lower, to brush her cheek and the tip of her nose. As his mouth moved lower still, he found her lips, eager and hungry for his.

His mouth moved over hers, lightly at first, then more firmly as the hunger grew. This was dangerous, he realized. This mysterious woman, with no name, no past, was not like any other woman he had ever known. She was soft and vulnerable. But beneath the vulnerability lay strength. This was not a village maiden who would teasingly offer her lips to a man. This woman was as reluctant as he to give in to the feelings that surged between them.

Megan held herself stiffly, fighting the feelings that poured through her, heating her blood, her flesh. Strange new sensations pulsed through her veins and curled deep inside her.

That first kiss they had shared, so brief, so shocking, had not prepared her for this. This time the feelings lingered and grew until they threatened to take over her very will. God in heaven. What was happening to her? How was it that this man's simple touch held such power? She gave a little sigh of pleasure and savored the dark, dangerous taste of him.

In some corner of his mind Kieran knew that he must end this. But not now. Not yet. As his mouth moved over hers, he forgot everything except the woman in his arms. His hands skimmed beneath her wet garments to seek her soft flesh. For a moment she stiffened. But slowly, gradually, as she began to strain against him, he heard her little sigh of pleasure, and he was lost. She breathed his name against his lips, and he felt his heart explode.

His kiss was no longer gentle as, driven by a desperate need, he kissed her with a savageness that left her stunned.

A part of Megan's mind warned her to beware of what lay ahead. But as Kieran's lips and hands continued their arousal, she could no longer think.

He lifted his head, his breathing unsteady. The need for this woman still shuddered through him, leaving his hands trembling.

Awkwardly Megan sat up, adjusting her wet clothing. She was grateful for the darkness that hid her from his view. Her cheeks, she knew, were flushed, her hands unsteady.

For no reason, tears filled her eyes.

Tenderly, Kieran touched a finger to her cheek. "More tears?"

He leaned on one elbow and studied her. She was crying uncontrollably. Great terrible sobs were wrenched from her. "What is it, Megan? What troubles you now?"

"You do not know the dark thoughts that I have been thinking." She struggled to stem the flow of tears and wound up crying harder. "If you did, you would never have risked your life to rescue me."

This strange lass sorely tried his patience. With a sigh, he said, "You make no sense, Megan."

Her voice rose. Her tears mingled with the rain that streaked her face. "You asked what troubles me? You. You trouble me, Kieran O'Mara." She turned away from him, mortified that he should see her cry like this. "You deliberately left your own brother and me out in the storm while you sat in the warmth of the inn pursuing the captain's daughter."

A smile touched the corner of his lips. "Is that what all this is about?" The smile became a deep rumble of roguish laughter. "I must remember that I owe a great debt to the captain's daughter." His eyes gleamed with warmth. "You are jealous of Nola."

"Jealous!" She pushed against him. Forgotten now were those precious kisses stolen only moments ago. Forgotten, too, was the ordeal of the ocean and her seasickness. Now there was only this terrible black rage building inside her. "I am not jealous of a tavern wench. Or of you, Kieran O'Mara. I am angry. Angry that I—" she felt her cheeks redden and forced herself to go on "—permitted a man like you to... take liberties with me."

"Liberties?" Kieran struggled to swallow his smile. If the lass were not so furious, this would be laughable. "Megan, listen to me. I knew that Nola was—" he chose his words carefully and kept his tone low enough that the captain would not overhear "—intrigued by a stranger to her island. And I surmised that by charming her I could persuade her father to take us across the channel. But the wench meant nothing more to me than a chance to escape."

"You would smile and be charming in order to get what you wanted?"

His smile faded. He was not proud of what he had done. "Aye."

"Then I must believe that you would do the same with me, my lord. That kiss we shared meant nothing more than that smile you gave to the captain's daughter."

"Damn you." He caught her by the upper arms and dragged her roughly against him until their faces were mere inches apart. Staring deeply into her eyes, he bit off each word with fury. Even now he wanted her with a desperation that left him trembling. "I will not be questioned like some smooth-cheeked lad. I make no apology for the captain's daughter. I would have done anything to escape the hangman's soldiers. I would beg, steal, even kill before I would return to that hell of a prison in England. I swear by all that is holy, I will remain a free man and return to my land. Land," he added with venom, "that no man will ever take from me again."

They stared at each other in silence. With the wind whipping his hair and clothes and his face a grim mask of fury, he looked at her with fire in his eyes.

"And as for what we just shared..." For long moments Kieran studied her, and she was struck by the depth of his anger. Through gritted teeth he said, "I suppose you expect an apology for my moment of passion. But I make no such apology, my lady."

As he strode away and took up an oar, Megan watched him with a look of wonder. Touching a finger to her lips, she heard his words echoing through her mind. A moment of passion. Aye, he had proven himself a man of many passions. But somehow, discovering how much he detested any weakness in himself, it only made their brief kiss all the sweeter.

Rolling herself into the sheepskin, she huddled in the corner of the craft and tried to blot out the sound of the raging storm. It could not compare with the storm that was suddenly raging in her heart. A storm of feelings so alien to her she could not even give it a name.

Chapter Eight

Megan rocked back and forth, cradled in the arms of an old woman whose face she could not see. But the woman's words were plain enough.

"Ye must not give in to that temper, lass. Ye've a temper as fierce as your father's. It is not proper for a lass to swear so. Ye must study your mother's gentle ways. She is a true lady, as ye will be when ye are grown. Make your old nurse proud, lass. Try harder for old Morna."

The old woman began to hum a tune as she rocked back and forth, back and forth.

The voice faded until it was no more than the sigh of the wind. But her name lingered. Old Morna. Old Morna.

A gentle breeze lifted a strand of Megan's hair, then just as abruptly dropped it. She opened her eyes. For a moment she had no idea where she was. Then, at the gentle rocking motion, it all came back to her in a rush.

She was on the boat crossing the North Channel. She gazed at the cloudless sky. The sunlight was warm upon her face. The storm had fled some time during the night.

Morna. A first glimmer of memory had returned. She hugged the thought to her heart. She had another name, besides her own. Morna. Old Morna. Megan wondered who she was. An elderly aunt or cousin perhaps? A servant? No matter. It would come to her. At least she had the beginnings of a memory.

She glanced around at the others, who lay sleeping. The captain had managed to steer the boat to land. Though the craft was not beached, it bobbed in the surf very near shore, held there by the force of the tide. The captain, exhausted from the night's ordeal, lay asleep at the tiller. Colin was stretched out in the middle of the boat, the oar still in his hand.

Only Kieran was awake. He leaned a hip against the rail and stared hungrily at the land beyond the rocky shore.

Megan studied his proud profile and wondered what drove him. He had survived brutal beatings in prison. He had risked death by drowning and by sword to reach this land. Now that he was here, would he find the peace he sought?

She got to her feet and stared at this land that claimed Kieran's heart. Long fingers of rock seemed to reach far out into the ocean. The shore was strewn with rock. In the distance were rolling green hills, dotted with thatched-roof cottages. Here and there sheep grazed. It was not unlike the land they had left behind. Her land, she thought with a sudden twinge. Her home now lay far beyond the body of water they had just crossed.

Seeing that she was awake, Kieran moved to her side, taking care not to touch her. He had become much too aware of the lass, a flaw he would take pains to correct.

"Welcome to Ireland, my lady."

She turned to him. "Is your home far from here?"

"Not far. A day's walk."

"Will we wake Colin?"

Kieran glanced at his sleeping brother. "Nay. Let the lad rest awhile longer. The crossing sorely taxed him." He held out his hand. "Come, my lady. I am eager to set foot on Irish soil."

She took his hand and once again felt the strength in his grip. The thought of the kiss they had shared last night sent her cheeks flaming. But though she ducked her head to avoid his gaze, she was still painfully aware of his nearness.

Together they climbed from the boat and picked their way
through foaming surf and over rocks until they stood on dry
land.

"Ahh. Smell it, lass. Feel it."

Kieran lifted his face to the sun and took in deep breaths
of air. "I carried the perfume of home in my heart all those
long days in prison."

"Did you fear you might never see your home again?"

"Never." His tone was low and deep with passion. "The
prison has not been built that could keep me from this place.
I always knew I would see Ireland again."

This was a passion she could understand and share.
Though her land lay far across the North Channel, she knew
she would see Scotland again. There was no man who would
say otherwise. When her memory returned to her, she would
claim her destiny.

They heard the others stirring and turned to see Colin
pulling himself over the rail of the boat.

"Are we really home, Kieran?"

"Aye. You fell asleep just before we touched the shore."

"'Twas a grueling journey. I thought the storm would
succeed where Fleet and the hangman's soldiers had failed."

"Aye. But we endured. And we are home."

As the captain walked to the side of the boat and peered
at them, she had a sudden thought. "What will happen
when Captain MacLachlan discovers that you have not been
sent by the Queen and that there is no fortune?"

Kieran touched a hand to the pouch of gold that hung
from his waist. "The good captain has earned his gold. And
as for the rest of my story," he added with a smile, "he need
never know. Let him boast to his grandchildren that he was
once in service to the Queen."

While Megan and Colin exchanged laughter, Kieran
climbed aboard the vessel and settled his account with the
captain. A short time later they stood on the shore and
waved as the boat headed across the North Channel.

"He will have much to relate."

"Aye," Kieran said with a laugh. "By the time the story is told and retold, Captain MacLachlan will probably have supped with the bloody English Queen in her ship's cabin."

"And advised her on the best route to England." Colin wiped tears of laughter from his eyes.

Watching them, Megan thought how wonderful it was to see these two brothers share a laugh. No matter what they had been through, they were home.

"The captain was good enough to leave us the food and water his daughter so generously provided." Kieran spread his cloak on the grass and handed Colin and Megan chunks of cold mutton. "Another debt I owe to Nola," Kieran said in an aside to Megan that had her blushing furiously.

Kieran was relieved to see that Megan's appetite had returned. Whatever sickness she had suffered at the hands of the storm was now gone. Even her color had improved since she had set foot on dry land. Her eyes danced with anticipation, and her cheeks bloomed a becoming shade of pink.

When they had eaten their fill Kieran picked up his cloak and led the way, with Megan and Colin following. They walked for hours beneath a gentle sun that warmed their backs.

"Is it not a fair land?" Kieran asked.

Megan had taken note of the lush green fields, the sparkling waters, the plump sheep. "Aye. It is a bonnie land."

For some reason that Kieran did not wish to dwell upon, her response gave him great pleasure. It should not matter to him that the lass liked his land. But it did.

In the warmth of the sun Megan had removed her cloak and draped it across her arm. Kieran watched the sway of her hips, the proud tilt of her head as she walked. He knew of no other woman who could look so stunning in shapeless men's clothing. He shot her an admiring glance. Another woman would have complained about the journey on foot but Megan simply strode along with all the grace and poise of a sleek young cat.

At midday they paused to cool their feet in the bubbling waters of a brook. Removing her kid boots, Megan rolled up her breeches and waded through the shallows. But when the image of Wilkes, the captain of the guard, flashed through her mind, her smile suddenly vanished. For a moment he thought she saw his bloated body floating toward her. She blinked, and the image disappeared. She felt a shiver of fear and wrapped her arms around herself.

From his position on shore Kieran saw her turn abruptly and retreat from the water. In swift strides he was by her side.

"What is it, my lady? What frightened you?"

She shook off his hand. "It was nothing. A sudden chill."

He watched as she pulled on her boots and turned away. Though they lingered there a short while longer, she resolutely refused to go near the brook. When at last they resumed their journey, she never looked back.

"There. See." Colin pointed. "Killamara. And just beyond, Castle O'Mara."

He ran until he was at the top of the hill. Behind him Kieran and Megan broke into a run. When they reached the top they stared in silence.

Below them the land was lush and green. In the distance were a series of small villages ringing a magnificent castle built on a hill. The turrets of the castle seemed to touch the clouds that hovered just above.

Megan glanced at Colin, then at Kieran. Their faces were transformed. Both men wore similar looks of naked hunger.

"Come." Kieran's strides were hurried, purposeful as he led the way down the hill. "We will be home before nightfall."

They followed a well-worn trail toward a small village. As they passed the first cottage, they saw a young woman stare at them, then lower her head shyly before disappearing inside a thatched-roof dwelling.

A few minutes later a man stepped through the doorway and called out, "Is it truly Black Kieran O'Mara?"

The three paused and turned. Kieran saw the way the man studied him, searching for some sign of recognition. His hand went to the growth of black beard that covered his neck and chin. Realizing that the beard obscured his identity, he raised his hand in a sign of welcome and the man strode forward to clasp it.

"God be praised. My lord. You are alive."

"As you can see, I am very much alive, Robert. You are a feast for my eyes."

"As you are, my lord. My Deidre said it was you. I did not believe her. We'd heard you were killed in an English prison." The man paused a moment. "Your mother does not know you are here?"

"Nay, Robert. No one knows."

"Then you must not tarry, for her grief has been great. I would be very honored, my lord, if you would accept the use of my horses for the rest of your journey."

Kieran smiled. "We would be in your debt."

Robert called out to several young lads who scurried away and returned leading three sleek horses, saddled and ready. As the three prepared to mount, Robert placed his hand on Colin's arm.

"Colin? You have changed even more than your brother." His eyes lit. "Oh, there will be much rejoicing in Killamara this night."

"Aye." Colin clasped the man's hand. "Was my death rumored, as well?"

"Aye, my lord. All of Killamara has grieved the loss of the O'Mara heirs."

"Then we will plan a celebration," Kieran said, winking at his brother. "For we have returned from the dead to assume our rightful place in our homeland."

As they wheeled their mounts, Kieran called, "Your horses will be returned to you on the morrow."

"They are yours for as long as you have need of them. God go with you, my lord."

"And you, Robert."

The three riders urged their horses into a run. As they passed through the village a great cry went up from the people, who spilled from their cottages to shout their welcome to the lords of the manor.

Megan sensed the affection of these people and was strangely moved by it. Tears filled her eyes, and she was forced to blink them away. What must it be like, she wondered, to be so loved by so many good people? Was there someone now, in that far-off land, mourning her? Had there been family, friends who loved her?

As Kieran led the way, Megan turned to Colin. "Why is he called Black Kieran O'Mara?"

Colin shrugged. "Some would say it is because of his dark hair and eyes. But those who have faced him in battle will tell you he earned the name for the black rage that drives him. Woe to his enemies who would deny him his birthright."

Black Kieran O'Mara. As they left the village behind and raced across a series of gently rolling meadows, Megan thought about the strange and complicated man who piqued her interest.

Megan stared at the turrets of the castle gleaming in late afternoon sunlight. Directly in front of the structure lay a glimmering lake whose smooth surface mirrored the castle above it. Swans glided across the water, adding to the peaceful beauty of the scene.

As the three entered a wide cobbled courtyard, a small, hunched gnome of a man hurried forward. For long minutes he stared at the two bearded men astride their horses. When recognition dawned, his face convulsed as he fought back tears.

"My lord Kieran. My lord Colin." His lips trembled, and he struggled for control.

"Aye, Padraig. We have finally come home." Kieran slid from the saddle and caught the man in a great hug.

The door opened and a plump woman paused a moment before letting out a shriek. At her cry dozens of servants came running. Soon they all milled around in the doorway and windows, shouting and crying.

Into this confusion a single figure strode. The sea of servants parted. The din of voices fell silent. From her position astride her horse, Megan watched as a beautiful woman paused for a moment in the doorway and stared at the two men. Her shock was evident. The woman put a hand to her mouth to stifle her little cry before she flew into Kieran's outstretched arms.

"Oh, Kieran. Kieran. My darling. You've come back to us."

"Aye, Mother." He lifted her in his arms and swung her around, then released her into Colin's outstretched arms where she fell against him with a sigh.

"They told us you were dead, that you had both died in Fleet Prison." Her hands stroked their faces, their arms, as if to assure herself that they were truly alive and not just something she had imagined.

"As you can see, we are very much alive." Kieran gave her another kiss before crossing to Megan. In one sweeping gesture he lifted her from the saddle and set her on her feet.

"Mother, I would like to present the lady Megan, who aided our escape. Megan, this is my mother, Lady Katherine O'Mara."

Choosing to ignore the odd clothing on the lass, Lady Katherine caught her hands in a firm grip. "You aided their escape? Then I am forever in your debt, my dear."

Megan found herself staring into deep blue eyes set in an exquisite face. Thick black hair had been fixed in a coronet of curls around a face that showed neither a wrinkle nor a line. Her somber black gown was of finest watered silk.

Megan became even more aware of her own shabby state in the company of this elegant woman.

A girl of about six, her feet bare, her dress stained with the juice of blackberries, pushed her way through the crowd of servants to stare at the strangers in their midst. A wild tangle of red curls fell nearly to her ankles.

"God in heaven. Bridget," Lady Katherine called, "were you off in the bog again?" Her face filled with pain as she drew the girl close in a fierce embrace. "My darling, you know it is forbidden to you. You could have been sucked down into the mire and never found." When the child made no response, Lady Katherine whispered, "Forgive my outburst. My heart, I fear, has been too battered of late." Catching the girl's hand she said, "Come and greet your uncles."

Seeing the bearded strangers, the girl hung back.

"Is it truly Bridget?" Kieran opened his arms. "You've grown so much, lass, I would not know you."

Still the girl pulled away, feeling suddenly shy.

Megan whispered, "It is your beard, my lord. The poor child probably does not know you."

The child glanced at Megan, then at the man who faced her.

"Aye." Kieran knelt on the cobblestones and opened his arms to the girl. "I am your Uncle Kieran, and this is your Uncle Colin. Have you forgotten us already?"

A shy smile touched the girl's lips. "You look like the drawings of ancient warriors Grandmother made for me."

Kieran touched a hand to his beard. "At this moment I feel like an ancient warrior, lass. Do I frighten you?"

There was a defiance in the lass that touched something deep inside Megan.

As she watched, the girl put on a brave smile. "Nay. I am not afraid of you. I am afraid of nothing."

"That's my lass. Then come give me a kiss."

With a laugh the girl launched herself into his outstretched arms. He swung her around and around, then gave her over to Colin, who was impatiently awaiting his turn.

The girl buried a hand in his beard and tugged it. "You cannot be my Uncle Colin."

"Well I am. And you," he said, tugging gently on a stray lock of fiery hair, "are the most beautiful girl child ever born in Killamara."

"Oh, you are Uncle Colin."

"How did I convince you?"

"You always call me the most beautiful girl child ever born in Killamara."

"You see. Now you know I have to be your uncle."

The lass giggled and buried her face in his neck.

"Come," Lady Katherine said, linking her arms through those of her sons. "We will prepare a feast to welcome you home. And you will tell me everything."

From her position behind them, Megan saw Kieran and Colin exchange meaningful glances. They intended, she realized, to spare their mother most of the horrors of their adventure.

They entered a great room where servants bustled around, stoking the fire, arrange a settle in front of the fireplace, plumping pillows. As they worked, the servants cast sidelong glances at the two men who had returned from the dead. Both men looked more like wild savages than men of noble birth.

The plump woman whose shrieks had first greeted their arrival took a tray from a servant's hands and bowed grandly before Kieran and Colin. "Welcome home, my lords."

"Ahh, Mistress Peake." Kieran bent low, for the woman barely reached his midsection, and planted a kiss on her cheek. "How I have missed your smiling face."

The housekeeper blushed with pleasure.

"Not to mention your biscuits and fruit conserve," Colin cut in neatly. He lifted her hands to his lips and murmured, "How many nights I lay awake in Fleet and dreamed of your partridges roasting over the fire. And the thought of your sweets nearly drove me mad with desire."

Mistress Peake's jowels quivered. "You always did carry on so about my food, my lord Colin."

"You spoiled me, Mistress Peake. I always knew that after you, no other woman would ever be able to please me. Except of course, this beautiful creature." Colin planted a kiss on little Bridget's nose and the girl collapsed in giggles.

Megan studied the housekeeper, whose gray hair fell in damp little wisps around her pudgy cheeks. Though she joined in their laughter, the woman's eyes filled with tears.

"I have missed your teasing," she said as she quickly brushed away her tears with the back of her hand then filled several goblets. "I will make you a feast this night that will make you forget every minute of your time away from Killamara, my lords."

She turned to Lady Katherine. Her voice took on a crisp, unpleasant tone. "Sir Cecil and his son have just returned from hunting and, when given the news, asked if they might join you, my lady."

Kieran's head came up sharply. "Sir Cecil and James Kettering? They are here?"

Ignoring the sharpness in his tone, Lady Katherine turned to the housekeeper. "Tell Sir Cecil and his son to join us, Mistress Peake."

"Aye, my lady."

When the housekeeper had left the room, Lady Katherine turned to her son. "Sir Cecil and James arrived only a day ago. They had heard the rumors and were concerned that I was alone during this trying time."

While Colin and Lady Katherine took up their goblets and sat together on the settle, Kieran lifted his goblet and stood beside the fireplace, his hand resting on the mantel.

Megan saw the frown that creased his brow before he turned to stare broodingly into the flames.

A moment later the door opened and two men entered.

"Kieran. Colin." The older of the two men hesitated for a moment, then strode forward and clasped a hand on Kieran's shoulder. He crossed to Colin and gave him a warm greeting. "We are still shocked at the news that you are alive." The man turned to Lady Katherine and lifted her hands to his lips. "As I am certain you are, my lady."

"Aye, Cecil." Her eyes misted and she blinked rapidly. "This is the happiest day of my life."

"And mine, my dear." He turned to glance at the younger man who had paused just inside the doorway. "Come, James. Why do you tarry?"

"Kieran," the young man said, continuing to pause in the doorway, "I cannot believe it is truly you. Am I looking at a ghost?"

"By all accounts I should be dead." Kieran extended his hand, and the young man crossed the room to grasp it.

"Elizabeth's court has been dull since you departed," James said. "Even the Queen herself misses your bold and lively debate on every issue that deals with the rebellious Irish chieftains."

"Is there no one left to fight the cause?" Kieran asked.

"Nay. No one with your gift of persuasion."

When James Kettering turned, he gave Colin a long look before crossing to him. Bridget still clung to Colin's neck. Since his arrival the girl had been unwilling to leave him for even a moment.

"Colin," James said with a smile, "I have not seen you in many years. According to your proud mother, the monks at Donegal Monastery consider you a prize."

Monastery? Megan glanced at the young man who had shared their adventure. An education at a monastery explained his formal manner of speech. But was he a priest? She tried to recall how many times she had muttered oaths in his presence. She must have been quite a shock to him. She stood very still, wondering how many other surprises would be revealed this night.

"It is good to be home," Colin said, accepting the young man's outstretched hand.

"Are you saying you do not miss the luxuries of Fleet Prison?"

"Oh, aye. I miss them terribly."

The two shared a strained laugh.

"There is someone here you must both meet." Lady Katherine led the father and son to Megan and said, "Lady Megan, this is one of my oldest friends, Sir Cecil Kettering, ambassador to Queen Elizabeth."

Megan was taken aback by his title. Ambassador to the very one who had imprisoned Kieran and Colin.

Sir Cecil was tall and slender, with pale blue eyes and gray, thinning hair. His features were finely chiseled, and Megan thought that most women would consider him extremely handsome.

"My lady." He lifted her hand to his lips in a courtly gesture, then said, "Welcome, my lady. May I present to you my son, James, Earl of Warfield."

"Lady Megan." James caught her hand and held it a few minutes longer than was necessary before lifting it to his lips. "I do not know where you have been hiding, lovely lady, but I find this bleak land suddenly far more... inviting."

James was a younger, paler version of his father. His eyes were as light as a summer sky; his brown hair was carefully brushed over his forehead. He cut a fine figure in his beautifully tailored silk tunic over black breeches. He was, Megan thought, like his father, a man who knew that women would find him most attractive.

"Lady Megan helped my two sons escape," Lady Katherine added with a touch of pride.

"How fascinating." Sir Cecil studied the young woman with interest. "Yours is not an Irish brogue. Where is your home, my lady?"

"Scotland."

"Ahh." His eyes narrowed. "And what is your clan?"

Megan swallowed. She had been dreading this moment. "I fear I do not recall."

Sir Cecil lifted an eyebrow. "Do you jest with me, my lady?" He cast a knowing smile at the others.

"She speaks the truth," Kieran said as he crossed to her. He seemed unaware of his suddenly protective demeanor. But it was not lost on the others. "Megan was wounded in battle. Her memory has been lost to her."

Lady Katherine studied her with a look of motherly concern. Sir Cecil and his son exchanged surprised glances.

"A woman of mystery. How intriguing." James touched a hand to the mane of hair that fell enticingly over her shoulder. "And so fetching in peasant's garb. I wager you would be ravishing in something more feminine."

For some reason Kieran could not explain, he found James's intimate demeanor offensive. He was not jealous, he told himself. He was merely looking out for this innocent. At the hands of a rake like James, she would be helpless. He had watched James cut a wide swath through the young women at court. No one, not even Elizabeth, was immune to his charms.

While Kieran watched, Sir Cecil placed an arm around Megan. "How terrible, my dear, to not know one's own family. Can you remember nothing?"

"Nay."

"A pity. It is most fortunate that you have all of us to lean upon in this trying time."

Without realizing it she straightened her spine and lifted her chin defiantly. "It will return to me. Until then, I am not some helpless female."

His eyes crinkled with laughter. "I can see that." With an admiring look he added, "What you need is rest, and Mistress Peake's fine cooking."

"That is what we all need." Kieran drained his goblet. "If you will excuse us, we will refresh ourselves before we sup. Mother, would you show the Lady Megan to her rooms? I would like her to have the chambers overlooking the garden."

"As you wish, Kieran." His mother shot him a disapproving look at his abruptness, then just as quickly swallowed her anger. Theirs had been a long and torturous journey. They all had a right to be short-tempered. She turned to Megan. "Follow me, my dear."

Wearily Megan followed Lady Katherine and the others up the broad stairs to the second floor.

"These will be yours while you are here," Lady Katherine said, leading Megan into a large sitting chamber with doors at either end. "If there is anything at all that you desire, you need only ask."

A cozy fire burned in the fireplace. A chaise and several chairs had been positioned in front of the fire. On a table rested a tray with a decanter and crystal goblets. Lady Katherine strode across the room and opened a door. Beyond Megan could see a large bed hung with delicate linens. Servants scurried around the room setting everything in order.

"Rest now, my dear. The servants will see to your every need."

"Thank you, Lady Katherine. You are most kind."

Megan was unaware of the weariness that was etched on her lovely features. But it was not lost on Lady Katherine. With quick, impatient gestures she ushered the others from the room.

When she was alone, Megan dropped down onto the bed. There was no time to remove her torn, faded clothes or to pull back the bed coverings. Within minutes she was sound asleep.

Chapter Nine

"My lady."

Megan was awakened from the sweetest dream. In it she had been a lass lying in a big feather bed with two other lasses near in age to her. They had been giggling about something, but now that she was awake she could no longer remember what it was. In the dream the lasses with her had seemed very important to her. As she opened her eyes and stared at the servant, she wondered idly who they were and what they had meant in her life.

"Lady Katherine instructed us to assist you in your bath and toilette, my lady."

Megan sat up. Across the room, set upon a sheepskin in front of the fireplace, was a tub filled with steaming water. While she watched, a succession of servants entered the room carrying gowns, petticoats, shawls, slippers. All were arrayed across the foot of the bed, awaiting her approval.

"Would you like to begin with a bath, my lady?"

"Aye." With a little laugh of delight Megan scampered from the bed and hurried to the tub. A servant removed her shabby clothes and helped her into the perfumed water. When she sat down, another servant began washing her hair.

Megan leaned her head back and gave a sigh of pure pleasure. How long it had been since she had enjoyed such luxury. When her hair was washed and dried with towels, the servant ran a comb through the tangles until it fell in silken waves down her back.

Another servant entered and poured a kettle of hot water into the tub, sending a fresh cloud of steam billowing toward the ceiling.

Megan closed her eyes and felt all of her tensions dissolve.

"Would you care to choose your gown now, my lady?"

"Nay." With her head back and her eyes closed, Megan waved a hand toward the door. "Leave me for a few minutes longer. I cannot bear to give up this comfort yet."

The servant gave a knowing smile and signaled to the others to leave. "Aye, my lady. You need only call when you desire our services."

"Thank you."

When the room was empty, Megan snuggled deeper into the warmth of the water and listened to the snap and hiss of the fire. Surely this was what heaven would someday be. When all the battles were won, this would be the reward of the faithful.

She heard the door open and waved the servant away. "Not just yet. I need another moment to revel in this luxury."

"Take all the time you wish, my lady." Kieran's voice was tinged with warmth. "I, too, desire many more moments to bask in a view such as this."

"Kieran." Caught by surprise, Megan started to stand, then, realizing her mistake, sank deeper into the water.

When she turned, she gave a little gasp and studied him with grave interest. "If I did not know your voice, I would think you a stranger."

A very handsome stranger, she realized. Gone was the heavy dark beard. Now his face was clean-shaven, revealing craggy, rugged features. Gone, too, was the shaggy hair. It had been trimmed to just above his collar. His brow was smooth, unwrinkled. His eyes seemed even more piercing and compelling. There was about him a look that both rightened and excited her. He was indeed a most handome man. And a dangerous one.

"You must leave. I have no clothes."

"So I have noticed, my lady." He walked closer. "But if our Creator had wanted your perfect body hidden by garments, you would have been born in them."

She could not see the humor of the situation. She felt her cheeks growing hot until they were burning. "You cannot stay in a lady's room when she is bathing. It is sinful."

"Aye. And I am a shameless sinner." He knelt beside the tub and brushed a lock of hair from her eye.

She slapped his hand away. "How dare you touch me while I am..." She swallowed and tried for a more commanding tone. "Leave my room immediately or I will be forced to..."

He grinned and touched his lips to a droplet of water that clung to her cheek. "To what, my lady?"

Heat raced along her spine. She could not think. Her mind refused to function.

He brought his lips along her face to trace one wet eyebrow.

She struggled to speak over the constriction in her throat. Her voice was little more than a whisper. "You must go, Kieran. The servants..."

"The servants will not return until you summon them." Picking up a soapy cloth he began to move it along the slope of her shoulder.

His touch left her paralyzed. She sat motionless while his cloth-draped hand moved slowly, seductively along her arm.

The sight of her took Kieran's breath away. Her hair fell in shiny waves down her back, then fanned out enticingly across the water. Her lovely face was beaded with moisture. The slender column of her throat invited his kiss. He could make out the shape of her breasts shimmering just beneath the water.

"God in heaven, Megan." He felt his throat go dry. "You are so beautiful."

He placed his hands on either side of her head, tangling his fingers in her damp hair. He saw the way her lashes lowered, veiling her eyes, and felt a rush of tenderness at the flush that colored her cheeks. Then she lifted her gaze to him, and he felt himself being swallowed up in a look so innocent and yet so alluring he knew he was lost.

He lowered his face until his lips brushed hers. The jolt between them was instantaneous.

Megan felt her heart stop. When at last it started beating again, its rhythm was so erratic she was certain Kieran could hear it. Shock and surprise jolted through her, leaving her senses reeling.

"And you taste as sweet as you look." Kieran grasped her shoulders and drew her firmly against him, covering her mouth with his.

This time the kiss was far from gentle. She felt her protest die in her throat as he took the kiss deeper. The fire of his touch seared her.

Kieran was achingly aware of Megan's softness as he pressed her to him. As her initial resistance faded, her lips softened and invited. Pressing his advantage, he changed the angle of the kiss and drew her even closer.

Water swirled around her, spilling over the rim of the tub and soaking the front of his tunic. But he was aware of nothing except the woman in his arms and the wonder of her lips.

Megan felt the warmth deep inside. A warmth that curled along her veins, heating her blood. She wanted to open to him, to kiss him as he was kissing her. And yet she was afraid. There was so much she did not know about men and women.

As he lingered over her lips, she felt herself beginning to fall under his spell. But as he drew her even closer, there was a knock on the door, followed by a servant's voice.

"My lady. Shall I assist you in dressing now?"

Kieran lifted his head and muttered an oath.

For a moment Megan felt strangely light-headed. Her heart was still tripping over itself. Her breath tumbled out in a long sigh.

Regret? he wondered. Or pleasure?

"God in heaven." Regaining her senses. Megan's hand flew to her mouth. What had she been thinking of? How had she so easily been tempted? "They cannot find you here."

"And why not? I am lord of the manor. I can go anywhere I choose."

"Kieran, they will whisper and gossip. I could not bear it."

He saw the way her cheeks flamed. "Have no fear." He brushed his lips over hers for one last lingering taste. Then he stood and walked to a door on the opposite side of the sitting chamber. "Beyond this door is my chambers."

"You sleep there, just beyond my door?"

"Aye, my lady. 'Tis why I requested these rooms for you." He gave her a smug, roguish smile that had her temper instantly flaring. "If you should ever awake and find yourself in need of... company, you need only knock."

Her hand closed around the soapy cloth. Seeing what she intended, he threw back his head and laughed as she flung it. His door closed a fraction before it hit, spattering soap and water in all directions.

Megan stared at the water that soaked the sheepskin beneath the tub, as well as most of the floor and hearth. Kieran would pay for this.

Despite her temper, she felt the laughter bubble up in her throat as the servants entered and began to assist her from the tub. Aye. He would pay dearly.

"Can this be the same lass we met earlier?" Sir Cecil Kettering exclaimed, looking up as Megan was ushered into the room.

Megan was shocked to see the room filled with men. Though arrayed in fine breeches and tunics, they wore swords in scabbards, and many had knives tucked into their waistbands.

She flushed when she realized everyone's attention was focused on her. If she was on a battlefield, she would know how to handle herself. Here, she felt shy and awkward.

From his position beside the fireplace Kieran studied her, unaware that his hand had tightened perceptibly on the stem of his goblet at the admiring glances of the men as she moved among them.

He had never dreamed she could look so regal. Her gown was crimson, worked with silver and gold threads at the hem and bodice. The neckline was modestly high, with a lace ruff in the latest fashion ringing her throat. A wide sash displayed her tiny waist. Her skirt fell in soft folds to the tips of crimson slippers. But though she was modestly attired, Kieran could still recall the flawless body she kept hidden from view.

"You look splendid," James said, catching her hand.

Megan gave him a shy smile and withdrew her hand from his grasp when he continued to hold it too long. "Thanks to the generosity of Lady Katherine."

"How could I not be generous to the woman who helped my sons return from the dead? I am forever in your debt, my dear." Lady Katherine watched the way her eldest son studied this young woman. Though he deliberately kept his distance, the look in his eyes spoke volumes.

"My dear," Lady Katherine said gently, "these men are all loyal, good friends, who have hastened to Castle O'Mara to welcome my sons back to their beloved land."

"Aye. As soon as we heard the news, we had to see for ourselves," a tall, raven-haired man said as he bowed low before her hand. His hair had gone silver at the temples, giving him a distinguished appearance. He had smooth, even features in a face tanned from years of working the land. There was a kindness in his eyes that touched something in Megan.

"This is Hugh Cleary," Lady Katherine said. "Hugh was friend to my husband, Sean, and has been friend to me since I first arrived in this land."

"I thought Sean O'Mara daft when he brought home a pale English beauty as a wife," Hugh said in his deep, lyrical voice. "But Lady Katherine soon showed me, and all of us, that she was deserving of Sean's love and trust. The lady has truly become one of us."

"Aye, 'tis true," the others echoed.

"It has been so long since I have heard the rumble of masculine laughter in this place," Lady Katherine said softly. "How I have missed it. Now, Megan," she said, shaking off the suddenly sad mood that possessed her, "come meet the rest of our friends."

Megan glanced at Lady Katherine and saw the wide range of emotions in her eyes as she moved among her late husband's friends.

Though the names and faces of the men soon became a blur, Megan found their smiles of welcome genuine. She returned their greetings as she was presented to over a dozen men whose names rang with the sound of Ireland. Their easy, teasing natures reminded her of Kieran and Colin.

Kieran watched the ease with which Megan handled the introductions to his old friends and fellow warriors. It was obvious that she was comfortable in a man's world. Further proof, he thought, that she had once commanded an army. And as strange as that would seem in this land, he imagined that she would be very good at it.

When all the introductions had been completed, Colin strode across the room and took both Megan's hands in his.

In a spontaneous gesture of affection she lifted her hand to his shorn locks, then to his clean-shaven cheek. "Why, you are hardly more than a lad without all that growth of beard."

"A lad?" He gave her a look of mock distress. "I am a score and two, my lady. Which makes me your elder. Mind your tongue."

They both shared a laugh.

He deliberately allowed his gaze to roam over her. "This gown suits you far better than the English soldier's breeches and tunic, my lady."

"English soldier?" Sir Cecil was abruptly alert.

Kieran shot Colin a warning glance, and the lad instantly regretted his outburst. But now that he had everyone's attention, he found himself stammering.

"Megan's gown was torn...and we found a pair of breeches...and a tunic."

"Where?" James asked with a scowl.

"Tied behind the saddle of a horse. So Megan exchanged her torn garb for that of the soldier."

"How do you know that the soldier was English?" Sir Cecil asked.

Colin could not lie. All his years of training at the monastery would not permit it. His cheeks grew red. He glanced helplessly at Kieran, then at Megan, who took pity on him.

"The man was following us." Megan glanced at Lady Katherine and saw the sudden look of fear that crept into her eyes. She must be careful not to add to this good woman's burden. "He identified himself as an English soldier and friend to the guard who was—overpowered at Fleet Prison." Megan knew that Kieran had killed the guard, but she dared not speak of such a thing in this company.

"A lone English soldier followed you?" Sir Cecil exchanged a look with his son.

"Nay. There were many. Perhaps a dozen or more."

"And you managed to evade all of them?" James shot her an incredulous look.

"Aye. There were three of us, after all, and they were mere English soldiers."

Hugh Cleary threw back his head and let out a roar of laughter. "By the gods, Kieran, she is the most beguiling woman I have ever met."

Kieran nodded. "Aye, Hugh. The lady is full of surprises."

The moment the words were out of her mouth, Megan had regretted them. She had no idea where such things came from. Perhaps in that other life she led, before the loss of memory, she had shared Kieran's hatred for all things English. But now, in the company of this titled gentleman and Kieran's obviously noble English mother, she felt ashamed of such boasts.

"How did you happen to take a man's clothes?" James Kettering asked sarcastically. "Did you hold him at sword point and demand his breeches?"

Megan's face grew scarlet. "We stole...helped ourselves to their horses. That is how we escaped. And among their possessions were the clothes I was wearing when I arrived here."

She wanted the questions to end, but she saw the interested looks of Sir Cecil and James.

Sir Cecil turned to Kieran. "How do you know they are not following you still?"

"I know not."

"You are not safe here," Sir Cecil said. "They will not stop until they have cornered their prey."

"This is my home," Kieran said softly. The very softness of his tone suggested danger. "I run no farther."

Sir Cecil seemed about to argue, then decided against it. Changing the subject he asked, "I suppose it was you, Kieran, who managed to overpower the guard at Fleet Prison?"

"With your connections at court, you surely know the details of our escape, Sir Cecil."

For a moment the older man seemed taken aback at Kieran's abrupt tone. Then he nodded gravely. "Aye. I have heard the version told to the Queen, though I will not repeat it in front of your dear mother." His voice took on a note of confidence when he saw that every man in the room was watching and listening. He paused while a servant filled his goblet. "I want you to understand, Kieran, that out of friendship to your mother, I did all in my power to have you set free. And I think I might have succeeded, had you not escaped before I could offer my petition to the Queen.''

"We were there a year, Sir Cecil. More than enough time to secure our freedom."

"So your dear mother has told me. But until her first missive, I knew nothing of your imprisonment. Nor did the Queen, I fear. But I did all I could."

"If Colin and I had waited until the Queen agreed to set us free, we would now lie buried in English soil, in an unmarked prison grave."

Seeing the troubled look on his mother's face, Kieran crossed to her and drew her close. "We will speak no more of this unpleasantness. Tell me the news from England, Sir Cecil. Have any of the restrictions upon our poor land been lifted?"

A ripple of tension could be felt by everyone in the room.

"As you yourself know, Kieran, Her Majesty desires no trouble with the chieftains of your land. But as she demands from all her subjects, Elizabeth demands a fair share of goods and taxes, as well as loyalty from the Irish."

The men shifted uncomfortably.

"Elizabeth is not our Queen, Sir Cecil. Though she may proclaim herself above England, Scotland, Ireland and Wales, she is only England's monarch."

The older man gave a negligent shrug of his shoulders. "I will not be dragged into a political discussion now, Kieran. Such talk is considered treason in my land. But I would remind you that the Queen has been more than fair with you. In fact, she has repeatedly asked you to step forward and reclaim your grandfather's lands and titles."

"Aye. Elizabeth made the offer if I would give up all claim to my land here in Ireland."

"This poor land is no substitute for what awaits you in England," James said passionately.

Kieran turned a black look on him, and the young man fell silent. Their many years together in service to the throne had taught him that Kieran's temper could be a frightening thing.

It was James's father who said soothingly, "You were one of Elizabeth's favorites at court, Kieran. She was very disappointed in you when you turned your back on her offer and returned to Ireland."

"Her offer." Kieran's words were a low rasp of fury.

Megan saw the effort it cost Kieran to hold his temper at bay.

"Elizabeth offered to restore your grandfather's estates and titles. And though they may mean little to you," Sir Cecil said vehemently, "they are much coveted in England. The title Duke of Harford has long been respected in my country."

Megan studied Kieran with new respect. Was he truly the Duke of Harford? The thought of the warrior she knew him to be seemed at odds with a noble English title.

Sir Cecil turned to Lady Katherine and his tone softened. "Your father was much loved by King Henry. The vast estates settled by His Majesty upon your father are the envy of all, my lady. It is a slight upon his good name that his grandson refuses to claim them. If not for himself, then out of consideration for you. You could be living in luxury in your native land, instead of—" he glanced around with a look of disdain "—this poor substitute."

Instantly Lady Katherine jumped to the defense of her son. "This is my adopted country, Cecil. I would remind you that I turned my back on everything English when I chose to wed Sean O'Mara. And I have never once looked back with regret."

For a moment Sir Cecil Kettering looked as angry as Kieran O'Mara. Then, swallowing his anger, he continued in reasonable tones, "Kieran's refusal to make peace with Elizabeth puts you at great risk, my lady. Would you make yourself an enemy of the Queen of England?"

Kieran's voice was low with feeling. "Tread softly, Sir Cecil. This is not my mother's battle. I do not impugn my mother's name. Nor her father's. I feel as much pride in my English heritage as in my Irish. And I tried walking the route you suggested. But if I learned anything in my years at the English court, it is that I am my father's son. Castle O'Mara and all of Killamara, humble though they may be by English standards, still hold my heart."

Sir Cecil directed his words at Kieran, but his gaze strayed to Lady Katherine, who stood proudly beside her son. "Are this ancient castle and these barren fields worth dying for?"

Kieran felt his mother's hand squeeze his in a painful grip.

"Aye. If necessary."

The two men faced each other. Kieran's jaw was set, his eyes as hard as flint. Sir Cecil studied him for long moments, then lowered his gaze.

The door opened. Mistress Peake broke the silence. "Dinner is ready, my lord."

Kieran nodded. Setting his goblet on a serving tray, he offered his arm to his mother, and they led the others from the room.

"Come, my dear." Sir Cecil caught Megan's hand and placed it on his sleeve.

Behind them Colin took Bridget's hand and smiled as she danced along beside him. This night she wore a dress of blue satin that fell to the tips of her dainty kid slippers. Her wild tangles of red hair had been pulled back with ribbons that matched the blue of her eyes.

Sir Cecil's son, James, trailed more slowly with the rest of the men as they made their way to the refectory.

The room blazed with light from dozens of candles set in sconces along the walls. On either end of the room were huge fireplaces where logs burned. The light was reflected in the gleaming crystal and silver on a table set with finest linens. At least a dozen servants scurried around, seeing to the meal.

Kieran took the seat at the head of the table. To his right sat his mother, with Sir Cecil beside her and his son, James, next to him. To Kieran's left sat Megan, with Colin beside her and Bridget next to him. The rest of the men took their places with ease, leaving Megan no doubt that they had often eaten together at Castle O'Mara.

Mistress Peake waddled around, furiously directing the servants with all the skill of a captain of the guards during battle. There were oysters, fresh scallops and salmon, followed by quail and pheasant. There were thick, crusty breads, still warm from the ovens, spread with freshly churned butter and sweet fruit conserves. With each course, the servants filled the goblets with hot mulled wine and ale.

Everyone at table looked up at the sound of a commotion outside the refectory. Suddenly a door burst open and a giant of a man strode inside, followed by a wide-eyed servant who had obviously been trying to subdue him.

"Where is he?" His voice boomed, causing a sudden silence.

Kieran pushed back his chair and stood with his hands on his hips. "Would you be looking for the lord of the manor?"

"Aye, lad. I've come to see for myself if he rose from the dead as the villagers have been whispering."

"Then see," Kieran said, striding across the room. "'Tis the truth they speak."

"By the gods." There was a long silence, in which everyone at the table watched the two with interest. "Kieran O'Mara. You're as ugly as ever."

The two men clasped each other in a fierce hug.

Seeing the stunned look on Megan's face, Kieran's mother called sharply, "Tavis, you've frightened our guest. Come meet the lady who brought our Kieran back to us. Lady Megan of Scotland," she said as the man made his way around the table, "fought beside Kieran and Colin, and according to my sons risked her life for their safety."

The man towered over her, studying her through narrowed eyes.

"This," Lady Katherine said with warmth, "is Tavis Downey. He and Kieran have been friends since boyhood."

Megan's hand was engulfed in a beefy palm. The man was so tall she had to tilt her head back to see his face. His blue eyes were warm with laughter. His hair was more red than brown. Though he could never be called handsome, his was a commanding presence.

"This slip of a lass fought beside you?"

Kieran nodded.

Tavis studied her for long moments, enjoying the fact that she blushed uncomfortably under his scrutiny. "'Tis sorry I am that you fought for such weaklings as these. I only tolerated Kieran all these years because he was easy to beat in a joust."

"Would you care to challenge me on the morrow?" Kieran asked.

"Nay. You need to build up your strength after all that time in a wretched English prison, lad. Your muscles will be mush and your limbs as weak as saplings."

"This may be the only time you can beat me then," Kieran shot back. "You'd best take advantage of any weakness while you can."

While the two men sparred, the others roared with laughter.

Tavis pulled up a chair beside Kieran, and with one arm wrapped around his shoulder watched as servants hurried to fetch him a meal.

"Mistress Peake, you have outdone yourself," he said as he wolfed down the food, washing it down with tankards of ale.

In an aside to Kieran he muttered, "I did not even take time to saddle my horse. When I heard the news, I set out for Castle O'Mara to see for myself that you were truly alive and well."

"And you did not take time to bathe, either." Kieran slapped his arm, then watched as his old friend polished off the rest of his meal.

When the meal was over, Mistress Peake approached Colin with a wide smile. She directed a serving girl to carve thick slices of a heavy, moist confection.

Colin's eyes lit with satisfaction. "Ahh, Mistress Peake. 'Tis your special cake, is it not?"

"Aye, my lord. And you must have the first taste."

The others watched as Colin lifted a bite to his lips and closed his eyes as he savored it. "It is as I remembered it all these long, dreary months."

"You do not think it too sweet, my lord?"

"Too sweet? Mistress Peake, it is perfection."

With a contented smile, the housekeeper ordered the servants to cut the rest of the confection and serve it.

"What think you, Megan?" Colin asked as she tasted it.

"Never have I eaten such a treat. Nor such a meal. You are blessed to have such a fine housekeeper."

Mistress Peake shot her a look of adoration that was not lost on Kieran.

"It was Mistress Peake who ordered your bath and toilette, as well," Lady Katherine said.

"Then I am doubly grateful," Megan said to the housekeeper.

"I thought a hot bath would be much appreciated after the rigors of your journey, my lady."

"Aye. It was indeed."

"The servants reported that you lingered overlong in your bath. We all feared you might catch a chill."

Megan felt Kieran's gaze on her and grew uncomfortably warm. "You may relieve their minds, Mistress Peake. I was careful not to grow cold."

"You must be careful, my lady," James Kettering said solicitously. "Even in summer the air on this island grows quite cool."

Kieran's voice was warm with unspoken laughter. "Aye, my lady. You must be careful not to linger overlong in your bath. Unless, of course, you take care to keep warm."

Feeling her cheeks flame, Megan shot him a look of pure venom. "I shall heed your advice, my lord. From now on shall take every care. Perhaps one of the servants can remain with me and hold a linen around me for warmth."

"'Twould be such a waste." With a chuckle Kieran drained his goblet and leaned back in his chair, feeling oddly contented. For the first time in a year he was replete, refreshed, at peace. He was once more surrounded by family and his dearest friends. And if he should find himself tempted to do battle, the woman beside him would be a most worthy opponent.

Chapter Ten

"That was a fine meal, Mistress Peake." Kieran set down his empty goblet and waved the serving girl away. "At last I feel as if I am truly home."

The housekeeper beamed with pride at the lord's praise.

Kieran scraped his chair back from the table. "We will take our whiskey in the library."

"Aye, my lord."

Kieran held his mother's chair and offered his arm. The others followed.

The library was a room with high beamed ceilings. Shelves filled with books lined three walls of the room. The fourth wall had a massive fireplace made of stone. A desk was piled high with books and ledgers.

Megan breathed in the fragrance of wood smoke, candle wax and leather and felt a wave of longing so acute it startled her. Had there been a room like this in her home? Oh, if only she could recall.

The men milled around, chatting, while the servants offered them goblets and tankards from trays.

Seeing some of the ledgers lying open, Kieran shot a questioning look at his mother.

"Forgive me," Lady Katherine said softly. "You have been gone a long time, my son. Sir Cecil offered to peruse the ledgers and help me settle some old accounts."

Megan saw the look that came into Kieran's eyes before
he strode toward the desk. Quickly scanning the open pages
he said, "Perhaps on the morrow, Sir Cecil, you can tell me
exactly what has been done in my absence."

"I would be happy to." The older man took a pinch of
snuff, then accepted a goblet from a servant. With a sigh he
sank into a chaise in front of the roaring fire and crossed his
legs. "This is a most interesting room. I would not have expected such a wealth of knowledge to be found in this poor
land."

Kieran's eyes blazed. "We may be poor by English standards, but we are not ignorant."

Though many of the men wore frowns, they tactfully kept
silent. They were, after all, guests in Kieran's home. And
this Englishman, though outspoken, was a friend to Lady
Katherine.

"I see I have touched a nerve." Sir Cecil shot an indulgent smile at his hostess. "I suppose we must expect this
from one who has only recently tasted freedom." He turned
his gaze on Kieran. "It is not your shame that your land is
poor."

Kieran's voice was dangerously low. "Nor is it the fault
of my people. If we are poor, it is because your Queen will
not permit us to use our rich resources to seek wealth for
ourselves in the marketplace. Our ancestral lands are being
taken from us by your countrymen, Sir Cecil. And those of
us who resist are dying in English prisons. Our goods could
be sold for twice the price in other countries, if we were allowed to trade fairly."

"Those are traitorous words," James Kettering hissed,
taking a step toward Kieran.

Sir Cecil lifted a hand to stem his son's angry words, then
turned to Kieran with a sigh. "Are you still hoping to lure
me into a political discussion, Kieran?" Emptying his goblet, he held it up while a servant filled it. Swirling the liquid
around, he stared deeply into it. "I would spare your poor
mother your ravings, if I were you. This good woman has

suffered enough, with both you and Colin gone now for over a year, leaving her to manage the estate alone.''

''My suffering was nothing compared to that of my sons.'' Lady Katherine took a seat beside Colin and touched a hand to his cheek. ''And now my happiness is so great, I fear my heart will burst. Just seeing my sons alive and well has wiped all the pain and fear from my memory.''

''You are most brave.'' Sir Cecil gave her a tender smile before turning to Kieran. ''On several occasions I sent emissaries across the channel to persuade Lady Katherine to return to England, at least until I could arrange your freedom. But her sense of loyalty would not permit her to leave this place until you returned.''

''Where would she have stayed in England?'' Kieran questioned. ''Her home is here.''

''Do you forget that her first home was England?''

''I forget nothing.''

Sir Cecil ignored the anger in Kieran's tone and continued patiently, ''I would have opened my home to your mother, Kieran. She still has many friends in England. They would have been overjoyed to see her return to take her rightful place at court.''

''Enough of this talk of England,'' Lady Katherine said. She had seen the flare of anger in her son's eyes and was determined that this night would be one of rejoicing. Lifting a goblet from a servant's tray she said, ''I drink to the miracle that has returned my sons to me.''

They all lifted their goblets to their lips and drank.

Colin's eyes twinkled. ''Then I suggest we drink to the lady who made that miracle happen.'' He lifted his goblet and said, ''To Megan.''

The smile had not yet returned to Kieran's lips, but his look softened as he turned to her. ''Aye. To our brave Lady Megan,'' he said, draining his glass.

The others did the same.

Across the room, Tavis Downey watched and listened. There was a subtle change in his old friend. But he had not

as yet figured out what it was. Of course, a year in Fleet
Prison would change any man. The rough edges were evident. The fire that burned in Kieran's veins was even fiercer,
if possible. As was the simmering anger. But there was
something else. Something...indefinable.

"From what I have heard you are a most fascinating
creature." James Kettering took a seat on the chaise beside
Megan and gave her an adoring smile. "You must relate to
us your adventures."

She shifted uncomfortably. "I fear there is nothing to tell,
my lord."

"You are too modest." When a serving wench offered
him more whiskey, he held out his goblet. "Surely you used
some trickery to escape the soldiers. Did you weep uncontrollably until they were driven to distraction? Or did you
faint, my lady?"

"Weep? Faint? What would those things accomplish?"

His hand paused in midair and he glanced at her in surprise. "They might have secured your freedom. What other
weapons does a woman have, my lady?"

Megan could only stare at him. He thought her incapa-
ble of wielding a sword. She glanced at Kieran and saw the
tight line of his lips. For a moment she thought he shook his
head ever so slightly. But when she looked again, he was
merely watching her intently. Perhaps she had imagined his
disapproval. Still, she thought he would be most reluctant
to discuss their adventures in front of Lady Katherine or
these strangers.

"Have you ever seen a doe and her fawn surrounded by
hounds, my lord?"

James blinked at the sudden harshness of her tone.

"That creature, who seems so docile, so helpless, will lash
out with her hooves and even her teeth if necessary, to protect the life of her offspring."

He allowed his gaze to roam her golden hair, her pale
coloring, and said admiringly, "Then I shall think of you
whenever I come upon a doe in the forest, my lady. Of

course I will still have to send my arrow to her heart, for that is the nature of the hunter.''

Restless and uncomfortable under his scrutiny, Megan scrambled to her feet. "If you do not mind, my lady," she said, turning to her hostess, "I should like to retire now. It has been a long and arduous journey."

"But what of the tales of your adventure?" James was offended by Megan's casual dismissal of him. He was not accustomed to being ignored by women, young or old. His surprise was evident on his face.

Colin had to swallow his laughter. He did not know which amused him more, James's mouth open in surprise or Kieran's black look as he had watched the handsome young Englishman sitting beside Megan in an attempt to charm her.

"How could I have forgotten. You must be exhausted, my dear." Lady Katherine stood and caught Megan by the arm. "Bridget and I will walk with you. It is long past her bedtime."

The little girl fondly kissed her uncles, then took Lady Katherine's hand.

"I am certain our men will find something of interest to discuss without us." She turned and met Kieran's gaze with a challenge. "Something that will not spark tempers to erupt into a battle beneath our very roof."

As the two women and the child disappeared through the doorway, Kieran's gaze lingered on them for several moments before he turned to his guests.

"I hope you are finding these rooms comfortable, my dear." Lady Katherine paused in the doorway as Megan stepped into the sitting chamber.

"Oh, my lady." Megan gave a little laugh. "Any room would seem a luxury after what we have come through. I cannot remember the last time I slept in a bed." She ran her hand lovingly over the smooth bed linens, then stopped abruptly at the sight of the soldier's garb she had been wearing when she arrived. The rough pants, tunic and cloak had been carefully washed and folded.

She did not need this reminder of her rough treatment at the hands of the soldiers. Megan tentatively touched them, then resolutely picked them up and placed them on top of a small chest, where she hoped she would not have to look at them again.

With Bridget still holding her hand, Lady Katherine crossed the room and took a seat on a chaise pulled up before the fire. "Was it terrible?"

"Aye. At times." Megan straightened. "But we endured. And we survived." She turned to her hostess with a wan smile. "And now I am grateful for your hospitality, my lady, until I can return to my home."

"Can you remember anything of your past, my dear?"

"Nay."

In agitation Megan walked to the fireplace and stood warming herself. There were so many times in the past few days when she had thought she would never be warm again. She shivered. Instantly Lady Katherine hurried to her side and drew her close.

"Do not try to force the memories, my dear. The best thing you can do now is refresh yourself both in mind and body. In time it will all come back to you." She smiled and embraced the young woman. "Perhaps when you least expect it."

"Oh. I pray it is so, my lady."

Lady Katherine heard the note of despair in Megan's tone and was touched by it. "We will all pray, my dear. Now—" she gave her a warm hug and walked with Bridget to the door "—you must sleep."

"Aye, my lady." Megan smiled at the little girl who clung to her hand. Bridget gave her a shy smile in return. Throughout the long evening, though the child smiled often at Colin, she had spoken not a word.

A servant hurried forward to help Megan undress.

Within minutes her gown had been replaced by a delicate nightgown of pale ivory linen. With her hair unbound and brushed loose, she was helped into bed.

When the bed linens were tucked around her, Megan gave a sigh of contentment. It seemed like an eternity since she had been so comfortable. Sleep came instantly.

The windows had been closed against the pleasant evening air and the draperies drawn. A table set in front of the fireplace held a decanter and two goblets. Sir Cecil Kettering and his son, James, faced each other. Their faces wore identical frowns.

"All our plans were for naught."

"Nay. We have come too far to be defeated now."

"Have you a plan?"

"Aye." The older man's eyes gleamed in the firelight. "I have not thought it through yet. But I will not let this opportunity slip through my fingers." He sipped his ale and muttered, "The lass may be the key. We need to learn more about her."

"But how? She is a woman of mystery."

He gave an evil, chilling smile. "I always enjoy solving a puzzle. Think of this as merely another hurdle before the final victory."

"You still believe we can win?"

Sir Cecil drained his goblet and strode across the room. At the door he turned. "There is no doubt. But we must move quickly, before the woman regains her memory. Now bring me her name. And leave the rest to me."

When he left, James stared at the fire for several minutes, deep in thought. He turned when the one he had been waiting for entered. Seeing the man's gaze go immediately to the decanter, he filled a goblet and handed it to him. In several gulps it was returned to the table empty. Once again James filled it and handed it to the other.

When the man drank his fill James said, "It is imperative that we learn the woman's identity."

"Where will I begin?"

James shrugged. "Locate something of hers that will link her to her past."

"Now?"

"Tonight. Do you know how to search a chamber without disturbing its occupants?"

"Aye. I have had occasion to deal with a few rogues and thieves in my day. More than a few owe me a favor."

"Then it is time to collect your debts. Make inquiries. Bring us the woman's name. We will do the rest."

Megan awoke from a deep slumber. Something, some sound perhaps, had disturbed her. In the darkness she listened, still fighting the mists of sleep that shrouded her mind.

There it was again. A shuffling sound. Footsteps? Perhaps a servant moving along the hallway outside her room, she thought, and made a move to roll over. There was a slight brushing sound, hardly more than a whisper. But something about it caused her to go perfectly still. It was not in the hallway. It was here in her room. Someone was going through her things.

She was instantly alert, straining to make out a form in the darkness. Why would anyone want to examine her belongings? She had nothing of value.

As she peered into the darkness she could make out the tall figure of a man moving stealthily toward the small chest beside the bed. She slipped from between the bed linens and stood to face her intruder.

"Who are you?" she cried loudly. "What business do you have here?"

The man stiffened in confusion. He had thought her asleep. Her voice did not come from the bed. She was somewhere beside him. He whirled to face her. A cloud obscured the moon, leaving them in inky blackness.

After years of habit, Megan reached a hand to retrieve a dirk from her waistband, then was shocked to discover there was none. She carried no weapon on her person. She had boldly challenged this intruder only to find herself helpless. But it was not her nature to back away from a fight.

"Answer me. Why are you here?"

In response the man brought his hand savagely across her face. Stunned, Megan dropped to her knees and let out a gasp of pain.

With only faint sparks of starlight to guide her, she saw the glint of a knife in his hand and knew that he meant to defend himself if she attacked.

"Nay." With a cry of alarm she got to her feet and tried to bar his way as he prepared to run.

His blade slashed through the air, missing her by inches.

"Megan." From beyond the closed door she heard Kieran's voice. But before she could cry out, a hand closed over her mouth.

She felt the terror bubble up in her throat when fingers covered her nose and mouth, cutting off her air. She put up a fierce struggle, prying at the hands that held her, until, feeling him weaken, she bit down hard. With a cry of rage the man pulled away.

"Megan. Your door is barred. You must open it." From the room next door Megan heard Kieran's angry voice.

When she looked up the intruder was scrambling over the balcony. Struggling to her feet, she closed the distance between them and fumbled to catch his arm.

He let out a low hiss of anger and gave her a shove that sent her crashing into the stone wall behind her. With a cry of pain she crumpled to the floor.

In some distant part of her mind she heard the splinter of wood as the door between the two rooms was forced open. But her only thought was of the man who had entered her room. Crawling to the balcony, she pulled herself up and peered over the edge.

The intruder had already dropped to the courtyard below. Though she could hear his booted feet as he ran in the direction of the stables, she could not make out his form in the darkness.

Wearily she sank down, her fingers curled tightly around the smooth stone of the balcony for support.

"God in heaven. Megan, you are hurt." Kieran dropped to his knees and touched a hand to the blood that seeped from a cut in her head.

He felt a rush of fury that had his blood pounding in his temples. That this lass should be harmed while under his protection was unthinkable.

"It is nothing." Dazed, Megan tried to study the man who bent over her. But his image seemed to swim in and out of focus. "Someone was in my chambers."

"Aye. Who was it?"

"I know not. I could not see his face."

"Did you hear his voice?"

"He did not speak, except for a cry of alarm when I bit him."

"You bit him, my lady?" Despite his anger, Kieran felt the beginnings of a smile. Though his features remained stern, his eyes crinkled.

"Aye. I found myself without a weapon." She caught his arm and drew him close. "You must find him, Kieran. He was running toward the stables."

"Nay, my lady. First, I must see to you."

"But he will make his escape."

"Hush, Megan." With great tenderness he lifted her in his arms and carried her to her bed. Lighting a taper, he examined her wounds.

"You are bleeding, my lady. But it seems to be nothing serious."

"I am fine." Tears of frustration filled her eyes. "It is the intruder you must see to, Kieran. I need to know—"

He placed a finger gently over her lips, stifling her cries. "My lady, I want to find this man even more than you do. But I have no intention of leaving your side until I see to these wounds."

"They are nothing."

"I will decide that."

As he poured water from a pitcher into a bowl and then dipped a cloth into it, she gave a sigh of impatience. But when he touched the cloth to the wound at her head, she felt the tenderness of his touch and was moved to fresh tears, which caused her grave embarrassment.

"You see. Your wounds cause you pain." He probed her wound, causing a quivering to begin deep inside her.

"Nay." She wanted him to stop touching her so that she could think. And yet she wanted him to go on touching her forever, so these strange new feelings would never stop. "The wound is not deep. I am . . . simply overcome. I fear I must be some kind of timid, weepy female. I seem to always shed tears in your company."

Kieran could not help smiling. His voice was low, soothing. "You are neither timid nor weepy, my lady. Now close your eyes while I assure myself that you are truly unharmed."

She did as she was told and lay very still, her eyes closed, while he washed the wound and stemmed the flow of blood.

How was it possible, she wondered, that a man as fierce as Kieran O'Mara could have such a tender touch? His hands, so calloused and battle-worn, felt wonderful against her skin. His breath, warm where it feathered the hair at her temple, was a dangerous reminder of his lips, hovering mere inches above hers. What would he think of her if he could read her mind and discover just how much she reveled in his touch?

As Kieran dressed her wounds he was achingly aware of the woman who lay quietly beneath his touch. He had promised himself that now that he was safely home, he would keep his distance and concentrate upon the needs of his family and countrymen. Yet here he was, allowing himself to touch her once more, and be touched by her. His gaze skimmed the pale ivory nightgown that revealed as much as it covered. Her high, firm breasts were clearly outlined underneath the sheer fabric. The thought of those shapely bare legs tangled with his in the bed caused a sudden shocking rush of desire. If the lady knew where his thoughts were taking him, she would order him from her room with great haste.

The growing silence in the room was unsettling. Kieran dragged himself back from the thoughts that disturbed him more than he cared to admit. "Have you brought something of value with you, my lady? Something you did not reveal to us during the journey?"

"Nay. I can think of nothing the intruder wanted." She met his dark gaze. "Everything I have belongs to someone else. The clothes I wore to sup belonged to Lady Katherine. The clean clothes folded atop the chest belonged to an English soldier. Even this gown I sleep in is not mine."

She saw the way his gaze devoured her and wished she had not mentioned her nightgown. She was uncomfortably aware of how she must look. Her cheeks grew hot. "Forgive me, my lord. In the confusion I forgot about my immodest attire."

His lips curved into the roguish smile she had come to know. How could a female be this innocent and still be a seductress? "Yours is a most...chaste gown, my lady. Why, it buttons clear to your neck." He ran a finger around the neckline, sending a series of tremors racing along her spine. "Such a pretty neck," he murmured, bending his face nearer.

He thought about kissing her neck and cautioned himself against it. One taste of her now would never be enough.

Megan swallowed the knot of fear that sprang to her throat. He was going to kiss her. She could see it in his eyes. She felt a moment of panic. His kisses were dangerous, like a healer's brew that dulled the mind and enhanced all other sensation. And yet, ever since their first kiss, she had been unable to forget the feelings he had aroused in her. Each time he touched her, those feelings came back with a rush that left her breathless and a little afraid.

His fingers began playing with a strand of her hair, sending new tremors rocketing through her.

"You have most unusual hair, my lady. It reminds me of a trail of moonlight on a warm summer night. A night that can weave a spell of magic around a man and woman." He plunged both hands into the tangles and drew her head back until he could stare into her eyes.

"Kieran..."

"And your eyes," he said, unaware of the protest that died in her throat, "are the most hypnotic eyes I have ever seen. At times they gleam with the fire of a warrior. At other times they reveal an innocence that makes me want to carry you off to some distant place where no harm can ever come to you again."

She saw his eyes narrow fractionally, and her throat went dry.

"Please, my lord..."

"Do you know how many nights I have thought about you?"

"You must go now." Her words were hardly more than a whisper.

His gaze fastened on her lips. "I fear I cannot."

As he bent to her he called himself every kind of a fool. This was not a woman with whom he could trifle. Each time he allowed himself to kiss her, he was drawn more firmly into the web of intrigue that seemed to surround her. And yet, there was no denying the desire that raged between them. He had to have one more taste of those lips.

At the first touch of his mouth to hers, heat poured through him. For a moment he was so stunned by it he caught her by the shoulders and drew back. Then slowly, deliberately, he bent to her, all the while watching her eyes. When his mouth covered hers a second time, his arms came around her, pinning her to the length of him.

All the feelings that had been growing between them were unleashed.

For Megan there was a wild sweep of pleasure followed by a low, pulsing need that seemed to build and build until she found herself clinging to him. The touch of him, the taste of him were pleasure that bordered on pain.

When Kieran took the kiss deeper, she moaned, inviting more, and he fumbled with the buttons of her nightgown until he found the satin skin he had long dreamed of.

She was firm against his palm. He felt the thundering of her heartbeat. Its rhythm matched his own. With a kind of reverence his hands moved over her flesh. His low moan of pleasure was matched by one of her own. The night closed around them as their passion climbed higher, then higher still, until they were caught in a hunger that threatened to devour them.

Kieran knew he had taken her too far, too soon. They both stood poised on the edge. One step more and she would cling to him and follow his lead. One step. He wavered, then pulled back. Though his mind rebelled against taking her higher, his body still strained toward her with a need that bordered on desperation.

Calling on every ounce of willpower, he lifted his lips from hers. He could read the confusion in her eyes as she lay very still, watching him.

Her body still hummed from his touch. Her lips were still warm and moist with the taste of him. When at last she could speak she whispered, "You must leave now, Kieran."

"Nay, Megan. I must stay." He resented the way his hands still trembled. Determined to put some distance between them, he stood and walked to the balcony.

"You are staying?" Her eyes widened. "But why?"

He turned. "The intruder may return. I cannot leave you alone and helpless."

"I am far from helpless, my lord."

She heard the warmth of laughter in his voice. "Aye. Of that I am very certain. Still, I cannot leave you."

"You cannot stay the night. It . . ." She struggled to calm her thundering heart. "It is not proper." She did not add that she would never be able to sleep, knowing he was watching her.

He shrugged, and from the sound of his warm chuckle, she knew that he was enjoying himself immensely. "You have two choices, my lady. You can sleep here, or you can sleep in the bed in my sleeping chambers."

"Your bed? But why?"

"Our intruder wanted you, my lady. Or something in this room. You will be safe only in my bed."

She thought about the logic of it for several moments. As long as he stayed in here, she was safe in his bed. It occurred to her that wherever Kieran was, she was no longer completely safe.

She resolutely slid from the bed. On legs that threatened to fail her, she made her way to his sleeping chamber. At the door, she heard his voice, warm and deep with laughter. "Sleep well, my lady. And if the servants should bring your bath on the morrow, I intend to enjoy it."

"My bath," she said with a little groan of dismay.

"If you are very nice to me," he added, laughing, "I may even allow you to share it."

"Kieran O'Mara. Before the servants arrive I expect you to wake me. I will not miss my bath. Besides," she added, sternly, "I will not explain to them why I am in your bed."

"A pity. It would have given them much to talk about."

"Give me your word, Kieran."

Instead he merely gave her a smile.

With a sigh of exasperation she said, "I do not need you to wake me. I will see that I am back in my room before the servants are up and about."

Megan turned and slammed the door harder than was necessary. But even that did not block out the rich, warm sound of his laughter as she crawled into his big bed.

Drawing the bed linens up over her, Megan inhaled the masculine scent of him that still lingered. Though she was loath to admit it, it was oddly comforting to lie in his bed, surrounded by the familiar scent and heat of his body. And though she was certain she would never be able to fall asleep again this night, she could not fight the exhaustion that slowly overtook her.

Chapter Eleven

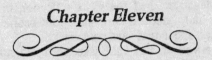

Megan heard the chatter of the servants as they moved around the room, drawing open heavy draperies, stoking the fire, laying out her clothing for the morning.

The servants. God in heaven. They had arrived before she had had a chance to slip out of Kieran's bed and into her own. With a little moan she pulled the bed linens over her head and wished she could sink into a hole and disappear.

"My lady, would you like to choose the gown you will wear this day?"

Reluctantly Megan pulled the blanket down and peered around. In the early morning sunlight she blinked. She was in her own bed, in her own sleeping chamber. Though she could not recall, Kieran must have carried her back to bed while she was still asleep. She breathed a sigh of relief and instantly regretted all the curses she had directed toward him.

Studying the lovely gowns being offered for her approval, she pointed to a dress of emerald-green satin. "That will do nicely."

"Aye, my lady."

Megan slipped from the bed and crossed the room to a basin of water. When she had finished washing, the serving girl helped her to dress.

"You chose well, my lady," the little serving girl said softly. "This gown is perfect for you."

"Thank you. But any gown would have done nicely. I wonder," she said idly, "if there was a time when I cared about such things as clothes?"

The servant began to arrange her hair in soft waves that spilled down her back and across one shoulder. As she worked Megan studied the girl's reflection in a looking glass. She had a natural curiosity about people. Was that another trait she had always possessed?

"What is your name?" she asked the maid, admiring her soft brown curls and lively green eyes.

"Aileen, my lady."

"Have you been at Castle O'Mara for a long time?"

"Since I was a lass. My mother and older sisters also work in the castle, my lady."

"Are you happy here?"

"Oh, my lady." Aileen gave her a wide smile that left no doubt. "'Tis proud I am to serve Lady Katherine. She is a fine lady who is kind to everyone. My father died in battle alongside Lord Kieran O'Mara, and 'tis the promise of Lady Katherine that every woman in Killamara who loses her man in battle will have a place here in the castle."

Megan was impressed. "She takes in every widow?"

"Aye, my lady. And their families. She cares for everyone of Killamara as though they were her own."

"What about Bridget?" Megan asked. "Whose child is she?"

"Lady Katherine had but one daughter, the sweet Lady Fiona. She was as kind as her mother and even more beautiful." The servant gave a little sigh. "She was the delight of Lord Kieran and Lord Colin."

"Where is Lady Fiona now?"

The girl's smile faded. "No one knows. She and her husband left their daughter, Bridget, with Lady Katherine before they sailed to England. They were never heard from again."

"How terrible. Has no one tried to find them."

"Aye, my lady. 'Twas the reason my lords Kieran and Colin traveled across the channel." Her voice lowered. "It has been rumored that Lady Fiona and her husband were killed at the hands of highwaymen, but my lord Kieran has never accepted that."

"Why?"

The girl shrugged her shoulders. "Their bodies have never been found. And Lord Kieran has vowed to search for them until he learns the truth."

She tied a ribbon through a cluster of Megan's curls and stepped back. "There, my lady. You look beautiful."

"Thank you, Aileen."

When Aileen left the room Megan walked to the balcony. Staring out over the lush green fields, she digested all that she had heard. Her heart went out to the child who had lost her parents. To have no knowledge of the ones she loved was, to Megan, as painful as having lost the knowledge of oneself.

"I see I have missed your bath. Alas. I had so looked forward to it."

At the sound of Kieran's teasing voice she turned.

Seeing the sadness that touched her eyes his smile vanished. "Had I known you would be so unhappy to be back in your own room, my lady, I would have left you in my bed and let the servants say what they will."

She was forced to smile at his humor. "Thank you for returning me to my bed, my lord. At least for the moment you have saved my reputation."

"It was my pleasure, my lady. You presented a most pleasant picture. One I will not soon forget." His words had her blushing furiously.

He thought about the way she had looked, her nightgown twisted in disarray around her hips, her hair spilling across his arm as he lifted her. It had taken all his discipline to keep from waking her with a kiss.

To ease her discomfort he asked, "Have you checked your room to see if anything is missing?"

"I fear I did not. As I said, I have nothing of value. But if it will make you happy, I shall do so now."

While Kieran watched Megan walked slowly around the room. When she came to the little chest, she glanced around in dismay.

"What is it, Megan?"

"The soldier's clothes. They were folded atop this chest. Now they are gone. Why would anyone want a stranger's clothes?" She glanced around, hoping she would find them lying elsewhere.

"I know not. Is nothing else missing?"

"Nay."

Kieran's look was thoughtful. Then, hearing the beat of booted feet upon the stairs, he offered his arm. "Come, my lady. We will break our fast with the others who already go below stairs."

"That will solve nothing."

"True. But troubles are always best faced after one of Mistress Peake's fine meals."

With only a little reluctance Megan placed her hand on his sleeve and allowed herself to be led downstairs.

"I must admit that Mistress Peake's food is far better than cold, dry partridge eaten in a damp forest."

"And I thought you were thoroughly enjoying your chance to live like a soldier, my lady."

They were both laughing as they followed the low rumble of masculine voices until they reached the refectory.

Bright morning sunshine poured through the windows, making patterns of light and shadow on the darkened wooden tables. The men looked up as they entered. The hum of conversation ceased.

"Ahh, lass." Hugh Cleary lumbered to his feet and held a chair for her. When she was seated, he sat beside her, leaving Kieran to take the chair on her other side. "Last night, after you departed our company and the Englishmen had retired," he added with a wink, "Kieran regaled us with stories of your adventure. We accused him of spinning tales

NO RISK, NO OBLIGATION TO BUY... NOW OR EVER!

CASINO JUBILEE
"Match'n Scratch" Game

Here's how to play:

1. Peel off label from front cover. Place it in space provided at right. With a coin, carefully scratch off the silver box. This makes you eligible to receive one or more free books, and possibly other gifts, depending upon what is revealed beneath the scratch-off area.

2. You'll receive brand-new Harlequin Historical™ novels. When you return this card, we'll rush you the books and gifts you qualify for ABSOLUTELY FREE!

3. If we don't hear from you, every month we'll send you 4 additional novels to read and enjoy. You can return them and owe nothing but if you decide to keep them, you'll pay only $3.14* per book, a saving of 81¢ each off the cover price. There is *no* extra charge for postage and handling. There are *no* hidden extras.

4. When you join the Harlequin Reader Service®, you'll get our subscribers-only newsletter, as well as additional free gifts from time to time just for being a subscriber!

5. You must be completely satisfied. You may cancel at any time simply by sending us a note or a shipping statement marked "cancel" or returning any shipment to us at our cost.

YOURS FREE!

This lovely Victorian pewter-finish miniature is perfect for displaying a treasured photograph and it's yours absolutely free — when you accept our no-risk offer!

*Terms and prices subject to change without notice. Sales tax applicable in NY.

like an old maid, but he insists every word is true. What say you, lass? Can you truly wield a sword like a warrior? Or has the man gone daft from his overlong stay in Fleet?''

Megan found herself relaxing in the company of this man. "Perhaps you would like to challenge me," she said with a laugh. "And see for yourself."

"Oh, lass. I could not lift a weapon against a lady. Especially one as pretty as you."

"She was counting on that," Kieran interrupted. "'Tis how she manages to best so many opponents. They think her too frail to be an adversary of any note. And by the time they discover their mistake, they are already disarmed and helpless.''

"Beware, my lord." Megan glanced around the company of men. "If you divulge any more of my secrets, I shall have to challenge you. And you would not want to be beaten by a woman in front of all your friends."

The men howled with laughter at the sudden frown that touched his lips. "You see what I had to endure since first I met this wench?"

Tavis Downey stared at his old friend from his position across the table, then turned his gaze on Megan. "Only Kieran O'Mara could come upon a lass who not only looks like an angel but fights like the very devil himself. The rest of us would probably find ourselves burdened with a female who looked like the devil and howled helplessly at every shadow that frightened her."

The men roared with laughter.

"What happened to your hand, Tavis?" Kieran asked suddenly.

Tavis dropped his hand to his lap. "I was helping old Padraig in the stables this morrow, and one of the horses took a bite." He grinned. "The old man is growing slower by the day. He should retire to a pallet in the corner of the scullery."

"To be denied his chance to work with the animals would be the death of the old man," Kieran said softly.

"If your wound pains you, Tavis," Colin said, taking his place beside Kieran, "let Megan care for it. She can grind herbs and roots into balm." He shot a grateful smile at Megan. "Thanks to you, lass, my wounds are completely healed."

"A healer." Hugh Cleary gave her an admiring glance. "I would hope to find you on my side, my lady, when next I go to battle."

Sir Cecil's voice reached them from the doorway. "We will not speak of battle while I am under this roof. We will speak only of a way to bring you to our side peacefully."

All heads turned toward the doorway, where Sir Cecil stood beside Lady Katherine. With a gallant bow he placed her hand upon his sleeve and led her to a place at the table. The intimacy of his touch was not lost on Kieran, who watched with no outward show of emotion. But Megan saw the way the little muscle worked in his jaw.

"Beware, my friends," Sir Cecil said as he took his place at the table. "For one of your countrymen to even think of battle is a crime punishable by death." He turned to Lady Katherine with a smile. "But I am here as your friend. I hear nothing; I see nothing." He filled his plate and began to eat as though he had not a care in the world. He turned to Kieran and added as an aside, "I would only caution you to think what would happen to your dear mother if you and your brother were imprisoned again. Or worse, killed in battle."

It was Lady Katherine who interrupted, hoping to defuse the tension. She glanced around at the men at table. "Enough of this talk of battle. Where is your son, Sir Cecil?"

"James is still abed. I fear the channel crossing, and our hunt yesterday, tired him. He will join us for a midday meal."

"When do you leave for England?" Kieran studied the man over the rim of his tankard.

Sir Cecil gave a lazy smile. "I have not yet decided. When I made plans to come here, I thought you were dead. And so I intended to stay on and help your poor mother with her affairs. But now..." He waved a hand. "I gladly offer my services to you, Kieran, if I can be of any assistance."

"You are too kind." When Kieran had finished eating, he scraped back his chair. "You will excuse me. I have much that needs my attention."

When he turned away, Megan had a glimpse of his eyes narrowed in thought. His smile, she noted, was wiped from his lips.

When he departed the refectory, Kieran made his way to the library. Once inside he closed the door, then strode to the fireplace and stared broodingly into the flames.

The jailer's taunt still rang in his mind. "And the best of all is that ye were betrayed by one who calls himself friend to ye."

Kieran began to pace, his mind in turmoil. Who among his friends would betray him to the English? And for what reason?

When their meal was finished Colin turned to Megan. "I was going to take Bridget for a walk. Will you join us?"

"Aye." She got to her feet and fell into step beside him.

As they exited the refectory he asked, "Have you seen the gardens yet, my lady?"

"Only from my balcony."

"Then we will walk there."

The door closed behind them, shutting out the hum of conversation.

Colin watched as Bridget danced ahead of them. They made their way between rows of carefully tended hedges. Here and there among the hedges were formal rose gardens and benches made from carved stone.

Megan glanced around in appreciation. A chorus of chirping birds hopped under the spray of water in a fountain, taking turns in a ritual of the bath.

The beauty of the garden seemed lost on Colin. He did not even see the lovely flowers or smell their glorious perfume.

"What troubles you, Colin?"

"So many things. Things I cannot speak of."

"Oft times a problem shared seems less troublesome," Megan said, laying a hand on his sleeve.

Colin gave her a long, silent look. "Aye, I think I could speak to you as I could not speak to many women, my dear Megan. But much of what lies in my heart cannot be spoken aloud. To anyone."

She had so many questions. Was he a monk? And if so, why had he not told her? Or did he hope to become a priest soon? Why would that be unspeakable? She wondered, too, about the crimes that had brought him to Fleet Prison. But she kept her questions to herself. Whatever troubled Colin must remain his private torment until he was ready to share it willingly.

"My little maid, Aileen, told me about Bridget's parents." Megan squeezed his hand. "I am sorry, Colin. You must miss your sister very much."

"Aye. I adored her. We all did."

"When you arrived in England, did you learn anything about her fate?"

"Nay. There was so little time. Almost from the moment we stepped on English soil, we were followed. It was as if someone knew our intentions."

"Had you confided in anyone?"

Colin shook his head. "Kieran and I have gone over this a score of times while we languished in prison. There were many who knew of our plans besides our mother and our friends. There is one among them who would betray us."

"How sad that it is often the one we love the most who causes us the most pain."

Colin glanced at her in surprise. "Aye. 'Tis true. But I cannot bear to think that it was a friend who sent us to that hellish place where we nearly lost our lives."

She drew him down on a stone bench. "Tell me about Bridget."

"I worry. She has been deeply affected by the loss of her parents."

"It is natural to worry about the child. But at least she has the love of her family to comfort her."

He watched as the little girl splashed in the fountain. "Aye. But she rarely speaks. It is as though she keeps all her thoughts locked inside. I spoke to my mother about it. She admitted that she cannot find the key to unlock Bridget's heart. The child does not open up to anyone."

"Give it time, Colin. The loss of both parents must be a terrible thing."

"Aye. Time. Why must everything take so much time?" He continued to watch as the child bent to smell a cluster of flowers.

Megan gave a gentle smile of understanding. "Tell me about Sir Cecil," she urged. "How did the ambassador to Queen Elizabeth become such a friend to your mother?"

"Sir Cecil was once much more than a friend to my mother," Colin said.

Seeing Megan's surprised look he added, "In their youth, it was expected that she and Cecil Kettering would wed. But when my mother met Sean O'Mara, in the court of Henry, she lost her heart. She defied her father and turned her back on a life of luxury to be with the man she loved."

"How exciting and romantic, to deny all except true love." Megan's eyes glowed.

He gave a short laugh. "It may be a romantic story, my lady, but though their love was a wonderful thing to behold, they chose a difficult path. King Henry desired my father's counsel. He commanded that my father and mother remain in England. My father refused, stating that his people had need of him in Ireland."

"Sean O'Mara defied the King?"

"Aye. He returned a hero to his people. But he incurred the wrath of many in Henry's inner circle."

"And Sir Cecil?"

"He apparently forgave my father for stealing away his first love," Colin said softly, "for he offered us the chance to be educated at court. Though I must admit," he said with a laugh, "my father resented it. He did not want his sons to have too much English influence. But my mother insisted that we accept Sir Cecil's generous offer. And when my father died, Sir Cecil was kind enough to use his powers of persuasion with Elizabeth to see that my mother did not lose title to her estates in England."

"It would seem that he is, indeed, a good friend..."

From the corner of his eye Colin saw a blur of movement. Both he and Megan turned to see Bridget standing on top of a narrow stone wall that ringed the fountain. Somehow she had climbed up and was starting to walk across. With her arms lifted for balance, she teetered perilously as she inched her way across.

"God in heaven," Colin cried. "Nay, Bridget. Stop."

Hearing his cry, the girl paused and turned her head. That sudden distraction caused her to lose her balance. With a cry, she toppled.

Megan and Colin raced across the garden.

Bridget lay in a heap on the ground. Blood seeped from cuts on both her knees, staining the torn hem of her pink gown. Tears ran in dirty little rivers down her cheeks.

With great tenderness Colin knelt beside her and touched a hand to her cheek.

"Can you stand, little one?"

"My knees hurt." She sniffed, wiping a grimy hand across her nose.

"I can see that." Lifting her gently in his arms, he murmured, "I shall take you in and have one of the servants clean you."

"Nay." Her eyes were wide with pleading. "Do not let Grandmother see me like this."

"But you must be cleaned. I cannot—"

"Nay. She must not see me bleeding. Please, Uncle Colin. You cannot tell her."

"Bridget, I must give you over to a servant."

The child began to cry harder.

Megan reached out her hand. "Please, Colin. Let me take care of her."

He would have argued. But the tears in the child's eyes were more than his tender heart could bear. "Will you let the lady help you?"

With a shy nod, Bridget wiped the tears from her eyes. "Please put me down. I can walk."

Megan caught the child's hand in her own and whispered, "Come. We will go around to the scullery, where no one can see us."

Megan gave Colin an encouraging smile and walked away with the child.

At the scullery she said, "I will fetch a bucket of water. I can clean you here, out of sight of your grandmother."

"Nay," Bridget cried. "One of the servants will tell. They tell Grandmother everything I do."

"I see." Megan mulled it over for a moment. "I wish there was some way to get you up to my chambers without being seen."

The little girl gave her a conspiratorial smile and caught her by the hand. "Follow me," she whispered. "We can use the servants' stairs."

Climbing stone steps lit only by an occasional candle, they made their way to the upper floors of the castle.

As they rounded a corner they nearly collided with James Kettering. After his initial surprise, he caught Megan by the arm to steady her.

"Your father said you were abed this morrow, feeling unwell."

"Aye. I was. But I am feeling better now. What are you doing here, my lady?" Though there was a smile on his lips, his eyes wore the hard glitter of barely suppressed anger.

Megan glanced at Bridget and saw the look of alarm that clouded her eyes. Thinking quickly she said, "We have been for a walk and had hoped to wash ourselves before seeing anyone."

He took note of the grimy little hand holding Megan's, and the dirty smudges that streaked Bridget's cheeks. Stepping aside he said, "I will not cause you delay, then, my lady."

As he swept past them, it occurred to Megan that James had not said why he was there. How did a guest discover these well-hidden back stairs, used only by the servants? And why would he choose to use them? Unless, she thought with a sudden chill, he wanted to hide his business from the view of others.

Bridget was already tugging on her hand, eager to be on her way. Without another word, they hurried away.

Except for a servant carrying firewood, they passed no one else.

When they reached Megan's chambers, she pushed open the door and led the child to a chair by the fireplace.

"First I will tend these cuts," she murmured, filling a basin with water from a pitcher. As she pressed a damp cloth to the cuts, she gave Bridget a warm smile. "Then we will see about cleaning you and that gown."

"You will not tell Grandmother?"

"Not unless you choose to."

The little girl made not a whimper while Megan cleaned the wounded knees and stemmed the flow of blood. With that done, Megan helped her undress and wash. When she was clean and bundled into a blanket, Megan began to scrub the stains from the filthy gown.

From her position on the chaise in front of the fire, the little girl watched with interest.

"Did you ever cut your knee?"

Megan winced. "I cannot recall. My childhood is lost to me." She squeezed the water from the garment and shook it. As she worked she glanced out the balcony and gave a sigh. "If I were to imagine my lost childhood, it would be in a place like this, with trees to climb and horses to ride." She turned to Bridget. "Do you ride the horses in the stable?"

"Grandmother has forbidden it."

"Why?"

The little girl sniffed. "She says my mother once fell from a horse and was nearly killed. She says she cannot bear to have anything happen to me, else her heart will surely break." Bridget's voice rose. "Grandmother says I am all she has left of her Fiona."

"I see."

Megan did see. With the loss of her daughter, in the care of her only granddaughter Lady Katherine had become overly protective of the child. And the more she tried to protect Bridget from all harm, the more the child struggled to break free.

She hung the wet gown by the fire, then sat on the chaise beside the little girl and drew her onto her lap. "Your gown will be dry in time for our midday meal. Until then, I will brush your hair and we will spend some quiet time here in my chambers."

As she ran a brush through the long, fiery tangles, the little girl relaxed. Soon her eyelids flickered, then closed.

While she slept, Megan watched her, feeling oddly moved by the little girl who struggled so valiantly to be independent. Though they barely knew each other, she sensed a kindred spirit.

From her balcony she watched James returning from the stables. Even from so great a distance she could see that his stride was brisk and purposeful as he made his way to the scullery. It was obvious that he intended to use the servants' stairway again. But did he use it for convenience? Or was there a more ominous reason he avoided being seen?

She chided herself for her thoughts. These people were, after all, friends to Kieran and Colin. She must make a move to curb her mistrustful nature.

Chapter Twelve

From the window Kieran watched as Megan helped Bridget into the saddle. Padraig, the stooped old groom who had been with the O'Mara family for over three generations, stood at the horse's head and held the reins.

It had taken two days of coaxing before Megan had obtained Lady Katherine's grudging permission to allow the child to ride.

Kieran felt a surge of pride as he saw the way his sister's child sat straight in the saddle. Leaning a hip against the windowsill, he crossed his arms over his chest and smiled at the sight of Megan, gowned in sunny yellow, calling directions as Bridget took the reins and urged her mount to walk in a circle.

The door opened. Kieran looked up as Colin crossed the room.

"They are good for each other," Colin said as he paused beside his brother.

"I am not so certain." Kieran frowned. "Mother is troubled by Megan's influence on the lass. She fears she will next teach her to handle a sword."

The brothers shared a laugh.

Colin's smile faded slightly. "It would not be the worst thing she could learn."

With a laugh Kieran said, "If the monks could hear you now, you would be expelled from their company."

"Perhaps that would not be the worst thing, either."

Startled, Kieran studied his brother's profile as Colin turned away. "What troubles you?"

"This." Colin held up a rolled parchment.

Kieran quickly scanned the message. "So. The bishop sends a delegation to welcome you home." He arched a brow. "Why do I sense that you are not happy about this?"

Colin shrugged, refusing to meet his look. With a sigh he muttered, "I have been away a year. I had hoped for more time here at Castle O'Mara before returning to the monastery."

"Take all the time you need."

"The bishop will want me to return with his delegation."

"I care not what the bishop wants. What do you want, Colin?"

Colin watched the little girl bounce in the saddle as the horse began a jarring trot. His hands, held stiffly at his sides, were balled into fists. "You will think me mad."

Kieran draped an arm around his brother's shoulders. "Tell me."

Colin's eyes were troubled. "All the time we were running, I was afraid. And sick and weak. And yet I have never felt more alive, more a man than I did then. The lass—" his gaze shifted to the figure who stood shouting encouragement to the little girl "—did not defer to me because I was a man. Nor did she treat me like a weakling. We were... equals. Can you understand?"

"Aye."

"And I know I must be mad because, given the chance, I would do it all again, if you and the lass were my companions."

A hint of a smile touched the corner of Kieran's lips. "I have always suspected as much about you."

Colin frowned. "You see? I am mad."

"You are an O'Mara. It is that simple. I have always known that we are not like other men."

"But I am not like you and Father. I have always been in frail health. And Father once said that my only salvation would lie in service to God."

"Colin, there are many ways to serve Him," Kieran said gently, "and every man must find his own way."

As Kieran walked to the desk and opened a ledger, Colin remained by the window. "If you had the chance to live our adventure over, would you?"

"Nay." Kieran's reply was instantaneous.

"Why?"

He placed both hands on the desk and lifted his head to meet his brother's eyes. "Because it is not over, Colin." He thought of the stranger who had invaded Megan's chambers and the taunting words of the jailer. "I fear it is far from over."

But though he could not admit it to his brother, there was another reason he would not care to live their adventure again. Megan. Ever since she had leaped into his life, sword drawn, eyes flashing, she had been on his mind far more than he cared to admit. The woman had him tied in knots. She was a complication in his life that he had not bargained for. And one that, in this uncertain time of his life, he should not permit.

Each day the throng of guests swelled as word traveled the countryside that the lords of Castle O'Mara had returned. The villagers called to pay their respects and to ask about the Lady Fiona, who had long been missing from their land. Often they brought gifts of welcome. The pens built around the stables soon filled with bleating lambs, squawking chickens and quacking ducks.

Warriors and chieftains came to welcome Kieran back to his rightful place as leader among their people. They came flanked by men hardened from years of battle.

Among such visitors was Terence O'Byrne, whose fierce orations at the court of Elizabeth in London had earned him the name Defender of the Faith by his loyal people.

He arrived at dusk, with a dozen riders accompanying him, just as the assembly had gathered to sup. Mistress Peake scurried around, ordering the servants to see to preparing additional rooms and readying extra places at the table.

While the others milled around, Kieran and Colin stood with their mother to greet their guests.

"'Tis true, then." Terence O'Byrne, a tall, handsome man whose hair was shot with silver, clasped Kieran by the arm. His dark eyes were piercing. His voice, when he spoke, was rich and resonant. "You have walked away from Fleet and lived to tell about it."

"Aye, Terence." Kieran greeted him warmly, then turned to offer his hand to the man's son, who stood proudly beside him. "Conor. Welcome."

Conor O'Byrne was a head shorter than his father and bore him little resemblance. His body was stocky and heavily muscled. His dark hair curled around a ruddy, handsome face. Unlike the voice of his gifted father, his quiet voice could barely be heard above the din.

"We feared for your safety," Conor said. "Few men survive Fleet."

Terence O'Byrne kissed Lady Katherine's hand, then turned to her younger son. "Colin," he said in a booming voice as he clasped the young man's arm. "You not only survived that evil place, you appear to have thrived."

"Aye. Though I would not recommend an English prison to restore one's health."

Colin's lips were curved in a wide smile when Terence O'Byrne suddenly stepped aside, revealing a beautiful young woman standing directly behind him.

She pushed back the hood of her cape, revealing a tangle of dark hair that fell nearly to her waist. Her dark eyes were downcast. Her full lips were rounded in a shy little pout.

Colin's smile disappeared. His mouth opened in surprise.

"My daughter, Cara, insisted upon accompanying us despite the long and difficult journey."

The two young people faced each other. Their faces mirrored a range of emotions—shock, confusion, extreme discomfort.

For a moment Colin said nothing. Then, regaining his senses, he brought her hand to his lips. "Cara. When did you leave..." He swallowed and tried again. "When did you come home?"

"I have been home a year now." Her voice was deep and rich with the brogue of her people.

"Aye. Cara has been home with us since you left for England, Colin."

"So long." Colin struggled to compose his senses.

"Come. Let us sup." Lady Katherine herded her guests across the room toward the long wooden tables where the others waited. Terence O'Byrne and his son and daughter were greeted warmly by those in attendance.

"Mistress Peake has prepared a special meal tonight," Kieran said as he led Terence to a place of honor beside his mother. Conor O'Byrne took a seat beside Tavis Downey. Cara was ushered to a chair across from Colin.

Throughout the long meal Megan watched as Colin and Cara glanced at each other, then away. When Cara turned to speak to Lady Katherine, Colin boldly studied her profile. But when she turned back, he busied himself talking to Tavis.

As always, Sir Cecil Kettering dominated the conversation. Turning to Terence O'Byrne he said, "Her Majesty still speaks of your powers of persuasion and expresses a desire that you return to court and accept a position within her council."

"Does she now?" Terence shot his son a knowing smile. "At least if I was in London, the Queen would know exactly what I was saying, and to whom."

"Aye." Sir Cecil assessed the man carefully. "Elizabeth would prefer to have you where she can see you. Her Majesty fears you are fomenting dissent here in your home-land."

"'Tis not dissent to wish to be left alone, my lord. I ask what any man asks. To live on the land of my father. To see my children, and my children's children. To welcome the spring rains on a crop that I am allowed to harvest for my own use. To grow old beside the woman I love. And to die in my own bed."

"That does not sound like the words of a man who claims to be a warrior," James Kettering said with a sarcastic laugh. He glanced around the assembly. "I thought all of you dreamed of dying with a sword in your hands."

"It is most probably the way we will all die," Kieran said softly. "But we can still have our dreams."

The others nodded.

At his brother's words, Colin chewed on his lip and stared at the ale in his goblet.

When the servants began serving thick slices of cake soaked in rum, Colin waved it aside. The smile on Mistress Peake's face dissolved.

Rushing forward, she whispered, "My lord. Are you dis-pleased with the meal?"

"Nay, Mistress Peake." Colin kept his voice low, reluc-tant to create a scene. "The food was as delicious as ever. I just have no room left for your cake."

"Then you are ill, my lord. Will I prepare a potion?"

"Nay, Mistress Peake. I am not unwell." He emptied his tankard and nearly slammed it down in his frustration. "Leave me."

"Aye, my lord." With a look of distress, the house-keeper hurried away.

When their plates were empty, Kieran pushed away from the table and led the way to the great room, where comfort-able chairs and chaises had been set in front of the fire-places at either end of the room. A musician and a dancer had been brought in to entertain. The musician began to play the lute, and the pretty young dancer began a series of steps. Kieran glanced toward Megan, who was seated beside James Kettering. Clinging tightly to her hand was Bridget, who had become Megan's shadow in the past few days.

Even now, in his mind's eye, Kieran could see the way the fiery lass had danced for the soldiers. Her hair had been but a veil of moon dust. Her eyes had gleamed like molten fire. In that forest stronghold she had been a temptress, a seductress. And he had no doubt that her clever, sensuous dance had saved their lives.

Kieran watched as James Kettering leaned close to whisper in Megan's ear. Kieran's hand closed around a tankard as the two of them shared a laugh. He turned away, emptying the tankard in several long swallows. Instantly a serving girl filled it. As he brought it to his lips again, his eyes narrowed on Megan as she crossed the room and paused to speak with Tavis Downey. At the sound of her laughter his stomach muscles tightened. God in heaven. He was jealous. Jealous of every man in the room.

He felt a moment of intense anger as he realized that she could have such an effect on him. Never before had a woman so besotted him.

Very carefully he set down the tankard. It was not whiskey he desired. The thought ripped through him, leaving him feeling decidedly unsettled. It was the woman.

In the middle of the great room the dancer whirled to the strains of the lute. All eyes were on her. All except Kieran's. He had no interest in the stranger. His only thought was of Megan. Across the room Megan felt Kieran's dark gaze burn over her, holding her even when she would turn away. With only a look he was touching her. Touching her as surely as if he were holding her in his arms. How was it possible that he could touch her from so great a distance? She shivered.

"Are you cold, my lady?"

Megan turned to James Kettering, who was watching her in a way that made her feel most uncomfortable. "Nay, my lord."

"You should have a wrap." Without waiting for her reply, he signaled to a servant, who hurried forward. "Bring the lady a warm cape," he commanded.

"Aye, my lord."

The servant whispered something to Lady Katherine, then left the room. A few minutes later she appeared holding an elegant velvet cape. With a feeling of importance, James took the cape from the servant and ceremoniously draped it around Megan, allowing his hands to linger at her shoulders.

Kieran watched without expression. He was suddenly weary of the company around him. Weary of their conversation, their laughter. But he could not leave his guests. Though he longed to be alone, to sort out his thoughts, he was forced to sit quietly and endure. But he did not have to endure young Kettering's hands touching Megan. Very deliberately he turned and began an earnest conversation with Terence O'Byrne and Hugh Cleary. But though they spoke of Ireland and her future, subjects dear to his heart, Kieran found his concentration broken frequently by the disturbing woman who sat across the room, talking and laughing easily with his mother and the others.

"You arrived at Castle O'Mara at the perfect time." Lady Katherine clasped hands with Cara O'Byrne. "The villagers are planning a celebration. Already the women have begun baking and sewing for the event."

"Oh, I hope Father will consent to stay." The young woman's eyes brightened.

"Kieran will convince him," Lady Katherine said. "It would be a shame to miss the games and feasting."

"Perhaps I could help prepare some of the food," Cara offered. Turning to Megan she said, "Would you like to help me? 'Twould be a chance to become better acquainted."

Megan smiled. "I do not know if I can cook, but I am willing to try."

"Of course you can," Lady Katherine said. Beside her, Cara nodded vehemently. "It would not be possible for a maiden to grow to womanhood without having learned to cook and bake and sew a fine seam."

Megan found herself wondering why the thought did not appeal to her. But she wisely kept her thoughts to herself.

"Cara, I will speak to your father," Lady Katherine said, getting to her feet. "I would so enjoy having you young women around while we prepare for the celebration."

As she crossed the room, Cara said to Megan, "Lady Katherine misses Fiona more than she admits."

"Aye. At times, when she thinks no one is looking, there is pain etched in her eyes."

Beside them, little Bridget listened in silence. Though she shared her grandmother's grief, she could not speak of it. The pain of her loss was too great to share with anyone. She kept all the terror of her loneliness locked away in her heart.

Without realizing it, the girl's fingers tightened around Megan's hand. Instantly Megan wrapped her arm around Bridget's shoulders and drew her close.

"Are you tired, Bridget?"

"Nay." Though she had to struggle to keep her eyes open, the child was reluctant to go to bed. It was in the dark of the night that the demons came, threatening to harm her the way they had harmed her father and mother.

Lady Katherine returned with a broad smile. "Your father has agreed to stay on until the celebration is over." At Cara's little laugh of delight she added, "Tomorrow we will invade Mistress Peake's domain and begin baking." Then, glancing at her elegant gown, she added with a smile, "And perhaps we should consider making some fine new gowns for the occasion."

"I am an expert with needle and thread," Cara said with authority. "I shall see to the gowns."

"What will Megan and I do?" little Bridget asked sleepily.

"You shall be forced to taste everything I bake," Megan said with a laugh. "And I shall happily wear anything Cara sews for me."

Lady Katherine's eyes danced with laughter. How wonderful it was to hear the musical voices of young women once more. And how good to see little Bridget join in the laughter.

Across the room, several pair of eyes watched with interest. Hugh Cleary was relieved to see his old friend's widow enjoying herself. He gave an admiring glance at the fine figure of Lady Katherine, then forced himself to return to the conversation that drifted around him.

Sir Cecil studied Lady Katherine with a practiced eye. She was still beautiful enough to turn heads. And young enough, he told himself, to miss the pleasures of the bed she had shared with Sean O'Mara. A calculating smile touched his lips.

Kieran heard the sound of his mother's laughter and felt himself relax. This was the first time, since Fiona left, that he had seen Lady Katherine let go of the pain that weighed so heavily upon her heart.

His gaze slid to the young woman who sat beside her. She held Bridget in her arms, with her lips pressed to the child's temple. She was unaware that the little girl had fallen asleep.

What a picture they made. She was a breathtaking Madonna, cuddling the child to her heart.

He felt a wave of tenderness as he stood and made his way to them.

Bending, he whispered, "I will carry Bridget to her bed."

Megan looked up in surprise, then down at the sleeping child. With a tender smile she handed Bridget over to him.

"Come," he said. "She would prefer that you tuck her in bed."

"Aye."

Megan got to her feet and walked beside him.

Cara went on chatting happily. But for a few moment
Lady Katherine heard not a word as she watched her so
and the young Scotswoman walk from the room.

There was a difference in Kieran since he had returned
But was it brought on by the time spent in prison or was
because of the young woman beside him?

There was a look in Kieran's eyes. A look she had see
before, in one whose eyes were so like her son's. It was
look that had made her pulse leap. And had finally stole
her heart.

Chapter Thirteen

Megan awoke to the sound of horses' hooves on the cobbled courtyard. For long moments she lay very still, resenting the intrusion into her pleasant dream. In it she had been carried in strong arms toward a bed. At first she had thought she was a child being carried by her father. But as they drew nearer to the bed, she realized that the man carrying her was not her father. He was strong and muscled, with dark hair and eyes. And the feelings that vibrated through her were not the feelings of a child. Even now, as she lay awake, those feelings lingered.

Sliding from the bed, she padded to the balcony to see what had caused the disturbance so early in the morning. Below, old Padraig took the reins of horses from a group of dark-robed men.

The heavy doors of the castle were thrown wide to admit them, and they disappeared from her view.

An hour later, when she was properly gowned and coiffed, she made her way downstairs to the refectory. The men looked up as she entered. In their midst were Kieran, Colin and Lady Katherine.

She felt Kieran's dark gaze touch her and knew there was a flush upon her cheeks. It had been the same last night, when they had tucked Bridget into her wee bed. Though he had not touched her, she had been achingly aware of him beside her in the darkened room.

Kieran watched her and felt again the familiar ache. Ther seemed to be no cure for it. Each time he saw her he felt strange warm glow, and each time he touched her he felt swift rush of heat that made him tremble with desire. Las night, when he had stood beside her in Bridget's darkened room, he had wanted her with a need that startled him. And when he had left her at the door to her chambers, it had cos him a tremendous effort to simply bid her a gruff good-nigh and leave her at her door.

"Ahh, my dear." Lady Katherine held out her hand "Come and meet our guests." As Megan paused beside the table, Lady Katherine introduced her to the cluster of robed priests, who smiled and nodded. Then, with obvious affec tion, Lady Katherine turned to a tall, robed figure whose dark, piercing eyes were startlingly like Kieran's.

"Megan, this is Bishop Seamus O'Mara, my husband' brother."

"Your Excellency." Megan curtsied and kissed his prof fered ring.

"Megan." Though his manner was kind, it was obvious that he was studying her carefully. "My sister-in-law has told me of your loss of memory. Have you begun to recall any thing?"

"Nay, Your Excellency."

"A pity. But you must be patient. All things happen ac cording to God's own plan. I will remember you in my prayers, my dear."

"Thank you."

When the servants entered bearing steaming trays of food, Megan took a seat beside Kieran and glanced at Colin, who sat across the table, to the right of the bishop. His eyes were downcast, his demeanor subdued.

"I had hoped that you would be ready to leave with us on the morrow," the bishop said to his nephew.

"Oh, but you cannot leave just yet," Lady Katherine protested. She related the plans of the villagers. "This cel ebration means so much to them," she said. "They cannot be denied the pleasure of welcoming Colin and Kieran home."

"I quite agree," said the bishop after hearing his sister-in-law. "We will stay until after the celebration."

Megan glanced at Colin's face. Though he struggled to show no expression, she saw the light that came into his eyes.

"You must eat something," Lady Katherine said as the bishop waved the servant away. "Yours has been a long journey."

"The others will eat. I will break my fast later. When you have eaten," the bishop said to Lady Katherine, "we will visit the chapel and offer a Mass of thanksgiving for the safe return of your sons." He glanced at Colin. "You will attend, of course."

"Aye." Colin pushed away his plate of food. "I will be there. But now, you must excuse me."

No one spoke as he crossed the room and let himself out. As the hum of conversation began to fill the room, Megan glanced at Kieran's face. His expression was unreadable.

Across the table the bishop had grown silent. On his face was a thoughtful expression.

The days leading up to the celebration were a blur of activity. People from the surrounding villages began arriving at Castle O'Mara. The grounds were abloom with colorful tents, carts and wagons of every shape and size. Standards bearing the crest of the O'Mara family billowed in the breeze.

The air was perfumed with the wonderful aroma of baking bread, pastries and sweetmeats. The pens built to hold the animals brought as gifts became empty as whole lambs and pigs were slaughtered and roasted, along with ducks, geese and chickens.

Throughout the preparations, Megan had discovered several things about herself. She had no talent for cooking or baking. And she detested sewing.

"If I have led a wicked life," she muttered to Kieran when he approached her in her chambers, "I know how God will punish me."

Her head was bent over the crimson cloth that draped over her lap and spilled onto the floor. Sunlight poured through the balcony window, casting her in a halo of gold. She was, he thought, the most perfect creature he had ever seen.

His voice was warm with laughter. "And just how will God punish you, my lady?"

"He will force me to sew gossamer gowns for all the angels in heaven." As Kieran began to chuckle, she muttered, "Aye. A hundred times a hundred of them. Until I have atoned for all my sins."

"That many? You must think you have committed a great many sins, my lady."

"If only I knew." As she looked up she pricked her finger and gave a little cry. Lifting her finger to her lips she said, "You see? I can wield a sword with authority. But I cannot manage a tiny needle."

"I can see that you must be rescued from this terrible doom. Come." He pulled her from the chair. The crimson fabric slid from her lap and lay in a pool of fiery sunlight.

"Where do we go?"

"We will ride the hills of Killamara, my lady."

"But the gown . . ."

"Perhaps we can persuade Cara to take pity on you. If not, there is always your maid, Aileen."

"Ahh." Her smile grew. "I would be most grateful to you if you could persuade one of them to take on this detestable task."

"How grateful, my lady?" He drew her close and she saw the laughter that lurked in his dark eyes.

"Grateful enough that I would warn you which of the pastries were baked by my hand. That way, you could avoid them, my lord, and live to a ripe old age."

Kieran roared with laughter. This woman was the most delightful creature. "How can I refuse such an offer? If Cara cannot help, I will fetch Aileen as soon as we return from our ride."

With their laughter ringing on the air, they made their way to the stables and helped Padraig saddle two horses. Soon, with sunlight warming their faces, they raced toward the distant hills.

"Oh, this is wonderful," Megan called. "I have missed this freedom."

Kieran studied the way she looked, her hair streaming on the breeze, her eyes glowing. There was a bloom on her cheeks that had been missing since their arrival at Castle O'Mara.

"You sit a horse as if you were born to it."

"Perhaps I was," she called, urging her mount into a run.

They let the horses have their heads until the animals were blowing and snorting from the effort.

Kieran shouted, "Let us rest awhile."

Bringing his horse to a halt beside a stream, he slid from the saddle and reached for Megan. As he helped her dismount, he allowed his hands to linger at her waist.

She steeled herself against the jolt that always came at his touch. "Your land is truly lovely, Kieran."

"Aye. Almost as lovely as you."

She felt her heart race and stepped back a pace. Whenever she was too close to him she seemed to lose all sense.

Seeing her uneasiness, Kieran caught up the horses' reins and led them through the shallows where they drank.

Megan stood on the bank and watched. Shielding the sun from her eyes she said softly, "Thank you for bringing me here. I am glad that you suggested we ride. I needed to get away from the tedious chores of the scullery."

Kieran left the horses in the water and walked toward her. "Is that the only reason you enjoyed the ride?"

"Nay." She laughed, and he found himself enjoying th
deep, husky sound of her laughter. "It is just good to tak
the reins, to feel a steed beneath me."

She stared at the horses moving slowly toward the shor
where the grass waving on the breeze beckoned them. "M
blood races at the sound of hooves pounding. My hear
beats faster when the wind catches my hair."

"Like this?" He caught a strand of her hair and watche
as it sifted through his fingers.

He saw the way her cheeks colored and felt a rush o
pleasure.

She swallowed and prayed her voice would not betray her
"We should get back now, Kieran."

"Nay." His eyes narrowed fractionally as he tucked he
hair behind her ear. "I prefer to stay here, where there ar
no gossiping servants or demanding guests. I am tired o
sharing you with so many people, Megan."

She ran a tongue over her dry lips, and he watched th
movement, feeling the first stirrings of desire.

"I promised Bridget I would let her ride in the court
yard." She looked up to see his dark eyes narrowed on he
and quickly looked away. "She has really become quit
good in the saddle."

"Aye." He ran a finger along her arm and felt her jum
at his touch. "She has a good teacher."

"I like teaching her." Megan stared, mesmerized by hi
big hand as it glided along her arm. Though she knew sh
ought to move away, she could not. "Bridget is quick an
bright and very brave."

"Like another I know." He brought his hand to her fac
and watched as her eyes clouded in confusion.

"Please, Kieran. Do not..."

He placed a finger over her lips to silence her. At the firs
touch of her lips to his flesh, he felt a surge of fire and nearly
drew back in surprise. Instead, he moved his finger along
her mouth, tracing its outline.

"You have perfect lips, my lady."

Her gaze flew to his face, and she saw the smoldering look in his eyes. They were treading on very dangerous ground. But she had nowhere to run. Besides, it was already too late. Though she might deny it to him, she could not lie to herself. She wanted the excitement he brought to her.

"I fear I must taste them."

With his finger beneath her chin he bent and brushed his lips lightly over hers. She stood very still, not daring to breathe. When he raised his head, her eyelids fluttered, then opened wide. He was staring at her with a strange, almost harsh look.

Kieran wanted the raging storm that exploded each time they came together. With his hands on her shoulders he drew her firmly to him and brought his mouth down on hers with a savageness that left them both shaken.

There was a wildness to the taste of her, and he was reminded of the highlands where they had first met. There he had found a primitive beauty unlike any he had ever seen. The highlands suited her. Strange, primitive, untamable. But there was a sweetness as well, an innocence that belied her ease in the company of men and the skill she displayed in the art of battle. She was a contradiction and unlike any woman he had ever known.

"Sweet. God in heaven, Megan, you are so sweet."

Megan's reaction to his kiss left her stunned. At first she stood very still, absorbing the shock that rocked her. Then slowly, tentatively, she touched a hand to his face.

"And you, my lord," she whispered against his mouth, "are very dangerous. And I find I like danger."

She offered him her lips and drew even closer, until she was pressed so close she could feel his heartbeat inside her own chest. With a sigh she brought her arms around his neck and clung as his lips claimed hers.

Each time they had come together, she had been forced to deal with strange, new sensations. And though these feelings left her oddly unsettled, she could not deny the excitement they aroused.

"I want to taste you, to feel you." His hands moved along her back, sending splinters of fire and ice along her spine.

His lips left hers to trail her throat, and she arched her neck, giving him easier access. He ran open-mouthed kisses along the sensitive skin of her throat and felt the little tremors that raced through her.

Heat poured through Megan and fire raced along her veins, threatening to consume her.

Though they were not aware of it, they dropped to their knees in the grass, still locked in an embrace. He feasted upon her lips while his fingers found the buttons of her riding gown and quickly unbuttoned them. With a moan he brought his lips to the swell of her breast and her nipples hardened.

Megan had never known such feelings. Her body quivered beneath his touch. A throaty moan was wrenched from her lips, evoking a new wave of passion in him.

"I want you, Megan. I must have you." The sound of his own voice startled Kieran. He had planned this seduction, had wanted to feel the thrill of desire. What he had not counted on was this wild, desperate need for her. A need bordering on madness.

The grass was a cool cushion beneath Megan's heated body. But nothing could offer her respite from the heat that throbbed and pulsed through her. Kieran's mouth found hers, lifting her high, then higher still, until she sighed and whispered his name. Or thought she did.

She knew she had to end this. All this was so new, so frightening, she needed time to sort it all out. But he was giving her no time. With each touch, each kiss, he took her higher, until she thought her heart would surely burst free from her chest. There were so many strange, unsettling feelings rushing through her, clouding her mind.

As his tongue tangled with hers, she struggled to hold on to her last thread of sanity. From somewhere deep inside Megan found the strength she had thought was lost.

"Nay, Kieran." With a long sigh she touched a hand to his cheek and drew back.

"Are you afraid, lass?" He lifted his head and stared into her eyes. Eyes that mirrored fear and something more. Something he could not quite define. "Do you think I would ever hurt you?"

"Nay. I know better." She drew in a long, steadying breath. "It is not you I fear. It is my own heart. I have never felt like this before, Kieran. I am so afraid."

"Aye." He uttered a low, fierce oath. "I have known little fear in my life, lass, but you frighten me." He gave a husky laugh. "In fact, you terrify me."

For a moment longer he held her roughly against his chest. Never before had he taken a woman against her wishes. But then, he had never before stood on the brink of madness with one like Megan.

"I will get the horses."

She heard the frustration in his tone. With quick, angry strides he caught up the reins and led the horses toward her.

She buttoned her gown and straightened her skirt with great difficulty, and found, to her amazement, that her hands were trembling. When she stood, she prayed her legs would hold her.

Kieran steeled himself against feeling anything as he helped her into the saddle. Pulling himself up, he gathered the reins and nudged his mount into a trot. Beside him, her horse kept pace.

His lips still burned with the taste of her. He glanced at his hands holding the reins. They were unsteady. As were his nerves.

This woman, with no name and no past, continued to turn his world upside down.

Chapter Fourteen

The day of the celebration dawned clear and bright. A chorus of sound filled the air as villagers spilled forth from their tents, carts and wagons and began the final preparations for their feast.

This was not a day made for danger or intrigue. Yet Megan could not seem to shake an uneasy feeling. As if something, or someone, wished her harm.

When Bridget rushed into her room and tugged on her skirts to hurry her along, she brushed aside her troubling feelings and caught the child's hand.

"My lady." As Kieran walked from his chambers he nearly collided with Megan, who was being led by an eager Bridget.

"Forgive me," she said, laughing. "I fear the lass cannot stand the excitement any longer. We must join the crowds below."

He put his hands on her shoulders to steady her, then allowed them to linger, enjoying the quick shaft of heat. "I see you managed to complete your gown." His gaze swept the scarlet satin that molded her breasts and waist and billowed around her ankles.

"Aye. With Cara's help."

"You look fetching, my lady." Such inadequate words to describe her. She was so lovely it almost hurt to look away.

"Will you join us, my lord?"

"Aye. I would not miss it."

They made their way from the castle, as eager as Bridget for the festivities to begin.

Behind them, taking great care to hide themselves in the crowd, two men followed and watched.

"It took you long enough to get here." James Kettering scowled at the stranger.

Malcolm MacAlpin, still garbed in traveling cloak and plumed hat, pulled himself up to his full height and surveyed the milling crowd. "Your servant bade me hurry. But I had important duties of my own to see to." He did not add that the minute he heard Megan's name mentioned, he dropped everything in his desire for revenge. Though he pretended to care little for the task before him, his blood ran hot with the thought that he would finally make the MacAlpin pay for the pain she had inflicted upon his dignity.

"Nothing is as important as this." James put a hand to his sleeve to caution him. "See that you maintain a discreet distance until you have had a chance to listen and observe."

Swallowed up by the throngs of people, they continued to trail behind Megan and Kieran.

The castle grounds were abloom with people in colorful garb. Elegantly attired men and women paraded alongside villagers in crudely patched garments of rough wool. The children of prosperous landowners played with the offspring of noblemen and simple farmers. Like innocents everywhere, they chased each other among the crates and vendors' booths.

A market had been set up in an open area of meadow. Seamstresses offered bright ribbons and bits of delicate lace. Cooks sold fragrant pastries they had prepared over hot coals. Farmers sold their fruits and vegetables and a variety of livestock. In wooden cages, piglets squealed and lambs bleated. Chicks, freshly hatched, were sold alongside baskets of eggs.

Through it all, Megan walked beside Kieran, her eyes aglow.

"You are enjoying yourself, my lady?"

"Aye. It is a fine day for a celebration," she said, holding firmly to Bridget's small hand.

"Does it bring back any memories of your own land?"

"Nay."

He heard the pain in that single word and instantly regretted his question. On this happy day, she needed no reminders of her loss.

He gave her a sidelong glance. "I must remember to thank Cara. You put all the other women to shame."

He enjoyed the color that flooded her cheeks at his words.

Seeing the way little Bridget eyed the food in the booths, he paused beside a table perfumed with the aroma of freshly baked goods. "You must each pick out a pastry."

With a laugh of delight, Megan and Bridget studied the assortment of sweets in a basket and made their choice. Kieran pressed a coin into the woman's hand and watched with amusement as Bridget and Megan savored the delicacies.

"This is wonderful." Megan held the small cake to Kieran's mouth. "Taste it."

He took a bite, then surprised her by drawing her close and running his tongue over her lower lip. At her look of astonishment he murmured, "You had a crumb on your lip, my lady. 'Twas sweeter by far than the pastry."

While Megan blushed furiously, Bridget giggled. When Kieran pulled Megan close and brushed a kiss over her lips, the little girl laughed in delight before running off to join in the games of a group of children.

From their position in the crowd, the two men watched through narrowed eyes.

James Kettering swore viciously before muttering, "Is she the one?"

"Aye." Malcolm MacAlpin's eyes narrowed on the woman who had refused him the chance to become her second in command.

"You are certain?"

"There is no doubt. Her hated image has been burned into my soul."

James was surprised by the anger in Malcolm's tone. "Then you would not shrink from inflicting harm upon the woman?"

"I would enjoy it."

An evil smile touched James' lips. "This is even better than I had hoped. Not only will we strip Kieran O'Mara of everything of value, but this time, when we return him to Fleet, we will use the woman to inflict even more torture." He cast an appreciative glance at the beautiful woman beside Kieran. "O'Mara will not be the only one to taste the nectar of that flower."

Both men threw back their heads and laughed. Then, seeing the startled glances of the villagers, they turned and fled.

"You should not do that in front of the child," Megan protested as Kieran's lips moved over hers. She was still held firmly in his arms.

"Why?"

"She might think that we—"

"—are in love, my lady?" He was laughing as he looked into her eyes.

At his words they both went very still. Then, as if on cue, they both pushed away and began to walk, taking great care not to touch each other.

Why had he said that? Kieran wondered with a frown creasing his brow. The words had startled him. He knew not from whence they came. Love. It was absurd. He had no time for such foolishness. He would leave that to the poets and dreamers. He had more pressing issues to deal with.

Love, Megan thought, feeling greatly troubled. Love wa
for people who could make plans for the future. She did no
even know her past. She could not afford to love this mar
She would not give her heart to any man until she knew wh
she was.

"Kieran." Tavis Downey strode toward them, shatterin
their somber mood. It was impossible to think gloom
thoughts in his presence.

Placing a beefy hand on Kieran's shoulder he said, "Sev
eral of the village lads have challenged us to wrestle. Cono
and I need you on our side."

"Why do you always seek me out when there is to be
fight?"

Tavis laughed. "I would rather see you take a beatin;
than take it myself."

In truth, Kieran was relieved to have something physica
on which to vent his frustration. "Aye. Let us give them
thrashing."

Tavis hesitated. "What of the lass?"

"I would like to watch," Megan said.

For a moment Tavis looked stunned. "It is unseemly, m
lady."

Kieran gave a roar of laughter. "When will you believe
me, old friend? This lady is not like any other. Though
doubt she will join in, she could probably give any mar
there a good thrashing."

"Come along then, lass," Tavis called to Megan. His face
was nearly as red as his hair. "We need someone to cheer u;
on. But mind you keep your distance. I'll not have a womar
fighting my battles."

Walking between Tavis and Kieran, Megan felt her spir
its begin to lift. She would dwell no more today upon love.
'Twas too vexing a thought for such a delightful day as this.

Colin trailed behind the group of black-robed figures.
Leading the way was Bishop Seamus O'Mara, who lifted his
hand in blessing as the sea of people parted to make way for

the men of the church. The women bowed as they passed and crossed themselves, while the men lifted their children aloft for a blessing.

The bishop was in high spirits, for he enjoyed nothing more than walking among the people for a few hours, feeling one with them. Of course, it helped to know that on the morrow he would return to his quiet life of prayer among the company of learned men.

He sighed. These few days at Castle O'Mara had served as a reminder of just how long he had been away from this life. He had been far removed from the smell of cow dung, the crying of children and the talk of war. Though he had grown up with them, he now discovered he much preferred the acrid scent of incense, the chanting of prayer and the calm reasoning that prevailed when men of the cloth met in the Queen's chambers to discuss ways to prevent war.

The English Queen. A nagging little thought persisted. While he met with the Queen's ambassadors to speak of peace, his countrymen were still being imprisoned for imagined crimes so that their land could be confiscated. He knew that his words often fell on deaf ears. Still, as a man of God, he had to keep trying to prevent battles that would cost even more lives.

He glanced at little Bridget, chasing after a crofter's son in a game of tag. He owed it to the lass to try to bring peace to this troubled land. If that meant dealing with the Protestant Queen, so be it.

As he paused at a booth to admire the plump hens being offered, he glanced around. Colin was no longer with them. It was apparent that he had slipped away again. The bishop frowned. The lad had been avoiding him ever since he had arrived from the monastery. First the lad had refused to confess, saying he needed time to prepare. Then he had not kept an appointment to discuss his future in the church. The bishop moved away from the booth, his gaze scanning the crowd for some sign of Colin. In his youth Colin had never seemed as headstrong as his brother, Kieran. Now he was showing signs of dissent. What he needed was more discipline. It might be best, he decided, to send the lad to Rome for a few years. He would not tell Lady Katherine. The dear woman was far too protective, especially with Sean dead and Fiona missing. He would wait until Colin was safely in the monastery to break the news to her.

Colin pushed his way through the thick hedge and stepped into the shelter offered by a stand of trees. As his eyes adjusted to the dim light, he saw her standing beside the little stream. She was wearing the heavy cloak she had worn the first night, with the hood pulled up to hide her face. His heart began a painful tattoo in his chest.

"I thought you might not come." Her voice, so low and musical, touched him as it had since they were children.

He took several steps toward her, then paused. "You knew I would come. But I had to be careful to slip away without being seen."

They stood without speaking, staring hungrily at each other.

"Cara." He heard the huskiness in his voice and cleared his throat. "Let me look at you."

She took a step into the shaft of sunlight.

"Nay. I mean really look at you."

She reached up with both hands to remove the hood. Her hair tumbled down her back in a cascade of dark waves. A thin sliver of sunlight fell across her face, revealing the uncertainty in her eyes. Then she slid the cloak from her shoulders, revealing a gown of pale pink silk that molded her slim figure.

"Why did you . . . leave the abbey?"

"I . . ." She swallowed, then licked her dry lips and tried again. "I found I was not suited to the life of a nun."

"But we talked about it. We agreed . . ."

She took a step toward him, then stopped. "We agreed to try. I tried my best, Colin. Truly I did. But I could not stay there." She hesitated, then asked, "And what about you? Will you go back with the bishop?"

How could he answer? How could he speak of the turmoil in his heart? Turmoil that he had been denying since he had taken that first step toward the priesthood.

He looked at her and knew that he had to try.

"Cara, sit down. What I have to say will take me a long time, for I have yet to sort it all out in my own mind."

Taking the cloak from her hands, he spread it on the ground. She knelt, then looked at him expectantly.

"Something happened to me in Fleet," he said softly.

"It must have been horrible." For a moment she covered her face with her hands as a shiver passed through her.

"Aye. It was cruel beyond belief. And I thought I would die. In fact, there were times when I would have welcomed death. But I survived. And by surviving, something strange happened to me." He began to pace as the words tumbled out. He told her of Kieran's capture in the forest and of the lass who risked her life time and again to rescue them. He told of the storm-tossed crossing and their narrow escape from the clutches of the hangman's soldiers who trailed them. And while he spoke, his eyes shone with a light that Cara had never before seen.

"The lass is like no other." He shook his head with a smile. "She taught me so much. Not just about battle, but about myself. Though my health is not robust, I realize I am no longer frail. I can survive heat and cold, floggings and starvation. That is not the sign of a frail man, is it?" Before she could respond, he went on. "I grew stronger with each recovery. And all this I learned because of the lass. She simply did what was needed at the time and expected me to do the same." He turned to Cara with a triumphant look. "And I did not fail in what I had to do."

Cara's voice was barely a whisper. "Do you love her, then?"

"Aye. I suppose I do." Seeing her stricken look, he fell to his knees beside her. "But not the way you mean. I love her the way I love Fiona, or Mother, or Kieran."

Relief flooded through her at his declaration. Her features relaxed into a warm smile.

It was as though a flash of lightning had suddenly illuminated the darkness of his mind. With a growing smile he said, "Do you not see, Cara? 'Twas Megan who showed me it is good to love. To love life. To love others unselfishly. And even to love a woman, if I choose."

Cara's eyes widened as the knowledge of what he was saying dawned. "But what of our promise to forsake our love and dedicate our lives to the service of God?"

"It was a noble vow. But we have both found that it is one we cannot live with."

Her eyes widened more. "Have you, Colin? Have you found that you cannot live with your vow?"

His voice was hardly more than a whisper. "Aye."

"Have you told the bishop? Or your mother, or Kieran?"

"Nay. I had to think it through, and tell you how I felt, before I face them. But now, having told you, I feel calmer about my decision. I have taken no final vows. I am not yet bound to the priesthood. I will not return with my uncle to the monastery. I will serve God in my own way, on my own land."

For long, silent moments they could only stare at each other. Then, slowly, tentatively, he dared to touch her. Reaching a hand to her cheek he whispered, "Oh, Cara. Do you know how long I have dreamed of this?"

She closed her eyes a moment, loving the feel of his hand upon her cheek. His fingers were strangely work-worn and calloused. His touch made it easier to say all the things she had kept locked in her heart.

"There was such a long time when I feared I would never see you again, Colin. And I grieved that I would never even have the memory of your touch to carry me through the endless years ahead."

"I know. It was the same for me."

"We should have at least touched each other before we parted."

"Aye. But we needed to avoid temptation in order to be strong enough to do what we thought right."

Growing bolder, he combed his fingers through the silken tangles of her hair and felt the need rising. "In prison I dreamed of your hair," he whispered. "And I was afraid it had all been cut off in the abbey."

"They would have cut it if I had professed my vows. But I could not." Tears welled in Cara's eyes as she whispered, "Mother Superior warned me that I am too vain. She said that my love of self was a stumbling block in the path of service to God. I think perhaps she is right." The tears slid from her eyes and spilled down her cheeks.

"Nay, Cara." With his thumbs he wiped the tears from her eyes. "You are neither proud nor vain. You are the most unselfish, humble lass I have ever known." Without thinking, he kissed the corners of her eyes and tasted the salt of her tears. "And the most beautiful."

His words unleashed a torrent of tears. "Do you know why I could not stay at the abbey?" she asked in a whisper. Without waiting for his response she stared into his eyes and said, "I could not bear the thought of never holding a babe to my breast. Your babe," she added fiercely.

"Oh, Cara." Colin felt a rush of longing so fierce it burned like a flame inside him. "I love you." He kissed her temple, her cheek, then whispered against her mouth, "God knows I tried to deny it. But I can no longer deny the heart that beats inside me. It is you, love. Only you."

With a moan he covered her lips with his. As the kiss deepened, she brought her arms around his neck and drew him to her. They fed from each other's lips, feeling the hunger grow and grow until the need overpowered them. And with murmured words of love they tangled together in the cloak and lost themselves in the love they had so long denied.

* * *

The tolling of the church bells for evening vespers marked the beginning of the feast. All day the people had frolicked, freed from their usual duties. There were contests of skill for the men where the young women could observe them and cheer for those who caught their eye. The married women exchanged recipes and remedies and repeated all the latest gossip. The children played until they collapsed in the grass to sleep. Old men leaned their backs against trees and related tales of their former glory.

Now, in the late afternoon sunlight, they came together to feast and celebrate the return of those who had been lost to them. As they took their places at long tables set on a grassy meadow, they feasted on deer and whole roasted pigs, partridge, goose and duck, and every manner of bread and pastry.

Megan sat beside Kieran. Though her plate was heaped with food, she ate very little as she sat stiffly, afraid to allow any part of her body to brush against his.

Beside her Kieran tasted the food and moved it around his plate. But he had no appetite.

Across from them, Colin sat next to Cara. They, too, ate very little. But their shoulders brushed often, and their hands were linked under the table out of the view of others.

Lady Katherine was seated between Sir Cecil and his son, James. Since the arrival of the bishop, both father and son had seemed extremely relaxed, as though they shared a very pleasant secret.

And as the ale and wine flowed freely, many of the villagers became orators.

"To my lords Kieran and Colin O'Mara," the village elder said in quivering tones. Several young men from the village had to assist him in standing, but he gamely continued. "They were not beaten down by the cruel taskmasters who held them against their will." He lifted a tankard and rasped, "Welcome home, my lords."

"Then we shall speak on the morrow. But first there is something I must attend to tonight." He caught Lady Katherine's hand in his. "You are cold, my lady." Taking his cloak from his shoulders, he wrapped it around her and said solicitously, "You need someone to take care of you, my dear. You have been too long neglected."

From his position at the head of the table, Kieran watched and listened. And though his hands tightened around the stem of his tankard, he showed no emotion as his mother was led away on the arm of Sir Cecil Kettering.

"You are overwrought, my dear," Sir Cecil said as he climbed the stairs beside Lady Katherine.

"It was the mention of Fiona," she said softly. "I cannot bear to think that I might never see her again."

"You need someone to care for you," Sir Cecil said, opening the door to her chambers.

He glanced around, pleased to note that the servants were still at the feast. "Your fire has burned down. I will see to it."

He crossed the room and tossed a log on the hot coals. Within moments flame licked along the bark and ignited into a roaring fire.

He turned. She was still standing where he had left her in the doorway. "Come, my lady. Warm yourself." Taking her by the arm he led her across the room and helped her into a chair by the fire.

From a table he lifted a decanter and filled two goblets with ale. Handing one to her he said, "Drink, little Katy." He cocked his head to one side and regarded her. "Do you remember how I used to call you that when we were young? My little Katy."

"Aye. The name no longer suits me." She sipped the ale and gave him a wan smile.

"To me, you are still as young, as lovely, as you were when we were in the court of Henry. You have not changed." He knelt and took her hand in his. "Nor have my feelings for you changed. I still want to look after you. want to see that you live out your life in luxury. Not—'' h waved his hand to indicate the rolling hills outside the ba cony ''—in this sad land so filled with bitterness and hatre for our kind.''

''Our kind, Cecil?'' She lifted her head. ''I do not un derstand.''

''Can you not see it, my dear? Did you not hear the rum ble of war from those who call themselves your friends?''

''Their anger is not directed against me, Cecil. It is agains a country that will not let them be free.''

''Aye. England. Your country, little Katy. And mine.''

''Nay. This is my country now. These are my people.''

''Do you really believe that? Do you think, if they wer to go to war against England, that they would forget you ar English?''

''Aye. I do.''

''And you would remain here in this land?''

''Aye,'' she murmured tiredly. ''It is my land now.''

Setting down the goblet, she made a move to stand. H put a hand on her arm to stop her.

''If you wish to save Killamara and the lives of your sons you need me.''

''Need you? Aye, I will need the friendship of my many friends.''

''I am not talking about friendship, my dear. It will tak much more than friendship to save the lives of your sons.''

''What are you saying?''

He gave her a smug smile. It was going just as he hac planned. ''I am the ambassador to the Queen, my dear. I an privy to much . . . secret information.''

She clutched his sleeve. ''What have you heard, Cecil? I there to be a war?''

He shrugged. ''It would seem that the whispers and ru mors have reached Elizabeth. She does not take kindly to threats from Irish warriors. Already ships cross the chan nel. Ships filled with soldiers loyal to Elizabeth. They shoulc each Ireland's shore within days. And it will take only scant days after that to march on Killamara.''

"God in heaven." Her eyes went wide with fear. "I have no fear for myself. But my sons..."

"Would be under my protection. As would all of Killamara. No English soldier could ever lay a hand on these lands or people. If you were my wife, no harm would come to you or yours.''

Lady Katherine stared at him, her heart beating wildly. "What are you saying, Cecil?"

He chose his words carefully. "There was a time, long ago, when you and I planned a future together. Was that such an unappealing thought, my dear?''

She avoided his eyes. "Of course not. But I could not help falling in love with Sean."

His eyes narrowed, but he forced a smile to his lips. "Sean is gone. But I can save everything of his that you have come to love.''

"By marrying me?"

"The Queen grants right of domain to loyal subjects. And I am one of her most loyal subjects. As my wife, you would be able to retain title to this land, as well as everything in your family estate in England. And, more importantly, I could order the soldiers from this land, for it would become English soil. That would provide a safe haven for your people and, of course, your sons.''

"You would do all this? Why, Cecil?"

"Because I am pledged to your safety."

"Do you give me your word on this, Cecil?"

His smile grew. It was so easy. "I have the ear of Elizabeth. She is a most generous monarch. I have but to ask, and it is mine." He pressed her fingers to his lips. "You need but say the word and we will pledge our troth. And the peace and safety you have always desired will be yours.''

Lady Katherine caught her breath and stared into his eyes. She did not love him. God knew she never could. But if this was the price that God required to grant her sons safety an her poor people peace, she would gladly pay it.

He caught her hand between both of his. "Will you marri me, Katherine, and save the lives of all you hold dear?"

Lady Katherine had a fleeting image of a bold, hand some warrior who had made her burn with a passion tha even now could make her blush. Though her eyes were clea she felt the tears against her throat as she swallowed the back.

And then she thought of the child, Bridget, so like he beloved Fiona. Bridget had the right to grow and live i peace.

She lifted her head proudly and said in a strong, clea voice, "I will."

Sir Cecil kissed her lips. It took all her willpower to kee from drawing away. And as he held her and kissed her, sh felt as if her heart had just shattered into a million pieces.

Chapter Fifteen

"**M**y lady."

Lady Katherine felt the tugging on her sleeve and was instantly awake. Her servant was standing over her, holding a candle aloft.

"What is it? What has happened?"

"It is one of the villagers, my lady. His daughter is burning with fever. His wife sent him to the castle to seek your help."

"Give him bread and ale while I dress." She was already out of bed and slipping into a gown, which was being held by a second servant.

Within minutes she was dressed and bundled into a warm cloak. When she paused at the foot of the stairs she was surprised to find Hugh Cleary waiting for her.

"Hugh." She gave him a warm smile. "What are you doing up at this hour?"

"I heard the arrival of a horse and the sound of the castle door being opened. I inquired of a servant and was told that you were going to the village to give aid to a feverish child."

"Aye. But what has that to do with you?"

"I would accompany you, my lady. You should not be out at this hour alone."

"The child's father is here. He will see to my safety."

"Perhaps. But humor me, my lady. I would feel better you allowed me to accompany you."

She caught his arm and smiled into his face. "I would b most pleased to have your company, Hugh."

She turned away too soon to see the pleasure that he words brought him.

In the dawn chill, old Padraig held the reins while the mounted their horses. Within minutes they were racin across the hills toward the lights of the village.

The crofter's cottage, at the far end of a lane, was sma and neat, with stone walls and a thatched roof. Inside a pea fire burned in the fireplace, casting a soft, smoky glow ove the single room.

Lady Katherine removed her cloak and gloves and stare around.

The child lay on a pallet in a corner of the room. Her dar eyes seemed far too big for her small, pale face. Tendrils o dark hair lay damply against her neck.

Lady Katherine knelt and touched a hand to the girl' forehead. Her touch confirmed what she already knew; th child was burning with fever. A sheen of moisture glistene on her ominously pale skin.

With a gentle touch Lady Katherine probed the girl' throat and behind her ears for swelling. Finding none, sh pressed her ear to the girl's chest and listened for severa seconds to the sounds of labored breathing. She could hea the rattle of fluid in the child's lungs.

Turning toward the crofter she said, "I will need coo water to bathe her."

Instantly the man lifted a bucket from a peg and hurrie from the cottage. When he returned, Lady Katherine dippe a clean cloth into the water and began to sponge the girl' body.

To the girl's mother she said softly, "You must bathe he like this several times a day, to keep the fever down. Whe you have finished, make certain that the linens around he are dry and warm."

"Aye, my lady. But we have few linens to spare."

"I will provide you with all you need. Give her hot tea or even a few drops of whiskey," Lady Katherine instructed. "And as much water as she can drink."

"She has been ill before, my lady," the child's father said with a worried frown. "But never like this."

"Aye. She is very sick," Lady Katherine affirmed. Squeezing their hands, she murmured reassuringly, "I will return this day with Mistress Peake's fine broth. And I will bring warm bed linens, as well."

Before leaving the cottage, she returned to the child's side for one last glimpse. When she walked to the door, there were tears in her eyes.

"Thank you, my lady," the father called.

"God bless you, my lady," his wife added.

"You must be vigilant," she said firmly. "See that she does not become chilled."

Outside the cottage, Hugh Cleary helped Lady Katherine into the saddle, and they rode through the darkened village in silence.

Seeing the tears that clung to her lashes, he said softly, "She will recover, my lady. You did all you could."

"Nay. I can do so little." She gave a deep sigh. "If only I had paid more attention to the Queen's physician at court. But I was just a maiden then, so young and foolish, and so certain that his help would always be there if it was needed. Little did I dream that I would lose my heart to this poor land, and feel so useless at times like this." Her voice trembled. "Oh, Hugh, I have seen so many of them die..."

Her voice trailed off as she choked back a sob.

Without hesitation Hugh slid from the saddle and pulled her into his big, strong arms. Her hood fell back, allowing her unbound hair to spill down her back.

She made a valiant struggle to hold back the tears. But the warm comfort of his embrace was her undoing. With great choking sobs she cried as though her heart were breaking.

"I want so badly to help them." Her words were issued between sobs.

"You do help, Katherine. Just by being here and caring."

"Nay. 'Tis not enough. I cannot save their young lives.'

"Shh. You are not God. You can only do so much."

"But it is never enough."

When at last her tears ended, Hugh pressed his lips to the top of her head and murmured gently, "She is young and strong, Katherine. She can fight this fever."

"Aye." With a square of finest lace she wiped her eyes but almost instantly fresh tears began. "I am such a fool,' she whispered. "But the child reminded me of Fiona. She was a frail child, much like Colin. And she fought many fevers in her youth."

"Aye. I recall," Hugh said softly.

She glanced at him. "How could I forget? You watched them all grow. You were always there when we needed you. And all of us came to depend upon your quiet strength. Oh, Hugh." She clutched his shoulders and stared into his eyes. "I have a terrible fear that I will never see Fiona again. And if that should be so, I could not..."

"Hush, Katherine." With great tenderness he touched a finger to her lips to silence her. "I have already spoken with Kieran. Two of my most trusted men have gone to England to continue the search."

Her eyes widened. "When did they leave? Why did you not tell me? What...?"

He chuckled low and deep in his throat. Again he silenced her. "I understand your heartache, and I share it, Katherine. But Kieran and I thought it best if no one knew."

"Aye. I agree. But at least let me tell Sir Cecil. He can arrange—"

"Nay." He cut her off sharply. Too sharply. Then, to soften his outburst, he said, "No one must know. This is to be our secret, Katherine. Do you understand?"

At her silence he said, "Too many people knew of the journey planned by Kieran and Colin. Their plans went awry. This time, no one must know. Do you understand?"

"I do."

The breeze caught and lifted her hair. Without thinking he caught a handful and stared as it sifted through his fingers.

His voice, when at last he spoke, was gruff with emotion. "I would do anything to ease your pain, Katherine. It breaks my heart to see you so unhappy."

"You have always been such a dear friend, Hugh. To me and my family."

His voice was as hushed as the breeze that whispered through the trees. "I would be more than a friend if you would let me."

The words hung between them for long, silent moments.

Lady Katherine looked up at him with wonder. "I never dreamed." She touched a hand to his cheek. Fresh tears sprang to her eyes. "Oh, Hugh. Why have you waited until now to speak of this?"

"I had no right. Out of respect for Sean, I have kept my feelings to myself, Katherine. But since his death, I have been watching over you, doing all in my power to keep you safe."

"I have been aware of your many kindnesses. And I am grateful, dear Hugh."

"I love you, Katherine. I always have," he said, tracing a rough finger from her eyebrow to her cheek, to the curve of her lips. "I did not know how to tell you."

"God in heaven. And I have for so long—" she looked away, struggling for the words "—cared for you as well." His eyes lit as she went on, "I think perhaps it is your gentle nature, and the way you have always preferred to stand aside and let others reap all the praise while you quietly go about doing what is needed." Her tears spilled down her cheeks and she brushed them away with the back of her hand. Her voice when she spoke was a cry of pain. "If only

I had known sooner how you feel. Perhaps everything would have been different.''

"I do not understand.'' He lifted her chin, forcing her to meet his dark eyes. "What is wrong with my telling you now how I feel? If you share these feelings, there must be some way we can find happiness, Katherine.''

"Happiness.'' She turned away and buried her face in her hands.

With great tenderness he turned her into his arms and lifted her face to him. "Tell me what troubles you, my sweet Katherine. Whatever it is, we will deal with it together.''

"Together.'' Her eyes brimmed. "We can never be together now, Hugh.'' She glanced at the sun shimmering on the horizon. "Already Sir Cecil is dressing for his audience with the bishop.'' She swallowed the tears that threatened. She would shed no more tears over the pain that wrapped itself around her heart. She had made her bargain with the devil. She would live with it, no matter what the cost.

"What does Sir Cecil's audience with the bishop have to do with us?''

"It has already been arranged. Cecil will seek a blessing from the bishop—'' she swallowed and took a deep breath "—upon our marriage.''

"You and Cecil Kettering?'' For long moments Hugh Cleary stared at her as if he could not believe his ears. Pain was etched on his handsome face, clouding his dark eyes.

His hands dropped to his sides. He took a step back from her.

"Forgive my boldness, my lady. I had no right to speak as I did. You will forget the declarations of an old fool?''

"We are both old fools,'' she whispered as she looked away, too overcome to say more.

Stiffly offering his hand, he helped her into the saddle, then mounted and led the way toward the castle. They rode the entire distance in silence, each lost in his own bleak, private hell.

* * *

Bishop Seamus O'Mara was furious. Despite the beauty of the morning and the grandeur of the Mass over which he had just presided, he could not shake his anger.

Last night he had granted an audience with his nephew and Cara O'Byrne. He had given careful thought to what he would say to both of them when they stood abjectly before him. He knew of the girl's hasty departure from the abbey, and suspected that Colin's imprisonment in England had been the cause of it. He had hoped that Colin would persuade the lass to return to the holy life from which she had fled. Colin had a good heart. And he had always been deeply religious. The bishop hastily pieced together in his mind the reason Colin had been delaying this meeting. It was the girl. Perhaps Colin saw the salvation of the girl's soul as his mission before returning to the monastery. A noble goal, but not one that should impede Colin's return to the monastery. The bishop intended to lecture both of them on the need for more discipline before giving his blessing on their return to the cloistered life they had chosen.

He had not guessed, when they arrived together and stood, heads bowed, hands carefully folded in front of them. Nor had he suspected when he began the lecture. It was only when he was finished, and ordered them to kneel for his blessing, that Colin had broken the silence to tell him that they had no intention of returning to a life of service to the church. That they were, in fact, planning to wed.

Bishop O'Mara had tried his famous powers of persuasion. When that failed, he had appealed to their faith. When they remained adamant in their decision, he had lost his temper and declared that they would have to live apart for one year before consummating their marriage if they persisted in this foolish intention to wed. But even that could not change their minds. And so he had been forced to give in to their wishes. At the end of one year, if their love prevailed, he would preside at his nephew's wedding. A wedding that he believed would be a disaster for both Colin and the church. He had been quick to point out to his nephew that a weak, frail man made a poor husband. Especially to one as headstrong as Cara O'Byrne. But Colin's quick mind and easy grasp of theology and language would have made him a respected leader in the church. Perhaps even a bishop or cardinal. Or even, Bishop O'Mara had suggested, the first pope to spring from their poor land. Even that lecture had not changed their minds.

He strode the distance from the chapel to the castle with hands balled into fists at his sides. He was not a man accustomed to losing.

In his chambers he was pleased to see that Mistress Peake had sent a tray of food to break his fast. He ate slowly, savoring the fine meal. He would miss Mistress Peake's cooking when he returned to the monastery.

When he had finished eating, he looked up as his aide, Father Malone, entered.

"Sir Cecil requests an audience."

"Aye. Send him in." With a frown the bishop strode to the fireplace and stood with his hands behind his back.

Bishop O'Mara had carefully cultivated the friendship of his sister-in-law's countryman. Cecil Kettering was, after all, a close confidante of the Queen. And the bishop knew that if Sir Cecil should be the one to bring about peace between Ireland and England, the powers in Rome would not be able to ignore him any longer. He was certain that Sir Cecil cultivated the bishop's friendship for the same reason. Elizabeth would be most grateful to subdue the troublesome island that continually threatened the peace of her empire.

"Excellency." Sir Cecil entered briskly and bowed his head ever so slightly before taking the seat Father Malone indicated.

The bishop's aide sat behind a desk and began to work on the bishop's mountain of papers.

"You told my aide that your business with me was most urgent, Sir Cecil. What is it you wish?"

"I wish your blessing, Excellency." Sir Cecil gave him a smug smile.

"Blessing? And what is it I will be blessing?"

"My betrothal."

"Ahh. You intend to wed again. That is good," the bishop said, lapsing into one of his favorite sermons. Cecil Kettering's wife had been dead for nearly a score of years. He had heard that Sir Cecil had become a bit of a rake at court. As had his son, James. A wife might be the very thing he needed to settle down into the proper life of a gentleman.

"It is not good for man to be alone," the bishop said.

"I quite agree. And I have been alone too long now."

"I do not understand why you need my blessing, Sir Cecil. Since you are not of our faith and your life in England does not affect us here in Ireland, I see no reason for this audience."

"Ahh, but my marriage will affect you and everyone here in Killamara, Excellency."

Bishop O'Mara lifted a brow.

"I have asked the Lady Katherine to be my wife." Sir Cecil nearly laughed aloud at the bishop's expression. The pompous old fool was choking on every word. "And she has graciously accepted."

When he could find his voice, the bishop said, "I could not possibly bless such a union. You are not of our faith."

"Such marriages are often allowed. It is within your realm of power to do so. And I believe, when I have finished explaining what I will do in return for your blessing, that you will see the wisdom of it."

Sir Cecil spoke briskly, enjoying every minute of the bishop's discomfort. He had no doubt he would have what he desired. He had carefully calculated every move.

Megan paced her room, feeling like a caged bird. All of the castle was buzzing with the news of Lady Katherine's betrothal to Sir Cecil Kettering. As they broke their fast,

James had boasted to everyone about his father's plans even before Lady Katherine had been given a chance to share the news with her sons.

They had taken the news badly. Colin had pushed himself away from the table and fled the castle. Terence O'Byrne had reported that Cara was missing, as well. No one had seen Colin or Cara since.

Kieran had closed himself in the library. He had spoken to no one since he had heard the news.

It was reported that the bishop was preparing to return to the monastery at Donegal as soon as the wedding ceremony was concluded. He had already presided over the official betrothal. Sir Cecil had insisted upon having the simple ceremony immediately. It had been performed in the chapel with only the priests and the lady's personal servants in attendance.

Even Aileen, Megan's little maid, had lost her smile, as had all the servants. It was as if there had been a death in the castle.

As Megan watched from her balcony, Lady Katherine and Hugh Cleary pulled themselves into the saddle. Sir Cecil and James, laughing together, rounded the corner. Sir Cecil's smile faded.

His voice, raised in anger, was easily discernible to Megan on the balcony. "What is this? Is my betrothed planning to travel in the company of another man?"

"We go to the village, Cecil."

"Or so you say. How am I to know this is not a tryst?"

Lady Katherine's face flamed. Hugh leaned down from the saddle. His hand snaked out and caught Sir Cecil by the front of his tunic. Instantly Lady Katherine lifted imploring eyes to Hugh, who promptly released his hold on Cecil.

"There is a very sick child in the village, Cecil. I must tend her."

Smoothing his tunic, Cecil took the reins from old Padraig's hand and shot Hugh a look of smug confidence. "I vill not have my betrothed caring for the villagers like some owborn midwife."

"Cecil, I have always cared for the sick and impover-shed of the village. It is expected."

He did not attempt to hide his disdain. In clipped tones ᴊe said, "They will soon learn that such things must ᴄhange." Without waiting for her approval, he hauled her from the saddle and caught her arm. "You will send one of ỵour servants, my dear."

Lady Katherine's face darkened with confusion. "You ᴄannot be serious, Cecil."

His voice lowered ominously. Turning to Hugh, he said, "Is the child in danger of dying?"

"Aye." Hugh's dark eyes burned with unconcealed ha-tred. Were it not for Lady Katherine, he could put a knife through this peacock's heart.

"Then I cannot have you exposed to danger, my dear." With a firm grasp of her arm, Cecil steered her toward the door of the castle and gave her a chilling smile. "We will fetch one of your servants immediately. And you," he said, turning once more to Hugh Cleary, "have partaken of our hospitality long enough."

Lady Katherine turned to Sir Cecil with a stunned look. "Hugh is a guest here. He is welcome to stay as long as he chooses."

"He will choose to leave as soon as we are wed," Sir Ce-cil said curtly.

Megan stood very still, unable to believe what she had just seen. Crossing her arms over her chest, she began to pace. How could a fine lady like Katherine agree to marry such a cold bully?

At a knock on her door she turned. She crossed the room and opened the door to find Hugh Cleary standing with his fist raised, about to knock again. Though the anger still seethed inside him, he had carefully composed his features.

"Forgive me, lass," he said softly. "But I recall that Kieran told me you are a healer."

"Aye. I...overheard Lady Katherine and Sir Cecil, Hugh I will gladly do what I can. Tell me what is needed."

He thought about his aching heart. But there was no cur for it. The child was another matter. "There is a child in th village who is dying, lass. Lady Katherine was about to vis again, since it is reported that the child grows weaker. Wi you see her?"

"Of course." Megan retrieved her cloak from a peg an tossed it over her arm before following Hugh Cleary to th stables. In his arms was a basket containing warm linens, a well as a flask of hot broth provided by Mistress Peake.

Within minutes they were racing toward the village.

At the crofter's cottage, Megan felt the suspicious stare of the child's father and mother as Hugh explained why the had come.

"If she is friend to Lady Katherine, why has she com alone?" the crofter asked, barring her way.

"You are wasting time," Hugh said with an edge to hi voice. "Allow the lass to enter."

"Nay." The crofter's wife joined him in the doorway "She is not one of us. She cannot touch our child."

"If Kieran O'Mara orders you to allow the lady to enter will you obey?"

"Aye," the crofter said, his eyes narrowed in anger. "Bu my lord O'Mara would never allow a stranger to usurp hi mother's place."

With an angry oath, Hugh led Megan to a grassy spo beneath a tree. "Rest, lass. I will return as soon as I can."

Hugh leaped on his horse and urged it into a run. Mega watched as the trail of dust marked his hasty journey to th castle. Within the hour another cloud of dust rose up, sig naling the return of Hugh. Riding alongside him wa Kieran. From the gossiping servants he had already heard the story of his mother's scene with Sir Cecil. His fury wa a terrible thing to witness.

"Have you insulted a guest in my home?" Kieran shoute at the crofter.

"Nay, my lord. But Lady Katherine has always cared for the sick among us."

"Lady Megan is here with my mother's blessing," Kieran said in thunderous tones. "Step aside and allow the lady to enter."

Inside the cottage, Megan examined the girl who lay so pale and still. While the others watched, she listened to the fluid that clogged the girl's lungs, then touched a hand to the fever that burned her skin. At first she was aware of the hostility of the parents, who hovered nearby watching her every move. But as she worked over the child, she soon forgot her uneasiness. The girl was dangerously weak. She would soon be lost to them.

"I need to find a damp, cool place, where certain herbs and roots grow."

"There is a river nearby. I will take you," Kieran said.

"I will return soon," Megan told the crofter. "Fill as many kettles as you can and put them on the fire."

"I will see that it is done," Hugh said, lifting a heavy kettle from a peg near the wall. He was taking no chances that the crofter and his wife might try to hide their child from this stranger.

With Kieran leading the way, Megan walked to the edge of the forest that ringed the village. Coming to a small stream, she followed it, picking herbs and roots as she did. When her arms were full, she returned to the cottage and began grinding the plants into a paste, while the crofter and his wife watched. When she had folded the paste inside a piece of soft cloth, she applied it to the girl's chest.

"This poultice will draw out the poisons," she explained.

The kettles, which had been filled at a stream and placed on the fire, began to boil. Soon a great cloud of steam billowed around the small cottage. "We must keep these kettles filled and boiling. The steam will aid in the child's healing."

Kieran and Hugh seemed relieved to have something important to do. For the next several hours while Megan knelt by the girl's side and applied fresh poultices, the men hauled water from the stream and kept the kettles boiling.

As he worked, Kieran studied the young woman who knelt by the child and labored, hour after hour, to ply her healing powers. Her hair had pried loose from the neat plait, sending little tendrils to curl around her neck and cheeks. The steam from the kettles caused the tendrils to curl damply. Her gown was stained from the plants she had picked. As the late afternoon sunshine slanted through the small window, lengthening the shadows in the cottage, he could sense her weariness. But she neither slowed her pace nor took a moment to rest. It was one more reason he loved her.

Love.

He stood, his sleeves rolled above the elbows, his arms straining beneath the weight of two buckets filled with water. Aye. There was no longer any way he could deny it. He loved her. Loved her for all the reasons he had tried to deny. And loved her for no reason at all. He simply knew that he loved her.

Chapter Sixteen

Megan lay on a pallet beside the child. Sometime after a hurried meal of cold mutton and crusty bread, she had fallen asleep. It had been her first food since breaking her fast early that morning. Now, in the hour before midnight, she awoke to find the child peering at her.

The steam from the bubbling kettles cast a hazy mist over everything in the cottage. For a moment Megan felt strangely disoriented. Then, recovering quickly, she touched a hand to the child's forehead. The fever was gone.

"How do you feel?" she whispered.

"Hungry."

Megan gave a delighted laugh and hugged her. "Then you shall eat. What is your name?"

"Roanna, my lady. Who are you?"

"I am Megan."

The child reached a hand to Megan's hair and said with a trace of wonder, "I thought you were an angel, my lady, sent from heaven to watch over me."

The sound of their voices roused the others. Within moments Hugh and Kieran, lying on pallets beneath the window, sat up and watched as the crofter and his wife rushed to the little girl's side.

"Oh, my darling," the mother cried. "Are you truly back with us?"

"I did not leave you," the girl said, her lips curving into a hesitant smile.

"Nay. But we feared for a while that you would abandon us for that other world." Her father wrapped his arms around his wife and daughter, then looked at Megan. "My lady, forgive me for my foolish suspicions. You have given us back our little one. Our humble cottage is yours. As is everything we own."

Megan's smile reflected her joy. "The recovery of your daughter is all the reward I desire."

"You performed a miracle, my lady," the child's mother said, wiping tears of joy from her eyes.

"It was no miracle. I am grateful that I learned the art of healing." Then, at a new thought, she said, "I could teach you and the other women of the village about the herbs and roots I use in healing. And you could pass it on to your children."

"We would be most grateful, my lady."

"It shall be done. I will leave it to Lady Katherine to choose a time and place."

The grateful parents fell on their knees and kissed her hand. Embarrassed and touched by their show of affection, Megan lifted shining eyes to Kieran.

He took her cloak from a peg and wrapped it around her. "Come, Megan. We must return to Castle O'Mara. Our work here is done."

"Thank you, my lord, for bringing this lady to us," the man said.

"Aye." Kieran studied Megan with a strange look in his dark eyes. "We are all blessed for having the lady here." Catching her hand, he gave a last glance at the happy parents and their smiling child and led her from the cottage.

As they made their way on horseback in the darkness toward the lights of the castle, Hugh said softly, "You may say 'twas merely the proper use of a few herbs and roots, my dear. But what I saw this night was truly a miracle. Your knowledge of healing goes beyond anything we know. Our

people have rarely taken to a stranger with such affection."
He turned to Kieran, whose look was devouring the woman
beside him. "Is that not true, Kieran?"

"Aye." Kieran smiled and Megan felt her heart leap.
"You have forever made a place for yourself among my
people, my lady."

His words touched her. For the rest of the journey to the
castle she felt bathed in a warm glow.

As they entered the courtyard, they saw old Padraig hob-
bling toward them from the stables, his hunched back covered by a warm cloak.

"Does he ever sleep?" Megan whispered.

"He naps. But the minute he hears the clatter of hoofbeats, he is awake and eager to perform his duties. It was
thus for my father and his father before him. He loves the
animals. And they return his love. They do not judge by his
appearance, as men do."

Kieran slid from the saddle and tossed the reins to the
waiting old man. Then he helped Megan from the saddle.

Hugh clapped a hand on Kieran's shoulder, then lifted
Megan's hand to his lips. "I am grateful for the chance to
share this day with you, my dear."

"It is I who am grateful, Hugh, for the chance to repay
the kindness I have been shown by these good people."

"I bid you both good-night," Hugh said before striding
away.

As Megan and Kieran made their way to their chambers,
Kieran instructed a servant to bring them food and drink.
Then, glancing at Megan, he said, "Perhaps you are too
tired to eat, my lady."

"Nay. I am far too excited to sleep just yet." She entered
the sitting chamber and began to pace in front of the fire
while he filled two goblets with ale. "And now that my task
is completed, I realize I am ravenous."

The little maid, Aileen, hurried into the room, eager to
prepare her mistress for sleep so that she could slip off to her
own bed.

"Oh, my lady. I have been waiting up for you," she said. Then, seeing Kieran in the sitting chamber, she bowed her head and began to withdraw. "Forgive me, my lord. I thought the lady was alone."

Megan knew that the servant could not retire until her task was completed. Recognizing her distress, she said to Kieran, "Excuse me, my lord. I will be but a few moments."

As she crossed the room she saw him stride to the fireplace and stare deeply into the flames as he lifted the goblet to his lips. He seemed filled with a restless energy.

Following Aileen into her sleeping chamber, Megan allowed her maid to remove her soiled clothes. While Megan washed herself in a small basin, the little maid brought forward a clean gown for her approval.

"Nay, Aileen. I will dress for bed."

"But my lord O'Mara . . ."

"Will not mind if I do not dress appropriately to sup with him." Her laughter trilled in the quiet of the room. "I know that Mistress Peake would have your hide if she thought you did not prepare me for bed before taking your own rest. So," she added conspiratorially, "you shall prepare me for bed and then you will retire for the night."

"Oh, my lady. You are so kind and thoughtful." Aileen laid out a nightgown of palest ivory.

"Nay. I am merely being practical. You need your sleep. And I needed to be rid of those soiled clothes." As she dressed, Megan felt the whisper of silk against her skin. Over the nightgown Aileen helped her into a flowing robe of ivory silk inset with delicate lace on the collar and wide sleeves.

Aileen brushed Megan's hair until it gleamed, then caught it up in two ivory combs.

"Do you require anything more, my lady?"

"Nay, Aileen. Go now and take your rest. Mistress Peake cannot accuse you of shirking your duties."

"Good night, my lady. And thank you." The little maid stifled a yawn as she made her way across the room.

In the sitting chamber Mistress Peake bustled around with an air of importance, taking care that every detail of the late-night meal was perfect. A table was set before the fireplace with snowy linens and gleaming crystal goblets. A sideboard groaned with hastily prepared dishes of cold venison, partridge and dove and breads toasted in the fire for the lord of the manor.

When all was in readiness, the housekeeper dismissed the servants and bowed her way from the room.

Megan stood hesitantly in the doorway, studying the man who still stood, his hand resting along the mantel, his brooding gaze fixed on the flames.

He had removed his cloak and tunic and tossed them carelessly over a chaise. He wore only an ivory shirt and slim fitted breeches.

Where did he go when he shut out the world and stared without seeing? Was there some secret place within him? A place where she could never go?

Gathering her courage, Megan lifted her skirts and entered the sitting chamber.

Kieran turned to watch her. God in heaven, she was beautiful beyond belief. When she crossed the room he was drawn to her. But he would not yet allow himself to touch her. For if he did, he feared he would take her like a brute.

He held her chair as she sat at the table.

"Ale, my lady?" He filled her goblet and offered it to her.

"Thank you." She sipped and felt the warmth of it swim through her veins, chasing away the chill that had suddenly come upon her.

Though he was attentive to her every need, he seemed aloof, as though his thoughts were far away.

He filled her plate and his own, and together they began to eat.

"I will have to remember to tell Mistress Peake she g[...] better with each meal. Or perhaps," Megan said with laugh, "I am so hungry that anything would taste good.'

Kieran leaned back, sipping his ale and watching her o[...] the rim of his goblet. His food was barely touched.

"You are," she said, taking a sip of ale, "a man of ma[...] surprises, my lord."

"In what way?"

"When I first awoke in the forest, I thought you wer[...] villain. And later, when you admitted having escaped fr[...] Fleet, I was certain of it."

"And now?"

She smiled. "There are so many Kieran O'Maras. T[...] fierce warrior, the loving son and brother, the loyal frie[...] the noble leader of his people." She arched an eyebro[...] "Which one are you tonight?"

He reached across the table and caught her hand in h[...] Instantly her pulse leaped.

He gave her a dangerous smile. "Which one would y[...] like me to be?"

"Be whatever you want to be." She was suddenly u[...] comfortable. He was so quiet. Quiet and thoughtful. A[...] she knew she was babbling. "I should retire now, my lord[...]

She set down her glass and got to her feet. But when s[...] stood, he was standing beside her. Their hands were s[...] linked.

He saw the confusion in her eyes. He looked calm a[...] determined.

"What is wrong, my lord?"

"Something happened tonight, Megan."

"Aye. A child stepped back from death's door."

"Nay. Something of even greater import."

She waited, watching his eyes.

"I realized I was in love with you."

Megan's heart seemed to stop beating for several se[...] onds. "You are confused, my lord. You are merely mirr[...] ing the gratitude of the crofter and his wife."

"Nay." His voice was low, almost stern, and his gaze was steady. "All the confusion is gone. I see clearly now what I have tried for so long to deny. I love you, Megan. What is more, I made a vow that I would share my love with you before the morrow." He gazed beyond her to the balcony window. "There are still several hours before the dawn."

Tremors rippled through her. Fear? she wondered. Or anticipation? She should be shocked. But though her pulse leaped at his words, she knew it was what she wanted, too. For too long she had denied the feelings in her heart for this man.

Love. Aye. She loved him. And had for a long time. But the very thought of showing him her love had her terrified.

"You do not know me, my lord. I am a stranger even to myself."

"I know everything I need to know about you, Megan. You are a rare woman. And you own my heart."

She backed away until his fingers laced with hers held her firmly. "I..." She licked her lips and tried again. "I believe that you care for me, Kieran, but..."

"Care for?" He drew her fractionally closer. "I care for my steed. I care for the people of my villages." His eyes blazed. "But I love only one woman, Megan. And I will wait no longer to show you how much I love you."

He brought his hands to her shoulders and stared into her eyes as he drew her close. His mouth covered hers in a savage kiss.

There seemed to be no gentleness in him now. He was all fire and passion and need. His lips moved over hers, taking, then giving, then taking, until she was drained. His tongue sought hers, thrusting, demanding, until she was breathless.

Feelings pulsed through her that only his kiss had ever awakened. Each time they had come together, he had uncovered another layer of passion. But this time the passion bordered on pain.

"Say you will stay with me this night." His words we[re] muttered fiercely against her lips.

Touching a hand to his proudly chiseled face she whi[s]pered, "I had once thought I could not give my love unti[l I] learned my name. But with you, my name no longer ma[t]ters. Show me, Kieran. Teach me."

For a moment Kieran was speechless as he stared at he[r.] Did she know what effect her words had on him? There w[as] nothing she could have said that would inflame him more[.]

"Oh, my lady." Lifting her hands to his mouth, he bu[r]ied his lips in first one palm, then the other. "I have thoug[ht] of nothing but you for so long now. God in heaven, I a[m] consumed with the thought of loving you."

Their gazes met and held, and he saw that her fear ha[d] been replaced with something else. Taking her hand he le[d] her toward his sleeping chamber.

The bed linens had been turned down. A fire burning [in] the fireplace was the only illumination in the room. It wa[s] so quiet Megan could hear the unsteady beating of he[r] heart. And then she became aware of the hiss and snap [of] the flames as they licked along the bark of a log.

Kieran crossed the room, leaving her alone for a mo[o]ment, and she glanced at the door. But though it tempte[d] her, she could not run. She was bound as surely as if he sti[ll] held her in his arms. Bound by a need as strong as his.

She watched as he held a taper to the fire. Setting it on th[e] bedside table, he moved to her, his eyes dark and unfat[h]omable.

"I need to see you while I love you," he said as his hand[s] moved to the combs that held her hair. As he removed them[,] her hair tumbled around her face and shoulders in a riot o[f] curls.

He plunged his hands into the tangles and drew her hea[d] back. "How long I have waited." Slowly, hungrily, he nib[b]led her lips until she sighed and drew him closer. He lin[g]ered over her lips, savoring the sweet taste of her.

With strong, sure movements he undid the buttons of her robe.

In the glow of the candle his face was dark and dangerous. And beautiful, she realized, as he slipped the robe from her shoulders.

He felt her tremble as the robe drifted to the floor. "Are you afraid, Megan?"

She swallowed and cursed the fear that coursed through her, leaving her shaking like the flower petals in the wind. "Aye."

He felt a rush of heat at the knowledge that his touch could affect her so. This proud, brave little beauty, who trembled before no man, was quivering before him. He touched a finger to her cheek in a gesture so achingly sweet she caught her breath.

"Do not fear, little warrior. There is so much we can teach one another."

He studied the way she looked, her slender figure barely covered by the sheer silk nightgown, her hair spilling across her shoulders in a tumble of curls. He drew her into the circle of his arms and covered her lips in a savage kiss.

He could feel her, soft and pliant, as his fingers found the ribbons that laced the bodice of her nightgown. He slid the fabric from her shoulders, then bent to follow its path with his lips.

He felt her shudder as she reached for the buttons of his shirt and struggled to undress him. When her fingers encountered his bare flesh, he gave a moan of pleasure.

"How long I have waited to have you touch me."

Her hands whispered over his skin until he could bear it no longer. With one fluid movement he picked her up and carried her to his bed. They lay tangled together in the bed linens. The only barrier between them was the silk of her nightgown, still clinging to her breasts. With soft, nibbling kisses he caressed her face. She sighed and gave herself up to his tender ministrations. But just as she relaxed, his teeth tugged at her earlobe and his tongue began thrusting, tor-

menting her, until she sighed and caught his face betwee
her hands, forcing his mouth on hers.

He was hungry to touch all of her, taste all of her. H
found her breast, small and firm, and he began to nibb
and suckle until she moaned and writhed beneath him.

With his teeth he drew the sheer bodice of her nightgow
away from her until her breasts were freed from that la:
barrier. His lips found her bare flesh, arousing her until sh
arched and cried out his name. And then, with a feeling (
desperation, he tugged and tore the last of her garment sav
agely from her, needing her warm and naked and willing.

He left her no time to think. Now she could only feel a
she moved with him, flooded by dozens of different sens;
tions that left her dazed.

Never before had she lost control. Never had she been s
assaulted by so many different feelings. Feelings that too'
her higher, then higher still, until she soared to the hea\
ens.

With his lips and fingers he took her to the first crest, unt
she shuddered and clutched at his arms, whispering hi
name.

He had a desperate desire to take her wildly, savagely, bu
he fought down the need. Instead, forcing himself to slowl
savor the moment, he rolled over, pulling her on top of him
and kissed her with a fierceness that left them both shaker

Leaning on one elbow, she tentatively touched a hand t
his chest. Abruptly he went very still, loving the feel of he
fingertips on his flesh.

"Did I do something wrong?"

From beneath lowered lids he murmured, "Nay, littl
warrior. Touch me again."

With awkward, halting movements she touched a finge
to the scars that marked his chest. "I cannot bear to thin
that a cowardly jailer inflicted these on you. Oh, Kieran.'
With an anguished sigh she bent her lips to the scars. "I
only I could take away all the pain you have endured."

His stomach muscles contracted violently. With a wild rush of heat he plunged his hands into her hair and drew her face down for a kiss. "You already have, love. All the pain of the past is forgotten when you touch me."

"I love touching you." Growing bolder, she knelt, and with her hair swirling around them both, traced a finger across his lips, then bent to follow the path with her tongue.

For long minutes he lay still while she kissed his throat, his chest, his stomach. But when she brought her lips lower, he moaned before catching her in his arms and rolling over her.

"Please, Kieran. Love me," she whispered.

But still he held back, raining kisses across her cheek, down her neck, across her shoulder.

Steeped in pleasure, she could only lie helplessly beneath him as his lips and fingers stripped away her last shred of control. She was no longer the fiery warrior. There was no thought of battle, of winning. Here there were no rules of warfare. There was only a wild abandonment, a wanton desire to glory in his touch and fill herself with this man.

Her stomach quivered as his lips moved across the flat planes and along the flare of her hip to her inner thigh. She arched toward him, begging him to end this torment. But still he drove her higher.

This was how he had dreamed of her. Passionate, desperate. His woman. Only his. He knew from her reaction that she had never before given herself to a man. That knowledge fueled his passion until he felt himself slip over the edge toward madness.

He could no longer bank his desire. He took her with a fierceness that left them both gasping.

She had known he would be a reckless, dangerous lover. From the beginning she had sensed the unbridled passion that lurked beneath his infuriatingly cold demeanor. Cold. Nay. There was nothing cold about the man who had taken her to the very edge of madness, then beyond. The heat, the fire, the passion burned her as they moved together in a wild, throbbing dance of love.

She moved with him, matching his strength, matching his needs, as they climbed higher. When they reached the crest her eyes opened, meeting his. Their breath trembled from between parted lips.

He wanted to remember her always like this, dazed with need, hungry for fulfillment.

He cried her name, or thought he did, as they soared through a black velvet night and lost themselves among the stars.

They lay, still locked in an embrace. With his lips pressed to a tangle of hair at her temple, Kieran held her as tenderly as if she were a fragile doll.

He kissed away the sheen that beaded her forehead, then lightly touched her lips with his.

He loved her. The thought filled him with such wonder he was still dazed by it. Love. That he should love this wild little creature, who had first captured his admiration as she stood in a meadow with a sword in her hand, was a source of amazement to him.

He saw her eyes fill with tears and quickly rolled to one side, gathering her close.

"God in heaven. I have hurt you."

"Nay." She turned her head, ashamed of the tears. "It is just that I have never known such a feeling. Oh, Kieran," she said, wrapping her arms around his waist and burying her lips in his throat. "I love you so much."

"You love me?"

She could not speak over the lump in her throat. Instead she merely nodded and began to weep.

"Oh, Megan. My wild little warrior." With his lips pressed to a tangle of her hair he began to murmur words of endearment. She loved him. It was more than he had hoped for.

He felt a wild surge of protectiveness toward this fierce, brave little woman. She was so far from her people. So alone. But, he vowed fervently, she would never be lonely again.

He kissed the slope of her shoulder, then buried his lips in the little hollow of her throat. It was not possible to want her again so soon. But as he held her and comforted her, he felt his passion rising. With kisses and touches and whispered words, they tumbled once more into a world reserved for lovers.

Chapter Seventeen

Pale dawn light filtered through the balcony window. Two figures lay tangled together, their breathing soft and easy.

Megan lay very still, studying Kieran as he slept. All night they had loved, slept, then loved again. And each time they had discovered something new about each other.

Shyly at first, then more boldly, she had explored his body as he had explored hers. How different his body was from hers. And yet how perfectly they complemented one another. Her gaze moved over him. How strong his jaw. How smooth his brow. His long lashes made spiky shadows across his cheeks. In repose he looked younger and much less fierce, as though he had not a care in the world.

She stared at his lips. Such inviting lips. She longed to trace their outline with a fingertip, but she feared waking him. Her gaze moved over his chin and throat, darkened with a stubble of growth. It was somehow oddly appealing to see him like this.

Who would have ever believed she could love that savage villain who had so frightened her during their early encounters? Yet she did love him. With a fierceness that astounded her.

"Do you like what you see?"

His words startled her. Glancing up, she saw his eyes, heavy-lidded, watching her.

Laughter lurked in her eyes. "I have always been fond of hairy creatures, my lord. Dogs. Goats."

"Goats? Are you calling me a goat?"

Sitting up, she touched a hand to the stubble on his chin. "A bristly boar, perhaps."

He caught her wrist and dragged her across his chest. Even now she was surprised by the strength in his grasp. "Be very careful, my lady. I expect a little respect from my wenches after a night like the last."

"Oh? Was last night any different from other nights, my lord?"

"Disrespectful woman. Unlike every other night of your life, you spent last night in paradise. As did I."

"Heaven last night," she said with a husky laugh, "hell on the morrow."

"This devil can be transformed into a saint by a single kiss from you, my lady." He pulled her face close for a long, satisfying kiss. "Is this the way you have been awakened in the past?"

With a giggle she replied, "I can truthfully say that I do not recall how I was awakened before I met you, my lord."

"If you had ever been this thoroughly kissed, I wager you would remember."

"Really?" She propped herself on her elbows and stared into his eyes. "Mayhap we should try it again, just to be certain."

He drew her close and nuzzled her lips until he groaned and, catching her by surprise, rolled until he pinned her beneath him.

"Now, my lady," he said, moving his mouth slowly, languidly along her throat, sending shivers of delight along her spine, "about that memory of yours."

She laughed as his mouth covered hers in a searing kiss. Her laughter became a low moan of pleasure as his hands, his lips, sent her once more tumbling into a world of pleasure.

* * *

Morning sunlight spilled into the room, and still Megan
and Kieran lingered in bed. Outside their room, in the hall
ways, in the sitting chambers, they could hear the sounds of
activity as the servants went about their daily chores. The
tantalizing fragrances of roasting meat and baking bread
wafted from below stairs, making them aware of their need
for food. But the hunger that gnawed at them could not be
assuaged by bread and meat. They filled their hearts and
souls with murmured words of endearment and whispered
confidences. They laughed easily, as the tensions fell away.
They feasted upon each other until they were filled to over
flowing with love.

Lying comfortably in Kieran's arms, Megan barely moved
when she heard the gentle knock upon the door to his sit
ting chamber.

"My lord" came Aileen's hushed voice.

"Aye." With his finger he traced the curve of Megan's
cheek to her jaw, then slowly across her lips. He swore when
she laughingly bit him.

"I did not wish to disturb you." All the castle was abuzz
with the knowledge that Lady Megan had not spent the
night in her own bed.

The little servant paused, then added, "I have prepared a
bath in the sitting chamber. Your mother and the others
have gathered in the refectory to break their fast."

"Thank you."

With a sly laugh Megan brought her lips to his throat and
began to move her mouth slowly, seductively, across Kier
an's chest.

"My lord?" Aileen's voice was muffled through the
closed door.

Kieran moaned softly as Megan's lips tormented him.
"Aye?"

"Do you desire anything further?"

"Nay." He caught at Megan and hauled her upward un
til their lips were brushing. "Tell my guests I will join them

n the refectory soon." His mouth closed over Megan's, tilling her words of exclamation.

"Aye, my lord."

As the maid's footsteps retreated, Megan burst into gales of laughter. "Did you speak the truth, my lord? Do you truly desire nothing further?"

"You little wench." With his lips crushing hers he muttered thickly, "Time with you is all I desire."

They came together with a rush of heat that had them both gasping.

Everyone looked up when Megan and Kieran entered the refectory.

Bridget, who had been waiting for Megan, flew into her arms and clung to her for long minutes. Their mutual affection was not lost on the others.

Lady Katherine's face was wreathed in smiles. "Hugh has told us how you saved the child in the village, my dear. I had feared the worst. I am so relieved. And so grateful."

As Megan took the seat offered her by Kieran, she lifted Bridget onto her lap. "It is I who am grateful. Grateful that, despite my loss of memory, I can recall the use of healing herbs. I would like to repay the generosity you have shown me by sharing my knowledge with the women of your villages, my lady."

"Oh, my dear. How generous you are." As she spoke, Lady Katherine was struck by the look of pride on her son's countenance. Did he not know how much was revealed in that look? Anyone could tell by looking at him that he adored the young woman beside him. Never before had he looked so relaxed, so content.

This young woman, with no past, no memory, was good for Kieran, Lady Katherine decided. She only hoped that her son would be wise enough to realize that and take her as wife. Perhaps she would find a time soon to speak to him about it. Or perhaps, she thought with sudden insight, she would be wise to say nothing. Kieran treasured his privacy.

And he had been especially withdrawn since his return fro~
England.

"Will you teach me, too?" Bridget chirped.

"Aye. It would be good for you to learn." Mega~
dropped light kisses on the girl's upturned face.

"If you would like," Lady Katherine said excitedly, "w~
can ride to the village today and you can begin the le~
sons."

"Surely you do not intend to pick herbs and roots wit~
the peasants?" Sir Cecil's voice held a note of contempt a~
he turned to the woman beside him.

The smiles froze on the faces of those at table. Megan fe~
the little girl tremble in her arms.

"Indeed I do. I have always regretted that I could not he~
Sean's people when they needed me," Lady Katherine sai~
softly.

"I need not remind you that Sean is dead. You are to b~
my wife now. If you become ill, the Queen's own physicia~
will see to you."

"And what about my people?"

"The lass will teach them what they need to know. Yo~
need not bother yourself with such things."

Kieran's mouth tightened into a grim, tight line, an~
Megan felt him stiffen beside her as he fought to keep hi~
temper under control. In low tones he said, "No man speak~
to my mother with such disrespect."

"The lady is to be my wife. Or have you forgotten?"

"I have forgotten nothing. Wife or no, you will treat he~
as you would your Queen."

Across the table James Kettering seethed with anger. Hi~
father, one of the most influential men at Elizabeth's court~
was being openly lectured by this traitorous rebel.

"Hold your tongue," Sir Cecil said sharply, "or you wil~
find yourself no longer welcome under my roof."

"Your roof?" Kieran's hands balled into fists.

Lady Katherine gently placed a hand on Kieran's arm~
then turned to Sir Cecil. "Castle O'Mara will always be~

long to Sean's sons, Cecil. I had thought you would understand."

"I understand that your sons, madame, will have to learn who is master of Killamara."

With a stricken look, Megan reached a hand to Kieran. With his eyes blazing he shoved away from the table and stormed out of the room.

Tavis Downey got to his feet and glanced around the table, then said to Lady Katherine, "You always said he inherited his father's temper, my lady. When he has a chance to calm himself, he will be back to beg your pardon." His boots beat a tattoo across the wooden floor as he followed his friend.

In the terrible silence that ensued, Lady Katherine turned to Megan. "As soon as we have finished breaking our fast, I will send a servant to the village to prepare the women for your visit." Shooting a quick, sidelong glance at Sir Cecil, she added softly, "I will be unable to accompany you."

Her deference to Sir Cecil's wishes caused another deadly silence. It was Hugh Cleary who finally spoke.

"I would be happy to accompany you to the village, my dear." To the others at table he added, "The Lady Megan is a most apt teacher. The lass's healing powers are nothing less than miraculous."

Megan shot him a grateful smile.

Across the table, James Kettering continued to fume. His eyes narrowed. Kieran O'Mara. How he hated him. The Irish scum was no longer trying to hide his feelings. It was obvious that he would not sanction his mother's marriage. He would have to be brought to heel. And soon. Or all would be lost.

James glanced at the young woman who had become uncomfortably silent since Kieran's departure. From the proprietary way Kieran had filled Megan's plate and watched with pride as she spoke, it was obvious that he had staked a claim on the Scotswoman. It was as if . . . James's eyes narrowed in sudden horror. Of course. There was no doubt in

James's mind. The two had become intimate. It was so li▌
O'Mara to win the most coveted prize of all.

James turned toward his father, who sat brooding besi▌
Lady Katherine. "I would speak with you, Father, abo▌
urgent business."

Pushing away from the table, James left the room wit▌
out a word. Within minutes his father followed.

Bishop O'Mara concluded the Mass and led the cluster ▌
black-robed priests across the courtyard toward the cast▌
doors. He had officiated in cathedrals in Rome and most ▌
Europe, as well as in Ireland. But there was something e▌
pecially satisfying about the simple chapel on the cast▌
grounds. As a lad he had found solace here, away from th▌
talk of war that always seemed to echo in the rooms of Ca▌
tle O'Mara. It was both a blessing and a curse that he w▌
descended from generations of warriors. He understood th▌
passion that drove a man to fight for what was his. But h▌
vehemently detested the violence of war.

As he entered the refectory, he glanced around. "Whe▌
is Father Malone?" he asked.

The priests shrugged.

One of them commented, "I saw him kneeling in praye▌
in the chapel."

"Ahh." Bishop O'Mara relaxed and began filling hi▌
plate. "He prays, no doubt, for a safe journey."

"When do you leave?" Lady Katherine, relieved that S▌
Cecil and James had left, taking the tensions with them▌
filled the bishop's goblet with hot mulled wine.

"Three days hence. As soon as your banns have bee▌
spoken from the pulpit and your marriage is blessed, I wi▌
have your servants pack our horses and carts with the nec▌
essary supplies, my dear."

"You will not reconsider and remain with us a whil▌
longer? It would please me greatly if you would stay on her▌
at Castle O'Mara. The villagers would welcome your heal▌
ing presence among them. And I would treasure Sean'▌

rother by my side." Especially now that Sir Cecil was
howing her another side of his powerful personality, she
eflected.

The bishop kept his features carefully schooled. He had
nade his bargain with Sir Cecil. In exchange for his bless-
ng upon this union, the innocent villagers of Killamara
vould be spared the ravages of war. The bishop admired his
ister-in-law for her willingness to make this sacrifice for the
ove of others. But he did not wish to stay and watch as his
amily holdings fell under the domination of this brute.

"I have already been away from my duties for too long. I
lare not tarry once you are wed." The bishop glanced
round and said, "I did not see Colin at Mass this morrow.
Nor do I see him now."

Lady Katherine, who had been too busy until now to take
notice, looked perplexed. "I have not seen Colin today."
She glanced at Terence O'Byrne, who sat beside his son.
Both men had been unusually quiet. "Have you seen Colin
his morrow?"

"Not I." Terence O'Byrne turned to his son. "Conor,
where is Colin?"

"Most probably he is still abed." Conor ducked his head
and continued to eat.

"Aye," the bishop said. "He always was a frail one."

Megan noted the flush on Conor's cheeks. He was hiding something. But what?

Conor thought about the things Colin had confided in
him. Though they had known each other for a lifetime,
Conor was still reeling from this latest surprise. He realized
that he ought to tell someone about Colin's plans, but he
could not bring himself to betray a confidence. Besides, he
was secretly pleased.

When they had finished their meal, Megan and Bridget
went off to fetch warm traveling cloaks. As they passed the
drawing room Megan saw Sir Cecil and his son standing
before the fireplace, their heads bent in earnest conversation.

Without another glance Megan caught Bridget's hand
hers and hurried away.

"How could you allow that cur to speak to you in such
manner?" James demanded. "I wanted to cut out I
tongue."

"And you shall," Sir Cecil said in a dangerously sc
voice. "Very soon now. The fool has no idea that he is on
again being betrayed by one who calls himself friend."

"Aye. But can we trust this...friend to remain loyal to u
Or will he turn on us as he turned on O'Mara?"

"We have the advantage. We trust no one. When this
over, he will die with the O'Maras, and no one will be tl
wiser."

James smiled for a moment, then his frown returne
"What of the Scotswoman? You saw the way O'Ma
treated her. I tell you, he has already made her his." Jam
paced in front of the fireplace. His eyes were dark with fur
"There is no mistaking the looks that passed betwee
them."

"All the better."

James turned on his father. "Are you mad? If she ha
tasted his love, she will not willingly leave him for anothe
no matter how compelling the reasons."

"We will give her no choice." Sir Cecil gave a chilli
laugh. "Do you not see? It will be even easier to overpowe
Kieran O'Mara if he is mad with distraction over the las
And he will go mad when he learns her fate." He clapped h
hands together. "Oh, this could not be better." Draping a
arm around his son he muttered, "The fish have all falle
into our nets. All we need do now is drag them in and watc
them slowly gasp for breath." As he led James toward tl
door he said, "Summon your man. It is time to introduc
the Scotswoman to her past."

Chapter Eighteen

Father Arden Malone was tall and slender as a sapling. Sparse brown hair fell across his high forehead. His fingers were long and tapered, and when he lifted a hand in blessing, the faithful felt as if they had been blessed by God Himself. His eyes reflected a kindness of spirit that invited trust. At the monastery he had been considered an outstanding scholar and would have surely climbed the ranks to bishop or cardinal, except for one thing. All he really wanted was to be a simple parish priest and minister to his flock.

He loved the people of this poor land. Loved them with the fierce protectiveness of a father. For so long now his people had been oppressed. He understood their fears for their children, their frustrations with the monarch across the sea and the pope across the continent who controlled their destiny. There were few decisions that were held in their own hands. But he was determined that he would honor what precious few decisions they could make for themselves.

Father Malone had grown up in a large, loving family. His father and brothers were men of the soil, who loved their animals and plots of land as much as their women and children. They were simple people, as proud of their eldest son, who had been born deaf and mute, as their youngest, whose mind was far superior to anything they could imagine.

Arden Malone had been hugged by his mother and sisters since he was born. He had watched his siblings fall in love, marry and bear many children. His nieces and nephews swarmed over him during his frequent visits to their homes. All of this made him, unlike many of the priests in his company, as comfortable with women as with men.

Thus it was natural that Cara O'Byrne, in her torment, had sought him out. He had listened with compassion as she told him about her feelings for Colin O'Mara, and their attempts to put aside their love in order to serve God. At Cara's urging, Colin had also turned to Father Malone after his unhappy discussion with his uncle, the bishop. The priest had listened in stony silence to the promise Bishop O'Mara had extracted from these two young people. And he had watched as they struggled heroically with their conflicting feelings of love. He knew, with a certainty born of faith and trust in the rightness of God's love, what he must do.

Now, as he stood in the silent chapel, he spoke the Latin words while he broke the bread and tasted the wine. Morning sunshine spilled across the polished wood of the altar. The sharp tang of incense still lingered on the air. Outside the window a bird sent up a plaintive cry, and far away another one responded. He turned to watch as the two birds soared together until they seemed to touch the sun.

"Two," he said aloud. "It is as God intended. In all of nature, there is one who fulfills the other."

Walking toward the young couple, who knelt with bowed heads, he touched a hand to their shoulders and said, "You have spoken your vows before God. Go now and love one another. You are one name, one heart, one spirit."

His words seemed to bounce off the walls and echo around the empty chapel.

With shining eyes, the two young people stood and faced each other. Tears ran down Cara's cheeks, and she brushed them away with the back of her hand. All her life she had dreamed of a joyous wedding, surrounded by her family and riends who would wish them well. But this ceremony, attended only by the gentle priest, had moved her to tears. She needed no wild celebration to mark this day. It was enough to know that she and Colin were wed.

Colin pressed a kiss to Cara's palm, then turned to Father Malone. "What about the bishop? Will he not seek to annul our marriage when he learns we have defied his rule?"

"Fear neither the bishop nor any man. What God has joined together," Father Malone intoned solemnly, "let no man put asunder."

As Megan, Bridget and Hugh Cleary returned from the village, they saw Kieran, astride his horse, approaching them from the surrounding forest. By his side rode Tavis Downey. Both horses, blowing and snorting from exertion, were lathered and covered with dust. It was obvious they had ridden hard for many miles.

Megan understood Kieran's need to ride, hard and fast, when his mind was in turmoil.

"How did the lessons go?" Kieran asked as he pulled his horse alongside Megan's.

"Very well." Megan felt her cheeks redden when Kieran unexpectedly caught her hand and laced his fingers through hers. "The women were eager pupils."

"Lady Megan showed us which herbs to pick and how to grind them into a paste for a soothing balm," Bridget said.

"I have had the good fortune to experience the lady's balm on my own wounds," Kieran said. "As did Colin. I believe he would not have survived the rigors of our journey without it."

Hugh and Tavis were aware of the passion behind his words.

"When we were leaving," Bridget said with awe, "the women kissed her hands."

"Like this?" Kieran lifted Megan's hand to his lips while the others laughed.

"Aye."

Kieran looked with pride from the woman beside him
the lass who sat her horse as easily as if she had been bo
to it. It was amazing what changes Megan had brought
their lives. There was color to Bridget's cheeks. And a fi
in her eyes that had been missing since the loss of her pa
ents. For the first time Kieran began to believe that his nie
would not only survive her loss, but would thrive.

"So, Bridget. Are you now going to grow up to be a so
dier or a healer?"

"Lady Megan says it is possible to be anything I choos
So I will be both a soldier and a healer. Like her."

Hugh Cleary chuckled. "Beware, my friend. It woul
seem the lady has an answer for everything."

"So I have noticed. Is she not a remarkable woman?"

Seeing the intimacy between Kieran and Megan, Tav
Downey arched an eyebrow in surprise. "So, Kieran, ha
someone finally laid claim to your heart?"

"Aye."

"Be warned, my lady," Tavis said with a laugh. "Man
a lass has dreamed of taming this rogue. But always, whe
he tires of the chase, he leaves them sobbing in their motl
er's arms."

Kieran squeezed Megan's hand. "This lady does not cr
easily, old friend. And I have no intention of leaving her.'

When they entered the castle, Bridget rushed into th
great room where her grandmother waited impatiently t
hear about her day in the village. But when Hugh and Tavi
glanced around for Kieran and Megan, they were nowher
to be seen.

With a knowing look Hugh said, "It would seem the lov
ers prefer their own company, my friend."

"Aye." Tavis looked perplexed. "Could it be he trul
loves her?"

Hugh glanced at Tavis in surprise. Beads of perspiratio
beaded his upper lip and forehead. He looked, Hug
thought, like someone who carried a terrible weight upon hi
shoulders.

* * *

"I needed you with me this day." Kieran's words were whispered against her throat as Megan lay in his arms.

"You had Tavis."

"He is a poor substitute for the woman I love."

She touched a hand to his face and stared deeply into his eyes. "Say that again."

"That Tavis is a poor substitute?"

"Nay." She laughed, then grew serious. "The rest."

"You are the woman I love." He leaned close, nibbling her lips and sending her heart soaring. "The woman who means more to me than life itself. God in heaven, Megan. I love you so much it frightens me."

With his lips, his fingertips, he led her on a slow, sensuous journey. Their lovemaking took on a tenderness, a gentleness that neither had experienced before. As if, she thought, steeped in pleasure, they had all the time in the world.

"Why do you suppose your mother agreed to a betrothal between herself and Sir Cecil Kettering?" Megan asked as she lay in Kieran's arms, her legs tangled with his.

She immediately regretted her words as beside her Kieran went very still.

It was many moments before he spoke. "Long before my mother lost her heart to my father, her betrothal to Sir Cecil was arranged by her family and King Henry."

"Aye. Colin has told me. But that was many years ago, when they were mere children. What has that to do with now?"

Kieran swung his feet to the floor and looked away, reluctant to reply. "Perhaps they have always carried a secret love for one another in their hearts." His voice was low, angry. "My father has been dead a long time. Colin and I have been in prison. My mother was left alone, with no one to comfort her."

"Lady Katherine is a strong woman, Kieran. She woul
not turn to a man simply for comfort."

Kieran's voice turned to ice. "Then perhaps she misses he
childhood home. Or the luxuries she has forsaken. Fo
whatever reason, she has pledged herself to a brute. N
matter what my feelings for the man, I have no right to in
terfere. She is free to marry again, if her heart desires."

"But I have watched them." Megan touched a hand to hi
shoulder to stay his departure from the bed. "It is not lov
I see in their eyes when they look at each other, Kieran."

He turned on her, pain and anger blazing in his dark eyes
"I will speak no more of this." Then, seeing the way hi
words hurt her, he reached a hand to her cheek and felt th
anger slowly dissolve. "You can ask me anything else, m
little warrior. Anything. But I cannot speak of my moth
er's betrothal to Sir Cecil. Do you understand?"

She nodded and drew him to her. To ease his pain she of
fered her lips to him and felt the passion once more rise
This time their lovemaking was frenzied, as if to hold thei
troubled words and thoughts at bay.

But later, when she could once more gather her thoughts
she resolved that, though she would speak no more abou
Lady Katherine and Sir Cecil, she would watch and listen.

As he dressed for the evening meal, Kieran heard Meg
an's laughter in the next room as she and her maid talke
and laughed with each other. At the sound of a door bein
opened, he peered through the doorway at the sight of littl
Bridget rushing into Megan's arms. Together Megan and
Aileen brushed the girl's thick, tangled tresses. It was ob
vious, from her giggles, that she thoroughly enjoyed bein
fussed over.

How he loved the sound of laughter echoing once mor
through the halls of Castle O'Mara. It had been such a lon
time. And perhaps, he thought, thinking of his mother'
pending nuptials, the day would soon come when the
laughter would die again. This time forever.

He paused before pulling on his tunic. He had mulled
over many things this day while he rode the hills of Killamara. Though he had never confided this to his mother in
his younger days, Kieran had seen and heard much that
disgusted him while in service to the Queen. He had witnessed the underhanded way Sir Cecil had obtained wealth,
title, privilege through his influence with Elizabeth. The
man was ruthless in obtaining more wealth, more titles than
any other man in the kingdom. He had betrayed friend and
foe alike to take possession of their holdings.

During his ride, Kieran had come to a decision. He would
never be able to accept Sir Cecil as his mother's husband. It
would be like a knife to the heart to see the man assume his
father's place in Killamara. There was but one thing to do.
He must leave and make a life for himself somewhere else.
Somewhere far away from this place he loved as much as life
itself.

He glanced again at the scene in the sitting chamber and
felt his heart lift above the pain. Though leaving Killamara
would be the hardest thing he had ever done, there was one
thing that would make it all bearable. This night, when they
returned to their sleeping chamber, he would ask Megan to
be his wife. He would take her to Scotland, to seek her people. Even if her memory never returned, they would make
a life for themselves. And he would spend a lifetime trying
to make her happy.

With a smile he stepped from the room. The sight that
greeted him took his breath away. Megan wore a gown of
scarlet satin that molded her high, firm breasts and tiny
waist, then fell in graceful folds to the tips of her slippers.
Her hair had been brushed until it gleamed, then entwined
with scarlet ribbons and tiny red roses. It fell over one
shoulder, covering her breast, before spilling in soft waves
to her waist.

"Oh, my lady," he breathed. "You are magnificent."

She walked to him with a look of love and touched a hand
to his sleeve. "And you, my lord, are the reason I took such

pains with my appearance this night. I wanted you to s
only me."

"You are all I can see, Megan. And all I ever will."

They swept from the room, with Bridget giggling an
trailing behind.

The voices in the great room stopped abruptly as Mega
and Kieran entered. James, who had been boasting of h
life in England, could not tear his gaze from the woman b
side Kieran. She was a rare beauty. And soon, he thoug
with a cruel smile touching his lips, she would be his for th
taking. That knowledge made him more disdainful of thos
around him.

Kieran glanced around. "Where is my mother?"

"She and my father have not yet come below stairs. Pe
haps," James said with a sly smile, "they could not wa
until they speak their vows two days hence."

Hugh Cleary's eyes narrowed. "That is crude, James
And unbecoming in the lady's own household."

"No more crude than your insistence upon staying unde
this roof until the wedding."

"I am here at Lady Katherine's request."

"You are here," James said with a sneer, "because yo
desire the lady for yourself. And you foolishly hope that
even now, she will change her mind and you will becom
master of Castle O'Mara and all of Killamara."

Megan was stunned at James's outburst. But his word
made her think. Glancing at Hugh, she recalled the tender
ness with which he always treated Lady Katherine. O
course. It had been there all along, if only one took the tim
to look. He loved Lady Katherine. And if truth be told, th
lady shared his feelings. All Lady Katherine's features, eve
her voice, seemed to take on a softness when she spoke to
Hugh. Megan berated herself. Why had she not seen i
sooner?

The others had grown uncomfortably silent.

"Is that all Lady Katherine means to you and your father?" Hugh demanded sharply. "This fortress? This land?"

James's features twisted into a look of vicious hatred, and for a moment he forgot to be careful. "She has much more..."

"James."

At the sound of Sir Cecil's harsh tone, his son whirled. With great effort he controlled his emotions until his face took on a bland expression.

"Were you entertaining our guests?"

"Aye, Father." James glanced at the others, who were staring at him with stunned looks. "We were speaking of your impending vows."

"Two days." Sir Cecil turned as Lady Katherine swept into the room, followed by the bishop and his flock of black-robed priests. "If only it could be tonight, my dear."

Lady Katherine forced herself to show no revulsion as Sir Cecil lifted her hand to his mouth. But when he bent to brush his lips over her cheek, she drew quickly away.

Her reaction was not lost on Megan. But Kieran had already turned away to greet Terence O'Byrne and his son.

Terence glanced around the room, then turned to Kieran with a frown of concern. "Have you seen Cara today?"

"Nay." Kieran turned to Megan. "Have you seen Cara?"

She shook her head.

"Nor has anyone else," Terence said, his voice barely above a whisper. "I do not wish to alarm the others, but none of the servants have seen Cara nor Colin since early this morrow."

"Where were they seen?"

"Heading toward the chapel."

"You see," Kieran said, relaxing. "What could possibly happen to them in the house of God?"

Terence let out a sigh. "I suppose I am being a foolish old man. But my daughter has not been herself since her return from the abbey."

"Perhaps she misses the orderly life of prayer and meditation."

"Aye. Perhaps. But she left the abbey of her own free will." Terence accepted a goblet from a servant's tray and smiled. "She has always been a quiet, thoughtful child. never know what she is thinking."

"She is a fine young woman." Kieran clapped his hand on Conor's shoulder and said, "I often thought we would become one family. When," he added with a laugh, "Colin and Cara grew up and wed."

Conor was strangely silent.

"I had thought so, too," Terence said. "That would have pleased me." Draining his goblet, he handed it to a servant and asked, "When does Colin leave for the monastery?"

Kieran shrugged. "He did not say. The bishop leaves in two days."

"Aye. As soon as the wed—" Seeing the look on Kieran's face, he left the words unspoken. No one wished to remind him of his mother's marriage.

"Dinner is ready, my lord," Mistress Peake said, bowing before Kieran. She deliberately ignored Sir Cecil.

"Thank you." Offering his arm to Megan, Kieran led the way to the refectory, with the others following.

Behind them, Sir Cecil reminded himself to be patient. In two more days, he would become the lord of this manor. And the housekeeper would have to answer to him.

As they entered, they were surprised to find Colin and Cara awaiting their arrival. The two young people stood very close together in front of the massive fireplace. The first thing everyone noticed was that their hands were linked. Their smiles dazzled.

"Cara." Terence O'Byrne hurried forward to press his lips to his daughter's cheek. "I had begun to worry over you. Where have you been?"

"With Colin." She gave a shy glance at the young man beside her, then cleared her throat. "We have something to tell you, Father."

Lady Katherine paused beside Terence and looked expectantly toward her young son.

"Colin and I were wed this morrow," Cara said proudly.

"Wed?" Terence gazed from his daughter to the beaming man beside her.

Bishop O'Mara, hearing Cara's words, lifted his head, then strode across the room to take charge of this impertinence. "Where were you wed? In a lowly crofter's cottage, by some itinerant preacher?"

"We were wed in the chapel."

For a moment the bishop seemed taken aback. Then, regaining his composure, he bellowed, "You would defy me and break your promise to wait a year?"

The others seemed shocked at his words. Lady Katherine, her eyes troubled, asked, "Seamus, what are you saying?"

In angry tones he said, "Colin came to me with a childish notion of leaving the monastery and marrying Cara O'Byrne. The church cannot afford to lose such as he. Besides, I pointed out that he would make a poor husband." At Lady Katherine's look of outrage he explained, "He is in frail health, after all. I knew that a year would cool whatever passion they had for each other and bring them around."

"Bring them around?" Lady Katherine stared at her brother-in-law as if seeing him for the first time. "Knowing how good and noble these young people are, you would ask such a sacrifice from them?"

"As you well know, Katherine, God asks much from those to whom He gave much."

"God, Seamus? Or you?"

In the silence that followed, the bishop turned to the young couple, who stood with hands linked. "By whose authority did you wed?"

Colin's voice sounded stronger and more assured than ever. "There is no higher authority than God. Father Malone said the mass and gave the church's blessings. But he

explained that we each wed the other, and that no power o
earth is greater than love.'' Ignoring the angry stare of th
bishop, he turned to Terence. ''I love your daughter, si
more than life itself. And I will do all in my power to mak
her happy.''

''I know you will, Colin.'' Terence accepted Colin'
handshake, then turned to embrace his daughter. ''An
judging by the way she looks, you have already made he
very happy.''

Lady Katherine, still reeling from the shock, hurried for
ward to embrace her son and new daughter-in-law. ''I de
sire only that you find happiness and fulfillment,'' sh
whispered.

Kieran strode forward and embraced his brother an
Cara. And then the entire company seemed to catch th
spirit of the moment and joined in the celebration.

Megan embraced Cara and Colin, then studied the loo
of radiance about them. Their open expression of love ha
transformed them. There was about them a glow of happi
ness that set them apart.

She glanced at Kieran and found him staring at her wit
the strangest look on his face. For a moment she could no
move. Then, starting toward him, she gave him a smile s
filled with love that it told him all he wanted to know.

The door opened. In the confusion of the moment, n
one seemed to notice the stranger who stood between Jame
and Sir Cecil. His gaze slowly swept the room, then settle
upon Megan.

''My dear,'' Sir Cecil said in silky tones. ''I have goo
news.''

Everyone turned toward him.

''After an extensive search, we have learned your name
And,'' he added slyly, ''a great deal about you and you
people.''

Megan glanced from Sir Cecil to the stranger. Though sh
did not recognize him, she felt a shiver along her spine.

Malcolm MacAlpin studied Megan's eyes. It was clear that she had still not regained her memory. There was not the slightest flicker of recognition. Oh, this was the sweetest revenge of all. Had he not vowed she would regret her mistreatment of him? All he had wanted was to be her second in command. Now, thanks to the fates, he could have it all—the leadership of the MacAlpins, the control of Megan's vast estates and, best of all, revenge upon the woman who had thwarted his manhood. Before he was finished with her, she would kneel, she would grovel, she would plead for her very life. The revenge he planned was worth all the waiting. When he and James were through with her, she would beg to die.

"Your name," Sir Cecil said, watching her eyes carefully, "is Megan MacAlpin."

"MacAlpin." Megan waited, hoping the name would trigger her memory. But she recalled nothing.

Satisfied with her reaction, Sir Cecil glanced at his son and the arrogant Scot who stood beside him. With a smile he said, "It appears the lady still cannot remember. Perhaps, Sir Malcolm, you should refresh her memory."

"Aye." Malcolm strode forward importantly. Bowing slightly before Megan, he caught her hand and drew her toward him.

Behind them, Kieran felt a growing sense of unease. There was something vaguely familiar about this Scot, but he could not place him. Still, his sense of unease grew. And at the Scot's next words, he felt his whole world begin to crumble.

"I am Malcolm MacAlpin, your distant cousin. And you, my beloved Megan, are my betrothed."

Chapter Nineteen

"Betrothed!" Megan stared at this stranger, then turned to glance at Kieran. "This cannot be. I . . ." She licked her lips, which had suddenly gone dry. "I would remember."

Malcolm gave her an indulgent smile. "They tell me you have lost your memory. Do you remember your sisters?"

"Sisters?" She felt a sudden jolt of pain. "I have sisters?"

"You see?" Feigning a look of concern, he dropped an arm around her shoulders and drew her close. "You cannot even recall the most important people in your life. That fool, Jamie MacDonald, will pay for this. I entrusted you to his care. And he failed me. Failed all of us."

Regaining his voice, Kieran said, "The lad you speak of told me that Megan was the leader of her people. And that she had chosen him as her second in command."

Malcolm's eyes narrowed dangerously. "MacDonald is a pompous fool. He was nothing more than a messenger, but I wrongly allowed him to accompany Megan to the Highlands."

"You allowed?"

"I am the MacAlpin, leader of our clan. And I allowed Jamie MacDonald to travel with Megan."

"For what purpose?"

Malcolm eyed Kieran with growing hatred. He was not about to be tripped up by these insolent questions. Sir Cecil d his son had warned him about Kieran O'Mara. "Megan has a sister in the highlands, wed to Brice Campbell."

Kieran recalled that name from his conversation with amie MacDonald. Brice Campbell was the infamous ighland Barbarian, a fierce chieftain loyal to Mary Queen f Scots.

"Megan was on her way for a visit, and I was unable to ccompany her." Pulling her close, Malcolm muttered gainst her hair, "I have punished myself a hundred times or letting you go without me, my love."

A shudder passed through Megan, and she struggled gainst the revulsion she felt at this man's touch. Pulling ack a step, she stared into his eyes, searching for anything at might jolt her memory. But when she looked at him she elt nothing. Nothing but a vague sense of unease.

Enjoying the attention, Malcolm played to his audience. What rejoicing there will be when I return with my beothed. We must make plans to return immediately, my ove."

Turning to Kieran, Malcolm said, "If you will allow us to artake of your hospitality this night, Megan and I will leave or Scotland on the morrow."

Kieran studied the tall, handsome man who stood with his rm possessively around Megan's shoulders. Was it possile that she had been betrothed to this stranger? All his enses rebelled against such a thought. But his heart reponded instantly. Megan would have been a catch for any nan. It would have been unlikely that a woman of her obious charm and talent would have remained unspoken for or so long.

"We were just going to eat," Sir Cecil said, catching Lady Katherine's hand and leading her toward the stranger. It leased him to usurp Kieran's position. And at the moent, it was obvious that Kieran O'Mara was reeling from his blow. Puffing up his chest Sir Cecil said, "You are more han welcome to partake of our meal."

"I thank you." Malcolm acknowledged the introdu‑
tions of those around him, then followed his host to the ⸳
ble.

As the servants began serving the meal, Terence O'Byr
said, "We were just about to celebrate the wedding of r
daughter to Lady Katherine's son." Turning to the hap‑
couple he said, "I ask that we all drink to the good fortu
of the bride and groom."

For a moment all eyes turned toward Colin and Car
who sat together, their hands linked, their gazes locked
love.

Everyone drank, and then Malcolm, warmed by the ⸳
and drunk with the power he wielded over his hated enem
stood.

"I would also propose a toast," he said. He bowed to t
young woman who sat beside him in a stunned trance. "'
my betrothed, Megan MacAlpin. And to our f
ture...together."

He lifted his goblet and met James's eyes across the t
ble. With a wicked smile both men drained their goblets.

Kieran stood by the balcony of his sleeping chambe
staring broodingly at the midnight sky. Just a room away l
his beloved, but he could not go to her. Nor had he any rig
to speak to her of the things he held in his heart.

Betrothed. She was promised to another. The thoug
gnawed at him, making it impossible to escape into sleep.

What a fool he had been, thinking he could walk awa
from Killamara with his woman and find happiness. The
was no escaping this hellish life. Now he was doomed to lo
all that he had spent a lifetime cherishing, and also th
woman he had come to love more than himself.

If only they'd had the wisdom of Cara and Colin. Th
thought of his brother, happily wed to his childhood lov
gave his spirits a momentary lift. How changed Colin wa
since his stay in Fleet. While he was not looking, Kiera

ought wryly, his brother had become a man. A fine man, ho had the courage of his convictions.

Slamming his fist into the wall, Kieran turned away and alked across the room. He would do no less than Colin. hough she was betrothed to another, he had to see Megan ne last time.

Dry-eyed, Megan sat in the middle of her big bed, star- g at the gleaming coals in the fireplace. She felt numbed eyond pain, beyond tears. The thought of leaving Kieran orever caused a tightness around her heart that made it ifficult to breathe.

Sisters. Malcolm MacAlpin had said that she had sisters Scotland. A family. She was about to discover all those eople who had once loved her. All the questions, all the ears she had harbored since that terrible day when she had ost her memory, would be resolved.

But it meant that she would have to leave behind these eople who had come to mean so much to her. Colin and ara, little Bridget, Lady Katherine. And most of all, ieran.

At the sound of the door opening, she looked up. A tall hadow fell across her bed, and for a moment her heart oared at the thought that Kieran had come to her. But as ne candlelight drew near, she realized her night visitor was ne stranger, Malcolm MacAlpin.

"You are not sleeping?" he asked.

"Nay." She gave an involuntary shiver and drew the bed nens around her shoulders.

"I thought you might be having doubts about the things told you this evening."

"Aye."

She saw the glint of a knife in his hand and shrank back or a moment. Seeing her reaction, he smiled broadly. Mal- olm had never before seen Megan MacAlpin as anything ut strong and unafraid. This was a new side to her—one he vas enjoying.

"I thought you might like to examine my knife," he sai
handing it to her.

She studied the MacAlpin crest emblazoned on the hi
then her eyes widened. "It is the same as the one I carrie
though mine has been lost."

"Aye. All MacAlpins carry this crest on their weapons.

"It is true then." She ran her finger over the crest and fe
the sting of tears. "You truly are the MacAlpin. And we a
betrothed."

He lifted her face and studied the tears that she tried
desperately to hide. "It is as I said."

"Forgive me, my lord," she said softly. A tear course
along her cheek as she added, "I hope you will be patie
while I learn all that I have forgotten about...us."

Malcolm sat on the edge of the bed and lowered his fac
to hide the smile that sprang to his lips.

"Aye, my lady. I will be patient. And now I bid you good
night."

This was even better than he had expected. He lifted he
hand to his lips. He would drag this proud woman to th
depths of hell before he was finished with her.

Kieran paused outside the door to Megan's sleepin
chamber. The flicker of candlelight told him that she wa
still awake. As he pushed open the door he was startled t
see two figures on the bed. Their voices were soft, mufflec
but he recognized Megan's voice. The other, he realizec
belonged to Malcolm MacAlpin.

By the light of the candle he could clearly see that the
were engaged in an intimate conversation. When Malcolr
lifted Megan's hand to his lips, Kieran turned on his hee
and stormed back to his room. He had no right to intrud
on Megan's life. She had finally found herself. And thoug
it would tear his heart out, he wanted only her happiness.

* * *

"Lady Katherine instructed me to pack all these gowns
r your trip home, my lady." The little servant lifted an
rmload of gowns to the bed.

"Nay, Aileen. Lord Malcolm said we must travel with
aste. I will take only the gown I wear and a warm cloak."

"Oh, my lady." Aileen burst into tears and turned away.
he bundle of gowns fell to the floor and drifted around her
et like so many bright flowers. "How can you leave with
his stranger?"

"Hush, now." Megan swallowed the little knot of fear
hat threatened to choke her. She must not allow herself to
ry or she would end up weeping like a child. "I am going
o my home, Aileen. Whenever you become sad, think of
hat happy thought."

It was what she had been telling herself all through the
eepless night.

As she lifted the heavy traveling cloak from the bed, she
oticed the glint of metal against the bed linens. Malcolm's
nife. He had forgotten it last night. Tucking it into her
aistband, she folded the cloak over her arm and headed for
he stairs. There would be time enough later to return it to
im. A lifetime, she thought with a shiver.

In the hallway she encountered Kieran, just leaving his
oom. For a moment they stared at each other in awkward
lence.

"So, my lady. You are ready for your journey?" He
tudied her hungrily, trying to burn into his mind every-
hing about her.

"Aye." How could she say what was in her heart? She
ought back the yearning to touch a hand to his cheek.

They both looked up as Malcolm and James strode along
he hallway, laughing together.

"Ahh, Megan."

When Malcolm reached Megan's side, Kieran took a step
ack.

Malcolm insolently looked her up and down, then said,
"I see you are eager to be off. As am I."

With a smug smile Malcolm took her arm and led h
down the stairs and out into the courtyard, toward t
waiting horses.

The entire household had assembled to bid her goodby

Lady Katherine, standing between Sir Cecil and t
bishop, strode forward to kiss her cheek. "Thank you, n
dear, for all you did for me."

"I did nothing, my lady."

"You brought my sons home safely. You touched t
hearts of my people. And best of all, you made me reali
that I was holding my granddaughter too tightly to n
heart."

Megan was shocked at the woman's admission. "Oh, n
lady, you were not..."

"Ahh, but I was." With a smile, Lady Katherine sa
softly, "Bridget was bursting to be free. And you unlocke
the door, my dear. For that we are both grateful."

Holding hands, Colin and Cara approached. Timidl
Cara caught Megan's hand and pressed it between both
hers.

"Thank you, my lady," she whispered. "For settin
Colin's heart free."

At her words Megan arched an eyebrow. "I do not u
derstand."

"It was you," Colin interrupted, "who made it possib
for me to declare my true feelings for Cara."

"I, Colin? How?"

"You are so filled with love for life, my lady." At her loc
of surprise, he bent and kissed her cheek. "I had never m
anyone quite like you before, my dear Megan. You are tru
the most amazing woman I have ever known. And I rea
ized that I could never return to my quiet life of prayer a
ter the excitement of our journey together."

Megan caught both their hands and held them. "I a
happy for both of you. I pray you find much happiness."

As they stepped away, Bridget broke away from Mistress eake, who was holding her hand, and launched herself into Megan's arms.

"You cannot go, my lady," she shrieked.

"I must, Bridget."

"You promised to teach me more about horses. And who ill teach me to hold a sword? You cannot leave until our essons are completed."

Megan looked beyond the little girl to the man who stood part from all the others. With unshed tears burning her hroat she murmured, "Ask your Uncle Kieran to teach ou. It will bring you closer to him. And that will bring you loser to me."

"Who will hold me when I am afraid? Who will keep my ecrets?"

"Oh, Bridget. Sweet, sweet Bridget." Megan buried her ace in the child's hair and felt the tears start. "If only I ould always be here for you."

"I will never see you again," the child suddenly screamed, ocking her arms around Megan's neck and holding on irmly. "You are just like my Mama and Papa. You will eave and never return to me."

Lifting Bridget, Megan carried her to Kieran and handed er to him. "Comfort her," she whispered. "And let her omfort you."

Without a word he accepted the little girl and watched as Megan made her way to the waiting horses.

"God go with you on your journey," the bishop called.

Megan crossed herself as he lifted his hand for a blessing. With tears blurring her vision, she allowed old Padraig o assist her into the saddle.

"Come back to us, my lady," he whispered.

It was the first time the shy old man had ever spoken to er. He placed his hand over hers and squeezed.

With a clatter of hooves, she nudged her mount into a rot. And as the tears streamed down her cheeks, she turned or a last glimpse of Castle O'Mara and its inhabitants. But

there was only one face she could see. Even when the cast
was nothing more than a blur of turrets gleaming in th
morning mist; even when the horses crested a hill overloo
ing tiny villages; even when she turned to study the glin
mering lake, with swans gliding across its mirrored surfac
she did not see the lovely, tranquil setting. She saw onl
Kieran's beloved face.

Kieran sat behind the massive desk in the library. Facin
him were Colin and Cara, and beside them, Lady Kather
ine and Bishop O'Mara. On their other side sat Terenc
O'Byrne and his son, Conor, who were dressed for trave
Hugh Cleary stood alone beside the fireplace.

To the untrained eye, Kieran's face showed no emotio:
But to those who knew and loved him, it was obvious tha
he was exerting great control over his feelings.

"I have summoned you here," Kieran began, "as my las
official act as lord of Killamara. On the morrow—" his eye
narrowed fractionally "—another will hold the future c
this estate and its people in his hands."

He turned to study his brother. "I envy you, Colin."

Colin's eyes widened. "You? Envy me? Why?"

"You have the courage of your convictions." He turne
to Cara, who held tightly to her new husband's hand. "Yo
are the only hope for the next generation of O'Maras."

"Do not speak so," Cara said softly. "You will one da
wed, Kieran. And you will have children of your own."

"Nay. One woman owns my heart. There will never b
another." His words were spoken curtly.

Turning to Colin he said, "It is only right and fitting tha
O'Mara heirs be bred on the land that was theirs for gener
ations. I cannot give you Castle O'Mara, for that will be
come part of Sir Cecil's estate. Therefore, I decree that th
land that had once been set aside for Seamus O'Mara—" h
inclined his head toward the bishop, who sat with hea
lowered, hands carefully laced "—including the lovel
manor house thereon, and the chapel, shall be yours."

Colin turned to stare at his uncle. "You had always said that your property would go to the church."

"Aye." The bishop glanced at Kieran, remembering their heated words. "But I have had a change of heart."

"Does this mean also that you will give us your blessing?" Colin asked boldly.

The bishop met Kieran's steely look. "Aye."

As the two kissed his ring and fell to their knees, he lifted his hand in a blessing, then drew them into his arms and hugged them awkwardly.

"Thank you, Kieran," Terence O'Byrne said, leaning over the desk to extend his hand. "I can leave now, knowing that my daughter's future is secure."

"Aye, Terence. And our family will treasure the knowledge that a great orator now shares a family bond as he pleads our cause before the English Queen. Safe journey," he added to Terence and his son.

"Oh, Seamus." Tears shimmered in Lady Katherine's eyes. "Your blessing of their marriage was what I have been praying for. You have made me very happy. As have you, Kieran." With arms outstretched she walked around the desk and embraced her eldest son.

"I would speak privately to my mother," Kieran said.

Though the others were surprised by his abrupt announcement, they filed solemnly from the room, leaving mother and son alone. Hugh was the last to leave. He knew that look in Kieran's eyes. He had seen the same look so many times in Sean O'Mara's eyes. They were harsh men, bred in a harsh land.

When the door was closed, Kieran pushed away from his mother's arms and strode to the fireplace. Turning, he said, 'I cannot stay for your marriage to Sir Cecil."

"But why? This is your home."

"On the morrow this castle and this land will no longer be mine. It will belong to your new husband."

"Nay, Kieran. We . . . have an understanding. Things will remain as they were. I have Cecil's word."

Kieran had long ago witnessed the lack of value of Si Cecil's word. But he could not speak of such things to hi mother. He said merely, "I cannot stay and watch you spea your vows. It would bring dishonor to me and to my fath er's name."

"Oh, Kieran. How can you say such things? What I do, do for you and Colin."

"I will not dignify that with a protest, Mother."

She stared at this son who was so like his father. "Wher will you go?"

"I know not." For the first time he allowed her a glimps of the depth of his anguish. "It no longer matters. But I wil say farewell to you now, quickly and without harsh words Know always that I love you, Mother, and would do any thing for you."

She knew that if she told Kieran the truth, he would ad mire her for her courage, as he had earlier admired Colin But he would also forbid her to pay such a price for peace And she knew that she had to do it. For the sake of all sh loved. And especially for the sake of Sean's memory. Bu she said merely, "Then stay, Kieran. And give me the com fort of your presence at the chapel on the morrow."

"That I cannot do." He walked to her and kissed her, then strode from the room.

For what seemed an eternity she stood, listening to the silence of the room. Then, with a sob catching in her throat, she hurried to her chambers.

She would face this heartache alone. She vowed to tell no one of Kieran's decision to leave.

The horses picked their way through the dense forest. It seemed to Megan that they had been riding in circles for hours. But when she called it to Malcolm's attention, he curtly advised her to follow his lead and trust him.

Trust. It did not come easily to Megan. She wondered if it had always been so. But though she longed to ask Malcolm questions about herself, she was loath to break through

is wall of silence. Ever since their departure from Castle
O'Mara, he had been lost in dark, brooding contemplation.

She watched as he reined in his mount and studied the
trees around him. Almost as if, she thought suddenly, he
was searching for some sign. After a few minutes of cir-
cling, he urged his horse farther into the forest, turning to
make certain that Megan was following. To satisfy her curiosity she peered closely at the trees as she passed them and
saw a small cross carved into the bark. Running her finger
along the indentation, she felt the moistness and knew that
the mark had been freshly made. It left no doubt in her
mind that Malcolm was following a trail. But who had left
it here for him? And where did it lead?

Chapter Twenty

"Are the soldiers in place?"

Sir Cecil helped himself to a goblet of whiskey from crystal decanter on Kieran's desk. The ledgers were strangel gone, as were all the account books. No matter. He had rea them carefully in the short time he had at Castle O'Mar before Kieran returned from prison. He knew every piece o property listed and how many crops were raised on the land No longer would these peasants work to fill their ow stomachs. In the next few years they would give their life blood to fill his coffers in England.

"Aye." James accepted a drink and strode to the fire place. The fire had burned down to ashes. Mistress Peake sulking, as were the other servants, would feel the sting o the lash when his father took possession of this estate. "I g now to meet the Scotsman."

"What of our...accomplice?"

"I have not seen him. But I told him where to meet us. fear he has become remorseful over his betrayal of hi friends. But I still think he will see this through."

"You realize what you must do?" In the privacy of th library, all pretence of honor fell away. Sir Cecil's eyes glit tered with evil. "You must kill him."

"Aye. Have no fear. It will be done."

Cecil lifted his goblet and met his son's look. "On th morrow, the lady will learn what it means to defy the Ket terings. I have waited a lifetime to avenge her casual dismissal of me when we were young. All that Sean O'Mara cherished will become mine. And his sons will die before their mother's eyes."

"Will that be enough to purge the hatred from your heart?"

The older man shook his head. "I think not. I have carried my hatred of O'Mara for so long, I cannot imagine life without it." He paused, staring into the ashes. "I had hoped to turn his sons against him in Elizabeth's court. But even in that I was thwarted. This time I will not be denied my vengeance."

The two men drained their goblets. "Go now," Cecil said, "and see that the soldiers are in place. As soon as the ceremony concludes and the papers are witnessed by the bishop, I want the O'Mara men seized."

"What about the bishop? His power in Rome and in England are legend."

"Aye." Sir Cecil barely paused before saying, "See that he becomes a casualty during the confusion. We will blame his untimely death on the discontented rabble of this untidy land."

Darkness came early in the forest. Overhead, the tall spires of ancient evergreens blotted out any trace of moonlight.

Megan shivered and drew her cloak tightly around her. Except for an occasional call of a night bird and the sound of insects, there was an eerie stillness in the chill air.

Malcolm's horse picked its way carefully through the dense woods. To keep them from becoming separated, Malcolm had insisted upon taking the reins to Megan's horse. When a wet tree branch brushed his face he swore viciously, sending a chill of alarm along Megan's spine. What sort of person had she been that she could have ever contemplated marrying such a man? Each time they had paused in their journey, she had felt his gaze upon her, soil-

ing her. And now, with the night upon them, she felt he
fear growing until it bordered on terror.

She thought about slipping away under cover of dark
ness. Had that same thought caused Malcolm to take he
reins. She glanced around wildly. But a single tantalizin
thought kept her from leaving. Home. At the end of th
journey she would see her home again and the people wh
had once mattered to her. As uneasy as she felt about thi
man, he was the key to her past.

At the same moment they both spotted a light in the di
tance. Malcolm muttered an oath and tugged roughly on th
reins. Megan swallowed her fear and concentrated instea
on the thought of a warm bed and dry clothes.

As they drew closer, Megan saw that there was a sma
cottage built along the far banks of the river. The horse
splashed through the shallow water and clambered up th
rock-strewn bank.

As they dismounted, Megan heard the whinny of a horse
Too late she turned and saw the cluster of horses sheltere
in a nearby stand of trees.

Before she could protest, Malcolm grasped her arm an
thrust her ahead of him through the half-open door of th
cottage. Inside, a dozen men were drinking from tankard
and warming themselves before a roaring fire. When the
turned, Megan found herself face-to-face with the hang
man's soldiers. Soldiers she had prayed had long ago re
turned to England.

"What is this?" As the men turned, one stocky guard
recognizing Megan, separated himself from the others.

Megan looked into the blazing eyes of Whip, the crue
guard from the forest.

"So. 'Tis our dancer." He advanced menacingly toward
her. "We found Captain Wilkes's body in the river, my lady
Where ye lured him. It would seem," the guard said, slam
ming down his tankard, "that we have been given anothe
chance to take our revenge upon ye."

"Aye," shouted another. "We have been too long without a woman. And this time we will need no dance to stir our blood."

His words were followed by a chorus of coarse laughter.

As Whip's hand snaked out toward Megan's bodice, Malcolm drew her away. "All in good time," he said with an evil smile. "But first I have a score to settle with the lady. As does the gentleman who paid for your services." As he dragged Megan toward a small room, he said over his shoulder, "When we are finished, you may have what is left of her."

James felt a wild exhilaration as he made his way to the cottage by the river. The deed was almost done. He and his father had had their differences in the past, but this would seal their relationship forever. His grateful father would be most generous. There was a house in London that James had been coveting, as well as an estate in Bedford. He had no doubt his father would now secure them for him. The women at court would fawn over him. The same women who had once vied for the attention of Kieran O'Mara.

O'Mara. How he hated him. Hated his calm assurance, the easy way he had with both men and women. Even in Elizabeth's court, the Queen and her ladies seemed taken with the Irish rebel who defied convention. James had resented the fact that his father had brought Kieran and Colin to England when he was a lad. He had seen them as rivals for his father's affection. But very soon he had realized that his father had other reasons for bringing them there. He had watched his father's manipulations. And he had learned.

Deep in thought, James saw nothing but the faint flicker of candlelight from the cottage. When he crossed the river, he dismounted and hurried inside, his blood hot for revenge.

"Where is the woman?"

One of the soldiers pointed and James strode toward the small room.

A single candle stood atop a scarred trunk. A filthy line
covered a pallet in the corner of the room. Malcolm held
tankard of ale to his lips. Against the far wall Megan stoo
stiffly, holding her cloak around her. Through the ope
window beside her drifted the chill night air.

"James." For a moment her eyes lit, but when he an
Malcolm began talking, her hopes plummeted. He had no
come to rescue her. He was in league with this devil.

"We only now arrived," Malcolm said with a puzzle
look. "How could you get here so soon?"

"You took an...indirect route. To confuse the lady.
James felt himself becoming aroused as he looked at Meg
an. It was not just her beauty; it was the knowledge that sh
belonged to Kieran O'Mara that tantalized him. How swe
would be the revenge.

Megan stepped forward. "Why are we here, James?"

He looked at her with an insolence that brought colc
flooding her cheeks. With the back of his hand he slappe
her so hard it sent her reeling. "You are here for our plea
sure, my lady."

She felt the sting of his blow, and the blood rushed to he
head. When had all of this gone wrong? And how had th
quiet, unassuming son of Sir Cecil become this cruel mor
ster?

James turned to Malcolm, coldly dismissing her. "Hav
the soldiers been given their orders?"

"They know only that they will finally have their re
venge upon the one who evaded them for so long now."

"As will we all." Striding to the door, James called to th
captain of the guard. "Your men will begin their marc
now. If you encounter any villagers who might reveal you
presence, kill them."

Kill the innocent villagers? At his harsh words, Mega
glanced from James to Malcolm. A rush of conflictin
emotions rippled through her. This man, who claimed to b
her betrothed, was in league with the English. That mear
that he was not who he claimed to be. Perhaps everything h

ad said was a lie. She pressed her fingers to her throbbing
mples. Perhaps she was not even Megan MacAlpin.
hrough a haze of confusion she heard James's voice issu-
g orders.

"When you reach Castle O'Mara, conceal yourselves
ntil the wedding party is inside. Then encircle the chapel
nd await my signal to attack."

"Attack? The wedding party?" Megan's breath caught in
er throat as James turned toward her with a chilling smile.
"You would send soldiers after your own father?"

"Little fool. This was all my father's plan." James stood
the doorway and watched as the soldiers filed from the
ottage and pulled themselves into their saddles.

As the hoofbeats faded, Megan stared at James with a
ok of stunned disbelief. God in heaven. Lady Katherine.
Ier marriage to Sir Cecil was all some terrible, elaborate
rap. But was that good woman the only prey? The answer
prang instantly to mind. She knew with certainty that the
apture of the lady's sons was the true quest.

"So. Kieran and Colin have not evaded the English sol-
iers after all. You and your father have merely been toying
vith them, accepting the hospitality of the mother to en-
nare the sons."

"Very astute, my lady." James closed the door of the
ottage and leaned against it. As he surveyed his prize, his
yes glittered with a strange light.

Megan felt a fresh wave of fear. She had seen that look of
ust before, when she had been captured by the soldiers in
he forest. Her mind raced. She needed to keep James talk-
ng.

Running her tongue over her dry lips, she asked, "How
lid your father persuade Lady Katherine to accept his offer
of marriage?"

James laughed. "Perhaps she loved him."

"Nay." Megan took a tentative step, hoping to inch her
vay toward the door. "It was not love I saw between them.
Yet she agreed to the marriage. Why?"

James's eyes glittered dangerously. "My father is a ve
shrewd man. He knew the one thing he could count on wi
Lady Katherine." At Megan's arched brow he added, "
mother's love. He offered his protection for her precio
sons and all in Killamara if she would but wed him."

"And his word meant nothing," Megan said with a to
of disgust.

"Beware, my lady." James watched her, anticipating h
next move. "Speak not against a Kettering in my pre
ence."

"But why marriage? What does Sir Cecil gain from this?

"The woman humiliated him in his youth. Do you thi
he would forget? Or forgive?"

"He would force a woman into marriage merely for tl
sake of revenge?"

James took a step forward and watched as she backed u
"Everything Sean O'Mara cherished will now be in n
father's hands. The woman, the land, and best of all, tl
fate of his sons."

"Enough talk," Malcolm said, advancing on then
"There is the matter of my revenge, as well. Or have yc
forgotten?"

Megan turned to watch him, gauging the distance to tl
door. "Why do you seek vengeance against me?"

As he advanced she took a step back, then another, unt
she felt the cold wall of the cottage against her back.

He reached out a hand and caught a strand of her hai
yanking her head painfully. His eyes glittered with hatre
"You are the MacAlpin, the leader of our people. And yo
refused my offer to become your second in command."

A leader. The thought sent her heart soaring. Had sl
somehow known that she was not born to follow?

"You would ally yourself with the English to avenge
personal affront?"

"I had already allied myself with them, my lady. It wa
the reason you would not accept me." His lips curled in

ィeer. "That, and the fact that I did not always adhere to ㄱur lofty code of honor."

With his hand still holding her hair, he drew her head ィck and lowered his face to hers. "We shall see how much ㄱur precious honor means when I have finished with you. ⅼ tried to punish you once, in a highland meadow. That blow ㄱst you your memory, but your life was spared. You will ㄱt be so fortunate a second time."

When Megan tried to pull away he caught her roughly by ィe shoulder, holding her still. With a mocking smile he ㅇvered her mouth with his and ground his teeth over hers ┒til she tasted her own blood.

"Relax and enjoy yourself, my lady," he said with a cruel ィugh. "I have only begun."

Across the room she could hear the sound of James ィughing as he watched her useless struggles. Malcolm ィessed his body against her until his thighs pinned her ィrmly to the wall, making her aware of his arousal. She felt ⅼ moment of sheer panic as she realized she was no match ㄱr his strength. He would take her savagely. And when he ィas through with her, James would use her, as well. For a ┒oment she went limp in his arms, and he seized the mo-ィent to capture her mouth with his. Then her fingers found ィe hilt of the knife at her waist. Malcolm's knife. With ィreat care she slid the weapon from its place of conceal-ィent. Her fingers were damp, and she feared she would ィrop it. She would have but one chance to find his heart. ⅈripping the hilt firmly in her hand, she drew back her ィead, as if offering her throat for his kiss.

"So," he murmured against her lips, "you are not so re-ㅣctant as you pretend."

He bent his lips to her throat just as she plunged the knife ┒to his chest. For a moment he stared at her with a look of ╷mazement. Slowly the look turned to one of horror, as he ╵ealized what had happened. His hands reached up to grasp ィe offending weapon, but before he could close his fingers ╷round it, he slid to the floor.

James was across the room in seconds. Stepping disdainfully over Malcolm's still form he said coldly, "You spare me the effort, my lady. I would have had to kill him befor I left here anyway. There can be no witnesses to what w do."

As she attempted to move away he unsheathed his swor and pointed it at her heart. "Now, my lady, it is my tur And I assure you, I am not the fool your Scotsman was. With the tip of his sword he cut away the cord that held he cloak. As it fell to the floor, he allowed his insolent gaze t roam her until her cheeks flamed. His voice was low wit desire. "Remove your gown, my lady."

When she merely stared at him he said, "Either you re move it, or I shall."

With a wave of revulsion, Megan clenched her hands a her sides.

He lifted the tip of his sword to her throat and met her ic stare. "I welcome the chance to inflict pain, my lady."

Before he could cut her, she reached for the buttons of he gown. His lips curved into a hint of a smile. "That is bet ter. Now you understand who is the master here." His shril laugh sent fresh waves of terror through her. "And you ar the slave, my lady."

As Megan slowly unbuttoned her dress, her mind raced This was a madman. He would stop at nothing to have wha he wanted. With hands, teeth, fingernails, she must figh him until he killed her. She would never submit.

When she reached the last button, he brought the tip o his sword to slide her gown from first one shoulder, then th other, until it joined her cloak on the floor at her feet.

She lowered her head in shame, that this man should se her in her chemise and petticoats.

"You are a vision, my lady. It is no wonder the lord o Killamara lost his heart to you." He closed the distance be tween them and caught her chin in his hand, forcing her t meet his look. "And now," he cried with a note of tri

mph, "the Ketterings will own everything once held dear
y the O'Maras."

As he bent to her, Kieran's steely voice stopped him. "Not
verything, James. The lady will never be sullied by you."

James and Megan looked up to discover that Kieran had
imbed in through the window of the cottage. Megan gave
little cry of joy at the sight of him.

"O'Mara." James swung around to find Kieran's sword
ointed at his heart.

Lifting his own sword, James lunged. The tip of his sword
issed Kieran's heart by mere inches, tearing through his
nic but failing to cut his flesh.

Kieran easily avoided his next thrust, then drove James
ack again and again until he tripped over the body of
Malcolm. As he fell, James' sword slipped from his hand.
Desperate, he pulled the bloody knife from Malcolm's chest
nd lunged at Megan. Holding her in front of him as a
hield, he placed the blade against her throat and snarled,
Now, O'Mara, you will drop your sword or I swear I will
pill the lady's blood."

Kieran felt a surge of helpless rage. There had been a time
hen he would have ruthlessly driven home the point of his
word without regard for such threats. But this was Megan
1 the hands of this madman. And he could not bear the
hought of any harm coming to her. "Let Megan go,
ames." His voice was low, deadly.

"I will kill her, O'Mara, and her blood will be upon your
ands."

"Nay, Kieran." Megan fought to keep the fear from her
oice. "You must not lower your weapon. He will kill us
oth."

With a glance at Megan, Kieran allowed the sword to drop
rom his hand. In the silence, it clattered to the floor.

Shoving Megan into Kieran's arms, James bent and re-
rieved the sword, then brandished it menacingly.

"The lady was right, O'Mara. Now I will have the pleas-
re of killing both of you before returning to the chapel to

witness my father's marriage to the lovely Lady Kathe
ine."

Megan felt Kieran's hands tighten at her shoulders, but |
continued watching James through narrowed eyes. /
James lifted his sword and advanced on them, Kieran thru
Megan behind him. But when James took another step, th
door to the cottage was thrown open. Standing in the doo
way was Tavis Downey. His face was red, his brow beade
with perspiration.

"You are late," James said before turning back to h
adversaries.

"Aye."

"So, Tavis, it was you." Kieran's tone was tinged wit
sadness.

"Aye. Your good and noble friend," James said with
laugh. "He has been most helpful in keeping us informed c
your plans. And now," James called to the man in th
doorway, "you may bid these two a final farewell. In fac
if you wish, you may join me for the final thrust."

As he once more lifted his sword, Tavis, looking fror
Kieran to James and back again, lifted his own sword an
shouted, "Kieran, I would make it a fair fight." He tosse
his sword and Kieran caught it and in a single gesture turne
to meet James's thrust.

"Fool," James cried. "You have chosen the wrong sid
in this fight. Now you can die alongside your old friend."

Megan and Tavis watched helplessly as the two me
fought, their blades slashing again and again until, at last
Kieran gave a triumphant cry and James fell to the floor i
a pool of blood.

Instantly Megan launched herself into Kieran's out
stretched arms and clung to him, tears coursing along he
cheeks.

"Are you unharmed, love?" Kieran whispered against he
temple.

"Aye. And you?"

She touched a hand to his torn sleeve and was relieved to see that he was not cut.

"Dress yourself, my love. I will stir the ashes."

"Nay, Kieran. There is no time. You must go and warn our mother. Her marriage to Sir Cecil is a sham."

"I have left Killamara. My mother's life is of her own making."

"You do not understand. This has all been a plot to steal our inheritance and return you and Colin to Fleet. The soldiers already ride toward Castle O'Mara."

From across the room Tavis said, "The lass speaks the truth, Kieran. We must ride."

"We?"

As Megan pulled on her gown, Kieran strode across the room to confront his old friend. The abject expression on Tavis's face left Kieran no doubt that the young man suffered great remorse.

"Forgive me, Kieran. I was jealous that you had gone to England without me. I intended only to vent some anger. But Sir Cecil and James, knowing my weakness for the ale, plied me with drink until my tongue was loosened. When I woke, they told me that I had revealed all your plans about England. I never dreamed it would lead to this. But I had gone too far. Sir Cecil and his son threatened to expose me to you and the others. I could not bear to have all of Killamara know of my dishonor. And so I continued to give them whatever knowledge they desired." He ran a hand through his hair in a distracted gesture. "It was I who invaded the lass's chambers, at James's command, and stole the soldier's clothes. But I swear, I thought it a harmless gesture. —" he swallowed and said softly "—never dreamed you would fall in love with her."

"Why did they want the clothes?" Kieran asked.

"They had to confirm that the soldiers you evaded were the ones in their employ. And that led them to Malcolm MacAlpin, who had allied himself with the English. It was he who knew the identity of the lass." Tavis lifted his head

and met Kieran's gaze. "I know you can never forgive me
But I pray you will not seek vengeance against my famil'
All they have ever wanted was to live in Killamara in peace.

"And you, Tavis? What is it you want?"

The man's voice was unaccountably contrite. "Forgive
ness. That is all I have ever wanted. To be your friend
Kieran O'Mara, and to live here among my people."

"It was a terrible thing you did. It cost us great pain. An
it nearly cost us our lives. But I believe you, Tavis. And
believe in second chances."

Kieran offered his hand. With a look of stunned disbe
lief, Tavis stared at it for long minutes before accepting it.

"Does this mean I can ride with you?"

"Nay, Tavis. The pain of your deceit is still too raw. I d
not wish to look at you. Go home to your family."

Kieran turned to Megan, who had hurriedly dressed an
was strapping on James's discarded sword. "Can you ride
my lady?"

"Aye."

"Then we ride to Castle O'Mara. And pray it is not to
late to save my mother from the devil who would claim her."

Chapter Twenty-One

Hugh." As Lady Katherine swept down the stairs, ugh Cleary paused with his hand on the outer door of the stle. She stared in dismay at the heavy wool traveling cloak ssed over his shoulders.

"Where do you ride so early?"

"I am preparing for the journey home, my lady."

"Now?" Her eyes widened. "But you promised to stay r my wedding."

"Aye. I did. But I find that I cannot stay."

"Oh, Hugh." She placed her hand on his arm. "What is ? What has happened to send you away so suddenly?"

"Do not be offended, Katherine." He touched her cheek, en abruptly lowered his hand and clenched it by his side. I cannot stay and watch you give yourself to Sir Cecil. It ould be more than my heart could bear."

She thought about her own breaking heart and pushed side the pain. "You were leaving without a word to me?"

His gaze roamed her lovely face that through the years ad become imprinted forever in his memory. "Nay, Kathine. I could not leave without a last look at you. I would ave sought you out for a final farewell."

Her voice lowered. "You speak as though we will never e each other again."

"Do you really believe Cecil Kettering will remain in Ire-nd after the deed is done?"

At her look of consternation he allowed himself to tou her hand. It was cold. So cold. "He will take his prize England and wear you on his arm for all to see and admir As any man would who was fortunate to win your hea And if you should ever yearn for this tiny island, he will mind you that your place is there beside him."

He saw the pain that came into her eyes. Growing bold he framed her face with his big hands and murmured, ' cannot bear to see you hurt, Katherine. And so I must g But know that I will carry you always in my heart."

"Oh, Hugh." Tears filled her eyes and spilled ov coursing down her cheeks.

With his thumbs he wiped her tears and lowered his he; until his lips brushed hers. It was all he could do to ke from pulling her into his arms and stealing her away wi him. But he had not the right.

Very deliberately he stepped back, pulled open the ma sive door and strode across the courtyard to his waitin horse. His men were already mounted. At a word from the leader they formed two columns and paraded smartly awa

Lady Katherine stood in the doorway and watched, h eyes misted with tears. Long after Hugh's horse had disa peared from view, she continued to stand, staring at t emptiness that lay before her.

Mistress Peake waddled around the scullery, driving t servants into a frenzy of cleaning. Hurrying to the refe tory, she lifted the heavy silver lid of a tureen and tasted t broth simmering beneath the plump partridges. On a tab groaning with sweets, she studied the row of her famo cakes and suddenly burst into tears. That was how La Katherine found her when she entered the room a few mi utes later.

"Oh, my lady." She lifted her apron to her eyes and wipe furiously. "You must think me daft."

Recalling her own tears, Lady Katherine caught the housekeeper's hands and squeezed them affectionately. Nay, Mistress Peake. It is a day of great emotions."

"I keep remembering how proud my Lord O'Mara was the day he brought you to his home, my lady. We were all so fearful of a noble English lady taking charge of the household. But you were so kind and patient with us. And so good." Mistress Peake's tears started afresh. Before she could stop herself she blurted, "He will hurt you, my lady. You must not wed him." At the enormity of what she had said, she gasped and covered her mouth. It was unforgivable for a servant to speak so boldly to her mistress.

After a lengthy, awkward silence, Lady Katherine composed her features and stiffened her spine. "Hush now, Mistress Peake. We will speak no more of it." She glanced round the room. "I will leave you to your tasks. There is much to be done yet before I leave for the chapel."

The housekeeper watched as Lady Katherine closed the doors behind her. Then she sank into a chair and fell into another fit of weeping.

Aileen's hands trembled as she lifted the combs to Lady Katherine's hair and secured the veil. Her mistress had chosen a simple gown of the palest pink silk. The neckline was modestly high, unadorned by jewelry. The sleeves were full to the elbows, then tapered, falling into points that covered the backs of her hands. Over her gown she wore a sleeveless cape of the same pink, lined with ermine.

"You look lovely, my lady. Shall I have Padraig prepare your carriage?"

"Nay, Aileen. I would walk to the chapel." Lady Katherine strode from the room. She needed fresh air, and quickly, else she would suffocate.

Sir Cecil studied his reflection in the looking glass. He knew that he still cut a fine figure. But, with his marriage to

Katherine accomplished, he would be the object of ev
more admiring glances. In England the O'Mara jewe
would bring a handsome sum. But more importantl
Katherine's holdings here and in England would enhance h
standing among the titled at court. More than a few wome
would find him fascinating when they learned of his wealt!
He preened a moment longer, then, seeing Katherine an
her servants heading toward the chapel, he strode from tl
room, savoring his victory.

As if in a trance, Lady Katherine moved up the aisle c
the chapel. Cecil looked supremely confident as he took h
arm and led her to the altar. The bishop wore a somber loo
as he opened the book and began the words that would fo
ever change all their lives.

In the first pew, little Bridget wept in Cara's arms as Coli
tried to comfort his wife and his inconsolable niece.

"Do you, Katherine, give yourself to this man of you
own free will?"

It was a most serious question, and one that Katherin
had asked herself many times in the torment of a sleeples
night. Was there really any choice left to her? Could
mother ever freely choose imprisonment for her belove
children over her own freedom? Even if Cecil had exagge
ated his influence with the Queen, she could not take th
risk, however slight, that he could spare her sons the ho
ror of imprisonment or that he might spare her people th
horror of war.

"I do."

The bishop turned to Cecil, then looked up at the sound
of a scuffle in the rear of the chapel.

Cecil felt a rush of fury. The fools had disobeyed hi
command to wait until the marriage vows had been spc
ken. Now the bishop and Katherine would have to be force
at sword point to complete the ceremony.

He turned with a scowl. But it was not only his soldie
who had created the disturbance. His mouth dropped ope

astonishment when he saw Kieran O'Mara and the lady Megan crossing swords with two English soldiers.

Though his men were able, they were no match for their opponents. Kieran quickly overpowered his man. Megan, fighting with all the skill of a man, backed one soldier to the wall, then easily disarmed him. As more soldiers spilled through the doorway, Colin, seated in a pew beside Cara, rushed forward and picked up a sword from one of the fallen soldiers. Instantly he joined Kieran and Megan as they battled the soldiers.

Outside, the sounds of blade striking blade and the cries of the wounded filled the air. There was a battle raging, though the combatants could not be seen.

Inside the chapel, there was a strange, eerie silence as everyone watched Kieran, Colin and Megan stride up the aisle.

"There will be no marriage," Kieran declared.

"Kieran," his mother said, turning to him in alarm. "You do not understand..."

"I understand everything, Mother." He placed an arm around her shoulders and drew her close. "I know that you agreed to this marriage because Cecil convinced you that Colin and I were in danger."

"There are soldiers..."

"Aye, Mother. Many English soldiers."

"God in heaven. You see, Kieran, we must..."

He touched a hand to her lips to silence her. "Your intended husband ordered the soldiers here. As soon as you were safely wed, Sir Cecil would have us returned to Fleet. Then you and all of Killamara would have been his to use as he pleased."

Lady Katherine turned on the man who stood scowling beside her. "Cecil, is this true?"

"Do you not see soldiers here, my dear? Did I not warn you the Queen was weary? But a single word from me will end all this. The choice is yours." Sir Cecil forced a tight smile to his lips. "Your son has always resented me. This is

a last desperate attempt to keep us apart." He turned to th
bishop. "Proceed with the vows. Quickly."

"Order your soldiers to cease their fighting, Sir Cecil, c
there will be much blood shed this day." Kieran's voice ros
with emotion. "My people will resist until their freedom
secured."

"Liar! I came here in peace to offer your mother a bette
way of life."

"Do you also call your son, James, a liar, Sir Cecil?"

Kieran saw the look that came into the man's eyes as h
turned toward him.

"What does that mean?"

"It was James who admitted your plot."

Sir Cecil's eyes narrowed, but the sudden fear was ev
dent in them. He glanced around the chapel. "Where is m
son?"

"He lies dead in a cottage in the forest."

"Nay." Cecil advanced on Kieran, his eyes blazing.

As the bishop and Lady Katherine reacted with growin
horror, Kieran said, "I followed James to the cottage, onl
to find Megan inside about to be brutalized by both Mal
colm MacAlpin and your son."

"Then James is dead by your hand?" Sir Cecil's tone wa
low, deadly.

"Aye. And I would do so again, with no regret, if some
one I loved was threatened."

"Then allow me to repay you for the murder of my son."
Sir Cecil lunged forward, twisting Lady Katherine in fron
of him like a shield. In his hand was a knife, which h
pressed to her throat. "You will drop your weapons." Hi
eyes glittered with hatred. He left no doubt that he woul
kill her if his command was not obeyed.

At the sound of running feet they saw the chapel fill witl
English soldiers, who stood awaiting Sir Cecil's command

"Now you will drop your weapons, or the lady's bloo
will be upon your hands."

Colin, Kieran and Megan allowed their swords to drop to the floor. Instantly one of the soldiers retrieved them.

"The lady will accompany me across this hostile land to the safety of my ship."

Kieran's hands clenched and unclenched at his sides. Never had he felt so powerless. Yet he knew, with absolute certainty, that he would never allow Sir Cecil to leave Killamara with his beloved mother. He would die rather than permit it.

"Now, my lady," Sir Cecil said in her ear as he made his way down the aisle, "you will not resist if you value your pretty neck."

When they reached the door to the chapel, Sir Cecil turned toward the ones who watched from the altar. "You will taste my wrath, Kieran O'Mara. Know this. I will spare no one in this miserable village. You will die knowing that your mother and brother and the woman, Megan MacAlpin, will all die with you. As well as the people of Killamara." To the soldiers who stood with upraised swords he ordered, "Kill them all."

Kieran pushed Megan behind him as he faced the enemy. Colin moved to stand beside his brother. Bishop O'Mara, who had been strangely silent throughout the entire revelation, suddenly seemed to come to life. Striding forward, he faced the soldiers.

"If you would harm these good people in God's church, you will have to kill me and my priests, as well."

From their places beside the altar the cluster of black-robed priests, led by Father Malone, strode forward, their hands folded as if in prayer. They positioned themselves around Colin, Kieran and Megan.

With eyes blazing, Sir Cecil shouted, "As emissary to Her Majesty, I order you to kill them all."

Still the soldiers refused to move until the swarthy guard named Whip, his gaze fastened on Megan, shouted, "The lady is mine. And I will kill all who stand in my way." Lift-

ing his sword, he charged into the crowd of priests. Relu-
tantly the other soldiers followed.

At the door of the chapel, Sir Cecil lifted the knife
Lady Katherine's throat. "Alas, dear lady, I only neede
you to escape your sons," he murmured. "Your presen
would slow me down as I make my escape."

"You are as evil as Kieran said."

"Evil? Nay, my lady. I simply seek to take advantage (
the opportunities afforded me by my position as Queen
emissary. And now I shall savor the vindication for the i
sult you hurled at me in my youth."

"Vindication?" She stared at him with horror. "All
this was done because I chose Sean O'Mara over you whe
we were young?" And then her horror turned to pain as sh
was struck by a terrible thought. "Have you also taken o
your fury on my daughter? Are you the reason Fiona di
appeared, Cecil?" Her lips trembled as she whispered, "Te
me where she is."

"She and her husband are prisoners in my country esta
in Essex, my lady. And when I return to England, I will hav
the pleasure of telling them that everyone they loved in thi
filthy land is dead. And while they are still weeping ove
your death, I shall have them killed, as well."

"It is enough to know that Fiona is alive." Lady Kath
erine faced him stoically, seeing the razor edge as the knif
flashed toward her.

Before he could finish the deed, Sir Cecil heard the thun
der of hoofbeats and turned to find Hugh Cleary, mounte
on a foaming stallion, bearing down on him. Sunligh
glinted off the sword in Hugh's hand.

"I have dreamed of this moment," Hugh said.

"I will kill the woman," Sir Cecil cried.

But before the words had escaped his lips, he let out
shriek as Hugh's sword found his heart. Before Sir Cec
crumpled to the ground, Hugh scooped Lady Katherine int
his arms and held her firmly against his chest.

"Oh, Hugh."

For long moments she could only cling to him as the
tmors shuddered through her. Then, composing herself,
e whispered, "I know not how you arrived in time. But I
n forever in your debt."

"Kieran met us along the road," he said. "And alerted us
the danger." He pressed his lips to her temple. "My life
uld not have been worth living had I not arrived in time."

"Fiona is alive in England," she murmured, wiping tears
om her cheeks.

"Aye. My men have found her. Even now, she and her
usband ride toward Killamara."

He breathed in the scent of her. Then, composing him-
lf, he set her down and said briskly, "Take the child and
e women and lock yourselves in the chapel's sanctuary.
hey cannot harm you there."

"But Kieran and Colin . . ."

"Your sons are men, Katherine. And capable of fighting
eir own battles."

His words were tempered by the look of love in his eyes.
eeing the wisdom of them, she nodded silently and went in
arch of Bridget and the women.

"Kieran," Hugh called, tossing a sword as he urged his
ount up the aisle of the chapel.

Kieran caught it and plunged into the cluster of unarmed
riests who bravely defied the soldiers. When the first sol-
er fell, Colin quickly retrieved the man's sword and joined
is brother in the fray. Moments later another soldier fell,
nd Megan scooped up his weapon. She felt a tug upon her
rm and found, to her astonishment, little Bridget clinging
► her skirts.

"Go," Megan cried. "Hide yourself beneath the pews."

"Nay, my lady. You taught me to hold a sword. I would
ght by your side."

"God in heaven. What have I done?" Lifting Bridget in
er arms, Megan began to run toward the sanctuary, where
e women had hidden themselves behind locked doors.
Vhen she reached the door she pounded with her fist,

shouting, "Lady Katherine. Bridget is with me. You m
open this door."

She heard the cries of relief. But before the lock could
thrown, Megan felt the child wrenched from her arms a
tossed aside. Stunned, she whirled and found herself face
face with Whip. In his eyes was a lust for blood.

"Now, my lady," he rasped, "we have some unfinish
business."

As he lifted his sword he was unprepared for her sudd
movement. Dodging his thrust, she brought her sword
barely missing his throat. His rage grew as he realized h
skilled the lady was with a weapon. She matched him thr
for thrust until, his breath coming in fast spurts, he fou
himself backed against the wall. His eyes narrowed as
fought off her advance and managed to pin her to the w
with the tip of his blade. As she struggled to free her slee
from the offending blade, he lifted his hand and caught h
with a stinging blow, sending her crumpling to the floor.
she fell she hit her head upon a protruding stone in the wa
Her sword slipped from her hand and clattered to the flo
beside her.

With an evil laugh Whip snarled, "So, my lady, at las
have my revenge. I have already disposed of the Irishma
And now I will rid the kingdom of you as well."

"Kieran?" As if from a great distance she heard his wor
and felt her eyes fill with tears. She was losing consciou
ness. Soon she would be as helpless as a bairn. "You kill
Kieran?"

"Aye. As I promised I would. It was my revenge for
murder of my friend at Fleet. And now, my lady, ye will jo
him."

He lifted his sword. Though she could barely make out
form in the blackness that clouded her vision, she heard
child's voice beside her.

"Here, my lady." The hilt of her sword was thrust in
her hand.

She felt the warmth of the hilt as her nerveless fingers apped around it. Relying only upon instinct, she lifted it d gave one final thrust. She felt the blade of Whip's sword rce her flesh. And then she was falling. Falling through lack cave that seemed to have no light.

Kieran picked himself up from the floor where he had len after an attack by half a dozen soldiers, including the zed guard, Whip. Blood seeped from a wound in his est. He stared at the number of bodies around him and ndered how he had survived. He remembered being uck by the guard's sword, then falling. But he could not all fighting all these men.

Out of the corner of his eye he saw a movement and irled. The man lying on the floor at his feet was Tavis wney. Kneeling, he swore when he saw the gaping wound his old friend's chest.

"I sent you home, Tavis. Why are you here?"

"When have you ever fought without me at your side, d? Once again I had to save your hide."

"Hush, old friend. You are losing much blood." As he ade a move to stem the flow, Tavis caught his hand in a ath grip. "Leave it. 'Tis too late."

Though Kieran's mind rejected such a thought, he knew to be true. His friend's face already wore the mask of ath.

"You gave your life for me, Tavis."

"Little enough price to pay for what I put you and Colin rough." His voice grew weaker until it was a mere whis-r. "I ask one favor in return."

Kieran leaned close. "Anything."

"Say I am forgiven."

"Aye. You were forgiven when I offered you my hand at e cottage."

"Then I die at peace."

Kieran grasped his hand and felt his fingers tighten fo
moment before they went slack. As he watched, Ta
breathed his last.

Through eyes glazed with pain Kieran saw Colin make
way toward him. He clasped his brother's shoulder as
tossed his bloody sword aside. The killing was done.

It seemed incongruous to see brilliant sunlight streami
through the windows of this holy building, bathing t
bloodstained bodies that littered the floor.

"Can you stand, Kieran?" Colin offered him an arm a
Kieran leaned weakly against him. Then, growing strong
he stood alone.

From the corner of his eye Colin saw the bishop fall to
knees. With a cry, he rushed to his uncle's side. The bish
was kneeling beside the altar, cradling a still form in
arms. Colin felt a lump rise to his throat as he gazed at t
bloodied body of Father Arden Malone. Even in death
face was serene.

"He gave his life for us," Colin said softly as Kier
walked over to join them.

"Aye. And he will earn a martyr's reward in heaven
Bishop O'Mara whispered. "I would gladly trade plac
with him. For his love was truly greater than any man
And his reward will be greater."

They all looked up as a child's whimper pierced the sti
ness.

"Bridget." Kieran glanced around, then set off at a r
to locate the child.

He found her standing before the door to the sanctuar
Tears streamed down her cheeks as she gazed at a crumpl
form on the floor. When he drew closer Kieran recogniz
Megan and felt his heart stop.

The door slowly opened and the women filed out, for
ing a circle around them. Lady Katherine tried to draw h
granddaughter to her, but the child pushed away and clu
to Megan's cold, lifeless hand.

"God in heaven." With a cry Kieran fell to his knees and
ew Megan into his arms. He felt a rush of relief when he
nd her pulse.

Blood streamed from the back of her head and from a
und to her shoulder. He could see, by the position of the
ad guard, that she and Whip had been locked in mortal
mbat. And though she had sustained a terrible blow to the
ad, she had once again bested her opponent.

"Can you hear me, Megan?" he whispered.

Her lids fluttered. "Aye." She jerked upright and reached
r a weapon. Then, glancing at the dead man beside her she
ispered, "Is it Whip?"

At Kieran's nod she whispered, "He said he had killed
u. And I feared that he had succeeded in killing me, as
ll."

"It was Tavis he killed. As you can see, Megan, I am
ve. And we need fear Whip no more. Your sword ended
s life."

For long moments she stared at him. Then, touching a
nd to the swollen mass at her skull, the realization
wned. With a note of wonder she proclaimed, "My name
Megan MacAlpin. I am leader of my people. My sisters'
mes are Meredith and Brenna. And Jamie MacDonald
d I were hunting in the Highlands when we were at-
cked."

"Oh, my beloved." Kieran pressed his lips to her temple.
t has all returned to you."

"Aye. Everything." She started to get to her feet, but a
esh wave of pain sent her swaying in his arms. She looked
ound as the others peered at her. "Is the battle over?"

"Aye, my little warrior."

"I regret I missed it." She gazed at him, and a tremulous
nile touched her lips. "Bridget was a fine pupil," she
urmured. "For it was she who saved my life."

A chuckle started deep in his chest and he threw back his
ad and roared. "Only you, my brave little Megan, could
ake me smile at such a somber time. In the blink of an eye

you have recalled your past, disposed of an old enemy a
regretted missing more of the battle, while praising y
youngest pupil."

"I was never known for my patience. Or my reticence

"Have you only now discovered that?" Though his wo
were teasing, his look was filled with love. "It is someth
I learned from our first encounter."

"Be careful, my lord. Or I will let you taste my temper,
well."

His laughter faded at the sound of thunderous hoofbe
growing nearer.

From his position beside the window Colin shout
"Kieran. Quickly. There are hundreds of horses advanci
upon us. We stand no chance against this army."

"English?" Hugh Cleary signaled his weary men to p
pare once more for battle.

"I know not." As Colin and the others hastily
sheathed their weapons, he watched the advancing army a
added, "They are as tall as giants, with shoulders as wide
longbows. Their hair is long and shaggy. They wear saffr
shirts beneath rough wool tunics. Their cloaks are of pl
homespun. And," he added with a voice tinged with av
"many of this wild horde are bare-legged, like savages."

"God in heaven," Megan cried. "It could be no one e
on earth."

Struggling to her feet, Megan leaned on Kieran's arm a
shouted, "Do not lift arms against them. They did not co
to attack. They are the Highlanders, come to rescue me."

Chapter Twenty-Two

pying the dead and wounded who littered the grounds, the ighlanders surrounded the chapel while their leaders made aight for the massive church doors. Before they could put eir shoulders against them, the doors were thrown open d Megan, leaning upon Kieran's arm, stepped forward ith a smile of greeting.

"Oh, Jamie. Jamie." With a cry of delight she launched rself into his arms and hugged him to her.

She was surprised when, instead of returning her em-ace, he roughly thrust her behind him and drew his sword.

"By all that is holy," he said through gritted teeth, "I ore to have my revenge against the one who gave me his ord to protect the lass and then stole her away."

Kieran faced the young giant in silence. Behind him, olin and Hugh drew their weapons. Hugh's army did the me.

"Jamie, you do not—"

"Nay, my lady. This is between the Irishman and me," he owled. "I have spent many a sleepless night," he said, viveling to face Kieran, "dreaming of this moment. Never s the lass been out of my thoughts. I have died a thou-nd times because I dared to entrust her to your keeping. ow you will pay for every harm inflicted upon my leader." is eyes were as cold as flint. "Draw your sword, Irish bas-rd. And face me like a man."

"Jamie, he is not your enemy."

The young Scot was beyond reason. Megan caught h arm, but he shook her off. It was then that she took the tim to really look at him. Since last she had seen him, he ha changed. There was none of the boy left in him now. H body seemed taller, leaner; his muscles were honed to pe fection. There was a haggard look to his red-bearded fac His eyes wore the haunted look of one who was driven.

He glanced at Megan, then to Kieran. "Has he b witched you, my lady? Is that why you stand with th monster against your own?"

"Oh, Jamie. Do you not see?"

In desperation, she looked beyond him and saw, for th first time, the face of her brother-in-law, Brice Campbel who stood at attention before his warriors.

"Brice. God in heaven, is it truly you?"

He held out his arms to her and she ran to him. Kiera watched as the giant lifted her as easily as a bairn an pressed his face to her hair. Though he showed no emotio Kieran's hands clenched at his sides. And though he hate himself for such foolishness, he felt a wave of black, blin ing jealousy.

"You must convince Jamie that Kieran O'Mara is o friend," she cried.

"A friend would not carry you away from all that yo hold dear, lass. It must be as Jamie said. You have been b witched by this monster."

Megan looked from Brice to Jamie and saw that both me wore the same determined expressions. They had com seeking vengeance. And somehow, she must find a way dissuade them.

Pushing free of Brice's arms she strode forward until sh was standing between Jamie and Kieran. "You must li ten," she said in clear, commanding tones. "It is true tha Kieran O'Mara gave his word to Jamie that I would be r turned to my people. But when I awoke from my wounds, had lost all memory of the past."

She heard the ripple of surprise that passed through the ˫nks of the Highlanders.

"Aye. I could not even recall my name. Nor could I re-ember Jamie, or you, Brice, or—" her voice lowered with ˫in "—even the names of my own sisters." Seeing the ˫ocked looks on their faces, Megan pressed ahead. "Kieran 'Mara and his brother, Colin," she said, turning to point ˫t Colin to the Highlanders, "had escaped from Fleet ˫ison and were being trailed by English soldiers. They ˫uld not tarry in our land."

"An escaped prisoner—" Jamie began, but Megan cut ˫n off.

"Being a man of honor, Kieran O'Mara refused to aban-˫on me in the forest. So his only choice was to take me with ˫em until I could regain my memory. Yet it was not until ˫is day in a battle with those same English that my mem-˫y returned to me."

In the silence that followed, Megan swallowed and prayed ˫e could quench the fire that still burned in Jamie's eyes. ˫would take more than a few words to quell the inferno ˫at had been building within him for such a long time.

"Had you not arrived when you did, I know that Kieran 'Mara would have surely returned me to my people as soon ˫ I recovered from my latest wounds."

Despite her assurances, Jamie stood his ground, his sword ˫ill clenched firmly in his hand. And though he felt a ˫udging admiration for the man who had eluded so many ˫llen English, he could not forget the hatred he had nur-˫red all these endless days and nights while he had searched ˫r the man who had stolen the MacAlpin.

Kieran was as unbending as Jamie. These savages had ˫red to invade his land and demand the return of their ˫ader. He found himself wondering if Megan had spoken ˫e truth. Would he, in fact, have offered to return her to ˫r people? Or would he have tried to persuade her to stay ˫ith him and make her home in Killamara? Now, it would ˫em, there would no longer be any choice.

Seeing the impasse, Lady Katherine stepped forward clutching Bridget's chubby hand in hers. "Megan's people are welcome in Killamara. I know you are weary, for Megan has told us of the perils of the long and difficult journey from your land to ours. Come." She gave a gentle, enigmatic smile as she thought of the servants who had labored so hard for this day. At least they would have reason now to celebrate. "We have a feast prepared. Let us talk among ourselves and find a path toward peace between our people."

Jamie glowered at Kieran. But at a pleading look from Megan, he sheathed his sword and, walking beside Brice Campbell, reluctantly agreed to the lady's suggestion.

Uncertain how to begin, Megan stood very still. Lady Katherine understood Megan's dilemma. If she walked with the Highlanders, she would appear to snub Kieran. If she walked beside Kieran, she would appear to choose him over her own people. Catching Megan's hand, she gently placed it in Bridget's and gave the two a shove. "Go now," she whispered, "and lead us all to the banquet table."

The Highlanders stood at attention as Megan and Bridget passed through their ranks. Then, following Jamie and Brice, they marched toward the castle.

Hugh Cleary caught Lady Katherine's hand and placed it on his sleeve. The tender, loving looks they exchanged said more than words. As they made their way to Castle O'Mara, Hugh's men followed, keeping a close watch on the Highlanders.

Colin embraced his beloved Cara, and with their hands firmly linked, they trailed behind.

Only Kieran remained at the chapel. For long minutes he watched as the bishop moved among the fallen priests, his hands forming the sign of blessing, his lips moving in silent prayer.

Death. It was all around him. Was that why his heart was suddenly so heavy? Or was it because he sensed that, now

at Megan had regained her memory, any chance for a fu-
re with her was also dead?

She was the MacAlpin, the leader of her clan. The loy-
ty of her people was so deep, they had reached beyond
eir own borders to find and return her to her rightful place
ith them. Now that she had attained her goal, he could not
and in the way of her happiness.

As he began the walk across the lawns toward the castle,
swallowed the bitter bile of defeat. Never had he felt so
ad, so lifeless. She had brought him so much joy and
ughter that he could not imagine life without her. But if he
ved her, he owed it to her to step aside.

The servants, under Mistress Peake's direction, were in a
yful mood. They moved among the men, bearing trays of
hole roasted pig, as well as venison, partridge, dove.
ileen and the other young women began to talk to the
ighlanders and even flirt openly. Tankards were filled and
filled until the bitter taste for vengeance was washed away.
he opposing armies realized they had shared a common
emy and began to exchange tales of their battles. Of
urse, each tale was embroidered until the soldiers draped
emselves in glory as, with their tensions behind them, the
en began to unbend.

Megan watched as smiles replaced the frowns. Laughter
ng through the great hall. But at the head table, where she
at between Kieran and Jamie, there were no easy smiles, no
entle laughter.

Beside Jamie sat Brice Campbell. Beside Kieran sat his
rother, Colin. The four men could have been carved from
tone. Their food lay untouched on their plates. Their
ankards still brimmed with ale, for not a drop had touched
heir lips.

"We offer you and your men lodging," Lady Katherine
aid. "Yours has been a long and tedious journey. You will
vish to tarry a few days and refresh yourselves before re-
urning home." She turned to her sons. "Is that not so?"

"Aye." Kieran's tone was flat.

"We are grateful for your kind offer, my lady." Jam
spared her a glance, then turned to look out over the sea c
faces. "But there are several hours of daylight left. Once n
men have eaten their fill, we will begin our journey home.

"So soon?" Megan felt her stomach lurch.

"Are you not eager to see your home, lass?" Bric
Campbell studied her, noting the sudden pallor.

"Aye. When I think about all those I had forgotten. Ol
Morna, my nurse." A wistful look came into her eye.
"Bancroft." To Kieran she added, "he is the keeper of th
door. Like your Padraig, Bancroft has been with our fam
ily for three generations." At the thought of her family sh
said dreamily, "And I shall get to see my sisters, Brenna an
Meredith."

At the mention of his wife's name, Brice said, "Mere
dith is with child again. She hopes this time it will be a gi
child. She sorely misses you and Brenna, and thinks an
other female will be a joyful addition to our home."

Kieran saw the look that came into Megan's eyes at th
mention of her sisters. He knew he was being selfish fo
wanting to keep her here with him. He had no right, whe
she had been separated from her loved ones for so long. Bu
the thought of seeing her go lay like a stone upon his heart

He looked up as Mistress Peake came bustling into th
hall, tears streaming down her face. Getting to his feet h
shoved back his chair and caught her by the shoulders.

"What has happened? Who has made you cry?"

"Oh, my lord." Her lips trembled and she could no
speak for the sobs that escaped.

"Tell me, mistress. What has..." He turned toward th
doorway, where a dazzlingly beautiful woman with coal
black hair and eyes as blue as a summer sky stood beside
tall, darkly handsome man.

"God in heaven..."

At his oath, everyone looked up.

Lady Katherine, deep in conversation with Hugh Cleary, ddenly gave a cry and raced across the room. Beside her, tle Bridget watched for several seconds. On her face was look of complete astonishment. Then, as recognition wned, she ran toward the couple screaming, "Mama. pa."

"Oh, Fiona. Is it truly you?"

The young woman scooped her little daughter into her ms, then drew Lady Katherine close and the two em- aced. Kieran and Colin followed, and the entire family fell to each other's arms, laughing and crying.

"My life is now complete," Lady Katherine said be- een bouts of weeping.

From her place at the table, Megan watched Fiona's mecoming and thought about her own. There would be uch weeping and laughing when she was once again re- ited with her family. But, she knew, a homecoming also eant a leave-taking. In order to return to her people, she ust leave Killamara. And Kieran.

She was happy for these good people. So happy. Then hy, she wondered, was her heart breaking?

Slipping unnoticed from the table, she made her way to r chambers to prepare for her journey home.

Jamie sat his steed proudly. He had come in search of his ader and he had found her. The hurdle that had once emed insurmountable was now crossed. The path would smooth once more. He was greatly relieved. For such a ng time now he had thought Megan lost to them forever.

He saw the way Megan's gaze followed Kieran O'Mara as led his mother and sister toward her for a last goodbye. here was something between the lass and this man. But at was not his concern. She was, after all, the MacAlpin. othing must prevent her from assuming her rightful place leader of the clan, as he and Brice had reminded her when ey had finally found some time alone.

He watched with pride as she kept her composure ev
when the child, Bridget, clung to her and wept. Dry-eye
she pulled herself into the saddle and gave a final wave
her hand.

"Safe journey, my lady," Kieran murmured, pressing h
hand.

She bit her lip until she tasted blood, but still she refus
to give in to the tears. They had said their goodbyes. A
she had been through all this before, when she had thoug
she was accompanying Malcolm MacAlpin home. But no
Megan thought, feeling her heart shatter into a milli
pieces, there was no hope left. He had his duties; she h
hers. And though she had always known that leadersh
demanded a terrible price, she had never dreamed it wou
cost her so much pain.

There was a lump in her throat that she could not swa
low. It threatened to choke her. As she nodded to Hugh ai
Lady Katherine, to Cara and Colin, to little Bridget hol
ing firmly to her parents' hands, she felt as if she were bi
ding farewell to her own family. She loved them, s
realized. All of them. And especially this man. Kieran. I
stood facing her, his features stern and unyielding. It tore
her to see him like this. But there was nothing she could s
or do that would make the parting less painful.

At Jamie's command the men formed neat columns ai
waited while Megan, followed by Jamie and Brice, rode b
tween them. With their leader finally at the head of h
troops, they started on their trek toward home.

As they crested a hill Megan reined in her mount ai
turned for a final glimpse of Castle O'Mara. Its turre
caught the glint of late afternoon sun. Swans glided on t
glassy surface of the lake. One figure still stood in t
courtyard, watching their progress. She knew it had to l
Kieran, but she could no longer see him clearly, because
the tears clouding her vision.

Kieran removed his shirt and crossed the room to poke
the ashes on the hearth. Beneath the layer of ash, hot co:

ɔwed in the darkness. Soon a thin flame licked along the ɪrk of a log.

He turned to glance at the night sky. Clouds scudded ɪross a crescent moon. After a day filled with pounding ɪd hammering, the night seemed unusually quiet.

He had spent the day at Colin's manor house, overseeing ɪe village workmen. Cara had ordered significant changes ɪ the old structure.

Changes. He leaned a hip against the rail of the balcony ɪd thought about all the changes that had blown through ɪeir lives like a whirlwind in the past few days.

The bishop had presided over the funerals of his brave iests. They lay buried beside the chapel. And though ɪshop O'Mara made plans to return to the monastery, he ɪll lingered, reluctant to leave the little chapel that seemed ɪ give him such a sense of peace.

Lady Katherine had wasted no time in marrying Hugh ɪeary and had returned with him and his men to his castle ɪ Armagh. Kieran had never seen her so radiant.

Fiona and her husband had bundled little Bridget off with ɪem to her husband's estate outside London, where they ɪould continue to work toward peace between their two ɪuntries. Kieran marveled that his sister could find such ɪppiness with an Englishman. But then, he thought with a ɪdden pain around his heart, had not he and Megan ɪemed an unlikely pair, as well?

Megan. There was never a moment in the day when she ɪd not crowd his thoughts. Even in sleep she slipped un- ɪdden into his dreams to torment him. He tried to picture ɪr aboard a ship bound for Scotland. But the thought was ɪo painful. With an angry toss of his head he turned.

The quick tap on his door deepened his frown. He wanted ɔ more of Mistress Peake's sulking complaints because ɪere was no one to eat the meals she prepared. She found ɪe castle too empty. As did he. But there was no solution ɔ it.

In quick strides he crossed the room and tore open 1 door. The words he was about to hurl died in his throat.

Megan, dressed in hooded traveling cloak, stared at h for long, silent moments.

"Since you do not invite me in, I invite myself." S brushed past him and crossed to the fireplace. "It is a c night, my lord. I feared my blood might freeze in my ve before I reached the warmth of Castle O'Mara."

He stood in the open doorway, staring at her as if he co not believe his eyes. Then, quickly composing himself, closed the door and leaned against it, crossing his arms o his chest.

"I thought you would be on a ship bound for yo home."

"Aye. I should have been." She turned to face him. " fact, I was aboard ship before I realized I could not go."

He dared not move as he drank in the sight of her. As s lowered the hood of her cloak, her hair tumbled down l back in a riot of golden tangles. Her cheeks were as red the roses in his mother's garden. Her eyes glowed with warmth that made his blood run hot.

"Will your Highlanders not come back for you and i mind you of your duties?"

"They tried to dissuade me. But I am the MacAlpin," s said with a trace of pride. "At least until another is chos from among our clan. For now, Jamie MacDonald will le my people. He has proven his love and loyalty. No one ne remind me about my duties. My duties lie with my hea Kieran." She untied the cords that held her cape and let drop to the floor. Beneath, she wore a gown of scarlet ve vet. In the glow of the fire, she shimmered and burn brighter than any flame. "And my heart," she added in lo husky tones, "lies with you."

He crossed the room and lifted his hands to her ha afraid for a moment that his heart had yearned so despe ately for her that he had merely conjured this image to ea him through his loneliness.

"Are you truly here with me, Megan?"

"Aye. And this time, nothing, no one, will persuade me go."

He put his hands to her waist and felt the blade of her dirk cked into her waistband. Lifting it to the light, he chuck- l low and deep in his throat. "Did you think you would ed a weapon to persuade me, little warrior?"

She took it from him, then dropped it to the floor. "I take chances, Kieran."

He felt the heat of her begin to race through his veins and cautioned himself to go slowly. But the hunger that awed at him had his hands closing around her arms, awing her close. Against her temple he murmured, "You ve given up so much to come to me, my lady."

"Nay." She turned her face until her lips were brushing s. The fire began, slowly at first, then building until she ought she would go mad from the heat. "I am greedy, ieran. I want it all. You, your love, this wild country. I ant the chance to fight by your side and sleep by your side l the days of my life."

"Oh, Megan." His lips found hers, warm and firm and illing, and his arms came around her, drawing her close ainst his chest. "I thought I would go mad from the neliness since you left." He lifted his head and stared eply into her eyes. "Promise me you will never leave me ain."

"I promise. Of course, I do expect you to make the jour- y to the Highlands when my sister, Meredith, has her third ild." An impish smile touched her lips as she added, "It ould be nice if we could bring a child of our own on the urney, to see his mother's land."

With great tenderness he lifted her face for his inspec- on. "The bishop is still here in Killamara. We will ask him preside at our wedding."

"Can we be wed immediately?"

"You mean this very moment?"

"Aye. We have wasted enough time."

"I fear we must waste a little more."

For a moment Megan's heart fell. Then, seeing laughter lurking in his eyes, she relaxed against him as [he] lowered his mouth once more to hers. Against her lips [he] muttered, "We will seek out the bishop on the morrow. [But] for tonight, let me feast upon you before I die of hunger[.]"

He plunged his hands into the tangles of her hair and dr[ew] her head back, plundering her mouth, as he murmur[ed] against her lips, "Welcome home, little warrior. I love y[ou] for now, for all time."

Love. As she returned his kiss, she felt her heart swell w[ith] the knowledge. Love. She had once thought it a foolish, si[lly] emotion. She had never wanted it. Had fought against it, [in] fact. But it had come, unbidden, into her heart. She lo[ved] him. So much, she had given up her reign, her family, [her] country. Ahh, but she had gained so much more. A li[fe]time of love. Love that would endure to the ends of tim[e.] And beyond.

*   *   *   *   *

HARLEQUIN

Romance

**This October,
travel to England with
Harlequin Romance
FIRST CLASS title #3155
TRAPPED
by Margaret Mayo**

I'm my own boss now and I intend to stay that way.''

Candra Drake loved her life of freedom on her narrow-boat
home and was determined to pursue her career as a company
secretary free from the influence of any domineering man.
Then enigmatic, arrogant Simeon Sterne breezed into her life,
forcing her to move and threatening a complete takeover of her
territory and her heart....

HARLEQUIN®
OFFICIAL SWEEPSTAKES
RULES

NO PURCHASE NECESSARY

To enter, complete an Official Entry Form or 3" × 5" index card by hand-printing, in plain block letters, your complete name, address, phone number and age, and mailing it to: Harlequin Fashion A Whole New You Sweepstakes, P.O. Box 9056, Buffalo, NY 14269-9056.

No responsibility is assumed for lost, late or misdirected mail. Entries must be sent separately with first class postage affixed, and be received no later than December 31, 1991 for eligibility.

Winners will be selected by D.L. Blair, Inc., an independent judging organization whose decisions are final, in random drawings to be held on January 30, 1992 in Blair, NE at 10:00 a.m. from among all eligible entries received.

The prizes to be awarded and their approximate retail values are as follows: Grand Prize — A brand-new Mercury Sable LS plus a trip for two (2) to Paris, including round-trip air transportation, six (6) nights hotel accommodation, a $1,400 meal/spending money stipend and $2,000 cash toward a new fashion wardrobe (approximate value: $28,000) or $15,000 cash; two (2) Second Prizes — A trip to Paris, including round-trip air transportation, six (6) nights hotel accommodation, a $1,400 meal/spending money stipend and $2,000 cash toward a new fashion wardrobe (approximate value: $11,000) or $5,000 cash; three (3) Third Prizes — $2,000 cash toward a new fashion wardrobe. All prizes are valued in U.S. currency. Travel award air transportation is from the commercial airport nearest winner's home. Travel is subject to space and accommodation availability, and must be completed by June 30, 1993. Sweepstakes offer is open to residents of the U.S. and Canada who are 21 years of age or older as of December 31, 1991, except residents of Puerto Rico, employees and immediate family members of Torstar Corp., its affiliates, subsidiaries, and all agencies, entities and persons connected with the use, marketing, or conduct of this sweepstakes. All federal, state, provincial, municipal and local laws apply. Offer void wherever prohibited by law. Taxes and/or duties, applicable registration and licensing fees, are the sole responsibility of the winners. Any litigation within the province of Quebec respecting the conduct and awarding of a prize may be submitted to the Régie des loteries et courses du Quebec. All prizes will be awarded; winners will be notified by mail. No substitution of prizes is permitted.

Potential winners must sign and return any required Affidavit of Eligibility/Release of Liability within 30 days of notification. In the event of noncompliance within this time period, the prize may be awarded to an alternate winner. Any prize or prize notification returned as undeliverable may result in the awarding of that prize to an alternate winner. By acceptance of their prize, winners consent to use of their names, photographs or their likenesses for purposes of advertising, trade and promotion on behalf of Torstar Corp. without further compensation. Canadian winners must correctly answer a time-limited arithmetical question in order to be awarded a prize.

For a list of winners (available after 3/31/92), send a separate stamped, self-addressed envelope to: Harlequin Fashion A Whole New You Sweepstakes, P.O. Box 4694, Blair, NE 68009.

PREMIUM OFFER TERMS

To receive your gift, complete the Offer Certificate according to directions. Be certain to enclose the required number of "Fashion A Whole New You" proofs of product purchase (which are found on the last page of every specially marked "Fashion A Whole New You" Harlequin or Silhouette romance novel). Requests must be received no later than December 31, 1991. Limit: four (4) gifts per name, family, group, organization or address. Items depicted are for illustrative purposes only and may not be exactly as shown. Please allow 6 to 8 weeks for receipt of order. Offer good while quantities of gifts last. In the event an ordered gift is no longer available, you will receive a free, previously unpublished Harlequin or Silhouette book for every proof of purchase you have submitted with your request, plus a refund of the postage and handling charge you have included. Offer good in the U.S. and Canada only.

HQFW-SWPR

HARLEQUIN® OFFICIAL
SWEEPSTAKES ENTRY FORM

4-FWHHS

Complete and return this Entry Form immediately – the m
entries you submit, the better your chances of winning!

- Entries must be received by **December 31, 1991**.
- A Random draw will take place on **January 30, 1992**.
- No purchase necessary.

Yes, I want to win a FASHION A WHOLE NEW YOU Classic and Romantic prize from Harlequ

Name _____ Telephone _____ Age _____

Address _____

City _____ State _____ Zip _____

Return Entries to: **Harlequin FASHION A WHOLE NEW YOU,**
P.O. Box 9056, Buffalo, NY 14269-9056   © 1991 Harlequin Enterprises Limi

PREMIUM OFFER

To receive your free gift, send us the required number of proofs-of-purchase from any specia
marked FASHION A WHOLE NEW YOU Harlequin or Silhouette Book with the Offer Certifica
properly completed, plus a check or money order (do not send cash) to cover postage and handli
payable to Harlequin FASHION A WHOLE NEW YOU Offer. We will send you the specified gif

OFFER CERTIFICATE

Item	A. ROMANTIC COLLECTOR'S DOLL	B. CLASSIC PICTUR FRAME
	(Suggested Retail Price $60.00)	(Suggested Retail Price $25.
# of proofs-of-purchase	18	12
Postage and Handling	$3.50	$2.95
Check one	☐	☐

Name _____

Address _____

City _____ State _____ Zip _____

Mail this certificate, designated number of proofs-of-purchase and check or money order f
postage and handling to: Harlequin FASHION A WHOLE NEW YOU Gift Offer, P.O. Box 905
Buffalo, NY 14269-9057. Requests must be received by December 31, 1991.

ONE
PROOF-OF-PURCHASE

4-FWHHP-2

To collect your fabulous free gift you must include
the necessary number of proofs-of-purchase with
a properly completed Offer Certificate.

© 1991 Harlequin Enterprises Limited

See previous page for details.